THE SONS OF RED LAKE

ZHOU DAXIN

Translated by
Thomas Bray and Haiwang Yuan

SINOIST

Published by
Sinoist Books (an imprint of ACA Publishing Ltd)
University House
11 13 Lower Grosvenor Place,
London SW1W 0EX, UK
Tel: +44 20 3289 3885
E mail: info@alaincharlesasia.com
www.alaincharlesasia.com
www.sinoistbooks.com

Beijing Office
Tel: +86(0)10 8472 1250

Author: Zhou Daxin
Translators: Thomas Bray and Haiwang Yuan

Published by Sinoist Books (an imprint of ACA Publishing Ltd) in arrangement with People's Literature Publishing House and with special support from China Translation & Publishing House

Chinese language copyright © 湖光山色 (*Hu Guang Shan Se*) 2008, Zhou Daxin

English translation text © 2022 ACA Publishing Ltd, London, UK

ALL RIGHTS RESERVED. NO PART OF THIS PUBLICATION MAY BE REPRODUCED IN MATERIAL FORM, BY ANY MEANS, WHETHER GRAPHIC, ELECTRONIC, MECHANICAL OR OTHER, INCLUDING PHOTOCOPYING OR INFORMATION STORAGE, IN WHOLE OR IN PART, AND MAY NOT BE USED TO PREPARE OTHER PUBLICATIONS WITHOUT WRITTEN PERMISSION FROM THE PUBLISHER.

This novel is entirely a work of fiction. The names, characters and incidents portrayed in it are the work of the author's imagination. Any resemblance to actual persons, living or dead, events or localities is entirely coincidental.

Paperback ISBN: 978-1-83890-522-4
Hardback ISBN: 978-1-83890-543-9
eBook ISBN: 978-1-83890-523-1

A catalogue record for *The Sons of Red Lake* available from the National Bibliographic Service of the British Library.

THE SONS OF RED LAKE

ZHOU DAXIN

Translated by
THOMAS BRAY AND HAIWANG YUAN

Sinoist Books

PART ONE

sky

WATER

Nuannuan's biggest dream was to earn ten thousand yuan. The digits in her account were slowly approaching that dream. Sometimes, she even dreamed of how she would spend the money. What she never dreamed of was the call that came, informing of her mum's dire situation. When the call arrived, she was busy cleaning a recently furbished apartment in Chaoyang District, Beijing. The smell of paint solvent in this new apartment had given her a headache, but Nuannuan did not stop: she scraped the dirt from the floor, cleaned the glass in the doors and window panes, washed the stains off the rags and mops, and carried the garbage away... The cleaning company had assigned the job to her and two other girls. The faster she could finish her part, the earlier she would get her share of ninety yuan. Just as she was wiping her sweat off – the mop in her hand and her T-shirt all soaking wet – one of the other girls' phone rang. The girl passed it to Nuannuan. "It's for you."

Nuannuan was surprised. "Who is it?" She felt nervous when she saw the number indicating her hometown. She had asked Dad not to call unless it was urgent – after all, it was not her phone.

"Nuannuan, I'm calling from the post office on Juxiang Street. You must hurry back. Your mother is very, very sick..." Dad's voice was shaky.

Her legs went shaky too. Leaning against the closest windowsill, she responded: "Dad, take her to the township hospital – I'm coming home…"

When Nuannuan arrived at the east bank of Red Lake on a bus, after a train ride to Nanfu City, it was noon the next day. She made a run for the pier as she got off – if she could catch the boat to the west bank, she would make it home at sunset. Yet the boat had already left her sight. Unwilling to give up, she ran to the ticket kiosk and asked: "Is there another boat today?"

"No. You'll have to come back tomorrow," the man answered as he closed the ticket window.

What shall I do? Standing by the lake, Nuannuan peered into the west bank. The lake surface extended a dozen kilometres wide, so vast that her eyes couldn't reach its limit. But she roughly knew Chu Wang Village's location, and she gazed in that direction with extreme anxiety. At this moment, resentment for Red Lake welled up in her heart. *Why are you so big?*

Nuannuan, whose village was on the west bank, had found the lake too big since her childhood. It wasn't easy to cross the lake to get to Nanfu City. Nuannuan knew that Fengyang River was the cause of the trouble. After being pampered by the Qin Ranges for a long time and flattered by the bowing Funiu Mountain, it reached this part of the world with extreme arrogance and would lose its temper without reason. It caused trouble to the people here almost every other year. The flood Fengyang River generated during the Guangxu reign alone took eighty thousand residents from here. Red Lake was slowly formed on a river beach and a large depression after the previous floods. However, the lake area was limited at that time, and the opportunity for it to become such a large body of water came when a dam was built downstream to divert water to the north. The people around the lake gradually got used to its presence, but Nuannuan could still hear some older villagers complain: "When the lake was small, it took us only a mealtime to get to the west bank from the east. But now, you must scull your boat for nearly a day. When Li Zicheng crossed the lake with his troops in the late Qing Dynasty, his horses swam across it. Which horse can do it today?"

"Hey, girl, would you like to have some fun on the boat?" shouted a shirtless man who had got off a nearby fishing boat. As he yelled to Nuannuan, he made a gesture of hugging.

Nuannuan looked daggers at him and responded sternly: "Go and get your sister to have fun with you." The man forced a smile of embarrassment and went back to the shelter on board.

Do I have to spend the night by the lake? Upset, Nuannuan threw her bag to the ground and sat down. Her hand touched the pouch next to her waist. It was filled with eight thousand yuan in cash; that was all the money she had earned in the past two years. *Mum, don't be afraid, your daughter has the money for your treatment...*

Nuannuan was sitting there worried, staring at the lake surface, when a motorboat hurriedly came from the lake and quickly reached the shore. Then she saw a few police officers pull a man in handcuffs from the boat, jump onto the beach and rush to a police car parked not far away.

"What did this man do?" someone asked the motorboat pilot.

Nuannuan pricked her ears to listen.

"He robbed a Chu tomb."

"What's a Chu tomb?"

"It's a tomb of the Chu State. When they sank a well near Juxiang Street on the west bank not long ago, they discovered two ancient tombs. The authorities of the county and Nanfu City had demanded no one touch them. But this guy chiselled a tomb open and got some badly rusted bronze ware, thus breaking the law."

"Do you mean the tomb belonged to the Chu State?"

"Yes, the county and the city authorities both said that the area around Red Lake used to belong to the Chu State."

Nuannuan turned her head back. She was not in the mood to listen to the story about the Chu State. She needed a boat that could take her to the west bank. Even a raft would be fine.

Nuannuan was feeling anxious when she heard a call from nearby. "Black Bean – remember to bring more magnolia buds next time."

Black Bean? She turned her head and saw Uncle Black Bean from her village, a frequent visitor to the east bank to sell his herbs. Nuannuan picked up her bag and found herself staggering towards him.

"Uncle Black Bean, did you row yourself here?"

The man, who was middle-aged, tanned, skinny and short, turned to look at her. "Ho-ho! Nuannuan! You're home? That's lucky. Come here and take a ride home on my boat."

The boat was miserably small, but Black Bean had installed an engine on it. With a continuous *whooshing* sound, the boat picked up a good speed. It was not windy, and the waves were gentle on the lake. Several white birds were flying close to the blue surface, and once in a while a small fish or two would jump up and back down again. Far beyond, fishers were collecting their nets from a handful of small boats.

"Nuannuan, I haven't seen your dad fishing in the lake for days."

"He must be busying himself attending to my mum. Her illness is getting worse."

"What's your mum's illness? I often see her buying medicine in the pharmacy, and she looked pale."

Nuannuan sighed. "I wish I knew."

"Nuannuan, how much do you earn a month in Beijing?"

"A little over five hundred yuan."

"Do they provide food?"

"We can have a lunch box at noon for five yuan."

"How are the sleeping conditions?"

"A few female co-workers and I rent a room."

"You've got a better deal than your Sister Luo from my family. She's working in the capital of the province, earning only 380 a month. She has less than two hundred pocket money after she pays for her meals."

"So, Sister Luo also works away from home now?" In Nuannuan's memory, Luoluo, Uncle Black Bean's daughter, was still a young girl.

"Yes, she works away from home now. She went with a few others, including Wei Liang from the Wei family. It's better to earn some cash working outside than farming at home. Farming can only keep your stomach filled…"

When the boat anchored, the sun had fled to the other side of the village hill, and smoke was rising from every chimney. Nuannuan said a quick thanks and hurried into the village. She walked underneath the stone pillar with a heavily weathered inscription of the village's name: *Chu Wang*. When she caught sight of the houses of various heights in the village that she had not seen for two years, Nuannuan suddenly had the illusion that the majestic place she left had shrunk: its tall, pretty houses shortened and broken; its wide, unwinding road narrowed down to an ugly trail. Yet the magnolia tree in front of her house seemed the same. Tall and robust, the tree had a crown like a giant umbrella. Then came the same birds that had flown on and off the branches when she left, chirping their last gossips before nightfall.

Only her little sister Hehe and Grandma were at home. Grandma, as usual, was wearing nothing on top while lighting the fire in front of the range. She was coughing loudly as she fed wood and grass to the fire, her withered breasts shaking back and forth. Hehe was chopping sweet potatoes into the pot, every piece splashing minute droplets of water on Grandma's naked body.

Hearing the steps, Hehe turned her head and saw Nuannuan entering the house. She stopped chopping and called out: "Sister..." Tears dropped from her eyes.

It made Nuannuan's heart ache. She stepped up and called "Grandma", bowing down to kiss her wrinkled forehead. Then she turned and asked Hehe: "Where's Dad?"

"He went to take Mum to the township hospital on Juxiang Street. Grandma and I were left to guard the house."

"How is she?"

"I heard the surgery will be this afternoon."

"What on earth does she have?"

"Breast cancer."

"Breast?" Nuannuan gasped.

"Mum's got cancer in one of her breasts," explained Hehe.

Nuannuan flopped into the chair next to Grandma. She buried her head in her hands.

"It's your dad's fault," Grandma said. "He always catches fish, shrimps and crabs in the lake. Aren't fish, shrimps and crabs belongings of the lake god? How can the god be happy if you always take his belongings? I asked him to pray to the lake god once a month, but he never listens. He always says that it's enough to burn incense at Lingyan Temple. Which god is worshipped in the temple? The Buddha. The lake god doesn't live there. They have their own territories, but both require prayers and incense sacrifices. But he doesn't listen to me. Now, you see, the punishment befalls your mum. She's got breast cancer."

Nuannuan didn't respond to Grandma. After a while, she raised her head again and said: "Is the bike here?"

Hehe answered: "Dad used it to take Mum to the hospital."

"Go to Shallot's and borrow her bike."

"What for? It's already dark," said Hehe, her eyes widening.

"I need to ride to the hospital. I need to see Mum."

"That far? On your own?"

"Go and borrow the bike now."

Turning away, Nuannuan helped Grandma throw a bunch of wood into the pit. The fire was lit again, and she quickly washed her hands in the basin. She started neatly chopping the sweet potatoes left by her sister. Once she had thrown all the chopped potatoes into the pot and closed the lid, Nuannuan took out a short-sleeved blouse from her bag. "Grandma, I bought a top for you. Come and try it on."

"Later. It's too hot in here," Grandma answered.

"You'll look better wearing it. Old ladies in Beijing never go topless, no matter how hot it gets." Nuannuan had grown uncomfortable with her grandma's naked body.

"Bah! We peasants can't be compared to the city people." Grandma was not convinced.

Nuannuan did not wait for her consent but put the blouse on for her. "How's that? It fits," Nuannuan said as she checked it out from a few angles.

Grandma smiled and grasped the front in her hand. "Good, it's good. It's just a bit posh…"

Footsteps and the sound of rolling wheels on the ground were heard before the sweet potatoes were done. Nuannuan knew it was Shallot without even looking.

"You're home! I thought you'd come back one of these days. Changlin got his job in Nanfu City, so I'll ride to the hospital with you." Shallot was a healthy, robust-looking woman, the product of long years working in the fields.

Turning her head, Shallot asked Grandma: "Have you eaten yet?"

Grandma did not answer. She raised her cane and knocked it softly on Shallot's arm. "Wife of Changlin, you and Nuannuan, two women, can't go outside together after nightfall. What if some bad guy follows you?"

Shallot answered with a smile: "Don't worry, there are no bad guys out there."

Grandma did not give up. "Eek! You can't be careful enough. I heard Old Tung's wife was mugged on the road the other day. The bad guy took all thirty eggs from her."

"I'll take this sickle with me then." Shallot pulled a sickle off the wall, its blade shining from the sharpening, and she waved it in front of Grandma. "If any bad guy as much as shows up, I'll chop his head off."

Grandma laughed with her mouth open, showing the only two teeth left. "Big talk. You haven't got the guts. A shout from the bad guy will send you to your knees."

"I've got Nuannuan with me."

"That's true. My Nuannuan has got some nerves." Grandma seemed proud. Again she said: "It's dark. You be careful when riding the bike. The road to Juxiang Street is by the lakeside, so watch your mouth. Don't say anything that displeases the lake god. You hear that?"

As she turned to push the bike, Shallot answered: "Yes, Grandma."

Nuannuan reached for the sickle on Shallot's back and followed her out.

Grandma also followed them out and asked: "Hey, Wife of Changlin, let me ask one more question. Are you carrying a child again?"

"What? Grandma is going to give me the approval for another child?" Shallot laughed in the dark.

"I'm only worried – if you're pregnant, you can't give a ride to Nuannuan. If something happens, we can't afford to compensate you."

"Don't worry, Grandma. Since Changlin isn't home, I've got no seeds sowed in me…"

The journey from King of Chu Village to Juxiang Street was 4,500 metres on a dirt road. Despite the mountain on the right side, the road was still suitable for a bike as it closely followed the lakeside on its left.

Nuannuan was sitting on the rear saddle while Shallot rode the bike. She could hear Shallot's heavy breath in the endless darkness.

Autumn crickets were chirping happily. But when the bike approached, they paused their songs. Just last night, she was in noisy Beijing, a city ablaze with lively brightness. Nuannuan felt that riding in this scary, silent darkness was surreal, as if she were in a different world.

Shallot's breath got heavier. Feeling guilty, Nuannuan whispered: "Take a rest. I can ride."

"I'm all right," answered Shallot as she reached into her pocket. She stopped the bike and put a small, warm pack into Nuannuan's hand. "You should just sit there and relax. You must have hurried to the train station yesterday. A train, a bus, then a boat. You must be hungry. And you didn't take a rest at home. You must be exhausted. It's pan-fried bread with egg in it. Eat it. We'll find you some proper food on Juxiang Street."

Nuannuan could feel tears in her eyes with the bread in her hand. Two teardrops fell on her front. Among all of her girlfriends, Shallot was the most trustworthy. Though neither Shallot nor her husband Changlin was related to Nuannuan, the two young women had become good friends simply because they admired each other's tempers. Shallot had married into the village five years earlier, and Nuannuan liked her quickly for her good nature, helpful heart and skilful hands that made embroideries and wicker baskets. Before she went to Beijing, Nuannuan would go to Shallot's house whenever she could; she kept no secrets from her.

"You must not worry too much about Auntie's health. I heard this disease is curable today." Shallot was trying to offer her some consolation.

Nuannuan sighed. "Mum is not living a charmed life."

"You were out there for two years. Any fine lads? Didn't you bump into a likeable one or two?" asked Shallot as she rode.

"No. The cleaning company is small, and I didn't meet anyone presentable. And I was out there for the money. I didn't spend much time thinking about that," answered Nuannuan as she gazed upon the pale white lake.

"Don't lie to Shallot. Don't you surprise me with a handsome young guy tomorrow."

"Make me your guard dog if I lied to you."

"You remember Kaitian from the village, right? Have you made up your mind about him?"

"Kaitian..." Nuannuan hesitated. She didn't know what to say.

Kaitian was from Chu Wang Village too. Nuannuan grew up with him. She remembered meeting him for the first time on a trip to offer incense in Lingyan Temple with Mum. Mum was one of the two most passionate visitors to the temple. The other one was Kaitian's mother. Mum eagerly offered the incense so that the Buddha would watch over Dad's fishing in Red Lake. Kaitian's mother went for the harvest. Kaitian's family farmed their fields. For the sake of a harvest, Kaitian's mother would kneel in front of the Buddha and kowtow during the New Year. She would also offer incense before every spring seeding, autumn harvest and summer plough. Nuannuan met Kaitian for the first time in front of the temple gate. She remembered how both of their hands were nervously clutching the edge of their mothers' blouses as they followed the crowd slowly into the temple.

When Mum greeted Kaitian's mother, she stole a look at Kaitian and caught sight of him placing a sweet into his mouth. He was gazing at the gate of the temple with curiosity. "Is it the first time you've come here?" asked Nuannuan.

Kaitian only smiled because of the sweet in his mouth, but he quickly removed it and said: "My mum told me that we're too young to be allowed in by the Grandpa Abbot."

"Why?" Nuannuan was amazed.

"He fears that children may pee in the temple," said Kaitian, who replaced the sweet in his mouth after he finished.

Nuannuan broke into a smile. "I've come with Mum many times, and I've never peed." As she said so, she watched Kaitian sucking his sweet, and her mouth watered. "Does it taste sweet?" she asked. She knew she might sound greedy asking this way, but she couldn't help it because she hadn't had sweets for a long time. Each time she had hinted to her mum that she wanted them, Mum would have said: "What's the use of eating sweets? We can buy salt with the money."

"Yes, it tastes sweet. Would you like one? My mum bought me three." As he said this, he took a sweet and placed it in Nuannuan's hand. Hesitating a bit, Nuannuan accepted it. While peeling off the wrapper, she glanced at her mum, but luckily she didn't notice it. This was Nuannuan's sweetest trip to offer incense because it always made her remember that autumn day with Kaitian.

Before that, Nuannuan had always been reluctant to go to Lingyan Temple to offer incense. She was unwilling because she begrudged the offerings. She felt sad each time she saw Mum place on the Buddha's altar the steamed buns made from the little wheat flour the family had. She felt miserable each time she found Mum buying incense sticks with the money exchanged for the family's chickens or eggs and burning them in the incense burners in the temple. Each time, she would think: *It'd be better to let me eat the delicious buns to satisfy my hunger and buy me some tasty sweets to please my palate.*

Once, she told Mum about this idea, but Mum, who had never been angry, spanked her and growled: "How can the Buddha bless you if you don't burn incense, sacrifice offerings, or say prayers in the temple?" For her words, Mum kowtowed a few more times in front of the Buddha statue in the main hall that day. While doing so, she apologised to the Buddha. "My daughter is too young to be sensible. I beg you not to blame her."

The trip from Chu Wang Village to Lingyan Temple was one and a half kilometres. Whenever Mum took Nuannuan there, she would be exhausted. Sometimes, Mum would carry her on her back for a while. But she didn't want Mum to be too tired and hated to hear Mum's heavy breathing, so she always asked Mum to put her down and insisted on walking to the temple. The trip not only tired but also starved her. Once, she was so unbearably hungry that, taking the opportunity of Mum praying somewhere else after setting her offerings on the altar, she tore a piece from one of the buns and stealthily ate outside the hall. She was happily munching when Mum came over and discovered her. Mum was so scared that her face turned a ghastly pale. She said in a teary voice: "You greedy rascal! You must have offended the Buddha this time. You can't blame your mother if you face difficulties in your life."

Pleased with her full stomach, she whispered to Mum: "The Buddha won't know who I am if you don't call me by my name. Then he won't be able to find and punish me."

Mum smacked her on her head and said: "Do you think the Buddha is easy to fool? Whose name doesn't he know? Even your life is in his hands, let alone your name."

From that sweet-tasting trip, Nuannuan and Kaitian started spending playtime together and realised that they both lived in Chu

Wang Village. The village was a big one. Since Kaitian's house was in the centre and Nuannuan's was at the far south end, it was no wonder that they had never even heard about each other before. The more time they spent together, the more they knew about each other. Kaitian learned that Nuannuan's dad, Chu Changshun, fished in a small boat in Red Lake every day; and Nuannuan learned that Kaitian's father, Kuang Baogu, was one of the old-timers who farmed the fields.

Nuannuan also learned that Kaitian had an enormous appetite and always felt hungry. Ever naked in summer, his belly bulged like a watermelon after every meal. It swayed when he walked. When some adults tapped his belly, it sounded almost the same as a watermelon. Whenever he trotted, his stomach would bounce so hard as if it were about to drop. Sometimes, Nuannuan would timidly step forward and gingerly touch his belly with her fingers. From then on, Nuannuan became worried about Kaitian's chronic hunger, and she would often secretly give him a bun from her home. As soon as Kaitian saw it, he would unceremoniously take it and gulp it down no matter how full he was. Later, when Nuannuan went to school, she happened to be in the same class as Kaitian. They had fun going to school and returning home together, and they began to feel closer. In summer, they caught grasshoppers and tried to tell which one was a better jumper. In winter, they would make snowmen together and try to find out the best fit for their eyes. In spring, they would pick wildflowers here and there, and select ones that looked the best on their warm heads. In autumn, they would break off the cornstalks to eat as canes in the cornfields and champ until their mouths blistered. The two cared about each other. Whenever Mum made delicious food at home, Nuannuan would bring some to Kaitian. Sometimes it was a boiled egg, sometimes a meat bun, sometimes a piece of fried carp and sometimes an ear of boiled corn. Kaitian's family was so poor that he couldn't get Nuannuan anything except lake water, which he filled in an empty wine bottle. When Nuannuan said she was thirsty, he would pass it to her. Sometimes, Nuannuan wasn't thirsty even after school, so Kaitian would let her wash her hands with the water. He held the bottle and poured it slowly while Nuannuan washed her dainty hands hard until she rubbed them pinky-red and spanking clean.

When they grew up and entered junior high school, they felt

embarrassed to be as close as before. They dared not to be as inseparable on the way to and from school. Often, one walked in the front while the other tagged after. Sometimes, when they got a bit closer, their fellow schoolmates from their village would jeer: "Hey! You're a match! They're so scared that they quickly separate!" Though they appeared estranged, they still felt as close as they used to be. Sometimes, when Nuannuan brought food to Kaitian, she would wrap it up in a handkerchief and hang it from an elm tree's branch by the roadside without the other students noticing. She would raise her hand and make a leaf-picking gesture under the tree. Kaitian, who walked behind her, would get her message loud and clear, and he could identify the branch to get the package.

The two would often talk about their future careers when they grew up. Nuannuan said she wanted to be a teacher at an elementary school, whereas Kaitian said he wanted to be a township mayor and manage hundreds of thousands of people.

One evening before they began their second year at high school, Kaitian walked unusually slowly. The abnormal distance from her told Nuannuan that something had happened to him, so she also slowed down. After the other students had gone far, Nuannuan rushed over, and only then did Kaitian tell her everything in a choking voice. Kaitian's father, eager to have the field ploughed, had been too harsh with a bull. The bull twisted its head around and, with an angry strike, broke his father's legs. Kaitian had to quit school after this to undertake the farm work instead of his father. He took out his fountain pen and notebooks from his schoolbag and stuffed them into Nuannuan's hands, saying: "I don't need them any more. You can have them." Nuannuan held Kaitian's hand in tears, not knowing what to say to console him. Nuannuan made up her mind to work hard in school. She was determined to go to college and help Kaitian afterwards. However, things did not go as she wished.

She took the exam but did not make it to college. Mum accompanied her to read the red-paper name list of college student candidates posted in front of the Juxiang Street High School. Nuannuan couldn't find her name after searching the list for a long time. She was so shocked that her feet seemed planted in the ground. Mum didn't blame her for not studying well. She only said that this must have been the Buddha's retribution. He must have remembered her stealing the offerings. Mum said: "He isn't joking when he gets angry. Be an honest fisher and work with your dad in the lake here."

The next day, Mum went to the temple with incense, steamed buns and other offerings. There, she kowtowed to the Buddha to express her willingness to accept the punishment. With her dream shattered, Nuannuan fished with her dad for a year. Then she was determined to leave and pick up work in the city.

Shallot's voice rose in the darkness. "Since you're home, you should think about marriage when your mother recovers. As for Kaitian, I know he still cares about you. He never stopped asking about you. You have to make up your mind now. If it's a yes, it's a yes. If not, you have to tell him, or he will grow bitter soon."

"Right," Nuannuan whispered, her eyes gazing upon the dark mountains on the other side of the dirt road. It was already ten o'clock in the evening when they arrived at the hospital.

Dad told Nuannuan that the surgery had gone well as a doctor from the county hospital had come to help. Mum was still in the intensive care unit, but everything was fine. At last feeling assured, Nuannuan sat down on the staircase in front of the hospital, with no strength left.

"You may rest assured. Anyone can get sick, right?" Shallot consoled Nuannuan in a heavy breath. "Auntie will be OK."

"Thank you, Sister-in-Law. You must be very tired," said Nuannuan, holding Shallot's hands tight in hers and feeling a bit guilty.

"It's all right. How can this short trip kill me?" With that, Shallot rose. "I'll find an eatery to fix you a bowl of noodles…"

Nuannuan kept Mum company in the hospital for a month and a half. The surgery was scary; one whole breast had been cut away. Some flesh around the breast was taken too. But everything was OK. The doctor said that the chemotherapy and radiotherapy had driven all of the cancer cells away. Yet Mum was too weak to even walk because of the blood loss, chemotherapy and radiotherapy. Nuannuan felt sad seeing Mum like that; she remembered how Mum would carry more than fifty kilograms of corns and potatoes home during harvests. *Cancer, why do you pester my mum? Hasn't she suffered enough in her life? Isn't our family's life hard enough? Why do you bother us while staying away from the rich and powerful? Oh heavens, what have we done to offend you? You're so unfair. So unfair.*

Mum's two-month stay in the hospital had cost all the money Nuannuan had earned, and they paid for the rest with the only income Dad had from fishing. Grandma used to say that there are only three things for rural folk like them to do: build a house, get married and keep sickness away. It was not until then that Nuannuan had understood the weight of those words. The price of keeping sickness away is truly high: it turns one into a penniless pity overnight. After Mum returned home from the hospital, it was natural that Nuannuan was responsible for everything around the house because Hehe had her school, Dad had his fishing in the lake and Grandma was too old to pick up anything at all. Nuannuan set aside thoughts of Beijing and focused on the housework and her family's contracted farmland. During her break between farm work, Nuannuan always thought about the joyful time she had with the girls she worked with in Beijing. Every time she had these thoughts, she would sigh. *Now I'm trapped here in Chu Wang Village.*

Nuannuan had lost all her fondness for Chu Wang, the village where she was born.

In fact, Chu Wang Village was quite famous among the villages on Red Lake's west bank. It was famed for its good location. Hidden in a col covered with green trees and grass, facing the endless Red Lake, standing on the top of the mountain behind the village, one could see the water extending far into the distant east with fishing boats coming and going on it. If the weather was good enough, one could enjoy the misty view of the lake's east bank, as well as the rolling peaks of the Funiu Mountains and the sea of woods to the south, north and west. The wintry northeast wind would weaken when it arrived here, and the intense summer heat would lose its prowess when it came. Another reason for the village's reputation was its connection with the ancient Chu State. According to legend, when the Chu State made Danyang its capital, King Zhuang of Chu frequented Chu Wang Village because of its geographical features and its proximity to the capital.

She loathed the village primarily because she loathed farming. Farmlands in Chu Wang Village were fine. Though most fields were on small hills, the irrigation worked thanks to the lake nearby. They had a full water supply in drought, while the fast flow of water also tackled flooding. Nevertheless, what youth would favour a life of planting crops? Everyone knows the sufferings of a farmer. The unpredictable weather gives you physical misery, then the meagre price of crops gives you poverty.

Nuannuan knew that Kaitian was no exception. When he was still in school, his father wanted to train him on the farmlands, but he despised the work with a smirk. "No."

His father glared at him. "You little prick, stop being so proud. You're so certain about going to college and working in the uppity air as a government official. What if the odds only give you a chance to work in the field? You listen to me. Little people like us, as long as we are capable of farming our fields, we know two things for sure – we won't starve to death, and we can afford to get married..."

Those words were an unfortunate prophecy of Kaitian's life. He reluctantly started his life as a farmer after his father's injury. At this moment, he was already a proper farmer. Whenever Nuannuan could not keep up with all the work around the house, he always came over to help.

Nuannuan noticed that Kaitian would stop to gaze at her when he came to help. One day, she asked, blushing: "What are you looking at? You don't know me any more?"

Kaitian hung his head, smiling. "I think you've learned how to look prettier. You know how to wear your clothes better than other girls of your age. Your hairdo looks excellent too – it makes you appear more urbane."

"Nonsense! Who has taught you to become so glib-tongued? Your flattery makes you sound as if your mouth were honeyed up."

"I'm telling the truth. As soon as I saw you, I felt awed and pleased."

His remark made Nuannuan happy. But she still pretended to reprove him. "You're trying to butter me up."

Nuannuan's benefit from working in Beijing in the past two years was twofold: in addition to earning a few thousand yuan, she also opened her eyes and learned how to dress. Nuannuan paid particular attention to the urban girls' knack for matching clothes with jewellery. A smart high-school graduate, she soon got the hang of it. Unable to afford high-end clothes and jewellery, she looked presentable, dressed in clothes for twenty or thirty yuan, and adorned with jewellery for nineteen yuan. Coupled with her pretty face and shapely body, she was dressed more like a city dweller than any of the girls working with her in Beijing.

Nuannuan had found it difficult to reconcile with the fact that she could no longer go back to Beijing. With her determination and pride, she had always wanted her life in Beijing. Apart from the money, she had also hidden a secret wish of getting to know more people, which of course included young men in the big city. What if she eventually met someone agreeable, someone who adored her? Every time she thought about this, she felt guilty in front of Kaitian. Though she never promised anything to him, she had to admit that Kaitian had always been in her heart. But life in the city was too exciting, and it attracted her so much. Nuannuan felt quite defeated now that her days to come would be spent here in Chu Wang Village with Kaitian. Maybe she could still go to Beijing after Mum's recovery... Nuannuan was thinking of this when something happened in the village.

One morning, the villagers had just got up when a *suona* suddenly sounded at the village's southern end. It was clear that the cheerful tone could only reflect the sentiment of someone getting married. Nuannuan got up and combed her hair. She wondered who it could be as she had not heard anyone in the village would be having a wedding. At this time, firecrackers blasted, followed by the sound of footsteps of many people towards the village's end.

Nuannuan came out, saw Shallot and asked her what was happening. Shallot gave a wry smile and said: "It's not a wedding but a funeral. Zhan Tongfang is getting his dead son married with a dead girl's corpse."

"Dead people's marriage?" asked Nuannuan in astonishment.

"Yes, Zhan Tongfang's son couldn't find a suitable partner because his family was poor, but his parents kept complaining about his lack of skills. He was so angry that he killed himself by drinking pesticides last year. His parents felt guilty and had been busy finding a dead partner to marry him. A girl in Chenjia Village died of a sudden illness a few days ago, so the Zhan family asked someone to talk with the girl's family and got their consent. Zhan managed to borrow four thousand yuan to get that girl's body over.

Before sunrise today, the girl's coffin will be buried together with that of Zhan Tongfang's son."

Nuannuan was startled. "I see. I've never heard about this kind of marriage before. The woman's family is willing to give up her dead daughter's body?"

"Why not? Money talks nowadays, right? As the daughter can still bring money to her family in death, she's worthy of her parents' upbringing."

"Zhan Tongfang's son was pretty good-looking, so why couldn't he find a girlfriend when he was alive?" asked Nuannuan again.

Shallot sighed. "It isn't easy for presentable young men to find lifetime partners today. Every family in this area expects to have boys. Pregnant women try to get CT images of their foetuses in the township hospitals to determine if they have one. If not, they'll have an abortion. As a result, we've got fewer and fewer girls. Plus, most young women have gone out as migrant workers in the past few years. As our girls look pretty, few want to come back. They all want to find either city residents or male migrant workers. Consequently, our young men are having more and more difficulty finding spouses. Zhan Tongfang's son dated a girl, but she had a change of heart after working away from home and seeing the world. She thought that his family was too poor, and she broke up with him. He then dated a few more girls, but none ended up in marriage. His parents were so anxious that they blamed him, thus leading to his suicide."

Shallot's remarks saddened Nuannuan, who wondered why things like the marriage of dead people should happen in a modern age. She couldn't help walking to the end of the village. There, she caught sight of a yellow coffin with the symbol of marital happiness pasted on it. She also saw the percussion band with the *suona* as its lead instrument. Then, her eyes fell on the newly dug-out grave of Zhan Tongfang's son on the hillside.

"Nuannuan, do you believe in souls?" Kaitian suddenly asked behind her.

Startled, Nuannuan turned around.

"Do you believe in them?" asked Kaitian again, in all seriousness.

Nuannuan shook her head. "I don't know."

"A few days ago, I took Jiuding's boat across the lake to Deng

City. On our way back, we passed the Soul-Bewildering Zone. It happened that it was enshrouded in mist and fog. We stopped to watch the mist. Guess what we saw above it?"

Nuannuan didn't ask about the Soul-Bewildering Zone because she knew the triangular area in the middle of the lake was often covered in something like cooking smoke. It rose from the water surface and spread out, sometimes imbued with a burning smell, similar to what could be sniffed at the village's outskirts in the early evening. If standing on a boat close to the clouds of mist or smoke, one could even see images of people or objects. It was said that some single people even saw pretty girls. Some fisherwomen saw soldiers marching with swords, and some people claimed that they had spotted a large pile of gold. If a boat happened to venture into the smoky fog, the people on board would immediately feel dizzy, see stars and subsequently lose their bearings. They would be unconscious of what they were doing. Since accidents often occurred there, it was known as the Soul-Bewildering Zone. The triangular zone wasn't big, with the central area's linear distance measuring about a kilometre. People throughout the ages had tried to figure out why the smoke appeared in this area, but no one had come to a convincing conclusion.

Many stories were handed down from the past. One of the stories went that a dragon king's daughter lived under the water. Whenever she fixed her meals, smoke would rise from the water. According to another account, a hot spring irregularly erupted under the water and sent smoke out of it. Some claimed that the image was the manifestation of the lake god and the smoke its protection. Some people said that when the Qin army defeated the Chu army, the latter retreated southward. In the process, many military ships overturned and sank. It was the souls of those dead soldiers who were at work. Other people maintained that the King of Hell spewed smoke from time to time and hid countless ghosts in each cloud. After the founding of New China, the county organised scientists to investigate. But in the end, they reached no definite conclusions. They said it could be the abnormal changes in water temperature that produced the phenomenon. However, some bold people ventured in to gauge the temperature and found it not different from elsewhere in the lake. The county authority marked this area with three navigation marks to prevent people from entering it by mistake.

"Are you sure you don't want to know what I saw?"

"What?" Nuannuan's tone was unfriendly as she was not in a good mood.

"I saw Zhan Tongfang's son waving at me."

"Nonsense!" Nuannuan shot a glare at Kaitian. "The image in the smoke is the result of light reflection. It's a phantom. The tall tales are not true."

"It's true. Zhan Tongfang's son stood on the top of the smoke and continuously waved at me. I was panicky and showed Jiuding by pointing at it, but he said he saw nothing."

"You're trying to scare me." Nuannuan stamped her foot on the ground.

"I think Zhan Tongfang's son was inviting me," Kaitian joked. "If I can't marry you in the future, I'll die first like Zhan Tongfang's son. Then, we'll be buried and married together afterwards."

"You're talking nonsense." Nuannuan threw her glare at Kaitian like a dagger, turned around and left. She was antsy the whole day, troubled by a lingering fear arising from what she saw in the morning and what Kaitian told her. She had heard Grandma telling her about dead people's marriage, but she had never expected to see it with her own eyes. *Good heavens!* She couldn't help contemplating that Kaitian might be unable to get married if she went out to work again. But she said to herself: *Kaitian, you think I'll die for you? No, no, no.*

Nuannuan's return not only cheered up Kaitian for various reasons, but other young men in the village were quite excited too. One of them, Zhan Shiti, the brother of the committee leader, owned a consignment shop in the village. His excitement for Nuannuan was truly excessive. He would wait to chat with Nuannuan at the entrance to the village. At first, Nuannuan paid no attention to him. Since they had gone to the same secondary school, it felt natural to talk to him as friendly classmates. The conversations were nothing more than small household affairs, and they went on until one day when Zhan Shiti suddenly placed a plastic bag containing a brightly coloured shirt into her hands. Nuannuan had some idea about his intentions, so she quickly placed the bag back into his hands and said: "Thank you, Shiti, but I already have a shirt."

Nuannuan became more cautious about Zhan Shiti's advances after that. Her impression of him was not a very good one. She remembered him with bad grades and bad habits of copying other students' homework. His family had money, yet he was reluctant about school. After spending his first year in high school, he quit to open the shop in the village. Because of his brother's position, he always picked quarrels and fights with other people. Nuannuan told Kaitian about the shirt. Kaitian laughed and said: "He wants my wife. No way in hell."

Nuannuan gave Kaitian a soft punch and pretended to be angry. "Who promised you a wife? You wish."

One morning, Dad was still not up after Nuannuan had made breakfast. She thought Dad had overslept, so she went to call him outside his room. Mum, still weak and skinny, came out and said: "Dad wanted to get up, but he felt dizzy. My guess is he got too tired."

Nuannuan went out to get the doctor from Mei's Pharmacy, but Dad stopped her, yelling from the window: "Don't spend money on the doctor. I'm just tired. All I need is a couple of days. You take the boat to the lake today. The boat can't be idled. One idle day will cost us more than ten yuan."

Nuannuan did not hesitate. "Got it."

She took the boat out after breakfast. It was windy that day. Waves rushed towards her, one after another, rocking the boat from left to right, up and down. But Nuannuan felt at ease.

Nuannuan wasn't afraid of being in the lake even when she was a child. Grandma told her that she had been born at the lakeside and had described the circumstances of her birth many times. She said it had been at dusk when a fierce wind suddenly sprang up from the water and swept up huge waves, which looked scary. "Seeing that your dad hadn't come back, your mum was anxious. I tried to stop her, but she insisted on heading for the lakeside with her bulging belly. So, I had to follow her. Your mum was standing by the lake, shedding tears. She was sorrowful until she saw your dad returning. Seeing your mum holding her back with her hands while her big belly bounced up and down, your dad was unhappy. He asked: 'Why are you here?' Your mum smiled and said: 'It's because of the wind. I was worried about you.' Your dad mumbled as he threw the mooring rope to the shore. Usually, he would have jumped onto the beach and tied the rope to a stone column before carrying the net of fish from the boat. But that day, he just cast the cord onto the shore when your mum stooped down to help. Before your dad had time to stop her, things happened. Your mum stepped on the water that had splashed from the lake, and she slipped. She flopped to the ground, and I heard an 'ouch' from her. I went up, only to see blood streaming from the crotch of her pants. Panicked, your dad hurriedly jumped to the beach, trying to hold your mum with his clumsy hands. Your mum shook her head and said: 'I've probably given birth.' Both your dad and I were in a frenzy. I had just pulled your mum's pants down when your head stuck out. Your mum bit the umbilical cord off with her teeth, and I held you to the lakeside to rinse you. The water that day was pretty warm, so you took your first bath in the lake. As we had nothing to wrap you up, your mum held you close to her chest. Fearing you might feel cold because you had just taken a bath, your mum repeatedly said: 'I'm warming you up. I'm warming you up. I'm warming you up.' That was how you got the name Nuannuan. The monk Tianxin from Lingyan Temple came to the village on an errand a few days later. After hearing about your birth, he paid a special visit to the location by the lake and examined it. Then, he gave his prophecy, saying: 'This child chose to come into this world at this particular venue. I'm afraid that she and Red Lake will depend on each other for survival for her lifetime. Her life bounds in water, which will nurture the soil.'"

Nuannuan had to suppress her laughter every time she heard Grandma telling her the story. "Thank God it was summer. If it had been late autumn, I would have been miserable taking a bath in the lake."

She rowed the boat into the fishing area and stopped to put down the net. She was quite efficient. The large net was set in position after a short while, and she sat down in the boat, waiting for the moment to haul.

Nuannuan had been going to the lake with her father ever since she was four. Dad took her so that she would not bother Mum at home. He also wanted to raise her game so that she could inherit his fishing skills in the future.

Nuannuan was worthy of being born by the water because she wasn't afraid of it at all. When she was four years old, she dared to walk around on the boat without a care.

Dad would ask Nuannuan: "Are you dizzy?"

"No, I'm not."

"Nuannuan, are you afraid of seeing the lake water?"

"No, I'm not."

Dad would pull up the fishing net from the water. Nuannuan would hurry forward to hold down the flipping fish and try hard to put them in the tank. When they went to the lake to fish, the father and daughter always ate their lunch on board. Whenever the sun was above their heads, Dad would cast the net, stabilise the boat and say: "Let's eat." Nuannuan would hurriedly carry the cloth bag of food Mum had prepared in the morning and place it under Dad's feet. She would take out a bun and hand it to Dad before taking out another for herself. When she felt Dad was about to crave water, Nuannuan would reach over the side of the boat to scoop a bowl of the lake water and serve it to him. He would gulp it down in one breath and return the bowl to Nuannuan, who would scoop another bowlful and drink it herself.

Nuannuan remembered Dad teaching her to swim as soon as it was warm that year. How could fishers not know how to swim? He instructed his daughter how to paddle the water with her hands and kick it with her feet. He then demonstrated it a bit before tying a rope around Nuannuan's waist and pushing her splashing into the water. Dad's act caught Nuannuan off guard, and, finding herself in the water, she screamed in terror. She paddled with her dainty hands randomly out of her instinct to survive, and surprisingly her floundering kept her afloat. Dad laughed on the boat and reached his hand to pull his daughter on board. After she took her breath, he pushed her back into the water again.

Repeated pulling and pushing relieved Nuannuan of her fear so that she was no longer panicky. She could swim freely in only half a month. One afternoon, a gust of wind blew Dad's straw hat off and into the water a few metres away. Nuannuan said: "Dad, I'll get it for you."

Seeing the distance, Dad was worried that his daughter might be exhausted before she could swim back. He said: "Wait till I scull the boat closer." But before his words died off, the young Nuannuan had plunged herself into the water. Dad fixed his eyes on her, ready to throw himself into the water to her rescue. He had never expected that Nuannuan would manage to struggle back after retrieving the hat. Watching Nuannuan climbing into the boat, he broke into a smile and said: "You're incredible. You're as strong as your dad now."

Once she had mastered swimming, Dad began to teach her how to fish. He first told her how to distinguish fish, asking her to remember what silver carp and white carp were. He also taught her the different features of crucian carp, grass carp and catfish, and how to distinguish black carp and yellowhead catfish.

After that, Dad taught Nuannuan to know the water, instructing her to judge the depth by its colours, the wind speed by the size of the waves and the climate by observing the clouds.

By the age of six, Nuannuan understood Dad's intentions: he had no son, so she must be trained to be a fisher and thus pass the family skills down. More than once, Dad had said to her: "Once you have learned this job, you will not be afraid of any disasters. As long as Red Lake lies here, we Chu family will survive."

But Nuannuan had never been keen... she wanted to stay in the village and go to the neighbouring village's primary school with the neighbours' children. Whenever she saw the neighbours' children carrying their bags to school, young Nuannuan would gaze with envy, but she didn't dare to tell her father about her intent. She knew Dad's bad temper: he would slap people if he got angry.

When her discerning mother discovered Nuannuan's desire to go to school, she quietly discussed it with her husband. "Shall we send Nuannuan to school so that she'll learn for a few years? Otherwise, she'll become illiterate and won't even be able to spell her name. It will invite others' contempt."

Dad shot a glare at Mum and yelled: "Can we eat literacy? Satisfying the stomach is the top priority. Only by catching fish can we keep our stomachs full. Do you understand?"

Seeing Dad's anger, Mum didn't dare to insist.

So Nuannuan continued to go fishing with Dad in the lake. It wasn't until an accident happened when Nuannuan was seven years old that Dad changed his mind. It was an autumn afternoon. Dad sculled the boat with Nuannuan on it to fish in a rivulet flowing into the lake. He had just finished the second round of net casting when suddenly he fell onto the boat with his hands pressing against his chest.

Nuannuan was taken aback and hurriedly stepped forward,

asking: "Dad, are you OK?" With his teeth clenched, Dad couldn't speak. Nuannuan realised that Dad was suffering from a sudden illness and started to cry in fright. But she quickly stopped crying, knowing that tears alone couldn't save Dad. She tried to scull the boat to the shore, but the oar was too heavy. Only seven years old, she wasn't strong enough. She could only propel the boat a few dozen feet.

Standing on the bow, she cried for help, but the people on the other fishing boats were too far to hear her. *What to do?* In a hurry, she struck on an idea. She took off her red *dudou*, tied it to the harpoon, stood on the bow and shook it vigorously from side to side. She waved for half an hour before she attracted the attention of a fisherman on a boat in the distance. The fisherman thought it was strange initially, but he then realised that something serious might have happened and approached Dad's boat.

By the time they got Dad to Mei's pharmacy in Chu Wang Village, he was already breathing weakly. The veteran physician practising medicine in the pharmacy said that Nuannuan would have lost her father if they had been a few minutes later.

After his recovery, Dad learned from the fisherman that his daughter had saved him. Staring at his daughter by his bed, he was silent for a while. On the day he was fully recovered, Dad thanked the fisherman. He then called Nuannuan over, and said in a rare gentle tone: "Because you saved your dad's life, he wants to reward you. Tell me what you want the most from me."

Nuannuan lowered her head and said: "I don't want anything."

"Go ahead and ask me. I'll give you whatever you want."

Nuannuan hesitated a second and said: "I want to go to school."

Her reply caught Dad off guard. He hadn't expected that she would request this. But he nodded and said: "Fine. I'll send you to the elementary school in the neighbouring village when it opens. You can go to school now."

Nuannuan was so happy that she turned and threw herself into her mother's arms, her face blushing…

Though she had not been practising for some time, the first haul was satisfying. She got three silver carp, two grass carp and a mullet. She did an estimation in her mind: they would weigh at least four kilograms altogether. *My hands are still good, and so is my luck. Dad, I'll show you my day's work.*

She put the fish into the water tank and arranged a second net...

Nuannuan had been working like this for over a month. Dad had asked to go fishing several times, but she was worried that he was not fully recovered and might worsen his physical condition, so she insisted that he work in the fields.

When he wasn't working, Kaitian would stand by Red Lake to look out for Nuannuan's fishing boat. When it was close to the shore, he would spend a long time gazing at the lithe, slender figure moving on the vessel. Nuannuan was conscious of Kaitian's gaze. In the evening, when there were fewer people on the beach, Nuannuan would wave him over, take a fish from the basket, and throw it at his feet. Kaitian would crouch down, and when there were no people around, he would take it home.

An excellent farmer now, Kaitian had some savings, with which he would buy something for Nuannuan from time to time. One day after selling his cotton, he bought a blouse for her on Juxiang Street. He wrapped it up with a plastic bag and then with old kraft paper before returning to the lakeside with the package under his arm.

That same day, Nuannuan had been with her dad. Father and daughter had each brought a fish basket ashore, with Nuannuan following behind him. As Nuannuan walked by Kaitian, the boy tucked the packaged blouse in her hand. However, Nuannuan failed to hold onto it, and it fell to the ground. At that moment, her dad had just turned to talk to her, so quick-thinking Nuannuan crouched abruptly and yelled: "Who dropped this on the ground?" She then picked up the kraft-paper package and made her dad believe she had stumbled upon it.

Dad said with great interest: "I didn't see it." Then he whispered a warning: "Don't open it until we get home."

At home, Dad opened it and patted his daughter on her shoulder, beaming. "You're so lucky that you picked up a blouse for yourself."

In those days when Nuannuan went fishing, Kaitian repeatedly told her to be careful not to enter the Soul-Bewildering Zone. He was worried that the foggy smoke might trap her. Each time, Nuannuan would smile and say: "It might not be too bad if I go in there. If I fail to come back, you can buy blouses for other girls." Her remark angered Kaitian. He raised his hand and meant to slap her, but he loved her too much to do that, so he put it back down.

Grandma, Mum and Dad all knew about Nuannuan's close relationship with Kaitian but thought they were simply friends from the same village. With Nuannuan's pretty face and Kaitian's poor household, no one ever considered marriage. Mum was a little worried seeing Nuannuan single at the proper age to marry. Then one day, she saw the village matchmaker, Mr Tianfu, walking to their door with a cigarette in his mouth. She hastily stood up and said: "Mister, please take a seat."

Mr Tianfu did not decline and entered the house. Dad dared not treat him without courtesy. He gave Tianfu his own seat and offered him cigarettes and tea. After smoking for a while, Mr Tianfu slowly asked: "Our child Nuannuan hasn't got any arrangement, right?"

"Not yet. You know anyone suitable?" asked Grandma.

Mr Tianfu flicked the tobacco ash off his fingers and said: "Go and get her over here." As soon as Nuannuan entered the room, Mr Tianfu asked her in all seriousness: "Nuannuan, what kind of a husband are you looking for? Tell your grandpa."

Only then did Nuannuan know that Mr Tianfu was there to act as a matchmaker. Rubbing the tips of her toes on the ground in embarrassment, she asked with a smile: "Who do you have in mind?"

"I've got two candidates for you to choose," Mr Tianfu said, stroking his beard. "The first is Huang Biaozi from Huanjia Village on the west bank. He's tall and stout and so strong that he could lift a millstone. He's from a well-to-do family that has a TV set and a newly bought tractor. He can use it for transportation and ploughing the fields. He's as old as you are. His only blemish is that one of his eyes is a bit slanting. But that's not a big deal. It won't affect his ability to drive the tractor fast. Neither will it affect his married life. The second one is Liu Shengcai, a handsome young man with fine features. He smiles at everyone as if he were a teacher. He lives in Liujiaqiao Village and works as its accountant, so he has a great time every day. His birth year zodiac animal is compatible with yours. The only thing that might not be satisfactory is that he was married. His wife died in a car accident last year. But he has no child, so you wouldn't have to be a stepmother after you marry him."

Nuannuan immediately pulled a long face. Her dad hastily cut in for fear that she might say something unpleasant to offend Mr Tianfu. "Nuannuan, we can't be too ambitious. It would be best if you remembered you're a village girl yourself. We can't afford to choose. A village girl who's looking for a husband has two things to consider. First, your would-be husband's family must be rich enough to prevent you from living a harsh life. Second, he must be strong enough to support the family. All the other conditions are nothing but nonsense. If you only think of looks, you must consider whether appearance can feed you."

"Grandpa Tianfu, after listening to what you said, I feel you're selling second-class goods to me. Aren't you?" said Nuannuan coldly, in defiance of her dad's advice.

Mr Tianfu unexpectedly broke into a smile. "All right. I'm glad we're on the same page. I anticipated that you wouldn't like them. I was just teasing you. Our Nuannuan is so pretty that everyone would fall in love at first sight. You're also a high-school graduate and have seen the world in Beijing. How can Grandpa have the heart to send you to families like those? I'm here to tell you that Grandpa has found you a good match. This future groom's name will surely please you as soon as you hear it."

Mum smiled and had to ask: "Whose son is he?"

"Zhan Shiti. Little brother of the leader. That boy asked me several times to come here and talk about this marriage. Yesterday, the leader called me to his office about it. I'm here today exactly for this."

The whole family was shocked, and nobody said anything. Nuannuan was speechless, as she had not expected Zhan Shiti to do this. The other three were surprised. *The leader's brother has his eyes upon Nuannuan?*

Dad spoke first. "This... is good, of course good. The leader's family... Nuannuan is lucky to have this."

"With marriage to the leader's family, no one will bully us ever again," Mum said, shooting a glance at Nuannuan.

Nuannuan was worried. She did not want things to go this way. She had to speak out. "Mr Tianfu, if you truly wish me a good marriage, go and talk to Kaitian's family."

Tianfu did not recognise the name. "Who is Kaitian?"

"Son of the Kuang family. The farmers," reminded Grandma.

Mum looked at Nuannuan, beginning to understand her thoughts.

"Humph. You want him? Are you out of your mind?" said Mr Tianfu, glaring. "His house is a pit of poverty. Once you jump into it, you'll never get out of that life. Don't you know about his disabled dad? Their lands are all farmed by Kaitian alone. If you marry him, you'll become their lifetime servant at once."

Nuannuan smiled. "I want to work for a longer time. All the jobs I had in Beijing were short-term. The boss kicks you out whenever he wants."

Mr Tianfu glared even harder at her and sighed. "You must think about this. It's about your life. It's not a game…"

The next day, everyone in the village heard the news about the leader sending Mr Tianfu to Nuannuan's house. Shallot came over immediately to verify the gossip. Nuannuan nodded. "He offered me Zhan Shiti, the younger brother of Zhan Shideng. I prefer Kuang Kaitian to him. I can't leave to work in the city any more, so I have to find someone here. I prefer Kaitian. What do you think? Which one of the two do you think suits me better?"

Shallot hesitated. "I can't be sure. But if we look at how things are now, Zhan Shiti is not that reliable. Kuang Kaitian is more down to earth than him. But I must be honest with you – there's something about Kuang Kaitian that I don't like."

Hearing this, Nuannuan's almond-shaped eyes opened wide. "What is it?"

"He's ruthless."

Nuannuan was surprised. "Ruthless? What do you mean?"

"I don't know how to put it. He's just quite ruthless with stuff. If he needs to carry something in his farm work, he'll carry more than 150 kilograms at one time. If his bull eats the crops, he'll tie it to a tree and whip it for two hours – the bull even weeps. The last time he accidentally broke a new water jar, he slapped himself in regret until his mouth bled."

Nuannuan smiled. "Ahh, you mean that. I think he's got character. And I like men with character."

"I'm just saying… anyway, a woman looking for a man is just looking for someone she likes. Once you like him, you'll want to sleep in the same bed with him for 365 days a year, you'll want to eat from the same bowl with him for 365 days a year, and you'll want to have children with him and wash his clothes."

Nuannuan blushed. "Thank you, Shallot…"

Kuang Kaitian heard about the gossip in the afternoon of the next day. He was fertilising the fields. He dropped the cart filled with shit and ran to the bank of Red Lake, waiting for Nuannuan's boat to arrive. Nuannuan saw Kaitian from afar and knew he must have heard something, so she turned her head away, pretending she hadn't seen him. As soon as the boat arrived, Kaitian jumped aboard, but Nuannuan did not look at him, and he had to cough loudly. Nuannuan turned her head back and asked in a cold tone: "What's up? Have you got a sore throat?"

Kaitian's face turned red. After a while, he said: "I heard someone is going to marry the leader's brother."

"Oh yeah? It's a blessing to marry into the Zhan family. They have the money and the authority. The marriage will make life so easy." Nuannuan stood up, showing no emotion at all.

Kaitian's face turned white. "So you do want to marry him."

Nuannuan felt satisfied seeing him like that. But she kept a straight face and asked: "Who said that?"

"Didn't you just say so?"

"That's what Mum and Dad want."

Kaitian got more worried. "What about you?"

"Do you care about this?" said Nuannuan, her voice sounding bitter. "You don't seem worried at all. You only worry about farming. Your corn, potatoes, wheat, beans. Do you care about me? You think of your wheat more than you think of me."

"I thought we were an item already."

"What item? When did you talk about this item with Mum, Dad and Grandma? Do you think I'm a radish, a pak choi, that you can buy from the market?"

"What do I do now? Who do I speak to?"

"Are you asking me? What use is your head? Is it broken? Why didn't you go and find a matchmaker? Why am I rushing you to do this? I'm in high demand. It's not like I'm dying as a spinster, lying in a spinster's tomb."

"All right, all right. I'll go to Mr Tianfu." Kaitian jumped out of the boat in a rush and ran into the village…

The sky was not even dark when the leader, Zhan Shideng, walked into Nuannuan's yard. Nuannuan and her family were sitting there having dinner.

As he opened the gate, Zhang Shideng called out: "Uncle Chu, are you having dinner?"

Dad was flattered and in shock. This was the first time Zhan Shideng had come to their house in a dozen years as the village committee leader. It was also the first time he had addressed Dad as Uncle Chu. Every time they saw each other, the leader either paid no attention or simply called him by his full name. Sometimes he would call him Old Chu, which was not as respectful as Uncle Chu.

Dad hastened to put down his chopsticks and offered a seat. "Mr Leader. Sit. You are a rare guest. Have you eaten? I'll get Nuannuan to give you some noodles. They're made of green beans. Nuannuan, come."

Zhan Shideng waved his hand. "No bother. I've eaten."

Nuannuan did not make a big move. She stood up to show courtesy, but her bowl was still in her hands. She figured out the guest's intentions almost immediately: Mr Tianfu must have failed to express her refusal, and things had just got more complicated.

"Uncle Chu, you know me. I'm a straightforward man. I come here tonight for no other reason – the marriage of Shiti and Nuannuan. Has Tianfu given you a clear picture of this? I'm here to make sure you understand. I, the leader, the big brother, sincerely support the marriage. After Nuannuan enters my family, we Zhans will make sure of her happiness. I had a good idea and made a decision about Shiti's shop. I will put Nuannuan in charge, and she will lead a good life, sheltered from the wind and the rain..."

"I believe you. I do." Dad nodded and glanced at Nuannuan, his face lit up with a smile.

Nuannuan sneered silently. *I didn't agree to anything at all, yet he is already talking about married life and the shop. He's so sure about this.*

"If you ask me, both Shiti and Nuannuan have come of age. So if both of you agree, let's choose a good date for the wedding. And you need not worry any more." Zhan Shideng also looked at Nuannuan. The glance seemed unquestionable.

Nuannuan anxiously put down her bowl and said: "I'm afraid..."

"I agree." Dad spoke out before her, his eyes more serious than before. Nuannuan looked at him in surprise. She hadn't expected Dad to say that because he knew it was Kaitian she wanted to marry.

"I will not bother you any longer. Please continue eating." Zhan Shideng didn't give Nuannuan the opportunity to talk as he quickly rose and walked towards the door. "Uncle Chu, you always ride your bike to Juxiang Street to sell the fish. I'll have Shiti buy you a motorcycle soon. It will be faster and lighter."

"No, no, I'm OK." Dad waved his hand. He looked very happy.

Dad seemed quite excited when he came back from sending the leader off. He kept rubbing his hands. "Who'd have known? Who'd have known?"

Nuannuan threw her chopsticks away in anger, making a loud noise against the bowl. "I decide my marriage. What time are we living in? Are you trying to arrange my marriage?"

"What are you talking about?" said Dad in a cold voice. "Mum and I, we wouldn't give you anything bad. It's all for your own good."

"For my own good against my wish?" said Nuannuan as she glared. "You hear me now. I lived in Beijing. I know things. I'm in charge of my marriage. No one tells me what to do."

Mum tried to make peace. "Nuannuan, we can talk about this."

"Talk? I already told you I want to marry Kaitian. But Dad just agreed to marry me into the Zhans. What do I do?"

Grandma suddenly spoke. "Nuan, I have been in your place. I wanted to find someone I liked. But days are days, and you can't pass even one day without money and food. Kaitian is a good boy, but his budget is always tight. It'll be too late to regret after you marry him. Young people always talk about feelings and love, but you'll understand after you get married. Those things never last. Only your days last. Besides, I'm not so sure about that Kaitian. I always see him hanging his head low when he walks. There's a saying that a man is afraid that he might get a cocky woman, and a woman fears she might marry a man who's always brooding. I'm worried that you may suffer in his hands in the future. And there's something else. I asked Grandpa Elm to read your and Kaitian's fortune yesterday. Guess what the fortune teller said."

"What did he say," asked Nuannuan's mum in anxiety.

"He said if Nuannuan marries Kaitian, she'll drink from two water wells."

"What does that mean?" asked Nuannuan, staring at Grandma with raised eyebrows.

"It means that you'd be married to one man but drink water from another man's well."

"Grandma, what stale gossip and trivial superstitious nonsense are you telling me? So, a man looking up every day is a good husband? A woman who drinks from the same well every day is a good wife? People in the city drink from many wells. Does it mean that their women remarry all the time?"

Nuannuan walked out with a pout. She didn't want to listen to Grandma's nagging any more. The village seemed at peace after a busy day. Some people were still doing their dishes, while some others had already gone to bed and turned their lights out. The dog next door heard her steps and growled quietly. Then it paced away, wagging its tail. Maybe it recognised her figure. Nuannuan strolled down the road towards the lake. The sky had turned dark, but the reflection on the lake lit up the road for her. Truth is, Nuannuan knew the road by heart. She could tell all the bumps and puddles, even with her eyes closed. How many times had she walked on this road in her life?

"Who is it?" someone shouted suddenly.

Nuannuan realised that she had reached the doorstep of Mr Tianfu's house. She responded: "Mr Tianfu, it's me. Are you still up?"

"Ahh, Nuannuan. That boy, Kaitian, he ruined my rest. He asked me to make sure that I go to your house again and talk about his marriage with you. How dare I? I just went there for the Zhans. I asked the boy: 'What are you doing? Nuannuan is promised to the leader's little brother. They are planning the wedding now. If you step in now, what will the leader do? Isn't it easy for him to give you a hard time? You'd better give up as early as you can. There are so many girls under heaven, so why don't you cling to one till you die?' Don't you think what I said to him makes sense?"

"Where is he?"

"He left in anger. Oh well, what a bad matchmaker I am. If I knew you both had this thought, I wouldn't have helped the leader and let Kaitian step in now," mumbled Mr Tianfu as he walked back into the yard.

Nuannuan stood for a while in silence. Then she turned back to walk to Kaitian's house. Before entering, she heard Kaitian's mother. "Marriage is prearranged by the gods. If she's yours, she can't escape. If she's not, you can't push her. Think about this – without Nuannuan, are you never going to marry?"

Next was the voice of Kaitian's father. "If you ask me, all that men want from their wives are children. Whoever can give birth to your child, marry her."

What she heard next was Kaitian's mother's voice. "Marry whoever can give birth? You're talking nonsense. Why didn't you find a limp girl to marry instead of me?"

Kaitian's father said in a subdued voice: "I was trying to help Kaitian to get over his sadness."

"Step aside. It isn't the right way to make him feel better."

Nuannuan did not want to listen. She raised her hand to knock on the door.

Kaitian opened the door. His parents were surprised to see Nuannuan, and they didn't know what to say. Before his parents reacted, Kaitian took Nuannuan's hand and walked her towards his room. In his room, Kaitian said in desperation: "Mr Tianfu told me that he dare not be part of this any more. He told me the little brother asked the leader in tears. He told me the leader promised his mother that you'd be her daughter-in-law. He told me that your parents and grandma all agreed."

Nuannuan sneered. "What a joke."

"What joke?" asked Kaitian, puzzled.

"Like I'll just marry because the leader wants me to."

"So what are you going to do?" Kaitian's eyes were wide open. He noticed the tear marks on Nuannuan's face, as well as her red eyes.

Nuannuan stared at Kaitian in expectation. "The two of us are the only people who have a say in this."

Kaitian shrugged. "What about the two of us?"

"Can't you use your head?"

"My head?" Kaitian stared at Nuannuan. All of a sudden, he

patted her on the head and said: "We can run away. Far away. To Zhengzhou, Beijing or even Guangzhou. And they'll never find us."

"No running," said Nuannuan. "Our families will suffer if we do. The leader will be so angry. Not to mention how much both of our families need us. My mum is sick. Your dad is disabled."

"What now…"

"Use your head."

"I'll go to your house and give your family hundreds of yellow soybeans, all that we got from last year's harvest. Your parents and Grandma will think again about this marriage."

"How can your gift compare with the leader's? They're talking about a motorcycle for Dad's fish selling on Juxiang Street."

Kaitian took one step back. "Oh dear."

"Use your head. C'mon."

"I'll go and persuade your parents and the leader. I'll tell them we've been an item from the beginning."

"Persuade? How do you persuade them about this? Even my parents won't listen to you. Not to mention Zhan Shideng."

"Then what…"

"Your head. Use it."

"I don't know." Kaitian touched his head, looking helpless.

Nuannuan suddenly dropped her voice. "When I worked in Beijing, I heard of this thing called a de facto marriage."

"De facto?" Kaitian did not understand and just gazed at her.

"It's like… two people did not get a marriage registration but live like husband and wife without their parents' permission. Others have to recognise their marriage in this case." Nuannuan lowered her head to hide her blushing face.

Kaitian bit his tongue in surprise. "So you mean…"

"You should sneak out to buy a couple of cracker strings from Juxiang Street and some papercuts of the Red Double Happiness."

Kaitian stared at Nuannuan in shock. But his eyes revealed his fast thinking.

"I'll drop by your place in secret tomorrow after breakfast. You will light the crackers as soon as you see me. Then we'll stick the Red Double Happiness on the doors. The neighbours will come over to see what happened and you should tell them that you just married me. We'll see what the leader can do about that."

Kaitian hesitated. "What if the leader sends people over to force you?"

"What? They dare not. It's not like the old times any more. We've got the Women's Federation, the police and the courts."

"What if he thinks of other ways to make trouble?"

"If you're so scared, well, I'll leave. You can just wait for the Zhans to take me as a bride." Nuannuan turned her back.

Anxiously, Kaitian pulled her back and gave her a regretful smile. "I just want to make sure everything's right. If we do it, what about your parents and grandma?"

"There's no other way. I have to ignore how they feel. They are the ones who insist on going against my wish." Nuannuan sighed.

Feeling quite moved, Kaitian pulled Nuannuan into his arms. "Nuannuan, I don't know what to say. I'll pay you back in the future. I'll give you a good life. I'll be good to you. I'll love only you my whole life. I won't glance at any other woman…"

Once Nuannuan had left, Kaitian rushed to tell his parents about her idea. His parents were in shock. After a while, his mother said: "Good Gracious. What if Nuannuan's dad and the leader's brother come over to make trouble?"

"That's nothing," answered Kaitian's father. "We didn't force Nuannuan into the house – it was her own wish. What can they do about it?"

Kaitian's mother put her hand on her chest. "I'm scared. I haven't seen anything like this in my life."

Kaitian answered in a deep voice: "Mum, this is the only way I can marry Nuannuan. Nuannuan's a girl, and she's not afraid. So why should we be? Bolt worked in Guangzhou, and he told me that a lot of people in big cities live together without getting married. It's legal now. They call it a common-law partnership. All you need to worry about is cleaning the house…"

The next evening after dinner, Nuannuan went into the thick bed of reeds by Red Lake where Kaitian was waiting for her. He whispered his achievements to her. "This morning after breakfast, Mum cleaned the house, and Dad gave me a roll of cash. I rode to Juxiang Street and bought a couple of cracker strings, each with five thousand salutes. Then I bought six Red Double Happiness papercuts, some lamb and some pork. I even got you this outfit from the shop. In the end, I also bought new bedsheets and two pillows. I put it all in the wicker basket on my back and covered it with my shirt and some green leaves on top. Then I rode back to the village. Nobody realised what I was doing. Dad did not go to the fields today – he helped Mum with the housework. The two of them tidied everything and paid special attention to our room, the one we are using for the wedding. They changed the sorghum mat on the bed and put on new blankets and sheets. They put a red string strap on the water vase so that we can use it as the potty underneath our bed. They were in a rush, so the bedside table was not replaced. But Mum covered it with a plastic tablecloth, so it looks nice."

Nuannuan interrupted Kaitian with a sigh. "All right."

"Are you angry with me?" Kaitian held tight to her hands.

Nuannuan shook her head in silence.

"What else do you want me to do?" Kaitian asked carefully.

"Nothing. Go home." Nuannuan waved her hand.

Kaitian tried to pull her into his arms, but he saw that she had no intention to come close. So he gave up and left, turning his head to look at her repeatedly as he walked.

The lake reflected a dense cluster of stars waving on the surface like struggling fish in a net. Standing by the lake, Nuannuan gazed at the stars in the water silently. She yelled in her heart: *God of Red Lake, you can read my mind. Please tell me if my de facto marriage is OK. Am I crossing the line? Am I breaking the rules Chu Wang Village has followed for so many years? Am I going to be spat on and cursed? Will my decision make me a slut? Will it offend you too? Well, I think Kaitian will make my life happy. I must fight for my happiness. I can't care that much any more.*

After a long time, Nuannuan went to the water again and scooped some up to wash her face. She then walked towards the village, step by step.

Nuannuan didn't sleep that night. She thought about the next day when she would become Kaitian's woman. She would live and eat with him every day. She could cover his forehead with her kisses, hold up his clothes to see what she had desired to see, and do that thing she had craved but dared not to elaborate in her imagination. Her heart flew up to such a height that she felt drunk in sweetness. Yet again, she thought about the impact of this on her parents and grandma. Her heart ached. *Dad, Mum, am I a bad daughter? Grandma, will you see me as the shame of the family?*

Nuannuan was up before sunrise. She lit the fire and started making breakfast. *Dad, Mum, Grandma, it will be the last meal I make for you as an unmarried daughter...*

Hehe ate first before school. Nuannuan went to sweep the yard and clean the pigsty. Dad sounded bitter when he got up. "What are you doing so early?"

"I woke up early," Nuannuan answered vaguely. She carried the basin in front of Mum's bed.

Mum was surprised. "I can walk around on my own now. You don't have to do this."

"It's easier for you this way." Nuannuan put on a smile, but inside she wanted to cry. "Mum, I may not find the time to do this even if you want me to in the future."

Grandma was about to comb her hair, but Nuannuan took the comb. "Grandma, let me do it for you."

Grandma was surprised. "Aha! You want to comb my hair."

Nuannuan smiled again. "I guess the sun is rising from the west today." Combing Grandma's thin grey hair, she felt tears in her eyes, as she realised that she might not be able to help Grandma every day...

After breakfast, Dad left to farm the field, Mum was feeding the chickens and Grandma was weaving a yarn. Nuannuan walked towards the yard gate in her old clothes. She paused at the doorstep and took a look at her familiar house. Then, after some hesitation, she stepped out.

The village was running as usual. People were getting ready to work in the fields after breakfast. Bulls were shaking the bells on their necks. The ploughs and sickles were tinkling. The sheep were *mehh-ing*, and the donkeys were *bahh-ing*. The dogs were barking as they played. Nuannuan walked towards Kaitian's house quietly. She knew that what she was about to do would engulf the village. But right now, no one knew what was about to happen. They greeted her as usual. *What will they do once they find out about this?*

Closer and closer was she approaching Kaitian's house. Clearer and clearer could she see Kaitian standing in front of the gate in his new clothes. Nuannuan picked up her pace.

At that moment, Kaitian's neighbour, Spotty Laosi, saw Kaitian and called out: "Ho-ho! Looking sharp. You must be going on a blind date. Tell me, tell your old bro, which pretty girl are you seeing? Is she from here or elsewhere?"

Kaitian was apparently scared, and he went back into the house. Nuannuan slowed down and waited till Laosi had gone. Kaitian was waiting for Nuannuan by the door. He ran out and pulled her in as if he was afraid that someone would take her away. "Your parents don't know, right?" Kaitian sounded worried.

Nuannuan nodded. Kaitian's parents came to welcome her. "Come inside, my child."

Kaitian took out the clothes he bought the day before and said: "Put these on." The style of the clothes was all right, but they were a bit large on Nuannuan. "Put them on for now, and I'll buy you something new to wear."

With that, he went to paste the Red Double Happiness. Only then did he notice that his family dog was eating the wheat paste and had almost finished it. "Bitch!" Kaitian kicked it, sending it rolling on the ground and scurrying out of the courtyard.

His mother said: "Don't worry, you can use the leftover rice in the pot as wheat paste."

He put the six papercuts on the yard gate, the house door and the kitchen door. Then he went to light the crackers, but his hands were too shaky. He used three matches, but none lit the fuse. Nuannuan had to step up and light the crackers. As the crackers went off, all the dogs in the village started barking. Despite the noise, Nuannuan and Kaitian heard their neighbours open and close their doors. The children came over first, followed by the young wives and young men.

Spotty Laosi's wife saw the Red Double Happiness on the yard gate and cried out in surprise: "Ho-ho! Kaitian, you dog. You didn't tell us about your wedding. We could at least give you a present. Were you hiding your pretty bride from us?"

Jiuding, also a fisher, laughed. "Kaitian can really keep a secret. We neighbours didn't know who the bride is, and there she is, marrying into his family."

The wife of Zhan Datong, a pig castrator, laughed even louder. "Kaitian, drag your bride out so we can examine her belly. Are the seeds you sowed already geminating so that you have no choice but to marry her?"

The crowd were laughing and talking as they entered the yard. Kaitian's mum brought out peanuts, melon seeds and sweets and thrust them into the hands of the children and the neighbours. People pushed each other inside the house in excitement. When they saw Kaitian holding Nuannuan's hand, they stopped talking and laughing in shock. None of the guests thought Nuannuan from the village would be the bride. Everyone knew Nuannuan's family was richer than Kaitian's. And a girl like Nuannuan, who had always stood out in the village, and had been chosen by the leader's family, could never marry Kaitian.

Nuannuan broke the awkwardness. She smiled gently and said: "Come sit down. Don't you all recognise me? Spotty's wife and Jiuding need a cigarette. Kaitian, come over and serve them."

By then, the crowd were noisy again. Jiuding was amazed. "My goodness. Who'd have known this."

Spotty's wife said: "Kaitian, you fucking rascal. You planned this to put us all in shock."

Zhan Datong's wife was laughing. "Kaitian, your secret is like a sorghum field at midday in July – not even the wind can sneak in or out."

Kaitian could not speak. He just stood there, smiling in happiness. Children ran out with sweets, peanuts and melon seeds in their hands. They called out: "Come and check out Nuannuan the bride."

Kaitian's mum walked in and said: "No one leaves this afternoon. We have a wedding feast for you. We're all drinking."

Spotty's wife said: "I don't even have a present with me. How can I drink your wine like this?"

Nuannuan hurriedly cut in. "Don't mention presents. Kaitian and I will be happy as long as you stay and enjoy the feast with the wedding wine."

Spotty, who had just pushed himself through the crowd inside, said: "Drink, drink. You're a fool not to drink when they offer. But Kaitian, you must tell us in detail how you lured Nuannuan into your house. I want to get a pretty girl myself someday."

Before Kaitian could respond, Spotty's wife punched him on his shoulder and reproved: "You're fucking daydreaming. How can you think of getting a pretty girl since you're so ugly?" The crowd burst into guffaws.

As the crowd was laughing and joking, they heard a noise from the yard gate. Nuannuan's dad walked in with a serious face. Jiuding did not realise the problem and thought he was here for the wedding. He laughed and said: "Kaitian, come here to greet your father-in-law."

Unexpectedly, Nuannuan's dad yelled at Jiuding: "Bullshit. I'm no one's father-in-law."

Everyone went stiff at his words. All eyes fell upon Kaitian. Prepared, Kaitian smiled and walked up to him. "Dad, you're here. Come in-"

Before he could finish, Nuannuan's dad raised his hand and slapped him. "Arsehole! How dare you seduce my daughter."

Everyone was too shocked to help.

Nuannuan stepped forward. "Dad. What are you doing? I wanted this. It's not his fault."

"You – you." Chu Changshun pointed a shaking finger at his daughter. "You're the shame of the family. I've lost face, and my ancestors' face, because of you."

"Dad! I'll be good to Nuannuan." Kaitian resumed his smile. "I'll help with your fishing and take care of you, Mum and Grandma. I swear-"

"Fuck off!" Dad yelled in anger and staggered out. The crowd felt the awkwardness and began to walk out quietly too. The yard, filled with laughter a moment before, suddenly became quiet.

Kaitian said to Nuannuan: "Go and rest in the room. We saw this coming. It's fine. He's your dad. It's nothing if he takes it out on you."

Nuannuan smiled bitterly. "It's not my biggest trouble. I'm worried about the leader..."

As she said those words, loud steps could be heard outside. Kaitian realised who they belonged to and whispered: "Mum, come and sit down with Nuannuan. Dad, don't move. I'll do the talking."

A cry came from outside the yard. "Kuang Kaitian! Get out here!"

Kaitian pretended that he didn't know anything and called out as he walked: "Are you here for the wedding? Forget about the present. Just come in and drink with us."

It was Zhan Shiti, the leader's brother, standing there with his male cousins. The leader himself was not among them.

"Have a cigarette." Kaitian took some out of his pocket.

Zhan Shiti shouted: "Beat him up!"

The cousins went forward in a flash. Kaitian tried his best to resist, but they were too many, and he was pinned down on the ground.

"What are you doing? And in broad daylight?" Kaitian cried out.

Nuannuan could hear everything, and she was about to walk out, but Kaitian's mum held her back. "You can't go. They'll hurt you too."

"So you know it's in broad daylight. Why did you abduct my woman, then? I'll show you," Zhan Shiti shouted as he kicked and punched Kaitian.

Kaitian, who could not fight back, did his best to cover his head and crouch so that they could not hit his critical parts. His only hope was the village people nearby, watching all this happen. He hoped some would come up and help him out. But no one came. They did not want to cross the leader's brother and the Zhans. He regretted the de facto marriage in excruciating pain, but it was just a flash and immediately gave way to anger. He now regretted not taking a cleaver from the kitchen when he had come out. Kaitian was worried about his parents. *What if they hurt them too?*

As he was thinking about all that, he heard Nuannuan's loud voice from the yard gate. "Zhan Shiti! You don't get to hurt people as you like."

Zhan Shiti paused as he did not expect to hear that. "You said that Kaitian abducted your woman. But I, Chu Nuannuan, am no woman of yours. You hear me now. I married into the Kuangs because I wanted to. What you just did is against the law. If you keep it up, I'll kill you. I'll call the police, and they will not let you off."

Zhan Shiti did not expect Nuannuan to interfere and make a loud speech in front of all the villagers. He could not speak.

At that moment, an authoritative voice came from the wall next door. "Shiti. Go away." It was Zhan Shideng, the leader. He was walking towards them, his face motionless. "Street fighting in broad daylight! You outlaws. Get away."

Zhan Shiti and his cousins had no choice but to retreat in

disappointment. Zhan Shideng bowed down to pull Kaitian up. "My apologies. My little brother is a mule. He knows nothing. Don't worry about it. Go back to your wedding. The world today is all about freedom to marry, and no one should have a say on this."

Kaitian wiped the blood from his mouth and answered in a deep voice: "Mr Leader, thank you."

"Here, take this present. It's not much, but I want you to have it." Zhan Shideng put twenty yuan in Kaitian's hand.

"No, no, I can't take this." Kaitian raised his arm to give the money back. It hurt so much that he drew a cold breath.

"I have a meeting in the township this morning. So I can't drink with you. Sorry about that." Zhan Shideng smiled at Kaitian and Nuannuan, then quickly walked away. The villagers looking on all around also scattered. Silence reigned in front of the Kuang house.

Nuannuan came to hold Kaitian. "Where does it hurt?"

Kaitian forced a smile. "They didn't break any bones. It's OK. It's OK. It was to be expected."

Nuannuan helped Kaitian into the courtyard. Kaitian's parents rushed down to take off his shirt and check his injuries. It was OK. The injuries were not deep.

That afternoon, the wedding was predictably unpopular. Friends and family didn't get invited, and the neighbours were too scared to come. But the four members of the Kuang family were happy to sit around the table. Kaitian's parents were happy because they did not expect such an agreeable daughter-in-law without any money spent. The young couple were happy because, as wished, they finally were married.

Just before they started eating, Shallot's voice rose in the yard. "Kaitian, Nuannuan. Do you have a drinking cup for me?"

The whole family went out to welcome her. Shallot passed two colourful pieces of cloth and a new washing basin to Kaitian and said: "I just heard about the wedding. I ran to Chen's shop and bought these presents."

Nuannuan hugged Shallot and teared up. "Sorry I didn't tell you this earlier."

Shallot patted her back softly. "I was surprised. But I'm still happy for you. You should do whatever you like. Now let's drink."

Shallot was not a drinker, but that afternoon she got herself tipsy. Her legs were shaky when she raised the last cup. She grabbed

Kaitian's shoulder and said: "Kaitian, as a woman, I know how difficult it was for Nuannuan to make this decision. There's no way that she would do this if not for the true feelings she has for you. You must be good to her. In truth, we're not related. But Nuannuan is more than a sister to me. If you treat her bad, I'll show you."

Kaitian raised his hand as he promised Shallot: "Rest assured. Nuannuan will be my precious for a lifetime…"

Unsurprisingly, no one came to visit the wedding chamber and act out the customary horseplay to tease the newlyweds later that night. Kaitian and Nuannuan were not surprised. They were more at ease without the crowd. Kaitian whispered comforts in Nuannuan's ears so that she would not feel disappointed. Afterwards, he went to the wedding bed to get ready for the long-anticipated wedding night.

Nuannuan might have been bold in deciding to marry Kaitian de facto, but she was timid on the bed. After Kaitian carried her to bed, she covered her face with her hands. Kaitian undressed her with great effort. When the snow-white breasts presented themselves to his surprised eyes, Kaitian covered them with his hands as if they were birds ready to fly away. He buried his face in them and said in ecstasy: "I've been dreaming of them for many a night. I'm looking at them finally. Good heavens, whenever I saw them bouncing on your chest under your clothes, I couldn't help trembling all over. Do you know how fascinating your breasts are?"

Nuannuan, who was beyond herself with bashfulness, turned the light off.

Grabbing her breasts in the dark, Kaitian said: "It must be the Buddha in Lingyan Temple that blesses us so that you're mine now. Don't you think so, Nuannuan?"

Gently pinching Kaitian by his ear, Nuannuan whispered: "Don't talk too loud. Someone might hear us."

It was an enchanting moment for both of them. They were excitedly busying themselves when a loud noise came in front of the window. The couple went stiff.

"Someone must be throwing bricks," concluded Nuannuan as she patted Kaitian on his back.

The couple rose to put on some clothes. Kaitian picked up a stick and walked out to check with the dog. It was all dark. The yard was silent. Kaitian found the brick next to the window and showed it to Nuannuan in his hands. Nuannuan gasped.

Kaitian patted her hands and chuckled towards the yard wall. "Zhan Shiti, you can toss bricks all you want. But that's all you can do. Nuannuan is my wife now. Eat your heart out."

Nuannuan sighed...

Kaitian and Nuannuan went to the township office for their marriage registration a couple of weeks later. As they were walking out of the office, Kaitian raised the red certificate in his hand and shouted out: "Now that my marriage is guaranteed by law, I will not worry about anyone trying to take my wife away!"

Nuannuan patted his arm, pretending to be angry with a smile. "You're crazy!"

Kaitian was smiling too. He said: "Truth is, I was still worried about what the leader may do to part us before getting this certificate. But now I am assured."

"Don't scare yourself. A leader doesn't have too much power in this capacity. How can he punish us? We farm our land, reap our crops and eat our grains, unlike our older generations who had to rely on leaders for recording our work points, allocating food and distributing ration coupons. He couldn't do it. Besides, leaders are elected every few years – who can guarantee that he'll be elected next time?"

"You're the one who can look on the bright side of things," exclaimed Kaitian as he kissed her affectionately, holding her in his arms. "If I were the leader one day, I'd..."

"You'd what? What could you do if you were one?" asked Nuannuan with a smile.

"I'd better not talk big. Who'd elect me as a leader?" said Kaitian, shaking his head.

Kaitian's first thought now was to visit his in-laws. He had wanted to go a couple of times, but Nuannuan had stopped him, saying: "They're still mad about us. Even if you go, they may not want to see you. Let's wait till the registration's done."

With the marriage certificate in his pocket, Kaitian felt obligated to make the visit. He picked up several things on Juxiang Street with

Nuannuan. In addition to the ordinary presents of pork, lamb legs, desserts and coloured cotton prints, they bought new clothes for Dad, Mum, Grandma and Hehe.

Around midday the next day, Kaitian walked towards his in-laws' house with the presents. Nuannuan was walking behind him. The couple were quite nervous and unsure about how they would be treated. Luckily, the yard gate was open. Hehe, Nuannuan's little sister, was washing some clothes in the yard. She rose and called out in excitement: "Mum! It's Nuannuan and my brother-in-law."

Mum came out of the kitchen with flour sticking to her hands. She looked at the couple first, then she glanced at the living room and said: "Come insi–"

Before Mum could finish, Dad's angry voice came from inside. "Go away!"

Kaitian gave Nuannuan a confused look. He did not know what to do. Nuannuan was calm. She took the presents from Kaitian and put them in front of the kitchen door. She whispered to Mum: "We'll leave now. Take care of yourself, Dad and Grandma."

Mum started crying. She nodded and answered: "Dad will come round..."

Nuannuan and Kaitian left the yard. Unexpectedly, Dad rushed out and yelled at them: "Take your things with you. I don't need those. I don't have anything to do with you."

They did not move. Seeing them, Dad picked the presents up and threw them out of the gate. Grandma came out to help. She walked out with her cane and said to Dad in a deep voice: "Changshun, you're throwing away my granddaughter's present to me. How dare you? Hehe, go and bring them back."

Then she waved her hand to Nuannuan and Kaitian, telling them to leave...

The couple were not upset about it. They had foreseen things like that. Nuannuan comforted Kaitian. "It's only natural that Dad needs more time to think this through. After all, we got married without telling him. We'll wait and see."

"One day he'll see the good son-in-law in me."

That made Nuannuan laugh. "You and your big talk."

Their marriage was a bomb drop in the village too. All the seniors disapproved, accusing them of being audacious; no one had ever seen anything like that. Some parents warned their children against hanging around with Nuannuan and Kaitian. Mr Tianfu was in shock too. He told people that this audacious deed was caused by Nuannuan's time in Beijing. Unmarried girls, according to him, should not leave the village to work. Some young people in the village were quite sympathetic and praised the couple's courage – they thought a marriage should be made according to the couple's wishes. During that time, everybody talked. But that did not last as days passed by. The villagers gradually accepted the marriage, and no rumours could be heard any more. Kaitian and Nuannuan ignored all the talk and worked in the fields as normal every day. All they wanted was a better harvest so that their life could get better.

Their days were quiet and peaceful. They couldn't love too much, so their life was harmonious and happy. They worked in the fields together during the day and enjoyed themselves in bed at night. Since they were both young and vigorous, they didn't care too much when they were together. Unlike the springy mattress in cities, their sorghum-matted bedding made loud noises as the bed shook. When they found themselves carried away in their lovemaking, the noises could be earth-shaking. One day, Spotty's wife ran into Nuannuan and whispered with a smirk: "Your sound of ploughing and sowing is pretty loud. I could hear it from the other side of the wall."

"When did I plough and sow?" asked Nuannuan, perplexed. She didn't quite catch what the woman had said.

"At night. Your Kaitian shook the seed plough rattling, rattling." As she spoke metaphorically, she demonstrated it with gestures.

Nuannuan suddenly realised what she meant and blushed from head to toe. Back home that day, she asked Kaitian to fix the sorghum mat to the bed frame with ropes.

Time went by fast when the couple felt happy. That day, only when she saw snowflakes flying in the north wind did Nuannuan realise that she had been married for two months. She got up in the morning and carried some firewood from the stack. When she caught sight of Shallot, she remembered that she hadn't visited her since she got married. She had been to her home regularly before.

After breakfast, seeing the snow was too heavy for her to do anything else outdoors, Nuannuan said to Kaitian: "I'm going to see Sister-in-Law Shallot."

Shallot had a son named Daming and a daughter named Xiaoming. They were sweeping the snow in the courtyard when they saw Nuannuan entering it. They each called her Auntie and ran away to play. Shallot was making padded clothes in the house. Seeing Nuannuan, she smiled. "Wow, what brought you here today? Why aren't you lying in Kaitian's arms in bed on such a snowy day?"

Nuannuan gave Shallot a gentle punch. "You're talking nonsense."

"You forgot your sister-in-law altogether after your marriage. These days, friendship is no match for love," joked Shallot with a smile.

"Who forgot you? I'm thinking of you every day. See, I'm here to see you now that I'm free." Nuannuan felt guilty indeed upon the thought that her mind was on nobody but Kaitian in the past months.

"You think of me every day? Only ghosts would believe you. Truth is, you have Kaitian on your mind daily. How many times did he do it every night?"

"Do what?" Nuannuan was bewildered.

"I mean busying with that thing." Shallot fixed her eyes at Nuannuan with a meaningful smirk.

Nuannuan suddenly understood what she was referring to. Her face blushed, and she gave Sister-in-Law Shallot another punch, pretending to be angry. "I'll leave if you're going to keep talking nonsense."

"OK, OK. No more joking. Sit, and I'll tell you something serious."

"What is it?" Nuannuan picked up the needlework and, together with Shallot, began to sew a piece of clothing for either Daming or Xiaoming. Nuannuan had always helped Shallot do needlework when she visited her before.

"Do you want to have a child earlier or later?" Sister-in-Law Shallot gazed into Nuannuan's eyes with a smile.

Nuannuan felt her face blush again and muttered: "I haven't consulted with Kaitian. What's your take?"

"If you want to have it later, you have to have some safety measures. It would help if you bought something from Mei's Pharmacy. Every time Kaitian does that to you, you must force him to wear it. Otherwise, you'll have to have an abortion, which will not only be painful but affect your future fertility. Then you'll have difficulty conceiving when the time comes for you to crave a child."

Nuannuan was shocked. "Really? According to you then..."

"Have it earlier. A woman must give birth anyway. It's better to do it earlier than later. Besides, the younger you are, the less effort you've got to make in the delivery. You have more strength to use when you're younger. You don't know how much of it you need to push a baby out."

Nuannuan listened with her eyes wide open.

That night, as soon as they got on the bed, Nuannuan told Kaitian everything she had heard from Sister-in-Law Shallot. Then, she asked: "Do you want a baby earlier or later?"

Burying his kisses in Nuannuan's breasts, Kaitian laughed. "I want one now."

Nuannuan got pregnant three months after the wedding. Once her pregnancy was confirmed, she was filled with joy and satisfaction. She felt relieved that she had resisted an arranged marriage. Otherwise, these happy days she had would not be hers. However, once in a while, she felt a slight dissatisfaction when she thought of her time in Beijing and the exciting life of people in the city. As a result, that night when Kaitian pulled her into his arms, she stopped him by pressing his hands and said: "We need a goal."

"What goal?" Kaitian was surprised.

"The two of us are stuck in Chu Wang Village in this life. But it can't be the life of our children. If they spend their life planting crops by Red Lake, knowing nothing about hairstyles, fashion and beauty, ignorant of cafés, theatres and parks, I will not rest in peace."

"What do you want, then?"

"We have to send them to schools in the city, to live a city life."

"OK." Kaitian shrugged. "Even I want to live a city life. I will not say no to our children's bright future."

"It's not about saying yes or no. It's a difficult goal. We need money first. I've seen it all in Beijing. With money, you can buy an apartment in the city for the children, and only then can they truly have a city life."

"OK. I need to make money. Your dad didn't want you to marry me because I'm poor. Money, the son of a bitch, never visits our Kuang family. What can I do? It's useless you urging me." Kaitian did not sound happy.

Nuannuan did not expect him to say that. "Don't get me wrong. I'm not urging you – I'm reasoning with you."

"All right, all right. I understand."

Kaitian was very happy to see Nuannuan's belly getting bigger every day. He did not allow her to do any work, and he made sure that his mother made her good food. Nuannuan would protest with a happy smile: "You're making a lazy pig out of me."

When the Dragon Boat Festival came, Nuannuan could hardly walk because of her big belly. Her mother-in-law did some calculations and predicted the birth would come in the next few days. She told her to be more careful. But Nuannuan could not simply sit and do nothing. She got up early, made *zongzi*, steamed the garlic, and boiled the eggs, getting the festival feast ready. Yet when she was about to start eating, she felt the pain. Her mother-in-law saw her sweating and told Kaitian to get Wheatleaf, the midwife in the village. Shallot also came over when she heard the news.

Aunt Wheatleaf smiled after examining Nuannuan. "No big deal – the baby is just eager to come out to share in the celebration of the Dragon Boat Festival."

Holding her hand, Sister-in-Law Shallot tried to alleviate Nuannuan's fear. "Don't be afraid. When a melon is ripe, it doesn't matter if you pick it a day earlier. It would help if you were stoic. Every mother is bound to taste the throes, which is a test from heaven. After this pass, there will be the plain. I went through it by closing my eyes and clenching my teeth. When heaven gives you a lively baby, how can you not pay some price?"

As she was eating an egg peeled by Kaitian, Aunt Wheatleaf watched Nuannuan wriggling and moaning with gnashed teeth. She smiled. "The way Nuannuan is reacting shows that the baby won't be a girl." When Nuannuan began to scream at the top of her lungs, Aunt Wheatleaf ran her hand over the head that had just come out and concluded: "It's a kettle with a spout." This is the Chinese euphemism for a boy. Sure enough, a boy swam out of the bloody waters. His cry resounded throughout the Kuang family's courtyard. Patting himself on the buttocks, Kaitian jumped with joy.

The Kuangs got a boy on the Dragon Boat Festival. Many neighbours came to the house to give their congratulations. Kaitian offered everyone a cigarette with a happy smile on his face. Spotty Laosi took a big puff and laughed. "Your boy certainly knows how to pick a good date. He will never lack food on his birthdays – *zongzi*, eggs and steamed garlic, whatever he wants. What a good birthday."

Jiuding said: "Qu Yuan would be happy if he knew about the boy's birth."

Spotty Laosi was in the dark. "Who's Qu Yuan?"

"You celebrate Dragon Boat Festival without knowing Qu Yuan? This festival celebrates him," responded Jiuding with a bit of contempt.

"Don't show off to me, Jiuding. I may be unaware of Qu Yuan, but I still celebrate the festival. No one can keep me from it. Besides, why don't you go to Beijing to teach the pretty girl students since you're so learned? Why don't you stand on a rostrum to give lectures every day as an intellectual does? Why don't you earn a salary? Why do you have to scull your boat to fish and grow wheat and sweet potatoes instead?" yelled Spotty Laosi unconvincedly.

At that moment, Sister-in-Law Shallot came smiling out of the room where Nuannuan was resting. She said: "Brother Laosi, don't be defiant. You don't read as many books as he does." Then she turned to Jiuding. "Please explain Qu Yuan to us."

Jiuding was happy to hear the compliment and, rolling up his sleeves, began the story. "Qu Yuan was a high-ranking official of the Chu State. He often drank and ate with the king, and he sometimes watched girls dancing. Later, however, he was at loggerheads with the king. Some wicked high officials drove a wedge between the two and caused Qu Yuan to lose the king's favour. The king didn't want him to work in the court, so Qu Yuan wandered here and there. Legend has it that he was in this area once…"

Spotty Laosi interrupted him. "You're telling a tall tale. If Qu Yuan was a high official, what did he come to our Chu Wang Village for? Did he want to drink our Red Lake's water to quench his thirst, or was he out of his mind?"

Jiuding responded in all seriousness: "I didn't make up the story.

A bald-headed leader of the county's Culture Bureau told us at the village entrance when he came to inspect the ancient tombs. That bureau head had only a tuft of hair on the top of his head. As he stroked his tuft, he said our village and its surrounding area used to be the Chu State's birthplace."

Spotty Laosi was about to dispute Jiuding's claims when the newborn boy suddenly burst out crying – no one knew why. Kaitian and Sister-in-Law Shallot hurried into the room. Seeing the hosts gone, the crowd lost their interest in staying further, and they left one by one.

The next day, Kaitian named their son Dangen, meaning "red root". Nuannuan thought about it for a while and then said: "All right."

The night before Dangen was one month old, Mum came over to see her grandson in secret. She brought noodles, eggs, red cotton fabrics and two sets of baby clothes. She said to her daughter and son-in-law: "I prepared these in secret. I couldn't visit you. But when I saw Nuannuan's figure from afar, I knew I needed to get you these things."

She kissed Dangen's small face and cried in happiness. Nuannuan threw herself in Mum's arms and sobbed. Mum tried to comfort her. "You can't cry now – if you get sad in the first month after giving birth, you'll get sick in the future..."

After the birth of his son, Kaitian felt more responsibility on his shoulders. He would always sigh and say to Nuannuan: "The income of a farmer is too petty. I just hope my luck will come and I can get a job in the government. I'll settle for the leader's position – then I can support both of you with the money."

Nuannuan smiled. "Money won't come just because you wish hard. You need to find other ways."

After that, when he was not working in the fields, Kaitian began seeking opportunities to earn more money. He heard that Leader Zhan Shideng had come from the township seat with a newspaper, and it had an article on how to get rich. Even though he knew the leader and his family had a grudge against him, he still went to the village committee office to ask the leader for the newspaper.

Unfortunately, the methods of getting rich weren't for people like Kaitian who had no means. When he returned the newspaper to the leader, the latter squinted his smiling eyes and said: "Great! It's good that you're thinking of making a fortune."

One month after childbirth, Nuannuan had her mother-in-law take care of the baby, and she resumed her farm work. One day, the couple were working on their contracted farmland by Red Lake when a motorcycle stopped in front of them. A young man of Kaitian's age jumped off and called out: "Big Brother! You want some weedkiller for your leafy crops? These are all imported from America. I've got three tonnes, but now only three boxes are left. I don't want to run around any more. So if you want these, I'll give you a discount. You can sell the extra to others and earn some pocket money."

Kaitian looked at him in surprise. He knew that weedkiller was useful: farmers in the village had used them on the green beans since the previous autumn and saved much effort, with the beans thriving and no one needing to worry about digging out weeds in the fields any more. He looked at Nuannuan, then turned to ask: "Imported from America?"

"I'm not lying to you." The young man took a bag of weedkiller out of the case on his motorcycle. "Look at the trademark – it's in damn English. Here, take my name card. Representative, China International Agriculture Limited. I'm in charge of Juxiang Street. Here's my number. If you find anything wrong with it, just call me, and I guarantee a full refund. Do you know why American farmers have time to dance, sing, watch films and go whoring? It's because they're using this fucking weedkiller. They sow the seeds in the fields, spray the chemical and just wait for the harvest time to come. They use all the time saved to have fun. You tell me why we Chinese farmers can't use it. Are we stupid?"

"How much for a bag?" Kaitian looked at Nuannuan again as she stepped up and took the bag.

"The market price in Nanfu and the provincial capital is between three and a half yuan and four yuan. But because I have something urgent to deal with, I'll give you one and a half yuan a bag wholesale. If you retail them to other people, you can make a profit of two to two and a half yuan per bag. How good is that? I only give you this special offer because I see you as a friend. So many fields in the village, yet I chose yours to park my ride. Why? Because I trusted you at first sight."

Kaitian nodded in satisfaction. One year ago, he bought some weedkiller from a shop at four yuan a bag. This price was a lot better, and he could see a profit. "How many bags are there in three boxes?"

"Thirty bags a box, so it's ninety bags in total. Put one bag in water, and it'll cover one acre. In total, it kills weeds in ninety acres. As for the money, just give me 135 yuan." The young man summed it up quickly.

Kaitian wanted to know what Nuannuan thought. "Are we taking that?"

"Only a fool would reject this special offer," Nuannuan said. "Take it. Even the richest man earned his wealth penny by penny. Even a small profit is better than nothing."

The young couple led the man to their house, and Nuannuan went in to get the money. She handed over the cash one by one. When the amount reached 130 yuan, the man waved his hand and said: "It's fine, I'll leave you the five yuan. Friends don't argue over small amounts of money."

That made Nuannuan quite happy. She saw the man off with a smile.

Kaitian was humming a happy tune when he returned to the field that day. The road was bumpy, and he was staggering, but it did not affect his humming. Two yuan from every bag, and he had ninety bags. That foretold an effortless profit of more than a hundred yuan in no time. Of course he was happy. Nuannuan, following his steps, said to him: "We'll keep two bags for ourselves and sell the rest as soon as possible."

Kaitian nodded. That day after working on the farm, he stood in front of the yard and shouted: "Weedkiller for leafy crops. Imported from America. Only three and a half yuan a bag."

The villagers, who had benefited from weedkiller before, all came over for the imported product and its low price. Kaitian sold eighty-six bags in a short time. It was a clean sweep, except for the two bags Nuannuan saved for herself and another two bags for Shallot. That evening, Kaitian was beside himself with joy. Not only did he eat four bowls of noodles, but he also wanted Nuannuan. The latter pinched him by his nose and said: "We still have tomorrow, don't we?"

That autumn, everyone used the weedkiller on their green beans, and it was very effective – not even a sight of weed could be seen. However, the green beans were killed too. The first to wither was the leaves on the sprouts; in the end, the farmers got nothing but the stems.

Everyone who had bought the weedkiller from Kaitian was in shock. *Good heavens! All the green beans are ruined!* Ninety acres, including Kaitian's own fields, had no sprout left. Things like this never happened in Chu Wang Village. It was the biggest shock ever. Before people came over to complain, the couple hastened to the village committee office and called the number on the name card. The number did not exist. By then, they finally realised that it was a scam. Losing a season's harvest was more than serious. People who bought from Kaitian forced him to look at their ruined fields and gathered outside his house to demand a solution. Kaitian had never been through anything like this. Nuannuan was stunned too. She held her breath and hid behind the door. The crowd was overwhelmed by anger. Spotty Laosi called out: "Fuck your sister! Even a rabbit doesn't foul his own hole, yet you are so rotten to trick your own people."

Zhan Tongfang, the tofu maker in his fifties, stepped into the yard and cursed: "You bastard! You ruined all the fields in the village for some money. You don't have a heart. You're killing us all."

Zhan Datong, the pig castrator, rolled up his sleeves, showed his fist and yelled in an agitated tone: "Boys, let's go and beat that scum to death. Or we'll squeeze his balls out. Castrate him."

As they were immigrants to Chu Wang Village, the Kuangs didn't have many relatives there. Therefore, at that moment, no one would help them. Kaitian had to apologise, so he went out and said in a small voice: "I'm a victim too. I trusted a stranger. It was all my fault. I'm the asshole."

Yet the crowd would not be appeased. Finally, Kaitian's dad walked out with his cane and knelt. "Neighbours! Friends! My stupid son Kaitian was tricked into this abomination. It's my fault. I didn't raise my son well. Here I kneel and apologise to you all. I beg you to allow him to find the person who cheated him. We'll compensate you as long as we find him..."

The crowd slowly left upon his words. Shallot, who stood away and watched in silence, came close and said: "Nuannuan, you must find that bad guy who sold you the weedkiller and make him pay."

Nuannuan answered in guilt: "Sorry to make you a victim too."

Shallot shook her head. "I never believed you wanted to hurt us."

Kaitian rode the bike with Nuannuan to Juxiang Street, hoping to find the man. But where could they go? The information on the name card was fake, and no one had heard of the man before. They did not have his address or motorcycle plate number, so they had to visit every shop and house in Juxiang Street. But they found nothing close to the Representative Person of China International Agriculture. *Maybe he's not from here?* At that thought, the couple went to a neighbouring town and township, but the search was a needle in a haystack; everything was in vain.

At sunset three days later, Kaitian and Nuannuan, both exhausted, had to go home. When they arrived in the village, Kaitian plopped down to the ground, too scared to face everyone he had harmed. He covered his face with both hands and cried: "You fucking liar! Fuck you and your ancestors! What have I done to deserve this?"

Nuannuan was leaning against a tree, gazing emptily into the lake, which was slowly falling into the night. It took her a while to speak out. "Let's go. What's happened has happened. There's no use hiding unless we jump into the lake. It's not worth it. Let's explain it to our fellow villagers."

Nuannuan held Kaitian's hand and led him home. They told Kaitian's parents about their useless efforts. Before dinner was served, the villagers knew about their return and formed a crowd outside their courtyard again. Kaitian was trapped inside. Cautiously, he offered everyone a seat and stammered to tell of his search in vain. People listened, looking grim.

Spotty Laosi interrupted before Kaitian could finish. "Cut your bullshit. I don't care if you've found him. I need a solution. If you can't make us happy, we won't let you go tonight."

As the crowd shouted and cursed, some motorcycles made a loud noise outside the yard, and several police officers ran inside.

They verified Kaitian's identification and quickly put a pair of handcuffs on his wrists. One policeman took out a paper and said: "You're under arrest. We suspect that you sold fake weedkiller and purposefully sabotaged agricultural production."

As they tried to push Kaitian out, Dangen and Kaitian's parents started crying. Nuannuan, also in tears, wanted to stop the arrest, but she was pushed away by the police. Kaitian was scared. As he walked, he cried out: "I didn't mean to..." But his cry faded away with the noise of the motorcycles.

Shallot, who entered without acknowledging anyone, spoke out in front of the crowd. "Go home, everyone. The man has been arrested. Money is not as important as him." The people stiffened at her words and started to leave in silence.

"Sister-in-Law..." Nuannuan threw herself into Shallot's arms and started crying loudly.

Shallot patted her on her back and sighed. "How did this get so serious? Who told the police?"

Nuannuan choked. "Maybe someone decided to report and sue us. I was so blind to trust that man. Kaitian asked me if we should buy that weedkiller, and I said yes without even thinking about it. I hate myself."

"Crying won't solve the problem. You have to do something about it," said Shallot. "I'm afraid you'll have to go to the village heads. The Party secretary is too old to help – he lies in his bed all day. You have to go to Zhan Shideng. He's the leader. He'll be able to bail Kaitian out."

Nuannuan nodded and wiped her tears. She passed Dangen to her mother-in-law and said: "Dad, Mum, stay at home. I'll go and beg the leader to help."

On the way to Zhan Shideng's house, Nuannuan hesitated several times, feeling embarrassed about refusing to marry his little brother. But what else could she do? She had to beg for his help...

The leader's house was a two-floored building, the best-looking house in Chu Wang Village. When Nuannuan arrived, the leader was sitting on a chair on his balcony, gazing into the village in the night with a cigarette. Nuannuan greeted his wife and followed her instructions to walk upstairs in quiet steps. Zhan Shideng seemed to be deep in thought, and he did not move. Nuannuan stood aside for a while and saw the whole village from the balcony: the houses, small and big; the small pier by the side of Red Lake; the winding road leading to Juxiang Street; the lake reflecting a pale light from the moon; the silhouette of the mountains hiding in the night... Under the pale moonlight, Nuannuan saw Zhan Shideng's big round wooden chair with an awning shaped like an umbrella on top. The chair amazed her. She had heard that the leader was a carpenter before he took office. He must have made the chair himself.

"Mr Leader," Nuannuan called out.

Zhan Shideng turned his head slowly. His sight seemed terrible, and it took him the time a man needs to puff up a pipe bowl of tobacco to see Nuannuan. "Kaitian's wife. What can I do for you?"

Nuannuan burst into tears and choked on her voice. "Something bad happened to my family. I beg Mr Leader to help."

"What happened?" Zhan Shideng stood up. His figure seemed tall and reliable in the moonlight.

Nuannuan spoke fast about the incident, her chest rising and falling as she sobbed. Her full breasts were bouncing up and down. Zhan Shideng listened with his eyes narrowed, yet he kept a gaze at Nuannuan's chest.

"Mr Leader, you're the only one I have."

"The police really took Kaitian away?" Zhan Shideng seemed surprised.

"It's true. They rode two motorcycles over."

"How could that be? They can't arrest him before an investigation."

The crescent moon had fallen behind the hill by now. The balcony was suddenly engulfed in darkness. Nuannuan couldn't see Zhan Shideng's face, but she felt a warmth from his words. A breeze swept over from Red Lake in front of the village, brushing the tips of the tree branches and rushing to the mountain woods behind the village. As it passed by, it brought a fishy smell to assail the nostrils. Zhan Shideng sneezed resonantly. He stooped over to press his cigarette on the floor and stub it out.

"His Dad, it's time to go to bed." His wife's angry voice came from the courtyard. Nuannuan knew this meant she had to leave.

"Go ahead and sleep yourself for now," responded Zhan Shideng with impatience.

"Mr Leader, you have to help us. Kaitian was tricked. How can he deliberately harm anyone in the village? He did not break any law."

Zhan Shideng sighed and said in a voice without emotion: "Kaitian did make a mistake with the weedkiller. He caused a big loss to the village, to the people he sees every day. Of course they're angry. Does he still want to live here? He would be so stupid to make money in this way."

"Mr Leader, we're victims too. You know Kaitian. He's not a liar. I was there too. The liar told us the weedkiller was imported from America, and the price was so good. We didn't think it through, so…" Nuannuan tried to defend her husband in a low voice.

"What do you want from me, then?" Zhan Shideng narrowed his eyes and looked at Nuannuan.

"If you can talk to the heads of the township police station and ask them to release Kaitian…"

Zhan Shideng did not listen to her pleading. He exhaled quietly. *Kuang Kaitian is in custody. Chu Nuannuan is in tears. How smug those two were when they silently got married.* Zhan Shideng still remembered that afternoon. A few children brought the news of Kuang Kaitian and Chu Nuannuan's wedding to this courtyard. *How stunning it was.* He had never expected that someone in Chu Wang Village would insult him in public like this and take away the woman who should have belonged to the Zhan family. He was in such shock that he didn't move for a long time. His first thought was that the children must have made a mistake. *How can such a thing happen in my territory?* He gasped and knew what had happened was real when he saw Mr Tianfu and his younger brother returning with sullen faces. His second reaction was fury: *Someone is rebelling. It's a genuine insurrection.* No one had ever dared to go against him since he became the leader over a decade before. Now, someone considered him to be such a pushover that they acted as if shitting on his head. *It's a disgrace to the Zhan family. Kuang Kaitian, who lent you the guts?* The rage could have brought him to Kuang Kaitian's home with a gang to smash it. He could have seized Chu Nuannuan, the slut who had decided to marry Kuang Kaitian herself. But he didn't have enough courage to do what he could have done. He often went to meetings in the township seat. He knew that those impulsive actions would have violated the law. The police had taken the Zhaojiazhuang Village committee leader for beating a villager not long before. *Fuck! Now people will sue you for the slightest reason. Fine, we have to abide by the law.* That was why he went to the Kuang family to stop his brother from creating the disturbance and gave twenty yuan as a wedding present. He had tried to suppress his anger several times before his law-abiding act – an impression he had wanted to give the villagers. *The fucking law!*

Zhan Shideng hadn't paid attention until Nuannuan returned from working in Beijing. He had never eyed her closely. As an old saying goes, gold phoenixes can fly out of a remote mountainous area. Located in Funiu Mountain and surrounded by Red Lake, the largest lake on the Central Plains, Chu Wang Village was a beautiful landscape. No wonder it was also a place that produced many beautiful women. All the girls in the village were slender, with red lips and white teeth. Some parents might look ordinary, but their daughters were gorgeous. Legend has it that many concubines in the harem of the Chu Kingdom came from this area. There were already many beautiful girls in Chu Wang Village, plus many good-looking women married from other places. Therefore, Leader Zhan Shideng grew a bit fastidious when it came to women. He seldom cast a look at ordinary females, let alone flirted with them.

Nuannuan caught his attention in that late afternoon. According to a request from the township's fishing affairs department, he gathered the few fishing families to Red Lake's beach. There, he told them not to use small-eyed nets to protect the fries in the lake. He was addressing the crowd when he caught sight of a shapely young woman with ample breasts coming over, dressed like a city resident. In shock, he thought she might be from somewhere else. He intuitively stopped to ask politely: "Excuse me, are you looking for someone?" The crowd burst into laughter.

Chu Changshun, who was sitting among the audience, rose and said: "Leader, it's Nuannuan, my elder daughter, who is coming to listen to your speech."

"I see," said Zhan Shideng in a subdued voice. In his memory, Nuannuan was still an ordinary girl. *How come she's turned into such an eye-catching beauty? It looks like the feng shui of the Chu family's ancestral cemetery was excellent. That's why they can have such a beautiful daughter.*

He often searched the women in the village for her figure from that day on. In his eyes, her face, breasts and buttocks were bewitching. Sometimes, his mouth would water as he ogled. For a time, he was contemplating how to get close to her. But at this moment, his mother came to tell him that his younger brother had a crush on Chu Changshun's elder daughter and wanted to marry her. She asked him to find a matchmaker for his brother. He didn't say anything for a while. Of course, he didn't dare to tell his mother that he had also fallen in love with Nuannuan. He was already the father of two children. He finally sighed and said to his mother with infinite regret: "My bro has good taste. OK, I'll do it." From then on, he kept Nuannuan away from his sight. He wasn't supposed to have a presumptuous desire for the woman his brother was after.

Not long after that day, he found Mr Tianfu and asked him to propose marriage on his brother's behalf. He hadn't expected Mr Tianfu to come to tell him that Nuannuan was unwilling to marry his brother. A little enraged, he went to the Chu family himself, confident of success as soon as he spoke. Sure enough, Chu Changshun quickly gave his consent. Zhan Shideng thought that, with Chu Changshun's endorsement, this marriage was a done deal, and there was no chance for a change. So he informed his mother and asked his younger brother to make all the marriage preparations, including cleaning the house, setting the wedding date and creating furniture. His mother and brother were both happy. Zhang Shideng had never expected that things would change. Less had he expected the insignificant Kuang Kaitian to take the Zhan family's woman away like a dog daring to grab the meat from a tiger's mouth. *You're way too audacious. You even have the guts to push me over. Maybe you're tired of living.* Nuannuan was the one who made him more furious. She had thrown herself into Kuang Kaitian's arms. *A slut deserving a good dressing down. Do you think an official Zhan is less attractive than a farmer Kuang? I'll show you.*

Truth is, he had seen Nuannuan coming towards his house on the balcony this evening. *You slut! You're coming after all as I expected. Didn't you try not to enter our Zhan family's house? You dared to marry that Kuang Kaitian out of stubbornness, didn't you? You had the guts to make a fool of our Zhan family and disgrace us in front of the whole village.*

Fine, let's have a contest. I don't believe you won't be lying submissively under our Zhan family's man. I don't think you can escape this fate. You sound pretty soft now – not as fierce as you did when you shouted at my brother. Zhan Shideng stood where he was, a cold smile flashing on his face.

"Please, Mr Leader, go to the police station. Kaitian is innocent…"

"If the police came down, then what he did is illegal. I'm only a village committee's leader. I can't deal with illegal things."

"But you're the leader. They all trust you," Nuannuan begged in a softer voice. "We'll think of ways to compensate those who bought our weedkiller."

"I'm afraid it's not that easy." Zhan Shideng narrowed his eyes further. *You bitch! Now you're here to beg me, eh? Why didn't you think of our Zhan family when you were eager to marry into the Kuang family?*

"Mr Leader, you're the best person to solve this. Everyone knows you in the township office. Please, save Kaitian." Nuannuan could not hold back any more, and tears ran down her face.

Zhan Shideng lit another cigarette and took a deep puff. *Now you know how to cry, eh? That's lots of tears. But you didn't cry when you rejected our marriage proposal. How smug you were then. How audacious you were to make yourself Kuang Kaitian's wife by having the pre-emptive wedding. You thought we Zhan family members could do nothing about it, right? You advocated free marriage, and you told us that was the law, thinking you were in the right and feeling self-confident. Now you're crying, eh? Shedding tears, eh? You're supposed to smile and to laugh at us, treating us as easy prey of your tricks. How smart you were.*

"Mr Leader, Kaitian belongs to your village. You can't abandon him."

"In Chu Wang Village, I won't ignore any house's business when bad things happen. All right, I'll go tomorrow and try to talk to someone." Zhan Shideng threw the cigarette on the floor and stepped on it hard. He said slowly to Nuannuan: "If I come through tomorrow, of course it's good. But if not, you can't blame it on me. What he did was illegal."

"Of course. I thank you, Mr Leader." Nuannuan bowed down…

The leader's attitude gave Nuannuan some relief. She knew words alone could not help solve a problem, so the next morning she went to buy two cartons of cigarettes and two bottles of wine. She put them in a bag and waited in front of Zhan Shideng's house. Seeing Zhan Shideng coming out with his bike, Nuannuan stepped up and hung the bag on his bike handle. "Mr Leader, take these. You can't simply talk. If you need to go out for a meal, do it, and I'll give you the money when you're back."

Zhan Shideng sighed. "You shouldn't have spent money on this. All right, I'll bring them as a present for the police officers."

That day, when he rode his bike out of the village, Zhan Shideng was all smiles. *Chu Nuannuan, you finally come to me for help. You're finally sensible. I'll teach you to be more sensible in the future...*

Zhan Shideng went straight into the police station on Juxiang Street, where the township government was. The police officers knew the village leaders very well, so they gave him a warm greeting.

Zhan Shideng took his time to take a carton of cigarettes out of Nuannuan's bag and said: "I came here today to reward your hard work. You arrested Kuang Kaitian, the liar who sabotaged farmers with fake weedkiller. You helped us all in Chu Wang Village. Everyone in my village is grateful, so they bought these cigarettes and wine, and asked me to bring them to you. We thank the People's Police."

He took out everything from the bag. The head officer felt a little embarrassed. "Leader Zhan, don't do this. It's our job to catch bad guys. You shouldn't say thank you to us."

Zhan Shideng pretended to be unhappy. "This is no bribery. Just presents from our people. If you reject them, you'll upset them."

The head officer waved his hand and had a policeman put away the presents. He led Zhan Shideng into his office, offered him some tea and said: "Leader Zhan, we did the investigation as soon as we received your call. We now have all evidence pointing to Kuang Kaitian's purposeful sabotage of farmlands. He also confessed to selling fake weedkiller. Normally we would send the case to the district attorney. But there's one thing that's not clear – he insisted that he bought the weedkiller from someone else without knowing the harm. But when we asked him to give us information about the seller, he gave us nothing. So we think he may be a victim too. That's why I haven't decided yet."

Zhan Shideng drank the tea, swallowed slowly and said: "I have a lot of experience with these criminals, and each of them has a forked tongue. Once caught, they'll tell every lie to get out of it. Kuang Kaitian has always been an ass in the village. There's nothing he dares not do. You must punish him."

The head officer looked at Zhan Shideng. "There are two ways to deal with the situation. We can make him write a guarantee, promising no further crime and compensation for those he harmed, then we'll let him go. Or we'll keep him in custody to find evidence of his deliberate crime, and then we can charge him. What do you think?"

Zhan Shideng jumped to his feet. "Head Officer, you can't let this bad guy go. I'm here today to give you a heads-up – the people who bought weedkiller from Kuang Kaitian are still overwhelmed by anger, and they're talking about petitioning. They want nothing but a harsh punishment for Kuang Kaitian. I was the one who persuaded them to stay at home. If they know that he's been released, they'll storm in here with sickles and axes."

The head officer got nervous hearing his words. "You must talk sense into them. I can't afford an angry crowd in the township hall. I'll make sure to advance the investigation. I won't let any bad guy go..."

At midday, Zhan Shideng walked into the most famous restaurant on Juxiang Street, the Eight Immortals, and ordered four dishes for himself: braised chicken with brown sauce, beef with soy sauce, fried lake prawns and fish head soup from Red Lake. In addition, he ordered a bottle of Crouching Dragon, a special yellow rice wine. He drank very slowly and did not leave on his bike until sunset.

He saw Nuannuan waiting in front of the village from afar. A smug smile flashed in his eyes. But immediately, he put on a disappointed face and slowly rode towards Nuannuan.

Nuannuan walked to him, full of hope. "Mr Leader, you must be tired. They must have agreed to let him go."

He jumped off the bike, sighed and said with sympathy: "Nuannuan, you have to be strong. It was not good at all. I pleaded with the head of the police station for a long time, but he insisted that Kaitian committed a serious crime of sabotaging agricultural production. They would not let him go. Moreover, Kaitian will face serious punishment. You must not be too sad. Maybe Kaitian is destined to suffer this."

Nuannuan's face went pale, and she began to sob. "How serious is the punishment?"

"They'll probably make him serve some years. But don't worry, what he did will give him five years at the most. Kaitian will be home after a couple of years," said Zhan Shideng with a relaxed tone.

Nuannuan started crying. She never thought of Kaitian being locked away. *A couple of years – what suffering! Even if he gets released afterwards, he'll become an ex-con. How can he live?*

Zhan Shideng directed his eyes at a pair of little egrets above the thin mist above Red Lake. He did this to mask the expression of satisfaction in his eyes. *Now you'll feel the same sadness that you made others feel. Did you know how my brother felt when you were having a good time in bed on your wedding day with Kuang Kaitian?*

"Mr Leader, is there any other way at all?" Nuannuan was still sobbing.

"I don't have anything to offer. I met the chief of the township today, and I talked to him. But he said the same thing – a serious punishment. What can I do? Nowadays, it's all about the law, and whenever the law is broken, things get difficult. If you ask me, you should not worry and take good care of your baby and your in-laws at home. When Kaitian gets released, you'll have your life back. Aren't you two still young? Everybody has their own trouble. It's nothing. Be strong and deal with it."

"No, no…" Nuannuan ran away, her hands covering her crying face.

Zhan Shideng was humming a happy tune when he walked home. As soon as he entered the house, he asked his wife to make some snacks to go with his drinks. His wife sniffed and mumbled: "You stink of alcohol, yet you're drinking again."

"Why not? Today is the best day to drink," Zhan Shideng cried in excitement. "I want a celebration. I want to celebrate the misery of those who dared go against the Zhans. I'll let everyone in Chu Wang Village know that whoever crosses me will end up in pain…"

Again, Nuannuan did not sleep. The first half of the night, she was crying in remorse. *I shouldn't have encouraged Kaitian to buy the weedkiller.* When it got closer to dawn, she was still striving to figure out a solution. *What to do? Who should I beg to help Kaitian?* Nuannuan thought of everyone she knew, but they were either peasants or fishers – none would be capable of handling something like this. *Maybe I should go to the township. Maybe I'll meet a kind official who will listen to me and let Kaitian go.*

Nuannuan made up her mind. In the morning, she handed Dangen to her mother-in-law. Then she got changed and took some money, ready to go. Her mother-in-law knew she was going to the township to seek help, so she followed her to the door and said in tears: "Only speak soft words, and never pick a fight. We can't lose you too."

Shallot heard about Nuannuan's plan. She gave her three cartons of Golden Leaf cigarettes. "Changlin got these good cigarettes as a reward for his pork sales last time. I don't let him touch them. You should have them with you today and offer them to the officials…"

Nuannuan had been to Juxiang Street many times, but she never paid attention to the police station. She had to ask several people to finally find the location. But when she arrived and stopped several police officers from walking out to ask about Kaitian, they either said they did not know anything or told her she could not meet him because the case had not been solved yet. So she turned to the township government in the hope of finding the chief of the township. He was, after all, the chief, and the police station was under him. Maybe he could make them release Kaitian.

Though Nuannuan used to live in Beijing, it was the first time she had been to the township government compound, and since she was there to beg for help, she felt very nervous. As a result, her steps were hesitant. The guard noticed that and stopped her. "What? What do you want?"

"I need to see the chief," Nuannuan answered timidly.

"Why?"

"I have an unjust case to appeal."

"The chief is not here. Go away." The guard waved his hand.

"Big Brother, please, I really have something important to

discuss with the chief." Nuannuan took out the Golden Leaf from Shallot and offered him a cigarette.

The man pushed her hands away. "I don't want it. Go away now."

Nuannuan did not know how to react. She burst into tears and begged: "Big Brother, please, my baby's dad was taken away by the police. But he's innocent. Please, I need to see the chief."

As she spoke, she forcefully put the cigarette in the guard's hand. The man looked less impatient and put the cigarette behind his ear. He said in a low voice: "No common people can come inside the government house with a petition. If you really need to see the chief, wait for him outside the gate. When he comes out later, I'll signal to you so that you can stop him and talk about your business."

"Thank you, Big Brother. Thank you." Nuannuan bowed down to the man.

Nuannuan stood outside the gate of the township government and opened her eyes wide to check everyone who went in and out. In a short while, two middle-aged men walked towards the gate. The guard rendered a soft cough and threw Nuannuan a glance. She hurried up and called: "Mr Chief, injustice..."

The bearded chief paused and asked: "Which village are you from? What injustice?"

Nuannuan hastened to answer: "I'm from Chu Wang Village. My name is Chu Nuannuan. My baby's dad is Kuang Kaitian–"

"Kuang Kaitian?" the chief interrupted her and thought for a while with his hand on his forehead. He frowned and asked: "Kuang Kaitian who sold fake weedkiller and sabotaged the fields of his own people?"

"Yes, him. But we only bought the weedkiller from another man. We had no intention to harm–"

"But the leader of your village committee reported that close to a hundred acres of green bean fields in your village were ruined. Your people are peasants. Don't you understand the difficulty of farming? How can you commit such a crime? The case is under investigation at the police station. I can't help you. Let's wait for the result. Is that OK with you?"

"Can't you tell them to let him go first? My baby is still small, and he's the only labour in the house. My baby's grandpa is not well. He can't handle this."

"I can't order the police to do anything. They are making the decision based on the investigation. All right, I have affairs to attend to. Goodbye."

The chief walked away in haste.

Nuannuan stood there in desperation. It seemed that all of her efforts to see the chief had been in vain. Kaitian would not be able to go home. What could she do? Once again, tears fell down Nuannuan's face.

The guard lowered his voice as he walked towards her. "Young sister, don't worry. What's the name of your man? What has he done? I'll call somebody at the police station and ask around for you. Crying will not solve your problem."

Nuannuan gave him the name and the story.

The guard told her: "You stay here. I'm just going back to the room to ask them about it."

He went inside the main gate while Nuannuan stood there, waiting in despair. After a meal's time, the guard came back as he promised and whispered: "Young sister, I asked. At this moment, it is not the police. It's the leader of your village committee. Once he agrees to let your man go, they'll send him home. So hurry up and beg him."

"What?" Nuannuan was stunned.

"The police concluded that your man only did bad things to others because he was tricked. Usually, with things like this, if you're willing to compensate the victims, your man would go home. But your leader made it clear that your man should not be released. And that's the big trouble here. Understand?"

Nuannuan shuddered. She bowed to the guard in gratitude. "Big Brother, you've helped me so much. Now that I know what has set my boat off course…"

Nuannuan jumped on her bike and cycled as hard as she could. She almost flew back to Chu Wang Village. When she entered the village, the sun had just set behind the hills, and chickens and ducks were retiring to their cages. She did not go home. Instead, she went straight to the small yard outside the office of the village committee. Zhan Shideng had not left yet. He was smoking a cigarette behind the desk, his eyes narrowed. The Party secretary was old and frail, so Zhan Shideng had become the de facto top leader in the office.

"I heard that you went to the township today, so I sat here all day, waiting for you to come back. What's up? Any good news?" Zhan Shideng pointed to a chair and gestured Nuannuan, who was still panting from the ride, to sit down.

Nuannuan did not move. "Mr Leader, you must not treat Kaitian like this."

"What's that supposed to mean?" Zhan Shideng's face gave no indication of his thoughts. "How should I treat him? Shall I praise him for what he did? Give him a big red flower to wear on his shirt? Take him to have some Lao Baigan liquor?"

"I've asked people. And I know everything now. You're the one who does not let Kaitian go. You!"

"Oh yeah?" Zhan Shideng laughed coldly. "You know everything now?"

"Of course I do."

"That's good. I thought they wouldn't tell you. But it seems that you know your way around. Who did you ask?"

"Mr Leader, please, let Kaitian go. Kaitian did not mean to harm anyone. He was tricked. Did you see our fields too? The two acres of green beans? Weren't they ruined too? We would never have used the fake weedkiller on our own fields if we had known."

"I'm afraid I can't. He ruined the crops in the village and sabotaged my people. I'm the leader, so I shall do justice for them. Kaitian must be punished," Zhan Shideng said sternly, though his voice was not loud.

"That's just your excuse. You want to punish him for marrying me, for my rejection of marrying your brother." Nuannuan stared into Zhan Shideng's eyes.

"Think what you like," said Zhan Shideng as he lit up another cigarette. He took a long drag and flicked the ash away. "Do not mix business with our private problems, all right?"

"Mr Leader, if you're angry about the marriage thing, just take it out on me. It was not Kaitian's fault. I made the decision to marry him. I don't know your brother well enough to love him. Though I don't think that I did anything bad, I'm still willing to offer an apology to you for harming the feelings of you and your family. Maybe I could have handled it all better." Nuannuan sounded very apologetic.

"Just an apology?" Zhan Shideng said, his narrowed eyes finally opening wide.

"What do you want from me, then?"

Again, Zhan Shideng narrowed his eyes. Yet again, his gaze was on Nuannuan's breasts.

"Money? Fine, give me a number first. After we get through this, I'll make sure to compensate for your loss. I'll write you a guarantee. Is that OK?"

"I never lack money." Zhan Shideng breathed out a perfect swirl.

"Then I shall offer my sincere apology," Nuannuan said as she suddenly knelt in front of Zhan Shideng.

"This does not mean anything," said Zhan Shideng, looking motionless. "We Zhans gave you an opportunity, but you and Kuang Kaitian threw that to the ground and made us lose face. You think kneeling can solve that? Do I look that cheap to you?"

"What do you want from me?" Nuannuan stood up, her face red as she was trying her best to contain her anger. "You name something, and I'll do as you say."

"You still don't understand?" Zhan Shideng squinted his eyes again and took a smoke. Then he simply stared at the small fire eating away the strips of the cigarette.

"I really don't understand you. Just say it. What do you want? Do you want Kaitian to help work in your fields? You know he's a good farmer."

"There's a field I'd like to plough. Your field is quite fine..." Zhan Shideng turned his eyes to look at the corner of the room.

Nuannuan thought about it for a short while, then her face suddenly blushed. She understood what Zhan Shideng meant by "ploughing a field". *Ugh!* She could not hold back her anger any more, so she growled quietly: "You dirty scoundrel. I didn't imagine you to be this disgusting. I treated you like a leader before, but I was blind. You're nothing but a pig. You swine."

"Are you done?" Zhan Shideng stood up, not affected by her words. He waved the keys in his hand and said: "We should both go back home for dinner. Your in-laws are waiting for your news. Go. Let's not waste our time on words."

Nuannuan exploded with anger. "You bastard! You pig!" Then she ran outside.

Nuannuan entered her yard with the bike, her face twisted in anger. The black dog was happy to see her home and ran towards her, wagging its tail. Nuannuan was so upset that she kicked the dog and cursed: "Stupid dog! Dirty bastard!" The dog, surprised and wronged, ran away with a bark of grief. Nuannuan's mother-in-law, Dangen in her arms, knew that things had not worked out as soon as she saw Nuannuan's face. She did not ask and passed Dangen to Nuannuan. Then she poured out a bowl of hot water, stirred in a teaspoon of sugar and gave the bowl to Nuannuan.

Tears rolled from her eyes before she drank from the bowl. *Zhan Shideng, you bastard! How dare you blackmail people like this? To seek justice for the villagers? What a high-sounding claim. It turns out that you've been harbouring such a filthy thought. Open your eyes to see who I am. Am I the one who can give you what you want?*

How could the innocent little Dangen understand his mother's mental torment? He grabbed his mum's chest, squirmed, and babbled for a breastfeed. Nuannuan gulped a few mouthfuls of water, untied her top, and placed a nipple into her son's mouth. While listening to him suckling, she let her tears trickle onto her clothes.

What now? There's no way that Zhan Shideng will be dissuaded from his vicious plan. But I can't simply wait for Kaitian's sentence to be finalised. Could I sue Zhan Shideng? But how? He said what he did was for the sake of justice in the village. How could that be wrong? He had all the good reasons in the world. Oh Kaitian, how could we have been so blind to buy the fake weedkiller and give Zhang Shideng an excuse to persecute us? How I regret our folly.

Nuannuan found it impossible to sleep that night. Her mind was filled with plans and despair. When it was close to sunrise, her mother-in-law knocked on her door and said to her from outside in a low voice: "Nuannuan, Kaitian's dad woke up with a stomach ache. He can't rest without news about Kaitian's return. I lied to him and said Kaitian is coming back the day after tomorrow. But he won't believe me and asked for you. Can you go to our bedroom and talk to him? Just offer him some comfort?"

Nuannuan's heart sank. She hurried to put on some clothes and went in front of her father-in-law's bed. She said: "Dad, I went to the township yesterday. The police promised to let Kaitian go home after a day or two."

"You're lying to me," said the old man lying in his bed under the lamp light, his gaze locked upon Nuannuan's face. "If you have such good news, you would've told me last night."

Nuannuan felt worse. She wanted to tell the truth, but how could she?

"Dad, I was too tired last night, so I didn't come over. What Mum told you is true. Kaitian will come home the day after tomorrow."

A faint flush emerged on the old man's pale face. He believed in Nuannuan's words. His eyes were reflecting joy as he said: "I can finally set my mind to rest..."

Nuannuan sat still on her bed for a long time after coming back from comforting her father-in-law. She did not leave her room until she heard the noise of the bellows. Her mother-in-law was starting the fire for breakfast. How would Kaitian be home while Zhan Shideng is not satisfied? Maybe she should go to the police station again and plead even more...

That morning, Nuannuan rode her bike to the township again. But they did not allow her to enter the police station. She begged and begged, but the policeman insisted that nothing could be done as the case was still being investigated. She had to go back to the guard in front of the township office. The man shook his head and said: "Didn't I tell you to go to your leader? What are you doing here?"

Nuannuan could not talk about Zhan Shideng's "offer". She teared up and answered: "The leader won't help us. He insisted on throwing my baby's father in prison."

The guard picked up his phone and called someone. After a short while, he put it down and said: "The people in your village who bought weedkiller from you have sent in a petition today. It just arrived. They demand serious punishment on your man. It's getting worse."

Nuannuan did not speak. Of course, she knew who was behind the petition and that there was nothing for her here. So she rose to thank the guard. "Big Brother, thank you for your help. I'm going home."

The guard followed her out and tried to comfort her. "You must go to the leader again and ask him to calm the village people down. You must do everything to stop the case from going to court. After his sentence, he'll be an ex-con. That'll be so bad for your children…"

The last sentence pounded on Nuannuan's heart. She immediately realised that a court sentence would not only make Kaitian suffer and cast shame on the family; it would also harm Dangen's future. *Heavens, Dangen, Mum won't let anything harm you. An ex-con's son would have no opportunity in education, in joining the army, in becoming an official and living in the city. No! But what can I do to persuade Zhan Shideng? Zhan Shideng, what you did to our family simply because I refused to marry your brother. What can I do? He doesn't want money. He surely has no need for presents, either. Do I have no choice but to accept his "offer"? That dirty swine! How could there be such a man like you under heaven?*

Nuannuan pushed her bike and measured every step she took to Chu Wang Village. With every step, she asked herself: *What now? What now?* Sadly, nothing came to mind by the time she eventually reached the stone pillar with an inscription of the village's name. She put her bike aside and leaned against the pillar, staring blankly at the village descending into the darkness. Slowly, tears began to fall from her eyes. She did not know how much time had passed when she finally raised her hands to wipe off the tears. Then she pushed her bike towards the village committee office.

Night had fallen, and the noisy village of the daylight was quieting down. Every noise, including the bleating sheep, was now lower. Nothing could be heard around the village committee office except for the sound Zhan Shideng was making as he locked the door. Nuannuan walked straight up and coughed behind his back.

Zhan Shideng turned his face and shouted out, his voice exaggerating his surprise: "Hey Nuannuan! You've come back. I heard you went to the township again today. Which official did you meet? Any good news–"

"Where do you want to do it?" Nuannuan did not let him finish. Her words were icy.

"Do what?" Zhan Shideng did not understand her at first. However, he knew everything from an instant glimpse at her cold figure. That coldness implied her willingness to sacrifice anything. His lip curved smugly. He turned to open the door and walked inside.

Nuannuan looked around and did not see or hear anyone else.

Feeling unworthy, she closed her eyes for a short while, and then she stepped up. The moment she entered the house, the door closed behind her. The room was dark. She could vaguely make out the shape of a bed in the corner. She closed her eyes again. She felt his breath behind her: he was next to her.

"My baby Dangen's dad must come home tomorrow."

"Sure."

"If your promise is not kept, I won't even cherish my life to–"

Before she could finish, she felt her feet fall away from the floor, and she was thrown onto the bed. Her instinct told her to cover her breasts.

"What are you covering yourself for? I didn't force you into this. Take off your clothes."

Nuannuan sat up and glared at Zhan Shideng. But after a short while, she raised her hands and unbuttoned her shirt, her teeth clenched...

"Look at that body. It's so white and tender. I thought we Zhans were not qualified to touch it. Now this proves that we can."

"Zhan Shideng!" Nuannuan was about to curse when she felt her breasts being clenched in his hands. She gasped.

"What a great cropland." As he mumbled, Zhan Shideng pushed open Nuannuan's snow-white legs...

EARTH

Nuannuan was still shaking in anger and hatred for Zhan Shideng as she stood in front of the door to the custody room. It was not until she saw Kaitian that those feelings were repressed by her love and pity for him. It had only taken a couple of days to change the look of Kaitian; he had been overtaken by despair and insecurity.

Even in his wildest dreams, Kaitian never thought of himself being handcuffed and locked up. At first, he would cry out in panic: "I'm innocent!"

After a while, the policeman would lose his patience and tap a finger on Kaitian's head. "Did you or did you not ruin ninety acres of green bean fields in your village?"

Kaitian had no choice but to nod his head.

"Then why are you yelling about innocence?" The policeman kicked his buttocks.

"But I only bought the weedkiller from someone else."

"Where is that someone else, then? Go and search him out if you can. Stop blaming others for your crime." He tapped on Kaitian's head again.

"I'm innocent!" Kaitian cried out again in despair...

Kaitian felt as if he were in a dream when he finally saw Nuannuan, and he raised a hand to rub his eyes.

A policeman unlocked his handcuffs and said: "You're only

forgiven because we need to give face to your Leader Zhan. Once you're home, you have to compensate every victim."

"Yes, yes," answered Kaitian vaguely as he walked towards Nuannuan. He threw himself into her arms.

Nuannuan did not say anything and shed no tears. She only patted his back and whispered: "Let's go home."

In the evening, men from every household that bought weedkiller from Kaitian were sent for and gathered in front of the village committee office. Kaitian stood in the middle of the crowd, bowing his head. Nuannuan stayed in the shadow cast by the wall in the corner. Seeing that Kaitian had been released, the crowd either whispered their criticism or shouted out curses.

The noise did not stop until Zhan Shideng came in with majestic strides. He coughed, then spoke out in an authoritative voice. "Shame on Kaitian for committing such a despicable deed. But shame on you all for making a scene here. We all live in this village, so why can't you solve anything by discussing it peacefully? Kaitian will pay for your loss. From today on, no one shall go to his house and point the finger at him. How much is he going to pay? An ordinary harvest will give you four hundred *jin* of green beans per acre, so we'll take that number. The market price is 1.2 yuan per *jin* – that makes 480 yuan per acre. Kaitian will pay you according to the acres of your ruined field. However, you all know about his household. He can't pay you all at once. So each year he will send some money to each of you until everything is even. OK?"

Hearing their leader's words, the crowd stayed quiet. Spotty Laosi spoke out. "OK. He can pay as the leader ordered. We don't want trouble with Kaitian, either. But we all have our lives to live, and no one can afford such a loss..."

After the people had left, Nuannuan tried to pull Kaitian home. To her surprise, Kaitian suddenly plopped on the ground, covered his head with his hands and sobbed. "Heavens! Eighty-eight acres, apart from our two acres to cover. Four hundred and eighty yuan per acre, that's more than forty-two thousand yuan to pay. All we've got is twelve hundred yuan in the bank. Where in the world can we find the rest of that money?"

Nuannuan whispered: "Heaven must have a way. Let's go home now."

Shallot walked over. "Don't worry about my two acres."

Nuannuan was touched. "My sister-in-law…"

Nuannuan supported Kaitian home. His mother held him in her arms and cried. Kaitian's father came over with his walking sticks and looked at him in tears. Nuannuan fetched water to wash Kaitian's face and feet.

That night, Kaitian lay in bed with his eyes wide open. Nuannuan put Dangen to sleep and turned her body. She held his head against her chest and whispered her comfort: "Stop worrying. Everything will be fine with you well at home. We'll figure out something about the money."

Kaitian burst out crying, his tears and snot dropping onto Nuannuan's chest. Nuannuan rubbed his back and said: "I did some calculation. Without Shallot's part, we have forty-one families to cover. Let's pay each of them one hundred yuan first, and they'll make peace with us for the time being. We have one thousand yuan in the bank, and we can sell the bike, the flatbed cart, the television and the watch I bought in Beijing. I'll go to my parents' house tomorrow and borrow some money from Dad. We'll have a better plan after paying one hundred yuan to everyone."

Kaitian was still sobbing. "Your dad hasn't forgiven us. How can we borrow money from him?"

"Don't you worry. I'll beg him to help. If he still doesn't agree, I'll figure something else out…"

The next morning after breakfast, Nuannuan departed for her parents' house. She knew that Dad was still angry, but she had no one else to turn to. Before she entered the yard, Mum saw her and hastened to pull her aside. "Dad is home. First, tell me about the money problem. How much is it in total?"

Nuannuan gave her the details. Mum was stunned by the number. It took her some time to say: "That boy Kaitian, he's so poor at dealing with things and has caused such a big mess. What are you going to do about it?"

Nuannuan said: "I told him to buy the weedkiller. It wasn't his fault."

As they were speaking in a whisper, Dad walked out. Mum pulled Nuannuan behind her in fear of his anger and said: "I told Nuannuan to come home. If you need to scold someone, I'm responsible for this."

Unexpectedly, Dad answered in a soft voice: "Let's go inside to talk about the matter. What's the use of standing here?"

Mum quickly led Nuannuan inside. Once they were in the house, Mum told Dad about Nuannuan's trouble. Chu Changshun stayed quiet for a long while. Nuannuan had her mind made up: she would leave if Dad spoke even one bad word. To her surprise, Dad only asked: "How much do you need?"

Nuannuan was speechless for a second. Then she quickly answered: "A thousand will do."

Dad did not say another word. He went into his room. After some searching, he came back and passed a roll of cash to his daughter. "Here's sixteen hundred yuan. You need some money for yourself."

Nuannuan instantly felt tears in her eyes. "Dad, I don't need that much."

Dad glared. "Take it as I ordered. Stop talking. You need to feed and clothe yourselves."

Nuannuan took the money. Before she left, Dad spoke again. "Remember, tears don't solve any problem when you're in trouble. You need to think, not complain. In moments like this, you must face the problems with Kaitian. Don't blame him, or it will cut deep. Do you understand?"

Nuannuan nodded.

"Go home. Comfort Kaitian. Don't let him get sick in desperation." Dad waved his hand.

Nuannuan was leaving when Grandma came out with her cane. "We people should be prepared when meeting with trouble so that it will never harm you. But when the trouble does fall on you, you must be bold and believe that there's nothing you can't conquer. Kaitian and you must be bold and think about a future where you are free of all this. Don't have your eyes only on the troubled present."

Nuannuan nodded again and wiped the tears off her face.

Then she left the house.

With more than a thousand yuan from Dad, combined with the money in the bank and the money from selling the bike, the flatbed cart, the television and the watch, Nuannuan and Kaitian paid two hundred yuan to several families who were most dissatisfied about

Kaitian's release, and a hundred to everyone else except for Shallot. By then, people finally made peace with them...

As Nuannuan and Kaitian were thinking about more ways to earn money, they did not expect Kaitian's father's bad health. Before that, though unable to move his legs, he could still walk around the house with sticks. But now he could not even get out of bed. He would cough all night and complain about an ache in his chest. Kaitian and his mother became flustered. The couple borrowed a flatbed cart and took the old man to the township hospital on Juxiang Street. The doctor performed an examination and talked about emphysema, which required Kaitian's father to stay in the hospital for treatment. The young couple were too shocked to speak. They went through the hospital admission documents. It was not Nuannuan's first time to deal with hospitalisation, but even she did not expect the cost. They spent the three hundred yuan they brought over in a couple of days. She urged Kaitian to go home and borrow some money. But he was too scared to face his neighbours. They could not get enough money from their relatives in other villages because everyone knew about their enormous debt. Kaitian pushed himself to the limit to persuade people but only got one hundred yuan in total. How could that be enough? Nuannuan made the decision to sell their cow. Kaitian panicked. "How about the field? That cow pulled the plough as hard as it could."

"We'll see. We have to get through this. We'll buy another one when we have money."

Nuannuan was determined. One morning when everyone was having breakfast in their yards, Nuannuan had Kaitian lead the cow outside. She called out: "A cow for sale. Come and buy it if you want it."

People came over with their bowls in hand. Spotty Laosi was the first to ask about the price. Nuannuan answered: "You all know about this good cow. It'll cost anyone at least 1,500 yuan in the market. But today, I'll give it to you for 1,300 yuan."

Spotty Laosi smirked. "You're asking way too much. Your cow has given birth twice. When a cow has a calf, its strength is halved, let alone two births. I'll give you 720 yuan. If you think it's OK, I'll buy it."

His offer pained Nuannuan.

Kaitian also shook his head. "Brother Laosi, your bargaining is too hard. How can you drive the price down so much? It's a cow, not a pig."

Spotty Laosi knew that the couple were in dire need of money and thought they would sell at a deeply discounted price. So he refused to compromise, saying: "Seven hundred and twenty is already a good price. These days, I can buy any cow or bull with the same amount. I offer you this much to help you out of your emergency."

Jiuding hated Spotty Laosi's attempt to fish in trouble waters and stepped forward, saying: "I'll buy it for a thousand yuan."

Before Nuannuan and Kaitian could respond, Spotty Laosi yelled at Jiuding with a filthy temper: "Jiuding, you son of a bitch! Are you so wealthy that you want to show off here? Why don't you buy a hundred plasters and put them on your body? Then everyone will know you've made a fortune, won't they? Why are you here to flaunt your money in front of me? Do you want to sabotage my deal on purpose?"

Jiuding smiled apologetically. "Anyone who wants to buy the cow can make an offer. How come I'm messing up your deal?"

Truth is, Spotty Laosi had taken a liking to the cow, knowing that he could quickly sell it in a cattle market for 1,600 yuan. How could he allow Jiuding to buy it? With a grim face, he offered 1,050 yuan. Jiuding bumped it up to 1,100, making Spotty Laosi so angry that his face went awry. He had to reluctantly raise the offer to 1,150. But Jiuding pushed it further up to 1,200. Stamping his foot on the ground, Spotty Laosi said with anger: "OK, OK. You've got money. You're wealthier than I am. Since we're poor, we won't compete with you any more." With that, he left panting with rage. As he took off, he cursed: "Jiuding, I hope you stumble over tomorrow and knock out a couple of your teeth. I hope robbers plunder your house and take your wife away so you'll still be in a mood to show off."

Nuannuan hurriedly said to Jiuding: "Please take the cow with you."

Jiuding shook his head. "You take it back to your yard. I'll come for it this evening." The villagers who had been looking on now scattered. Jiuding then led the cow back into the Kuangs' courtyard.

Jiuding said: "I know you don't want to sell this cow. You are peasants, and you can't work without cattle. Don't sell it at such a low price. Keep it, and I'll give you 1,200 yuan. Think of it as a loan, and pay me back when you have money."

Nuannuan burst into tears. Kaitian was touched too. He said: "Jiuding, I see you as a little brother. When I have the money, I won't forget about how you saved my life."

Jiuding waved his hand and said: "What are you talking about? Just remember to help me out when I'm in trouble..."

With 1,200 yuan from Jiuding, Nuannuan managed to afford her father-in-law's treatment.

The day Kaitian's father was discharged from the hospital, Nuannuan and Kaitian borrowed a flatbed cart again to take him home. When they reached the small ferry in front of the village entrance, they saw Shallot stepping off Black Bean's boat with her husband Changlin in her arms. Changlin had bandages all over his right arm. Nuannuan stepped up and asked in shock: "What happened to my Brother Changlin?"

Shallot wiped her tears. "It's been bad luck for both of our families. Changlin was working for a construction team in Nanfu City, and he fell off the scaffold. Now he has suffered a comminuted fracture in his right arm."

Nuannuan could not speak. Shallot had two children and her in-laws to take care of. With Changlin's injury, there was no way that she could manage the household on her own.

"Don't worry about me," said Shallot in a relaxed way, having recognised Nuannuan's concern. "It doesn't scare your Sister-in-Law Shallot. I can live through any day as bad as it gets. But you, with Kaitian, must not worry too much. You have so many problems coming your way..."

Kaitian's father's sickness pushed them another step closer to rock bottom. Kaitian's lips were covered in blisters due to their exhausting days. As Nuannuan spoke more comforting words to Kaitian, she hastened to find herbs to make a tea that would relieve his internal heat.

Kaitian sighed. "After this autumn's harvest, I'll go to the city to pick up work. We need money."

Nuannuan nodded. "That can work. I'll stay at home and take care of your parents and Dangen. You should go and find ways."

Soon, the busy autumn harvest season came. Every family in Chu Wang Village began to harvest millet, green beans, maize and cotton. Before the weedkiller incident, Kaitian had taken on all the farm work so that Nuannuan could concentrate on looking after their baby and doing family chores. He had seldom allowed her to work in the fields. But now, Nuannuan insisted on working outdoors because her mother-in-law could take care of their weaned baby. She argued that she could also decoct the medicinal herbs for her father-in-law. "Besides," she said, "I'll feel better helping you a bit in the fields."

That afternoon, Kaitian was going to harvest maize and had to take Nuannuan because of her stubbornness. Their family cornfields were on the hillside to the west of the village. It would take two meals' time to climb up to the hill. They were about to step out when Kaitian noticed the wet breakfast residue left on the front of her blouse. It reminded him of her busy morning. Seized with a feeling of love and pity, he said: "Forget it. Don't harvest the maize today. It's too tiring climbing the hill. How about cutting the half-acre millets by the lake? Cut as much as you can and wait for me to continue."

"Don't worry. I'm not a clay figure, so how can I get tired climbing the hillside?"

Pretending to be angry, Kaitian glared at her. "No more talking. Go back." And with that, he left.

Aware of Kaitian's kind intention, Nuannuan didn't insist. Carrying a shoulder pole with a basket hanging from each end, she went to harvest the millet. This year's millet grew very well. It had long ears with plump millet fruits. The ears were so heavy that they bent the stalks under their weight. Nuannuan put down the baskets and shoulder pole at the end of the fields and began cutting the millet. She estimated that it would take her this afternoon and tomorrow morning to finish harvesting the millet at her pace.

It was quiet in the fields in the afternoon. There was no sound except for the staccato grasshopper chirping. Nuannuan stooped down to cut the millet nimbly, the thick ears brushing her forearms. The sharp leaf blades relentlessly left bloody cuts on her wrists. The stalks fell, rustling beneath her swaying sickle. Beads of sweat gradually emerged on her forehead and from the hair covering her temples, trickling down her cheeks. She had to straighten up to wipe the sweat off her cheeks from time to time. Nuannuan didn't know how many times she had straightened up, but when she did it this time, she spotted Zhan Shideng passing by the edge of the field on his bicycle. She immediately bent down, pretending not to have seen him. *Pig! Son of a bitch!* After the humiliation at his hands that night, she would never see him again. She felt sick and hateful even at the mention of his name. She never allowed herself to recall that night. Whenever it flashed up, she immediately ordered herself to think of something else or find something to do to divert her attention. She decided to bury that night deep in her heart, trying not to reveal it to anyone, including Kaitian of course and even herself. How much she longed not to be able to recollect it. But she had glanced at Zhan Shideng a moment ago. That night's scene flashed back in her mind's eye again. She bit her lip and forced herself to concentrate on the millet stalks, attempting to push the memory back to the recess of her heart.

"Hey, is that Nuannuan?"

She heard Zhan Shideng calling her. Her entire body became tense. *Son of a bitch, you dare to call me!* These were the words she would have slung at him intuitively. But she decided to ignore him as if there were no such person in the world. A response would only invite more nonsense from him.

"Hey, Nuannuan, why don't you answer me since you're so close?"

Nuannuan heard him drawing nearer, but she carried on cutting the millet, bending her back.

"I was coming back from a meeting in the township and happened to see you. We haven't seen each other for a long time," said Zhan Shideng as he walked over. "Since that night, you—"

"Beat it!" roared Nuannuan, raising her head abruptly. She saw Zhan Shideng standing a few feet away, all smiles. She saw his beard stubble and nose and the sweat breaking out on it.

Still beaming, Zhan Shideng continued: "What happened? Why are you so angry? As the saying goes, 'A night's sleep begets an affection for a hundred years.' We've been a one-night husband and wife."

Nuannuan threw a handful of the millet stalks at Zhan Shideng's face. Then, bending down to pick up a clump of clay, she yelled: "Get out of my sight!"

Zhan Shideng remained undisturbed. He said with the same smile: "You're acting as if we're enemies. Truth is, we've had the closest physical contact. Frankly, I've been thinking of you every day since that night. Your body is indeed…"

The clump of clay whooshed towards Zhan Shideng from Nuannuan's hand. Unfortunately, it missed its target and smashed into fine pieces in the field behind.

Zhan Shideng remained calm and lowered his voice. "You see, there's not a soul around us here. Why can't we make love on the green grass by the lake again? It'll give us a different taste…"

Nuannuan couldn't hold back her tears because of anger and shame. Knowing that Zhan Shideng would say something more offensive to the ear if she stayed in the fields, she crouched down to pick up the shoulder pole and then left, carrying the baskets.

Nuannuan sat at home, seething with anger and shedding tears. She quickly wiped her tears when she heard Kaitian's footsteps.

Kaitian's work in the maize fields that afternoon had gone so smoothly that he had finished harvesting the ears before the sun disappeared behind the hills. As he carried two big baskets of maize ears into the courtyard, he saw Nuannuan already sitting in the main room. "You're back?" he asked in surprise. He set the baskets on the ground and went into the kitchen. He scooped a bowl of water from the vat and gulped it down in one breath. He then went into the main room and asked Nuannuan affectionately: "How much millet did you harvest? You carried it back yourself?"

Nuannuan didn't respond.

He was stunned. When he looked closer, he found the corners of Nuannuan's eyes had tear stains.

"What's wrong? Are you tired? Has something happened?" asked Kaitian. He was anxious because he knew Nuannuan had such a strong character that she didn't cry easily.

Nuannuan was still silent. Covering her face with her eyes, she started sobbing.

He walked up close to Nuannuan and stooped down to ask

eagerly: "What in the world happened? Is it because the baskets slid from the shoulder pole and dumped the millet out?" He looked around, only to find the baskets in the courtyard empty.

Nuannuan cried more bitterly. If it were not for the hands covering her face, she would have wailed at the top of her voice.

Kaitian's heart sank. He thought something grave had happened. He wondered if something had happened to his father-in-law, like a serious illness. But when he visited him a few days before, he had found him all right. "Is it because our dad went fishing on the lake?"

"No, no. It's that son of..."

Kaitian was puzzled. "Son? Whose son?"

Nuannuan's humiliation and anger would have driven her to tell Kaitian about everything Zhan Shideng had been doing to her. She wished that Kaitian would beat Zhan to a pulp. But she held back what she wanted to say, aware that Kaitian had a quick temper. If she had divulged her insult to him, she would have got him into big trouble and the family into a worse situation. She didn't want the family to suffer more. Therefore, she came up with a white lie. "It's the sun of the early afternoon. It was so hot that it hurt me when sweat got into the cuts on my wrists. So, I was no longer in the mood to work in the fields."

Kaitian laughed. "I see. I thought something terrible had happened. It turned out to be the sun. OK, OK, you don't have to work in the fields. I'll finish the work off when I have time tomorrow."

From that day on, Nuannuan didn't ask to work in the fields any more. She was afraid of running into Zhan Shideng again.

She had talked to Kaitian about finding work in the city after the autumn harvest season. After the incident in the millet fields, Nuannuan didn't dare to let Kaitian go. If he went, only the two aged parents and young Dangen would be at home. *What if Zhan Shideng keeps on harassing me? To fight him would lead to the exposure of what happened that night. It would make me and the family a disgrace. If I went with Kaitian to the city, bringing Dangen with us, who would take care of the old folks at home? Besides, Kaitian may find it hard to settle in a big city. Then how could he take care of me and Dangen?* After turning all these considerations in her mind, she decided to keep Kaitian home.

Even when they were at home, it was important for the young

couple to find ways to earn money. They could not afford to waste their time in Chu Wang Village, where their neighbours were waiting for payment. First, Nuannuan made Kaitian carry a big basket of garlic from the spring harvest and a basket of pumpkins from last autumn to the quarry several miles away in order to sell them to the kitchens. But it only earned them a few dozen yuan, which was far from what they needed. Later on, she thought about making ropes by twisting hemp fibres between the palms, but that would not bring them much either. It was then that Nuannuan had her eyes on Dad's fishing boat. *What if Kaitian went fishing with Dad in the lake? That will be a good way to make money.* Nuannuan told Kaitian about the idea. Kaitian nodded and said: "That's all well and good, but I'm not sure if Dad will take me."

Nuannuan said: "Dad needs a helping hand anyway. Hehe is helping at the moment, but you're definitely better than her. I'll take you to see Dad tomorrow morning."

The next morning, Nuannuan and Kaitian went to the small ferry just as Dad was about to row his boat into the lake. Nuannuan said to Hehe, who was sitting in the boat: "I have some needlework for you. Let your brother-in-law work on the lake today."

Naturally, Dad did not object. He waved at Hehe and said: "Go then."

It was the first time that Kaitian had been on his father-in-law's boat, and he was eager to show his capacity to work. As soon as he got in the boat, he reached out for the paddle to start rowing. But the boat would not move forward; he could only make it circle around. His father-in-law smiled. He sat opposite Kaitian and explained the rowing skills in detail. Kaitian, smart as he was, learned by heart very quickly. Before long, he could row the boat effortlessly. With his strength, the boat moved forward smoothly and reached the centre of the lake in no time. Kaitian paid much attention and modestly asked questions when his father-in-law put down the net. Dad had no son, so he was happy to teach his son-in-law. A curious student and a willing teacher, they got along quite well. At midday, Kaitian jumped ahead to make noodles from the coal stove. He poured garlic sauce on the noodles and reverently offered one bowl to his father-in-law. The old man sat on one side of the boat and ate in satisfaction. It was the first time that Kaitian had spent time with Dad alone since he married Nuannuan, so he was meticulous about everything. Though he did not catch a lot of fish that day, Kaitian left a fine impression on his father-in-law.

At sunset when they were anchoring, Kaitian tried to speak in an easy tone. "Dad, I've learned a lot from you today in the lake. I really want to continue practising fishing with you."

The old man quickly answered: "If that is so, come again tomorrow. Hehe can stay at home and help around the house."

Kaitian was hoping for that response. He nodded and said: "I will. I will."

From then on, Kaitian joined Dad in his boat, and eventually he was trusted to cast and draw up the net on his own. Every morning, he went to prepare for fishing very early. As soon as his father-in-law arrived, they would row the boat into the lake. Every day at sunset, Kaitian would carefully wash the boat while Dad went to bargain and weigh the fish with the buyers. Dad soon found Kaitian quite agreeable. He never talked about getting Hehe back on the boat and kept Kaitian as his assistant. Kaitian never asked about their fishing income because he knew that Dad would not let him work in vain. As expected, after several days, Dad halved the money from selling the fish every evening and gave Kaitian his share. So Kaitian had a stable income of a dozen yuan every day. He found it quite satisfying during the days when he could not work in the fields.

However, those days did not last for long. As the weather grew colder, fewer and fewer fishers worked in the lake. Fishing would gradually stop after the first snow. One evening when they were anchoring the boat, Dad said: "The season has arrived when we put the boat to rest. We're not going on the lake tomorrow."

Kaitian sighed. *Well, this income is at its end.* Seeing Kaitian returning home with a grim face, Nuannuan knew that Dad had stopped fishing for the year, so she tried to comfort him. "Don't frown. We'll think of another way to make money."

The next day was when Kaitian's mother would customarily go to Lingyan Temple to offer incense. Seeing her mother-in-law stagger when she walked, Nuannuan was worried that the distance would be too much for her. "It's too far away for you to go any longer. Please let Kaitian and I go on your behalf. You stay at home and rest."

Her mother-in-law gave in promptly, saying: "OK. It's getting more and more difficult for me to walk. You and Kaitian can do it for me in the future." She then handed Nuannuan the basket with incense sticks and steamed buns. Without work to do, Kaitian felt bored, so he was only too glad to go with Nuannuan.

It was the first time Nuannuan and Kaitian had been to offer incense at the temple since they were married. At the doorsteps of the temple, Nuannuan prayed silently: *Buddha, you're not blessing the Kuangs these days. Is it because I've offended you? If so, I'm here to apologise to you today.*

In the Mahavira Hall, she set the steamed buns on the altar, burned incense and prayed in secret: *My respectful Buddha, if you advocate rewarding good with good and evil with evil, please punish the weedkiller-selling con man and Zhan Shideng. Please take away their money or position. What they did was too low.*

After her prayers, she saw Abbot Tianxin coming into the hall. Nuannuan couldn't help going up to accost him. She bowed and said: "Your Reverend Abbot, may I ask you a few questions?"

"Please go ahead, our benefactor," Abbot Tianxin greeted her back.

"Can the Buddha answer pilgrims' prayers?"

"He can if the prayer requests are in line with heavenly principles and human reasons."

"Since there are so many pilgrims, will the Buddha forget some of their prayers?"

"The light of the Buddha is omnipresent. So how can he forget?"

"Will he keep his promise?"

"He will if you believe in him."

Before stepping out of the temple, Nuannuan laughed. "You weedkiller con man, and you Zhan Shideng, wait and see. Karma will get you soon."

After two snowfalls, Red Lake became absolutely silent. Except for a small boat carrying people over, nothing could be seen but the lonely waves swarming up and down.

Chu Wang Village, by the side of the lake, became quieter too. Only dogs and chickens would run around in the village while most people hid inside to stay warm. However, in the Kuang house, as soon as the lukewarm sun rose, Nuannuan got busy. She would hang a half-finished fishing net on the old magnolia tree outside the door and start knitting it. Selling fishing nets was one of her recent ideas for making money. She had to seize every opportunity since several people had come over again some days ago to press them for money. Kaitian went to hide in his uncle's house out of fear.

Money was what this family needed the most. As she was knitting the net, Nuannuan wished that this net would sell better. In the late morning, Dangen, carried out by his grandmother, reached out his dainty hands and cried for suckling. Nuannuan had to stop knitting. She took Dangen over, cuddled him in her bosom and placed a nipple into his mouth. She looked up at Red Lake and followed a flying gull in the sky with her eyes. *Heavens, please warm the earth up so that we can go fishing in the lake to make some money.*

Nuannuan suddenly saw a small boat coming her way on the lake. She recognised it as Black Bean's boat. Not many people visited the east bank – one or two maybe, but they were all offering incense in Lingyan Temple. However, this time, judging from the look of the visitor, he was from the city. He did not have any incense holder or offerings with him. Instead, he carried a canvas pack on his back. The man jumped off the boat and paid Black Bean. Then, maybe because he saw Nuannuan's figure, he walked straight towards the Kuangs' door and said: "Hi, friend. How are you?"

Hearing his greetings, Nuannuan turned her face towards him and answered: "Good." She noticed that the visitor was almost an old man – a very skinny yet fit old man. "Uncle, are you offering incense in Lingyan Temple?" she asked politely.

The old man shook his head. "No."

"Then what are you doing here?"

"I'm just showing myself around. I heard there's a long stone wall on the hill behind your village that extends along several mountains. Is that true?" asked the old man, panting heavily.

Nuannuan thought about it and answered: "It's true. But that wall is broken and leaning. It has no use any more." She was surprised to know that the old man from the city was interested in the plain stone wall.

"I met Black Bean, the owner of the boat, on the east bank of Red Lake. He told me there's a long wall on the hill."

"The wall really has no use any more," Nuannuan explained again.

"Can you, or anyone from your house, take me there to see it?" the old man insisted with a smile.

"There's nothing to see but some stones." Nuannuan had so much to worry about that she did not have any interest in taking him.

"Of course I wouldn't let you take me for free. I will pay."

Though not quite happy about the situation, Nuannuan had to laugh. "I don't need any payment. If you really want to go, I'll take you. It's just some walking around, and I don't ask for money for walking around."

"How about this? You take me there, and I'll give you twenty yuan."

Nuannuan was stunned. "Twenty yuan for that? Are you serious?"

The old man laughed. "You think I'm tricking you? How about that I give you the money right now to assure you." He took out two ten-yuan notes and passed them to Nuannuan.

Feeling slightly ashamed, Nuannuan pushed his hand away and said: "I haven't done anything to earn that yet. I can't take the money in shame. Wait here, and I'll take you there after I've put the baby down."

Nuannuan turned and entered the yard. She felt genuinely happy as she walked towards the house. Twenty yuan was the price for four hundred grams of wheat. *I'm just worried about money, and someone came with it. Was it because the Buddha saw me offer incense and found me pitiful, so he sent this person here?*

After passing Dangen to her mother-in-law, Nuannuan picked up a sickle for chopping up firewood and a rope for binding them, and led the old man to the small hill behind the village. She had visited the stone wall many times. When she was little, she always went to pick up firewood with Dad on the hill. When she had grown up, she always went there to cut weed to feed the livestock. Either way, she had to pass the stone wall. Sometimes she might even sit on top of its collapsed part to eat her meals. She could basically walk up the path into the hill blindfolded. She gave her name to the old man in courtesy, and he offered his in return. He called himself Tan Wenbo, and he was from Beijing.

"Uncle, where do you live in Beijing?" asked Nuannuan, who felt they had something in common because he came from where she used to work.

"Haidian, near Peking University. Have you been to Peking University?"

Nuannuan shook her head and asked again: "Uncle, why did you come all the way to this remote, poor village of ours? You can't have done all that travel to see this mere stone wall."

"Well, I read in a book that someone built a stone wall here a long time ago. But I wasn't sure about whether or not it was true. So I have travelled here to see if there is any of the relic left."

The path was winding, and the old man was carrying his bag as he talked. It did not take long for him to start panting. Nuannuan could not see him like that, so she lifted the bag from his back and said: "Let me carry this for you."

The old man accepted her offer and smiled. "Thank you, Ms Chu."

They ate their lunch while trudging along. The old man took some bread and sausage from his backpack and shared them with Nuannuan. Although she had worked in Beijing, she begrudged buying this delicacy, and it was the first time she had eaten sausages. After only the first bite, she was already enjoying its flavour very much, but she didn't have the heart to eat it all. She hid half of it in her pocket without the old man noticing because she wanted Dangen to have a bite in the evening. Since the old man could not walk as fast, it was already late in the afternoon when they reached the stone wall. Nuannuan thought he would be disappointed by the look of the wall, so she pointed at it and said apologetically: "You see, it's already collapsed. It's really of no use any more."

To her surprise, the old man grew quite excited. He almost staggered to the wall and quickly drew out a pair of glasses, a magnifying glass, a pen, a hammer and some other tools that Nuannuan did not recognise. He inspected the wall in detail, knocked on some parts and did some measurements. He then wrote everything down. Nuannuan sat to the side and had a little rest. Afterwards, she started chopping up firewood around the wall. Occasionally, she would look back at the old man, busy with his tasks, and found the scene humorous. *So much seriousness for a stone wall that's been here forever.*

The old man kept busy until dusk. He did not even touch the bottle of water he'd brought.

"We should go, Uncle. It'll be dark soon."

The old man heard her words and raised his head to check the sky. "Good. Good. We shall go," he answered, though he seemed reluctant to leave.

The old man was very happy on the way back and said to Nuannuan: "Young Ms Chu, thank you for taking me here. Do you know what I discovered today? A Great Wall."

"A Great Wall?"

"Yes. My estimation at this moment is that the wall was built by people of the State of Chu during the third century BCE to prevent invasion from the State of Qin."

"By the State of Chu?" Nuannuan looked lost.

"Yes. The village you live in today was historically in the domain of Chu. Their earliest capital was not far away from your Chu Wang Village."

Nuannuan smiled as she remembered the story about Qu Yuan told by her fellow villager Jiuding. "I... have heard of Chu, but I didn't know that the wall was—"

"Of course you didn't know. All that history is too far from your life. I only learned about it from a history book. After various wars between the two states, Chu constructed a Great Wall on hills in this area to stop the invasion. I did not travel here with much hope to find it. But who'd have known? With the help from you and Black Bean, I came and I found it. You have no idea how happy I am right now."

"But the wall is of no use any more." Nuannuan felt obliged to remind him again.

"No, no material use at all. But it's valuable in research. Do you understand that, my child?"

The old man could not stop talking in excitement on the way back. It was not until they reached the entrance to the village that he paused and looked at the dark sky. "Young Ms Chu, I'm afraid I'll have to stay in the village tonight. Is it possible for me to stay at your house for one night? I'll pay you."

Nuannuan hesitated and then answered: "Of course it's fine. But our place is not a big, bright house like those in the city. The bed is a wreck too. I'm afraid you won't like it."

"It's fine with me as long as I have a place to sleep in. I have travelled extensively, and I have been to worse places. Let's say I'll pay you fifty yuan for one night's stay in your house and another thirty for one dinner and one breakfast. With the twenty yuan I promised for taking me to the wall, you get one hundred yuan in total. Is that OK?"

Nuannuan smiled again. "Here, we do not take money if someone needs a place to stay for one night and a meal. Everyone needs help when travelling. I'll simply be happy if you don't find our rural life too meagre."

"I must pay you – you earned this money," said the old man as he thrust a hundred yuan into Nuannuan's hand.

Nuannuan did not expect to earn a hundred yuan with almost no effort at all. She clutched the note in her hand. Though she wanted to return it to show courtesy, she could not bear to lose this money. After a while, and with much hesitation, she put the money in her pocket.

Her parents-in-law were surprised to see an old man from the city coming to their house. Nuannuan offered her guest a seat and told them about the day. Her mother-in-law hastened to cook dinner after she heard what had happened. Nuannuan followed her into the kitchen and whispered: "Mum, cook him the best meal you can. That old man has already paid us thirty yuan for tonight's dinner and tomorrow's breakfast."

Her mother-in-law whispered back to scold her for taking the money as she pointed out again: "Everyone needs help when travelling."

Nuannuan told her that she did not ask for payment, but he insisted. "Cook him a good meal and let him eat his fill, then we don't have to feel guilty."

Her mother-in-law showed all her cooking skills that she had practised for years. She made four dishes: fried pumpkin flowers, chilli with green beans, chives with scrambled eggs and steamed purslane leaves. Nuannuan made the noodles herself. She apologised to the old man as dinner was being served. "We don't have any meat around the house, so you'll have to go vegetarian tonight."

The old man tasted the dishes happily and said: "Delicious. Everything is delicious. I like it. Vegetables are good for your health." He ate two bowls of noodles and smiled at Nuannuan when he finished. "I haven't eaten this much for a long time. If I could make noodles like you did, I'd open an authentic noodle eatery and make a lot of money."

Nuannuan blushed at his compliments. That night was her happiest in a long time.

After arranging for the old man to rest in a spare room, Nuannuan returned to her own bedroom. At that time, Dangen had laid down after being undressed by his grandma. Nuannuan was taking off her clothes when she suddenly remembered the half sausage in her pocket. She hurriedly took it out and placed it close to Dangen's mouth.

"What?" asked Dangen in surprise.

"The grandpa from Beijing gave it to you. It's made of pork. Very tasty."

Dangen bit a piece off, and as he chewed it, he nodded and said: "Yummy."

"Don't finish it off. Leave a bit for your dad to have a taste when he's back," Nuannuan whispered.

The next morning, the old man said to Nuannuan: "I'd like to work on the wall here for another couple of days. Can you take me there again? If you can, I'll add thirty yuan to your payment every day. And it will be 150 yuan every day with meals and bed included."

Of course, Nuannuan agreed quickly: money would come much faster from this than knitting fishing nets. How could she turn down such a good opportunity? Before breakfast, she went back to her parents' house and had Hehe bring Kaitian back from his uncle's because he had no need to hide any more. Later on, she prepared two packs of food for lunch on the hill.

After breakfast, Nuannuan carried the old man's bag and led him to the hill again. She kept him company through the inspection, measurement, calculation and recording by the side of the collapsed stone wall. When they returned home that evening, Kaitian had already come home. Nuannuan gave the money from the old man to Kaitian and told him everything.

Kaitian was happily surprised and said: "This is a god-sent opportunity to make some money."

Then, Nuannuan introduced Kaitian to Uncle Tan. The old man smiled and said: "Tomorrow, I'll have to trouble you to take me to the hill."

From the third day onwards, Kaitian became the old man's companion. Naturally, he was quite familiar with the wall too. The old man kept himself occupied for nine days with Kaitian by his side. During those days, Kaitian and Nuannuan learned a lot from him. He told them that people from Chu built the Great Wall but abandoned it afterwards; during the Song Dynasty, the Jurchens invaded China, so people of the Southern Song Dynasty re-established the wall in defence. Judging from the edges of the stones on the wall, some were obtained from the hill earlier than others. The old man also told them that the stone rubble behind the wall was foundations of camps for the army that guarded the wall. The big camps were built for the officers, while the small ones were for the soldiers. The open area separated by stone bricks on the far end was the army's exercise ground. Whenever there was no war to fight, soldiers would go to the ground and practise their martial arts. Kaitian and Nuannuan absorbed his words with great interest. They had never thought about the remarkable story behind those stones, which they had set eyes on countless times...

On the day of the his departure, the old man gripped Kaitian's hand firmly and said: "Thank you both for offering me so much help. I may visit again if I can in the future."

"If you come again, we'll keep you company," Nuannuan answered in sincerity as she felt a certain gratitude towards him. That day, Kaitian and Nuannuan walked the old man all the way to the ferry by the lake and saw him off as he went on Black Bean's small boat heading for the east bank. She truly hoped that the old man would visit again. The Kuang family had earned 1,600 yuan in eleven days. It was a precious income that had arrived with the best timing. Kaitian paid the most urgent households and bought medicine for his father. They could also cover their household expenditure through the winter.

Spring Festival was drawing near not long after this incident. Although the family budget was very tight, Nuannuan insisted that Kaitian buy two kilograms of peanut oil. She wanted her parents-in-law and her young son to have a decent New Year. On the afternoon of the twenty-ninth day of the lunar month, the day before New Year's Eve, she made some pastries, including fried dough, fried lotus pie and fried sesame crispy dough. After finishing, she picked some from each kind and carried them to Sister-in-Law Shallot's home.

Because she was managing an impoverished family, Nuannuan hadn't been to Sister-in-Law Shallot's home for quite some time. Only on entering her house did she learn that all her family savings had come to nothing because of Changlin's injury. She hadn't bought any cooking oil for the New Year. Neither could she afford to buy pork for making dumplings, which had to be vegetarian. Seeing Nuannuan's fried pastries, Daming and Xiaoming helped themselves after hurriedly greeting her. The way the two children were eating brought tears to Nuannuan's eyes. She said: "I haven't paid you a cent of what we owe you, so you have to live like this. I'm so sorry."

Sister-in-Law Shallot said with a smile: "Don't mention the payment. Both our families are unlucky at the moment. But the demon of poverty can't stop us from living a better life, which I think will come soon. As the old saying goes, people on both sides of a river take turns to be prosperous in thirty years. Life is full of ups and downs. Maybe we can become wealthy again."

Holding Shallot by her hands, Nuannuan said: "Sister-in-Law, each time I see you, I feel motivated."

When spring arrived, Kaitian and Nuannuan resumed their busy work in the fields. They fertilised the wheat field, looked after the sprouts, earthed up field ridges to regulate the water in the sweet potato fields, and planted pumpkins, green beans, chives, aubergines and chilli peppers. The workload was far beyond one household's capacity.

One day, the young couple were looking after the peppers in the field when Kaitian's mother came over with Dangen in her arms. "Dangen's dad! Two city people, one man and one woman, came to the house and asked for you. Come home and see."

Kaitian was confused. "City people? Who do we know from the city?"

Nuannuan was worried. "Do you think someone came over for the weedkiller problem?"

Kaitian clapped his hands to wipe off the dust and spit. "If it's good news, it's good news. If not, we can't escape anyway. Let's go home and see what happens."

Nuannuan couldn't stay in the field on her own, so she followed them home.

Kaitian walked into the yard and saw two city-looking young people sitting there. He asked nervously: "Are you sure you're looking for me?"

The young man stood up. He first looked at the newspaper in his hand, then took a look at Kaitian and smiled. "It is you that I'm looking for. We read Mr Tan Wenbo's article in the newspaper and saw the photos he took here. We came here specifically looking for you and Ms Chu Nuannuan."

"Tan Wenbo? Ohh, Uncle Tan." Kaitian and Nuannuan were reassured. Kaitian stepped up and took the paper from the young man. He saw not only a picture of the stone wall but also a photo of Uncle Tan, Nuannuan and himself. "Heavens, we're in the news! Dangen's mum, come and check this out." Kaitian gave Nuannuan the paper in excitement.

The young woman came close and said: "We are both majors in history at the graduate school of Tianjin University. His name is Xiao Jing, and I am Jing Xiao. We read the article written by Mr Tan and decided to see the Great Wall of Chu and visit you on the way. Can we trouble you to guide our tour, please?"

"It's the stone wall on the hill, right? Sure. You came all the way here. You deserve to see it," answered Kaitian immediately.

"Just one small thing – how much do you charge for that?" asked the young man.

"What charge?" The question put Kaitian in a daze.

"The charge for taking us to the Great Wall of Chu."

Kaitian burst into laughter. "How can we charge you?"

He was about to follow up his pronouncement with "It's free of charge" when Nuannuan said. "Thirty yuan." She looked quite calm.

Kaitian stared at Nuannuan with alarm.

"What about the fee for staying and eating in your house?" asked the young woman.

"Sixty yuan more each," answered Nuannuan. "We charged the same with Uncle Tan last time."

"Deal. I'll pay you for the first two days now." The young man happily took his wallet out and gave Kaitian three hundred yuan in cash.

Kaitian was so happy to have the money in his hand; it would almost cover the loss of one acre of green beans. Kaitian asked them: "When are we going up the hill?"

The two students answered: "Whenever you like."

Of course, Kaitian wished for them to stay for one more day, but before he could answer, Nuannuan said: "You should go tomorrow. Take a good rest in the afternoon and have a rural homemade dinner with us tonight so that you can happily start tomorrow's work."

The two students nodded and agreed. Kaitian and Nuannuan cleaned the warehouse that Uncle Tan had stayed in so that the students could put down their luggage and take a rest.

As there was only one bed, Kaitian was initially worried that they might need to sleep separately. When they didn't request another bed, Kaitian felt at ease and realised that they were a couple. He asked them what they would like to eat for supper and listed what Nuannuan could make: green-bean rice soup, steamed vegetable dumplings, fried sesame bean flour noodles and wheat noodles with wild herbs. Xiao Jing and Jing Xiao had a brief discussion and said they preferred green-bean rice soup and steamed vegetable dumplings. Kaitian then nodded to Nuannuan and said: "OK, let's fix them the soup and dumplings, plus four side dishes." After he made the arrangement, Kaitian said to them: "I need to go back to the field to plant peppers."

Jing Xiao was quite curious. "I have never planted peppers before. Can we go with you?"

"Of course. Let's go." Kaitian, still excited, took the students to the field. He had not felt so happy in a long time. *Two graduate students from the city watching me work in the field, in full curiosity... How could that happen?* With a dab of his hands, Kaitian split the dirt, slipped in the sprouts, poured the water and sealed the seeding pit with dirt again. As he worked, he explained the proper distance between seeding pits, the difference of sprouts, which kind of sprouts will yield more peppers, which kind was bell peppers, and which was chilli peppers.

The two students listened and watched closely. After a while, they asked: "Can we help you?"

Kaitian was waiting for those words, and he answered: "Sure. Roll your sleeves up first. Farm work is not the rocket science you study in university."

The students joined Kaitian in the field. Kaitian stopped working and started coaching them. Spotty Laosi was passing by the field at that moment and was surprised to see the scene. He walked up to Kaitian and whispered: "Where do these city people come from to help you work?"

Kaitian bore a grudge against Spotty Laosi because he had been demanding compensation for the loss caused by the fake weedkiller. So, Kaitian mumbled: "They're two of my relatives from a city. They're here to visit me, but they insisted on tagging along when they found out I was coming to the field to work."

Spotty Laosi was stunned. "You have relatives in the city?"

Kaitian pretended to be unhappy. "So what? We can't have them because we're poor? Let me tell you, my uncle and aunt are both living in Tianjin. Tianjin, you know? The city famed for its deep-fried twisted dough, you understand? Some of the money I paid you and the others after the incident came from them."

"Fuck! I didn't know all of this before. If I had known, I wouldn't have been so aggressive," said Spotty Laosi with a flattering smile.

Hearing his exclamation, Kaitian could hardly suppress a laugh.

The next morning, Kaitian took Xiao Jing and Jing Xiao to see the Great Wall of Chu on the hill. On the way, seeing the two students' excitement, Kaitian thought to himself: *It must have been a spell that brought them all the way down here to spend that much money, and just to see a collapsed stone wall. What a waste. With all that money, I'd go to the city and treat myself to some fried dough sticks and soup with pepper in a fine restaurant and a movie in the theatre. Well, at least I benefit from their visit – where else can I find money from?*

Jing Xiao suddenly said: "Mr Kuang, your lady is such a good cook."

Kaitian did not answer for a second. When he saw her fixing her eyes at him, he realised that Mr Kuang was himself, and his lady was, of course, Nuannuan. He felt somewhat flattered and said:

"She's a peasant's wife, and all she can do is cook. I'm happy that you didn't dislike the food. Hmm, I think it's better if you don't call me Mister. When you do, I don't feel like I'm being talked to at all. Just call me Kaitian, or Big Brother. How's that?"

"Yeah, yeah," Jing Xiao answered in Kaitian's accent, her laughter filling the air of the lonely hill.

Kaitian was worried about their disappointment in seeing the wall as it was: after all, it was old and had collapsed. He made up his mind that if they didn't like the wall, he would take them to see several caves on the hill. He used to herd the sheep and chop firewood on the hill, and those caves with stones in strange shapes inside were his favourite places. He thought the caves were the most worthy sites for visitors. However, the students gasped in full amazement at the sight of the wall and did not move for a while. Later on, they ran towards the wall and started their inspection and measurements as they talked and wrote down several notes. Kaitian was assured by their excitement and followed them in silence as they slowly moved forwards alongside the wall...

When the sun was above their head, Kaitian found a flat clearing and set the snacks he had brought. He then called Xiao Jing and Jing Xiao to join him. The snacks included boiled maize ears and steamed vegetable dumplings in addition to a few preserved eggs.

While eating, Xiao Jing asked: "Brother, you've made a great contribution by helping Mr Tan Wenbo find the Great Wall of Chu."

Kaitian broke into a smile. "It's been on the hill for generations. Except for you guys and Uncle Tan, no one else thinks of it as useful."

Jing Xiao said: "The discovery of the wall verified many things in history books. It was of significant help to the research in the history of the Chu State. People will see it as increasingly important. Maybe it can be a scenic spot for tourists."

Kaitian didn't quite understand her, and neither was he interested in it – he really couldn't see its usefulness. *Stone walls are stone walls, nothing more and nothing less. What does the Chu State history have to do with me? No matter how important it used to be, it can never be more vital than making money to compensate the villagers' loss. It'd be fine as long as you stay for a few more days, and each day you pay me 150 yuan.*

Xiao Jing and Jing Xiao did not return home until dark, and they talked about staying for several more days. Kaitian was happy about that: one more day for them meant more money for his family. He told them almost immediately: "You take your time to do your thing, and I'll keep you company."

That night at home, Xiao Jing and Jing Xiao went to their room after dinner. Kaitian said to Nuannuan: "You should go to the house of Men Kuan, the butcher, and ask him to cut one *jin* of pork for a couple of meat dishes for dinner tomorrow. The students will be happy. If they stay for even one more day, we could earn an extra 150 yuan."

Kaitian served his father as he took the medicine, and he helped Nuannuan steam the vegetarian buns for lunch the next day on the hill. The young couple cleaned up the kitchen and walked past the warehouse, now transformed into a guest room. They saw the light in the room off and went quietly down their steps, knowing that their guests had already gone to bed. Suddenly, Kaitian and Nuannuan heard the rustling of the sorghum-cushioned bed. The couple looked at each other with a knowing smile. Kaitian wanted to keep listening, but Nuannuan hurriedly dragged him away. Entering their bedroom, Kaitian whispered to Nuannuan with a smirk: "I didn't expect that people from the city could make such a big noise when they do something like this as we do."

Nuannuan didn't respond but blushed deeply.

Kaitian hugged her and said: "Let's follow their example."

Still quiet, Nuannuan undressed bashfully. That night, Kaitian was a little wild on top of Nuannuan, and as he banged her hard, he gasped: "Let's have a competition with them to see who's more vigorous and can make more noise."

Nuannuan was frightened by his boldness and hurriedly covered his mouth with one hand while holding him tighter by the waist.

Xiao Jing and Jing Xiao went up the hill every day for five days. Kaitian eventually stopped following them around after taking them to the wall and instead took the opportunity to get firewood on the hill and carry it home in the evening. He felt like he was killing two birds with one stone. In the evening of the last day when they were heading home, Xiao Jing said to Kaitian, who was carrying the firewood: "Big Brother Kaitian, Jing Xiao and I did some investigation, and we both think that this Great Wall of Chu was probably built around 312 BCE when Chu was already declining. The ruler did not realise the state's problems and invaded the city of Yongshi, which was reigned by the state of Han. Qin used the excuse of Han's defence to justify its attack on Chu. In Danyang, which today is the area north of the Dan River, Xixia County in Henan Province, Qin killed eighty thousand people and took captive more than seventy Chu generals, including Qu Gai. They also occupied most of Chu's land. As a result, this area became the frontline of the war between Chu and Qin. They must have sent civilians to construct this Great Wall here in the hope of counter-attacks and defence of Qin's southbound expansion."

Kaitian could only understand a small part of Xiao Jing's words, so he asked: "So how many years had passed since then?"

"More than 2,300 years."

"Yikes, that many years? My great-grandpa's great-grandpa wasn't even born by then. Why do you want to see a wall that old?"

Jing Xiao answered: "The basic idea was to find out how people carried out military construction during the time so that we could understand ancient Chinese ideas of defence and attack in wars. Of course, there is much more than that to follow."

"Can you make money out of this?"

Both students laughed."Probably not," Xiao Jing replied.

"Then I'll have to break it to you – don't spend time on things that don't give you money. That's just a waste of a life. Only a fool would waste their life. Maybe I shouldn't say this, but I get paid by you for bringing you here."

The students laughed again...

As Xiao Jing and Jing Xiao were about to depart, Nuannuan felt sorry. She took a picture with them and kept their phone number and address. Moreover, Jing Xiao insisted on giving one of her blouses to Nuannuan. How could Nuannuan take that? After declining several times, Nuannuan eventually offered Jing Xiao in exchange a colourful piece of cloth that Shallot had given her as a wedding present.

Holding Nuannuan by her neck, Jing Xiao said: "Sister, if you were in our Tianjin and dressed yourself up, I guarantee that many men would date you."

Her comment turned Nuannuan's face red.

Jing Xiao added: "The food you cooked in the rustic family style was scrumptious. I'll remember you. Come to visit me at home whenever you have an opportunity to tour Tianjin."

Nuannuan beamed. "We're clumsy and didn't have much to offer. We're sorry to have been poor hosts. Come again when you have time." Nuannuan gave the students some walnuts and salty-boiled eggs for the trip back. Kaitian and Nuannuan walked Xiao Jing and Jing Xiao all the way to the ferry by the lake and saw them off as they went on Black Bean's small boat heading for the east bank.

Kaitian had made 750 yuan in five days. He paid a hundred yuan to each of the seven families that had pressed for payment the hardest.

Nuannuan sighed. "It would be great if more people came more often, and they all stayed in our home."

Kaitian chuckled. "How could we be so lucky? You're daydreaming."

After breakfast on the day following Xiao Jing and Jing Xiao's departure, Kaitian went to the field to work. When he reached the entrance to the village, he ran into Zhan Shideng. Since the weedkiller incident, Kaitian had always felt embarrassed when he saw Zhan Shideng, feeling that he owed him for getting him free. Finding it impossible to shun him, Kaitian forced himself to go up to him.

"Hi Kaitian, I heard that your relatives in Tianjin visited you?" said Zhan Shideng.

"Hi Leader." Kaitian wanted to pass by.

"Did you borrow money from them to pay the compensation?"

Kaitian hemmed and hawed because he was unwilling to discuss the topic with the leader. "I borrowed some, but every family is having a hard time these days." Then, he hurried away.

At that moment, all that Kaitian wished for was his father's recovery. Once his father got better, he could leave him to his mother's care and then take Nuannuan and his son to Guangdong to find work. He would not stay in Chu Wang Village with all his neighbours' judgements over him.

However, he saw no sign of recovery in his father.

One afternoon, Kaitian was going home after buying some herbal medicine in the township hospital because he could not find it in Mei's Pharmacy in the village. As he passed by the small ferry, he saw several young people from the city stepping off Black Bean's boat and begin asking about Kuang Kaitian and Nuannuan. Due to his experience with the two students from Tianjin, he wasn't surprised by their visit. He stepped up and introduced himself. "I'm Kuang Kaitian. Are you looking for me?"

The young people cried out: "Yes, yes! It's you that we're looking for."

One of them showed him a picture in the newspaper. Kaitian looked and recognised the photo he took with Xiao Jing and Jing Xiao on the Great Wall of Chu.

"We are university students from Hunan, and our ancestors were people of the State of Chu. We really want to see the Great Wall after reading this article, and we'd love to stay in your place. Can you be our guide?"

Kaitian instantly knew that he had another opportunity to earn money. He smiled and answered: "Yeah, yeah. Come with me."

Kaitian led the four young people, all talking and laughing in excitement, into his yard. He raised his voice and said: "Dangen's mum, we have guests."

The experience with hosting the two graduate students from Tianjin told Nuannuan instantly what happened. She hastened to offer a bowl of plain boiled water to each of the students and poured out two basins of cool water for them to wash their faces and hands. Then, she pulled Kaitian into their room and said: "We only have one spare room in the house, but we've got two men and two women to accommodate. How will this work? We can't put them all in one small room."

Kaitian thought a second and said: "Shall we let two of them stay in the home of one of the neighbours?"

Nuannuan shot a reproving stare at him. "That's a bad idea. Wouldn't we put their accommodation fee in the neighbour's hands if we did that? How about we give them our room, and the two of us can sleep on the kitchen floor?"

Kaitian agreed. "Sure, we'll do as you said."

After a while, Nuannuan went to talk about the price with the students. "Last time when Xiao Jing from Tianjin was here, we took them to the hill and offered them food and accommodation for 150 yuan each. The price will be the same for you. Is that good?"

The students answered: "Good, good. 150 yuan it will be."

As soon as they agreed, their leader gave Kaitian six hundred yuan. Kaitian again felt the excitement. *Another roll of cash earned. I'm sure it's the Buddha of Lingyan Temple that's blessing us.*

Nuannuan intended to extend the students' stay as she did last time, so she tried to persuade them to take a rest in their house. But the young students were too vigorous to take a rest; they could not wait to explore, and they asked to go to the hill immediately. Kaitian had no choice but to agree. He pulled four turnips from the soil in the yard, washed them clean, handed one to each of the students and said: "Here, one for each. It can quench your thirst and satisfy your hunger." The four students laughed. They stepped out of the gate while champing the turnips.

Before he left, Kaitian whispered to Nuannuan: "Can you manage dinner for four more people? If not, go and ask Hehe for help."

Nuannuan shook her head. "Just go and entertain the guests. Don't worry about things at home."

Hearing her words, Kaitian put the six hundred yuan he had received from the students into her chest. "Keep it safe as you do with your breasts." With that, he gently punched Nuannuan on her breasts.

"Don't worry. When did I lose your money?" Nuannuan glared at him with feigned anger.

Since their wedding, Kaitian had always put the family's accumulated money in Nuannuan's chest pocket. He knew that was where Nuannuan cared the most. Before their marriage, he had tried to touch them, but to no avail. "I'll live a happy life when we get rich in the future. Then, I'll get you a few maidservants like the ones we saw in the operas."

Nuannuan broke into a smile. "You're daydreaming."

The four students were as excited as their predecessors at the sight of the Great Wall on the hill. They too took measurements, notes and photos. One of the male students leaned against the wall and recited loudly:

> Oh, Brown Stone, how many years have you been lying here?
> Do you remember my ancestors I hold so dear?
> Have you ever heard his cry that deafens the ear?
> Have you ever seen him wield a sharp sword or spear?
> Have you seen his blood splashing that the stone doth smear?
> Did you know that he died for the Chu State without fear?

Kaitian vaguely felt that he was composing a poem. But the other students burst into laughter. One of the girl students said: "He made me laugh so much that I spat out all my teeth. I'm afraid I can't enjoy the dinner this evening." The poetic student chased the girl until they ran a long distance, and both fell at the turn of the wall, one upon the other...

They stayed for three days and set out for the hill every morning after breakfast to inspect the wall. They walked and talked alongside the wall and sat down to make some notes once in a while. They spent all day on the hill and would not leave until dinner time. Kaitian led them all the way and showed them locations of the army activities, according to what Uncle Tan taught him – where the army camped, where the troops practised martial arts, where the soldiers ambushed their enemies and so on. He explained all the details in such a convincing manner that he seemed like an expert in history. He would go on the slopes to pick wildflowers for the two girls and rocks in exotic shapes for the two boys when they were too tired to walk. The students all spoke of Kaitian as a competent guide. On the last day, before they went down the hill, a girl student stood on the wall and shouted out towards the west:

> The days and months hurried on, never delaying;
> Springs and autumns sped by in endless alternation.
> I thought how the trees and flowers were fading,
> And feared my beauty's disappearance in the same fashion.
> Gather the flower of youth and cast out the impure!
> Why will you not change the error of your convention?
> I have harnessed brave coursers for your riding.
> Come, let me go before and show you the direction!

The other students applauded. Kaitian was confused and didn't understand what she was yelling about. He asked the three students, and the other girl student told him that they were lines from Qu Yuan's poem 'The Lament'.

Qu Yuan? Kaitian tried hard to remember what Jiuding had said about him.

The girl student explained it in detail. "Qu Yuan was a man from the State of Chu. He was a courtier of King Huai of Chu. His name Huai is the word for Chinese scholar tree. He advocated the strategy of 'passive joint front of defence' in the interest of the Chu State. The courtiers like Grand Master Shangguan opposed him and won King Kuai of Chu's trust at the sacrifice of Qu Yuan's. Consequently, the Chu army suffered a catastrophic defeat at Danxi. This Great Wall of Chu is in the vicinity of the ancient battle's site."

Without understanding her, Kaitian sighed. "You guys have too much time on your hands. If you were me who must worry about making money to pay a debt while supporting the family, you wouldn't have the time to meddle with the Chu State's affairs, would you?"

His remark elicited a burst of laughter from the students. One of them said: "Are you also concerned with the affairs of the Chu State by guarding their Great Wall? Judging from the location, your Chu Wang Village must have been in the Chu State domain. So, you are logically a descendant of the Chu people. Guard it well."

The students brought Kaitian and Nuannuan an income of 1,800 yuan. On the night after their departure, the young couple went to bed. The handsome income made Kaitian so happy that he wanted to have sex with Nuannuan. His wife stopped him and, holding down his hand, said in all seriousness: "You need to think about this carefully."

Kaitian did not understand. "About what?"

"The visits people pay to the stone wall."

"What is there to think about? It's good, isn't it? One visit, one more opportunity to earn money."

"Is that the only thing you can get out of this?" said Nuannuan as she glared.

Kaitian ran his hand over his head and mumbled: "What else is there to think about?"

"You! You never use your brains," said Nuannuan, tapping

Kaitian's nose with one finger. "Have you thought about this? More people will want to come and see the wall after they read the newspaper. Don't you think we can even create some wealth? A good business out of the old wall ignored by our old generations?"

"Are you serious?" Kaitian held tighter to Nuannuan's hand.

"Of course, the wall is useless to us who farm the fields. But now it seems to me that for well-educated people, and for those city people who like antique things, the wall is a big attraction. Therefore, there will be a lot more people visiting here soon."

"Hmm, you think so?" said Kaitian, his face brightening up. "And what shall we do about it?"

"The most important thing at the moment is accommodation for those visitors. It is already difficult for us to receive four guests, so we must find a way to build a new house. Otherwise, we won't be able to take more than five next time. If we send them to a neighbour's place, we'll miss the money they're willing to pay."

"Right, right." Kaitian patted Nuannuan on her breasts with excitement, which soon gave way to a frowning expression. "But we need extra land for the construction. Our house occupies all that we've got – three rooms, a kitchen, a warehouse, a pigsty and a coop of chickens. Where can we build another house?"

"Go and talk to the leader, Zhan Shideng. All you need is his consent to build any house you like. There's a big unoccupied space in front of our house. Mum said it was only empty because we did not build things on it, so the land is still ours. Moreover, the village committee hasn't given us Dangen's share of land after his birth." Nuannuan was reluctant to talk about Zhan Shideng. She felt nauseous even thinking of his face. But it was impossible to work around him.

Kaitian did not want to go to Zhan Shideng, either. He asked again in hesitation: "Must I go and see the leader?"

Nuannuan sighed. "Only when he stops being the leader can we stop asking him for favours. Yet it is impossible at the moment, right? He's the leader, and we have to beg him for help."

"Forget it. Let's leave this subject alone," said Kaitian. He held Nuannuan's breasts and covered her mouth with his…

After supper on the eve of the Mid-Autumn Festival, Kaitian was fretting about the site of the house they planned to build. The neighbour Spotty Laosi entered the courtyard, holding a pipe in his mouth. As soon as he stepped in, he called out: "Hey Kaitian. I smell some air of fortune in your yard. I saw city people keep coming and you leading them to the hill. Are you doing something that may bring your family good luck?"

Kaitian rose wearily. "What luck?"

Nuannuan chuckled. "Brother Laosi, some city relatives suddenly thought of us, their poor rustic relatives. So, they came to visit us. We took them to the hill because urban youngsters like to see wild plants."

Both Nuannuan and Kaitian understood that they were not supposed to tell this Spotty Laosi the truth. If he had known that leading city people to the stone wall could bring in profits, he would surely grab the opportunity from them.

"Well, living in this remote place, we're fucking suffering from both poverty and humiliation," exclaimed Spotty Laosi as he squatted in the yard puffing on his pipe. "When can we tour here and there like the city people and enjoy the view of pretty women of other places?"

Kaitian burst into laughter. "You've got so much cash in your pocket. Do you want them to give birth to baby cash? Why don't you take Uncle Black Bean's boat to the east bank, buy a train ticket, go to Nanfu City and have a good time there? I heard that the women there are very presentable."

"What? How can I squander that pocket money in Nanfu City? What about my family's life?" Spotty Laosi rose to straighten himself up and continued: "Wait till I'm reborn into the next generation. I'll be a city person and marry a city girl with a good complexion. Hey Kaitian, do you have some money now? If you do, you're supposed to pay me some. I need it to buy a calf."

Kaitian put on a long face instantly. This Spotty Laosi presses me for money every day as if he feared that I couldn't pay him at all. Son of a bitch! He has no consideration for our feelings. Kaitian went into the room, took two hundred yuan from Nuannuan and said: "This is all we've got. Take it for now."

Taking the cash, Spotty Laosi smiled with half-closed eyes. "Brother, I can say for sure that you've made some money from outsiders. Otherwise, you wouldn't have such big banknotes. Remember, we're neighbours. Don't forget your Brother Spotty Laosi when you've got a money-making opportunity."

After seeing Spotty Laosi off, a sense of urgency seized Kaitian. *Our activity of making money from guiding city people around and providing them accommodation at home will come to light in the village sooner or later. They'll eventually realise that they can get the guests to their houses if we don't have enough space. We must build a house right away. But to do so, we must ask Zhan Shideng for his approval for the building site. Truth is, after I married Nuannuan and had our son, I've added two more members to the family. They're entitled to a piece of land. All right, all right, I'll go and beg him for this once.*

Nuannuan was bending over to wash the dishes. Kaitian said to her: "Dangen's mother, I'm going to ask the leader for his approval now."

She gazed at her husband for a long time before uttering the words: "I'm sure there will come a day when we won't have to beg him."

WOOD

Kaitian had several mooncakes he had bought for Dangen in his left hand and a jar of yellow rice wine in his right hand. He was walking in full reluctance towards Zhan Shideng's house. He heard that the leader liked yellow rice wine, so he was going to offer the only jar brewed in the house to him.

In the evening of the Mid-Autumn Festival, the temperature in Chu Wang Village had dropped considerably. The cold breeze blowing from the depth of Funiu Mountain was brushing around people and giving them a chill. But Kaitian, while walking, was sweating profusely. He knew that his marriage with Nuannuan had greatly displeased the leader, and it would not be easy to ask him for help. He stopped and thought of returning home several times, but the overwhelming desire to make money drove him onward. The moon, almost in its full grace, was rendering a bright light of reflection on Red Lake, and Kaitian could see Zhan Shideng's new house clearly. It was the first time he had seen the house since the leader built it. *That motherfucking house sure is an exhibition! With a house that big, I could take in as many guests as I want.*

He entered the yard with the presents. The dog saw him and started barking. Zhan Shideng was sitting in the main hall, having dinner. He turned his head and seemed quite surprised to see Kaitian. He obviously did not expect Kaitian to visit his house. He offered a rare hospitality and stood up in courtesy. "Hey, Kaitian, come on in."

Kaitian, looking awkward, put the mooncakes and the jar of wine on the dinner table and said with forced easiness: "The Moon Festival is here, so I brought some mooncakes for your children. I see them as my own nieces and nephews. We brewed this wine ourselves, and it tastes really good. I hope Mr Leader will like it."

"Wow, I can't possibly take them," answered the leader politely as he offered Kaitian a seat. "Anything I can help you with?"

Kaitian could not wait. He told him about his plan to build another house. Of course, he kept his intention to himself and only talked about making room for his relatives who would come over to look after his father.

Zhan Shideng did not answer immediately, and it took him a while to answer. "Kaitian, my brother, you never asked me for anything before. And I shouldn't reject you if you do. However, you should understand this – the policy of land ownership is very strict, and the township office forbids us to increase anyone's without a good reason. Also, there are many others in the village who want the same thing. If I agree to your plan, everyone else will want their wishes granted too. Let's say I don't give you an answer today, and I'll think of something later."

Kaitian knew he was just making an excuse to turn him down, but he had to keep smiling and said: "Mr Leader, you are capable of doing anything you like. Please do see this through. I trust you on this."

"OK, OK, I'll think of something. You can start by preparing the materials you need for the construction. But do not start building anything without news from me."

Zhan Shideng's acceptance of the wine and mooncakes gave Kaitian some confidence that he would give his consent eventually. Besides, he had a large clearing in front of his house, saved from its construction. An approval was as simple as a nod from Zhan Shideng. It required neither procedures nor paperwork. According to Zhan Shideng's words, Kaitian started preparing planks, bricks, tiles, sand and cement the next day. Kaitian had cut down a dozen trees around his courtyard a few years before. They were piled up in the yard and already dried up, so he did not need to pay for the planks. He did not need to buy sand, either: he went to collect sand by the lakeside every day at sunset and had gathered a lot in a few days. He did need to pay for bricks and tiles, and he didn't have enough money, so he went to beg the owner of the kiln in the neighbouring village. Eventually, the owner agreed to sell him on credit, and the payment would be due after the autumn harvest. The owner had Kaitian sign an IOU; he trusted Kaitian because he still had a house of his own. If things got bad, he could at least take his house. Kaitian used his money mainly on the cement and put down an order with the plasterers and carpenters in the village. After that, the only thing he needed to do was wait for Zhan Shideng to grant his right to build the house.

Kaitian and Nuannuan spent the time finishing work in the fields. However, after a long time of waiting, not even a word came from Zhan Shideng. Autumn was about to come, and if they didn't build the house, they would have to wait till the next spring. Kaitian was anxious.

One day, a postman from the township brought him a registered letter from Beijing. It was a curious incident for the Kuangs because they never had any business with the post office since none of them were working outside the village. Kaitian, quite baffled, opened the letter and found out that it was from Uncle Tan in Beijing. Uncle Tan wrote to Kaitian about his plan to bring up to eight students to see the Great Wall of Chu during the winter holiday, and he wanted Kaitian and Nuannuan to offer them accommodation. Kaitian was apparently very happy about it: another opportunity to earn money. However, he became even more anxious because he would have to send Uncle Tan's group to other people's houses if they could not build the new house as soon as possible.

Kaitian went to Zhan Shideng's house that very afternoon. Before he could speak, Zhan Shideng smiled and said: "Kaitian, you must have come for the business about your land. I was about to pay you a visit first. I went to the township office about it, but it's so difficult."

"How difficult?" Kaitian's heart sank.

"The government won't approve an increase to your land ownership. They told me that you've already used your quota, and they're very strict about new constructions these days," said Zhan Shideng with a kind, sincere smile on his face.

Kaitian was not pleased. He eagerly answered: "If they don't approve, I'll build it on the empty land in front of my place."

"I'm afraid you can't do that. I may bring people over to tear it down if you do," answered Zhan Shideng coldly, resuming the authority in his voice.

Kaitian dared not say anything else, as he knew it would be his loss if he looked for trouble with the leader.

Kaitian arrived home with a forced smile and a heart full of anger. *Zhan Shideng, you motherfucker! You drank my wine and ate my cakes, but you did nothing for me. Do you still have any conscience?"*

Nuannuan knew what had happened simply by looking at his face. She did not ask anything and fed Dangen in silence. She had predicted the result. Yet she still held hope for Zhan Shideng's compassion and gratitude for the mooncakes and wine. As it turned out, she was wrong.

"Good heavens, what shall we do?" mumbled Kaitian as he gazed at the construction material in the yard. "Stop the construction? Let the money heading our way slip off?"

Nuannuan suddenly said: "I'll go and beg him again."

"Can you make it work?" said Kaitian as he looked at Nuannuan. "I'm afraid he's still bitter about our marriage."

"I'll try," answered Nuannuan, pretending to be calm. She knew Zhan Shideng was deliberately delaying the consent because he was waiting for her to beg him. She thought to herself: *I'll lower myself and beg him again, but only once more. What if he wants the same dirty business? I bet he dares not to ask me that with his family watching. I must go there when they're all eating together...*

Although she said she would go, Nuannuan didn't make a move until it was the second day. She didn't want to ask Zhan Shideng for anything any longer. But delaying was not the best option. Finally, she made the difficult decision. *Zhan Shideng, you son of a bitch! I'll beg you for the last time. The Buddha is watching. There'll always come a day when we don't have to implore you.*

Nuannuan picked breakfast time on the third morning. She thought he could not really try anything on her with his wife and children at home. She forced herself on the road with dozens of salty duck eggs. She forced herself again to knock on Zhan Shideng's door. As she had anticipated, Zhan Shideng spoke to her politely about how she should not bring the eggs over. He even asked why they needed more land and how they had prepared the construction material, as well as the intended date of construction. In the end, he said: "The township office require formal procedure for everything, and you'll have to fill in a form for the land ownership. Wait here – I'll bring you the form from the committee office."

Nuannuan agreed. She sat down and chatted with his wife while he was gone. However, it took Zhan Shideng a long time to come back. He did not get back to the house until it was time for everyone in the village to start farm work. Zhan Shideng claimed that it took longer because he had other affairs to look after in the office. At that moment, his children had already left for school, and his wife was about to leave for the magnolia forest to work with a basket in her hand. Though quite scared, Nuannuan knew she could not leave: it was her only opportunity to have him grant them the land. She became quite nervous on seeing Zhan Shideng's wife leave. "Where's the form?" she asked.

Zhan Shideng smiled and took a piece of paper out of his pocket. He pointed at the table and said: "Sit there and write down the reason for the construction. Write down the number of rooms and houses, and the time you want to start the construction. I'll stamp my seal on it once you finish. I'll be in the yard while you're filling it in. Call me when you finish."

"What form is this?" asked Nuannuan as she found out that it was a blank piece of paper.

"This is what I say is a form."

Nuannuan hesitated before sitting at the table. Zhan Shideng walked out.

Relieved, Nuannuan picked up the pen and started thinking about what to write down. She was frowning, deep in thought, when a small door leading to the room next door opened, and Zhan Shideng walked in. Nuannuan turned her head in shock. Before she could react, he had already locked her in his arms with great force. She now realised she had not been cautious enough. She tried her best to resist and opened her mouth to call for help. But Zhan Shideng forcefully covered her mouth with his hand. As she lost her strength to fight and dropped on the floor, she called out in her mind: *Kaitian*...

Silently, tears dripped down her face.

"It's done. Now you can get up," said Zhan Shideng. After he had vented his lust, he rose to dress and threw Nuannuan's clothes at her body.

Nuannuan cried loudly, covering her face with her hands.

"When you get back, tell Kaitian to build the house in front of your residence. You can make it as big as you wish. No one will prevent you. Frankly, there's no form at all, and you don't have to fill in anything. If I say it's OK, you can start your project."

Nuannuan was still crying.

"What are you crying for? This is not the first time. You're not a virgin any more. Are you worried that you can't find a husband after I fucked you? You're already a mother. Is my fucking once or twice a big deal? Don't pretend you're chaste. As I told you before, there's no woman in Chu Wang Village I can't sleep with if I want to. Now you believe me, right? You shunned me each time you saw me. Do you think you can?"

"You son of a bitch! You swine!" cursed Nuannuan.

"Go back to Kaitian. He's waiting for the news. Of course, you can keep crying here. You can also call for help, or you can sue me at the township court. You can do anything you want if you don't wish to preserve your reputation, live in the village and enjoy a peaceful life for your whole family."

Nuannuan spat at Zhan Shideng.

"OK, don't be angry any more. There's water in the basin behind the door. Go and wash your face," Zhan Shideng said without expression. "The first time, we were strangers. Now, we're acquaintances. The more we're together, the more enjoyable it'll feel. What's the big deal, eh? Is it misery that can kill you? Does it feel worse than a cold, a fever or diarrhoea? I don't believe it."

"You swine! You son of a bitch!" screamed Nuannuan.

That day, Nuannuan came out of Zhan Shideng's courtyard and arrived at Red Lake's beach. There, she stood a long time. Thinking of the deep humiliation, she wanted to jump into the water and drown herself. In death, she'd have no worries about compensating the villagers, no need to buy drugs for her invalid father-in-law, no concern with the house's construction, and she wouldn't have to look at Kaitian's gloomy face. In death, she'd forget everything in this mundane world and be free from such an insult. But there were also many things she was hesitant to give up, such as Kaitian, their son, her dad, her mum, her sister and her parents-in-law. Her son was the least she could part with. The mere thought of him losing her loving care ached her heart.

She pulled herself together and crouched down to wash her face. As she scooped the water and put it on her face, she cried silently. *Oh, heavens, the Buddha in Lingyan Temple, and you, the lake god, you've seen what Zhan Shideng has done to me, haven't you? Please answer my prayers and punish him.*

Nuannuan forced herself to look as if nothing had happened and walked home. Kaitian hastened towards her as she entered. "How did it go? Has he agreed?"

Nuannuan answered in a plain voice: "Let's build on the land in front of the house. Build whatever we like."

"Really?" Kaitian looked happy.

"Do you think I'm lying to you?" Nuannuan sounded angry.

"Great, great... Why are your eyes red?"

"I rubbed them too hard, and I've got some dust in them. Dangen, come to your mum and let her give you a kiss." Nuannuan had to change the topic, as she felt incapable of holding back her tears. Luckily, Kaitian did not ask anything else: he had gone out with great satisfaction to find the plasterers.

Nuannuan did not step out of her room on the day that Kaitian started the construction...

Kaitian was fully occupied by the construction. Building a house was a serious task for any family in the village, and especially for Kaitian's. He put everything he had into the construction, not to mention the bricks and tiles he bought on credit. To his satisfaction, the construction went very well. The plasterers, carpenters and painters all strived to their best efforts, so the work was neatly done. After the job was finished, Kaitian felt blissful, though he could not find anything other than a small amount of food around his house. He raised his son Dangen over his shoulder and laughed. "A serious job well done by the Kuangs."

Nuannuan did not say anything. She turned her face and wiped her tears.

People in Chu Wang Village could not understand why Kaitian would build another house. "His original house was enough for the family, his father is sick, he's got a big debt, yet he built a new house. What a silly ass. He can't afford to live like that."

Some who bought weedkiller from him walked in front of Kaitian's new house and said: "Kaitian, the house is proof that you have money. Why didn't you pay me first?"

Kaitian would fold his hands and answer in full respect: "I will. I'll pay you as soon as I have more money."

Winter came soon after the house was built. Kaitian made eight single beds with the timber left and put four in each new bedroom. He then prepared eight sorghum stalks for the mats and borrowed money from his cousin for eight bedsheets. Eight quilts were also prepared by Nuannuan and his mother. After all the work was done, Kaitian and Nuannuan anxiously waited for Uncle Tan's news.

What they feared the most now was Uncle Tan's change of mind. *Heavens! Please make sure you come. If you don't, we can't live any more. We've invested too much.* A few days before the winter holiday, Kaitian and Nuannuan felt uneasy, even when eating and sleeping. They went to the ferry at the lakeside several times a day for fear that Uncle Tan wouldn't come.

To their relief, Uncle Tan kept his word. One afternoon after a light snow, Kaitian was feeding the sheep with the haystack in his yard when he heard Uncle Tan's voice. "Kaitian, Nuannuan, are you home?"

Kaitian jumped up in excitement and ran out. It was such a great scene: he had brought a team of students with him. Kaitian counted and saw eleven people, including Uncle Tan: four women and seven men.

Uncle Tan smiled happily. "I wrote no more than eight in the letter, but I had to bring more. I'm afraid you can't let us all stay in your house."

"We can, we can." Nuannuan smiled too. She had not smiled for a long time. She had Kaitian lead the eight students, four men and four women, to the new house and had Uncle Tan stay in his old room in the warehouse. The two men left would stay in the couple's room while she would sleep with Kaitian and Dangen in the kitchen.

Uncle Tan saw the new house and could not stop complimenting their work. "Wonderful! I thought you would find us accommodation in your neighbour's house and our team would have to split up. This is better. We can still gather together during the night for discussions. This new house makes your place look like a hostel. How about I name this place for you?"

"Yes, yes!" Kaitian laughed happily.

Uncle Tan turned to one of his students. "When we left, I asked you to bring several writing brushes and some red paint for marking the site. Do you have it with you?"

The student took out the brushes and paint from his bag. Uncle Tan took a brush and dipped it in the paint. He wrote three characters on top of the gate: *Chu Di Ju* (Home in the State of Chu). The students clapped their hands in agreement. Kaitian and Nuannuan did not understand the name's literary value, but they clapped as well. After everyone had settled down, Nuannuan asked the question about her biggest concern. "Uncle Tan, can you give me the number you'd like to pay? We'll prepare things according to that."

"Nothing is a problem between us. I'll give you a number, and if you feel like more, just let me know. I say a hundred yuan per person, including accommodation, food and guidance from one of you two."

"Sure, sure." Kaitian dared not let out his happy laughter. That was 1,100 yuan a day. He had not even dreamed of earning that much.

"I'll pay you for the first six days so that you can use the money for rice, flour, vegetables and meat. You should also buy eleven pillows. Since we are in the guest house of Chu Di Ju, every guest deserves a pillow." Uncle Tan counted 6,600 yuan in cash and gave it to Kaitian.

Kaitian's hands trembled. He had never held that much money in his whole life. He went into the kitchen and showed Nuannuan the money. Then he put two hundred yuan in his pocket and gave the rest to Nuannuan: one note after another, he carefully put the money into the pocket on Nuannuan's chest, which made her breasts look larger.

"I'd better put the money away," said Nuannuan. "It will make my breasts look as ample as when I had just given birth to Dangen."

"I feel more reassured having the money in your chest. Who cares what it looks like."

Nuannuan prepared dinner for the guests while Kaitian rode the old bike he borrowed from Spotty Laosi and rushed to Juxiang Street for some pork, lamb, chicken and green vegetables, as well as a bottle of Chinese liquor worth 3.6 yuan. He stopped by his father-in-law's on his way home and asked Hehe to come over and help her sister the next day. He promised to pay Hehe a wage of six yuan a day. His father-in-law was not pleased to hear this. "What wage? When you need help, just ask her. Families don't ask for money from each other."

That evening they had dinner in the living room in the new house. They did not have a table big enough for eleven people, so Kaitian unhitched the two door planks in the kitchen and laid them on the floor to serve as a table. As it was the first meal, Nuannuan made a big welcome dinner for the guests. She cut the meat in large chunks so that people could enjoy the chewing. She poured the Chinese liquor into two big bowls and made people take turns to drink. Uncle Tan and his students had never experienced that in the city, and they felt curious and excited. Children in the village, also driven by curiosity, swarmed to their door to watch, as they had never seen that many people from the city. Kaitian shooed the children away when he heard Spotty Laosi ask him in the shade nearby: "Kaitian, what are so many of your relatives doing here?"

"They're here to see my parents," replied Kaitian. He would never let Spotty Laosi in on the secret.

"Relatives? Do you think I'm a fool? I asked a couple of the students a moment ago, and they told me they didn't know you at all."

"No, no. Only a few are my relatives while others are their friends who'd like to have fun with them." Kaitian hurriedly tried to hide the truth from Spotty Laosi.

"You son of a bitch! You're playing a trick on us. Go ahead, but I'll get to the bottom of it eventually," said Spotty Laosi as he spat.

"Come on, Brother Laosi, why would I lie to you?" Kaitian was a bit panicky, afraid that Spotty Laosi would take away his opportunity to make money once he knew everything. Kaitian knew that any family could entertain the visitors, and anyone could take them to the Chu's Great Wall on the hill.

The next day during breakfast, Hehe came over. Kaitian said: "Your sister is exhausted from steaming buns yesterday so that we can eat them on the hill. I hope you don't mind taking up more work today so that she can take a rest."

Nuannuan waved her hand to urge him off. "Don't worry about things at home."

Kaitian then took Uncle Tan's team up the hill. As expected, the students were amazed to see the Great Wall of Chu. Kaitian saw a young man take a machine out of a small trunk. Facing the wall, the machine made a small noise. He was curious and asked about it. The young man answered: "It's a video camera. We use it to make videos. You've watched TV, right? Things on TV are all made by this."

Kaitian stepped up to touch the machine and found it surreal. He asked: "Can you put the Great Wall of Chu on TV?"

The young man laughed and nodded. "Of course we can."

At that moment, a young woman started talking seriously in front of the camera with a corn-shaped microphone in her hand. "I am now standing on top of the hill behind Chu Wang, a village on the west bank of Red Lake. This stone wall behind me is a remnant of the Great Wall built by the State of Chu, according to Mr Tan Wenbo's research..."

Kaitian looked at the young woman. He found her voice quite agreeable. She had delicate features, but her chest was relatively flat. Her buttocks were so scraggy that they were unattractive to those who would otherwise touch them. He thought that if Nuannuan were dressed like her, she'd be more attractive. As he was thinking this, the camera, with its small noise, suddenly turned towards him. He was surprised and called out to Uncle Tan, who was making some measurements close by. "Uncle, take a look at this. Why is the camera facing me?"

Uncle Tan smiled and said: "You helped with the research of the Great Wall of Chu, so you deserve to be in the video. If you like, you can also talk about your knowledge of the wall."

"Talk about what? This thing has been here since forever. My dad used to herd the sheep here when he was little, and I myself came here all the time to pick up firewood. I used to sleep on the wall when I was tired. Sometimes I even peed on it. No one knew how precious it really is. We only started remembering its existence since your first visit..."

That day, Kaitian talked a lot with Uncle Tan, but he didn't realise the cameraman was recording everything he said. When they went down the hill, the cameraman played the video to him. Kaitian was delighted to see himself incessantly talking while gesturing on the TV screen. He yelled excitedly: "My god! My god! My god!"

Uncle Tan's team carried out their field research from that day on. At the start of the wall, they observed carefully and measured with steel tapes. They knocked on the wall with a hammer and wrote down notes with fountain pens. They took photos and made videos with the cameras… Everyone was happily busy at their work all over the hill. Kaitian's job was to introduce the hills, valleys, streams, rivers, villages and caves in the area. He taught them the names of different trees, bushes, weeds and rocks. He showed them the routes to go up and down the hill. He helped them tell if the weather would be sunny, cloudy or windy (and how windy exactly). He also carried two bottles of hot water and the meat buns and pickles for their lunch. The days were cold, and the wind was so much fiercer on top of the hill that it hurt their faces. Kaitian, seeing people working around the stone wall, their breath visible in the air, thought to himself in sarcasm: *What's the point of this?* Yet he hoped that they would keep busy for a long time so that he could earn over a thousand yuan, day after day.

One day, while Uncle Tan and the students were busy, Kaitian put down what he was carrying and went to pee in a col. Suddenly, he saw Spotty Laosi lying on his belly there. Kaitian asked in surprise: "What are you doing here?"

Spotty Laosi smirked. "What am I doing? I want to find out what tricks you're playing."

Kaitian pretended not to understand him and asked: "What tricks? What tricks can I play?"

Spotty Laosi responded: "Didn't you tell me these relatives and friends came to visit your parents? But why are they running around here?"

Kaitian laughed. "City people are curious and want to look around. They came up to the hill because they've never been here."

Spotty Laosi glared at him. "Go fucking trick the fools, but I'm not blind. They've been measuring the stone wall. Do you think I didn't see them? Tell me the truth. Are the visitors going to buy the stones?"

Upon hearing this, Kaitian almost burst into a guffaw. "You

fucking Spotty Laosi, how can you have such a thought?" But Kaitian secretly felt relieved, thinking that such a thought was better than his suspicion and interference with his money-making business. So, he said in a mysterious tone: "They did express their interest to buy the stones but didn't tell us how much they want."

At this, Spotty Laosi rushed to Kaitian, held his hands and pleaded: "When they decide how many, please let me know so that your brother can make some money. No one oversees stones on the wall. They're so easy to remove that I can pull off five or six slabs a day. If they want to buy them indeed, it would be a great opportunity to make a fortune. We may have different family names, but we're as close as biological brothers. We two must get rich together."

Kaitian nodded but coldly smiled in secret. *As close as biological brothers? You hardly seemed to be that when the weedkiller incident happened. Want to get rich together with me, eh? You're daydreaming!*

Spotty Laosi's shadowing made Kaitian further aware that the villagers would eventually discover that Nuannuan and he were making money by providing accommodation and guidance. Once they knew, they would follow suit. He told himself to get well prepared beforehand to be better positioned when others began to compete with them.

Uncle Tan's research project lasted twelve days. During that time, Kaitian and Nuannuan had been very careful and busy. But the income made them more than satisfied. Uncle Tan paid them 13,200 yuan in total, from which only 1,500 yuan was spent on purchasing goods for their stay. The rest of the money was put safely in Nuannuan's chest pocket. Upon his departure, Uncle Tan held Kaitian and Nuannuan's hands and said: "We'll give the videotape to the television company once we're back. A lot more people will know of the Great Wall of Chu, and they'll want to see it in person. By that time, even your Chu Di Ju will be too small."

Kaitian did not say anything. But inside, he felt excited. *Please send more people here, please…*

After Uncle Tan and his team left, Kaitian made the payment for the bricks and tiles he bought on credit to build the house and gave one hundred yuan to every family that bought weedkiller from him. He had Nuannuan sew the pocket on her chest close so that the rest of the money could be kept safe in it. Night fell. Kaitian held the pocket on Nuannuan's blouse in his fingers while Nuannuan sewed it. Kaitian exclaimed: "I've never imagined that a small family like us could have such a large sum of money. With this and the three-roomed house, I'm not anxious any more."

Without saying a word, Nuannuan sewed quietly. She hung her head down to bite the thread off. Then, she took off her clothes and went to sleep. The sight of her fine complexion and curvy body aroused Kaitian's sexual desire. He pulled himself up upon Nuannuan and started kissing her. When his kiss went up to her face, Kaitian's lips felt her cheeks wet. He paused a little and soon realised that she was shedding tears, which stunned him. "What's wrong? Why are you crying?" Nuannuan's sob now gave way to a wail. Kaitian panicked and asked: "What in the world happened? You should be happy." How could he know that Nuannuan was sorrowful because she suddenly remembered the humiliation she had suffered to build the house?

Seeing Kaitian freeze, Nuannuan had to tell him that she was thrilled by the money they had made.

Kaitian was happy again, and he laughed. "It's still early to get excited. Didn't Uncle Tan tell us that more people will come to see the Great Wall of Chu?"

"If more and more people come to see the wall, can we take them all in Chu Di Ju? The three of us had to sleep on the floor to receive eleven guests. What if next time there are thirteen of them? Where do we put them?" asked Nuannuan, her eyes gazing upon Kaitian's face.

"Is there really going to be a group of thirteen? That many?"

"Nothing is impossible. What if they do come?"

"What do you think we should do?"

"We shall build more houses and expand this hostel."

"More houses? Are you asking me to spend the money we just earned?" Kaitian was in shock.

"This is not simply spending. I learned from TV – it's called investing. Even here, people use the saying, 'You can't make omelettes without breaking eggs.'"

"Will Mr Leader Zhan grant us the land?"

Nuannuan looked resentful as she said: "When I went to see Zhan Shideng last time about the land ownership, he promised me that we could build as big as we want."

"Then... shall we?"

"We shall. In the worst case, we can just sell the houses if no one comes to stay."

The Kuangs started another round of construction without notifying anyone. With more money in their pocket, the young couple found it easier than last time.

They paid for the planks and cement, and again bought bricks and tiles on credit from the kiln. The owner had already built trust in Kaitian and agreed to everything he said. Out of sheer boldness, Nuannuan decided to build more than one house. So they built three guest rooms on both the eastern and western sides of the original Chu Di Ju, as well as a yard wall with an arch over the gateway on its southern side. Once it was finished, Chu Di Ju became a proper compound, ready to take in guests.

People in the village were even more surprised this time: Kaitian's son was still too young to get married, yet they spent so much money on these houses. Zhan Shideng did not expect their new project, either. He especially went to the construction site and inspected with suspicion. He asked Kaitian: "Are you planning on selling these houses?"

Kaitian only smiled at him. He dared not give away his true motivation. Chu Changshun, Nuannuan's dad, also felt unhappy about his daughter's expenditure, so he came over to warn them. "You must not do anything beyond your capacity. With so much debt, aren't you afraid of going bankrupt with all this construction?"

Nuannuan led Dad to her room and explained in a soft voice: "We're building these for the visitors."

Chu Changshun was more displeased to hear that. "What visitor will come to our poor village? Do you think we live in Nanfu City? I just hope you're not tricked, like last time with the weedkiller." He finished saying this with a sigh.

Dad's concern was not groundless. In the next few months, no one showed up to visit the Great Wall of Chu. As a result, no one came to stay in Chu Di Ju. So many empty houses sitting there unoccupied increased Kaitian's anxiety. One night, he sighed and said: "Have we been blessed with just a little good luck? Have our good days become history now? Maybe we shouldn't have recklessly invested so much money in the houses. Now we have no more cash in our hands. What shall we do?"

Nuannuan patted him on his back and said: "Don't panic. Stay calm and wait. I don't believe only those few city people are interested in the Great Wall of Chu."

But they waited and waited, and still no tourist showed up. Nuannuan became more nervous as their waiting extended without hope. They bought the bricks and tiles on credit with an interest of fifty yuan every month for one thousand bricks, and sixty yuan every month for one thousand tiles. If their houses stayed vacant for any longer, they could not even pay the interest. Then, she said to Kaitian: "Go and let our fellow villagers know that we're selling our houses. See if anyone is interested in buying them."

Kaitian pounded himself on his legs with regret while saying yes with repressed agony.

Long after Kaitian had put the houses on the market, a non-local man came to ask about the price. He had kept bees on the west bank of Red Lake for a long time. Kaitian hoped that he would make a fair offer. The beekeeper claimed that he didn't make much money in his trade and wanted to buy the houses for five thousand yuan. Realising that this offer was even less than the money they owed to the kiln owner, Nuannuan instantly shook her head and repeatedly said no.

After learning that his daughter and son-in-law were selling their houses, Chu Changshun rushed over and complained: "You aren't making a living – you're making trouble. Although you're both in your mid-twenties, you don't know how to budget your life yet, do you? As the saying goes, 'Neither eating nor dressing makes you poor, but poor management may throw you into poverty.' How can you get rich by managing your finances like this?"

Kaitian was initially afraid of speaking with his father-in-law. Now he hemmed and hawed. "It's... not my fault."

Nuannuan smiled and said: "Dad, Kaitian is not to blame. It was my idea to build the houses."

One night when the couple were sitting in the new house in anxiety, Shallot ran inside and cried out happily: "Kaitian, come and check this out – you're on TV."

The couple were stunned, so they did not react immediately.

Kaitian gathered himself first, then put Dangen down and ran out. Yet when they reached Shallot's house, he could only see Uncle Tan on the TV. He was introducing the Great Wall of Chu with a smile. He explained the length and width of the wall and the pattern of the rocks used to build it. The TV pictures amazed Kaitian. "Wow! They're so clear." They could see Uncle Tan's white beard, the clump of con grass under his feet, and the wall, with the crevices between the stone blocks.

Sister-in-Law Shallot jokingly reprimanded him. "You rascal Kaitian. You were only interested in getting yourself on TV. It would be great if you had let us know so that we could get there too."

Kaitian could only laugh. "Who'd have known?"

The next day, everyone in the village knew about the appearance of Kaitian and the wall on TV. Everyone was surprised, yet no one understood what it meant.

The villagers were wondering when the TV interview with Kaitian took place. Spotty Laosi said to Kaitian with contempt: "It turned out you were busying yourself for TV exposure when the city people were here. I don't think you're better than I am."

Zhan Shideng also smirked. "What's the big deal appearing on TV? When village committee leaders had meetings in the township, Nanfu City's TV station came to videotape us several times, only you didn't see me when you watched your TV."

Kaitian felt nothing but happy, having no false hopes at all. Nuannuan knew she had made the right decision to expand Chu Di Ju, and the opportunity to make big bucks was coming.

One midday, not long after Kaitian's appearance on TV, several boats that looked like Black Bean's anchored on the ferry outside Chu Wang Village. More than twenty university students stepped out, all laughing and talking, and walked directly towards Kaitian's residence. Kaitian was eating in the old yard when he caught sight of a group of students at the door. He was stunned, not knowing what was happening. Nuannuan realised it was the opportunity she had been waiting for. She stood up and said: "You must have come for the Great Wall of Chu. Welcome!"

One of them told her that they were students majoring in history at Hebei University and they had come for the wall. Kaitian put down his bowl immediately and took the students to the newly expanded Chu Di Ju. He counted his guests. There were twenty-two of them – seven women and fifteen men. It was easy to offer them all accommodation. However, Kaitian and Nuannuan hadn't had the time to buy pillows and bedsheets for the new guesthouses. Kaitian arranged for the women to stay in the main house and the men in the east and west wings of the guest compound. The students were pleased to see the new houses and new beds in such a tidy courtyard. Kaitian promised to bring bed linen before dinner time and talked to the leading student about the price. The student asked him: "How much did Mr Tan pay when they were here?"

Kaitian answered: "One hundred and twenty yuan per person including accommodation, food and a tour guide. But your group is larger, so I can give you a discount. How about 110 yuan every day per person?"

The student thought for a while and agreed. He gave 4,840 yuan to Kaitian and said: "Here's the money for two days. I'll pay you more if we stay longer."

Kaitian took the money and showed it to Nuannuan. Then he had her put two thousand yuan in the pocket she had sewed and gave her a couple of hundred for the dinner. He went to his father-in-law's later and gave him a little over one thousand yuan so that he could find a neighbour to get fourteen bedsheets and pillows from Juxiang Street. He asked that they return to the village before dark. He would pay them fifty yuan each. Chu Changshun glared at his son-in-law and said: "Don't mention money with your father-in-law, OK?"

Kaitian quickly answered: "OK, OK, no mention of money." Then he turned and said to Hehe: "We need you to come over and help your sister prepare dinner. I'll buy you a new dress and a new blouse after the guests have gone."

Hehe smiled and said: "My brother is most generous with his words."

Kaitian answered happily: "I'll give you my word."

The students washed themselves and rested for a while before they asked to see the wall on the hill. Nuannuan tried to extend their stay for the sake of two thousand yuan a day, so she said to them: "It's too late to go on the hill now. How about my baby's dad takes you around Red Lake for now? He'll take you to the hill tomorrow morning."

The leading student said: "Sure, we can go and see the lake."

Nuannuan pulled Kaitian aside and whispered to him what to do. He then left to guide the students.

The villagers were curious about the group of students from the city, and they all walked out their doors to watch Kaitian take them to the lakeside. They asked each other about the visitors. Zhan Shideng was in shock too. He thought to himself: *Damn! The visitors asked for Kuang Kaitian instead of me.* Children in the village also swarmed up to look at the students.

The small shop owned by Zhan Datong was close to the lakeside. He piled up dozens of dried sunflowers in front of it. The students had never seen such things, so they quickly bought all the flowers. Zhan Datong was more than happy: the sales had already surpassed his yearly revenue. He patted Kaitian's shoulder and whispered: "Thank you. Finally you are doing something good for the village."

There was nothing special to see by the lakeside except for some grass, herbs, willow trees and wildflowers. The students took several pictures and started asking about other places to go. Kaitian was nervous: it was still early before sunset, and the students would not be happy without things to do. Suddenly, he remembered that Uncle Tan told him about a fierce battle between Qin and Chu right here by the side of Red Lake. He announced in a tone of authority: "You must take this place seriously, for it is, in fact, an ancient battlefield. In the old days, the Chu army were defeated by the Qin army in Danyang, and they came here to take a rest before the next battle. But a hundred thousand Qin soldiers followed them and lit the fire of war again right here. The Chu soldiers had not recovered from their defeat, so the Qin army killed tens of thousands of our Chu people. What a cruel battle it was. Dead bodies were everywhere in this very place on that day."

"Wow!" The students listened to him carefully with their eyes fixed on the grass and the clear water.

One student said: "Maybe we can find some relics of the weapons they used in the battle." The others followed him as they carefully watched their steps in the grass. Kaitian was relieved, so he followed their steps too. He wished that they could really find a piece of weaponry. With the students occupied again, he hoped they could spend time here until sunset so that he could earn money for one more day.

"When I read Qu Yuan's work," said the leading student, "I read that his poem 'The Lament' was written in this area. He wrote the poem to commemorate soldiers killed in the battle. Do you think it was *the* battle?"

"It's possible," echoed one of the students.

Another student recited a few lines from the poem:

> *Grasping our great shields and wearing our hide armour,*
> *Wheel-hub to wheel-hub locked, we battle hand to hand.*
> *Our banners darken the sky; the enemy crowd like clouds:*
> *Through the hail of arrows, the warriors press forward.*
> *They dash on our lines; they trample our ranks down.*
> *The left horse has fallen, the right one is wounded.*
> *The wheels are embedded, the foursome entangled,*
> *Seize the jade drumstick and beat the sounding drum!*

Kaitian listened in silence. Though he did not quite understand what they said, he felt happy to see these students paying attention: *I can bring other guests down here by the lake again next time so that they can stay longer...*

The next morning after breakfast, Kaitian guided the students on the hill. They cheered in amazement when seeing the Great Wall of Chu and then spread out. Some took pictures of the surroundings, some sat on a rock to paint pictures, and some took notes of their observations.

The group stayed in Chu Wang Village for four days. Nuannuan and Kaitian earned close to ten thousand yuan in total. It was a net profit of seven thousand yuan. They quickly paid what they owed from the construction. Apart from the income, they felt happy because they were more confident in the future of Chu Di Ju. Moreover, three days after the group left, sixteen students from Shandong arrived. Following the Shandong group, twelve from Baoding in Hebei showed up. Before the Baoding group left, eleven from Kaifeng came to stay too. Spotty Laosi stopped the students from Kaifeng when they arrived at the ferry and said: "You can stay at my place and eat with us. You're all welcome in my house."

The students went with him. But they saw Chu Di Ju with its new houses and tidy floors, beds and tables, and they immediately moved out and asked to stay there. Spotty Laosi was furious, but he dared not stop them.

One night after receiving the groups of visitors, Nuannuan said to Kaitian: "We should help Shallot out. She didn't ask for compensation for the weedkiller. Now that we have more money, we can't forget about her."

"How should we help her? Give her money?"

"She won't take it. You know Shallot – she will not take money from you for no reason. I think we could hire her in Chu Di Ju and ask her to cook for the guests. I can't manage in the kitchen with so many people to feed. She's a better cook than I am. With her and Hehe, we don't need to worry about food at all. I can help you with the tour guiding if I'm not needed in the kitchen. We'll pay Shallot four hundred yuan every month, and she'll eat with us. She can use the money to help her family out."

Kaitian frowned. "Isn't four hundred yuan too much for a month?"

"Too much? Aren't we trying to help her out here? Changlin's arm is debilitated, and their life is even more difficult than ours before Chu Di Ju."

"We'll do as you say."

Nuannuan paid a visit to Shallot. She did not mention anything about returning a favour or offering some help; she only talked about the job opportunity and her payment. Shallot was very happy and agreed immediately. Farm work in their fields was not enough for her, and she was thinking of new ways to make money. The second day she showed up to work. Nuannuan told her what dishes to make, and she went to the kitchen and occupied herself in a very efficient manner.

Nuannuan knew about Spotty Laosi's remorse about the guests. She did not want to make an enemy of her neighbour, so she thought to offer him some opportunities too. She went to his house and said: "We will pay you twenty-five yuan a day if you take one group of visitors to see the wall. Are you in or not?"

Not able to attract guests to his house, Spotty Laosi had to compromise. And twenty-five yuan a day was a lot better than nothing. He agreed, though with reluctance. "All right. You Kuangs make your big money, and I'll take only a small slice out of it. Heaven knows how unfair this business is…"

After consecutive groups of visitors left, Kaitian locked the guest house's door in the evening and returned to his residence in the backyard. He counted the money with Nuannuan. Good gracious! Stack after stack of banknotes. After paying off all the debt, they still had a few thousand yuan. Beyond himself with joy, Kaitian somersaulted the room. Nuannuan also felt tremendous relief. She had never been so at ease since the weedkiller incident. She looked up and happily said to heaven: "Oh, money, we'll never have to submit to your humiliation."

Late spring was drawing closer and closer. The grass was pleasantly lush on the outskirts of Chu Wang Village, by Red Lake, on the hillside and over the ridges of the fields. Various kinds of flowers were also captivating. Nuannuan led Dangen to the Chinese chives plot along a field ridge, basket in hand. She was going to cut the first crop of the chives. The view of the wildflowers along the way lightened her heart further. She told herself: *A better life is ahead. Can we make more money with the Chu Di Ju property?*

"What's this, Mum?" asked Dangen, who toddled ahead and picked a string of flowers.

"Ivy morning glory. It's called ivy morning glory, honey."

"What can we do with it?" asked Dangen with wide-open eyes.

"We farmers enjoy looking at them."

"What's the use of us farmers looking at them?"

"When we look at them, we feel happy, babe."

"What can we do when we're happy?" Dangen looked into Mum's eyes for an answer.

"When we feel happy, we can…" Nuannuan couldn't answer her son's question. She then bent down and gave him a hearty kiss. "When I feel happy, I want to kiss you." As she said so, she tickled him, and the two hugged each other, laughing heartily.

Due to the continual arrival of guests coming for the Great Wall of Chu, a large quantity of vegetables was needed, and Nuannuan persuaded Kaitian to convert the family plot of land into a vegetable patch. They grew at least a dozen kinds of vegetables, including aubergine, chives, tomatoes, kidney beans, spinach, celery, pak choi and cucumber. Kaitian was a much better cereal crop grower than a vegetable grower, but the soil by the lake was incredibly fertile. Therefore, all the vegetables were flourishing.

Today, Nuannuan came to the plot to cut back the chives, as yesterday a group from Shandong had arrived and chosen to eat steamed dumplings with egg and chive filling. Nuannuan planned to cut back the chives before noon, clean them, prepare them as a filling, and in the afternoon give them to Shallot to prepare for the guests as steamed dumplings.

At the vegetable plot, Nuannuan left Dangen on the ridge to play and went into the field to cut back the chives. The first crop of chives was really tender. The sections of the cut chive leaves exuded a bit of garlicky aroma to assail Nuannuan's nostrils. She quickly pulled a blade from the chive leaves she had cut, the tenderest of the lot, and turned to call: "Come over, Dangen. Taste this." Dangen rushed over and opened his mouth wide. He chewed a little bit, but the chilli sensation forced him to stick out his tongue, which was stained with a juicy green. His grimace made Nuannuan laugh, and she immediately sucked the chive's sap on the tip of Dangen's tongue into her mouth.

The sun rose high without their knowing it. The sky was as blue as the lake. A few birds took off from the thickets on the edge of the field and flew into the silvergrass by the lake, chirping joyously. After showing her son the birds by pointing at them, Nuannuan went back to harvesting the chives. She hadn't had so many smiles on her face for a long time.

After cutting back one bundle of chives, Nuannuan turned around and suddenly noticed Zhan Shideng standing at the front of the house. Her smile suddenly vanished, like a startled bird in flight. She pretended not to have seen him, put her head down and continued to cut the chives, though it was easy to see that her hands were now slow and clumsy.

"Hey, I know you saw me, but not even a hello?" Zhan Shideng had a big smile on his face.

Nuannuan didn't lift her head for a while but kept on cutting her chives. Only when Dangen went to her side and said "Mum, someone is calling for you" did Nuannuan finally put down the sickle, lift her head to Zhan Shideng and say coldly: "What are you standing here for?"

"Now that you have money, you talk more arrogantly," Zhan Shideng exclaimed, pretending to be serious. "Hey Nuannuan, you never spoke to me like this before."

Nuannuan shot a glare of hatred at him and said: "Leave at once if you don't have anything serious to discuss. I don't have time to idle. I've got work to do."

"Well, I don't have anything serious indeed. I only want to tell you two things. One is that I miss you, and I especially want…"

"If you continue talking nonsense, I'll cut you with my sickle." As she said so, she glared at him and threw the sickle towards him. It fell and planted itself in the ground in front of him.

Zhan Shideng smirked. "OK, OK, I won't talk about this. Let's discuss the second item. You're allowing the stone wall visitors to stay in your home for lodging and have already earned a good deal of money. After today, I intend to set up a distributed accommodation system to send guests that come to Chu Wang Village into other homes and allow other families to earn a bit of money for the sake of our collective wealth. What do you say?"

Nuannuan's heart sunk, and, with much anger in her voice, she replied: "So, you've found another way to get at us. Do you think earning this money is easy for us? If we didn't do it like this, how could we pay back the families we owe?"

"Hey, don't forget that I'm the leader here, and the leader must be watching out for the good of the whole village. Haven't you heard the authorities talk about allowing wealth for all people? A good turn like this can't be left to a single household."

"You can't just force the guests to stay in other houses. It's only right that guests choose where to live."

"You should have reasoned with me earlier. Frankly, I'm longing for your presence every day." Zhan Shideng grinned from ear to ear. "You're the only one that I want to see every day in the entire village. Your breasts make me…"

"Dangen, let's go." Nuannuan knew what was coming next and, pulling Dangen by the hand, picked up her vegetable basket and rushed away…

She didn't realise that she still had the sickle in her hand until she and Dangen had walked a long distance. *Bastard! I wish I could slash you with my sickle. Only by killing you can I feel better. Oh heaven, if you can see everything he's done, kick him into the lake.*

"How are you, dear patron?" A greeting roused Nuannuan from her thoughts. She looked up, only to see Master Tianxin, the abbot of Lingyan Temple. He stood on the roadside, a small bucket in hand.

Nuannuan hurriedly bowed to greet him back. "Master, how are you? You're…"

"Thanks. I'm going to release life." Master Tianxin pointed at the bucket in his hand. "We do this several times a year, a convention passed down by our ancestral clergymen."

"Let me help you with the bucket," said Nuannuan. Suppressing her displeasure, she let go of Dangen's hand and reached out hers.

Master Tianxin hurriedly shook his head and said: "No, thank you. I'm almost at the lakeside. I'll feel more at ease if I can finish what I started." After that, he resumed his trip.

As the road leading to the village was by the lakeside, Nuannuan tagged along after the abbot, leading Dangen by his hand. When they arrived at the shore, Nuannuan saw Master Tianxin on his knees, closing his palms in front of his chest and chanting some Buddhist text in silence. Then, he reached his hand into the small bucket and fished out a few small-sized grass carps and a young turtle. He put them into the water.

"Fish, Mum! Fish!" Dangen cried out joyously before running to Master Tianxin.

Nuannuan was about to stop her son when Master Tianxin unexpectedly turned to scoop him up and hold him in his arms. As he watched the fish swim in the water, he tenderly patted Dangen on his dainty shoulder. "Son, they're fish. But in the eyes of us Buddhists, they're like humans. They're living creatures with souls. We have no right to take their lives."

How could Dangen understand the sermon? He said: "My grandpa can catch them. He can cast fishnet to catch fish."

His remark embarrassed Nuannuan.

When he rose, Master Tianxin caught the expression in Nuannuan's eyes, and he smiled slightly. "Buddhists and mundane people obey different rules. We do what we're supposed to do, and you do yours, for that matter. We are in two worlds and won't interfere with each other. So, you don't have to feel disturbed."

Nuannuan felt touched. She pulled Dangen over and said to him: "Bow to Grandpa."

Little Dangen did as Mum told him and bowed childishly. Master Tianxin patted Dangen on his head with a smile. Then, cupping his palm in his hand in front of this chest, he said goodbye.

Master Tianxin was about to turn around when Nuannuan impulsively shouted: "Master, may I ask you a question?"

"Buddhism maintains that only by asking questions can one enter a state of enlightenment."

"What can one do if one harbours a hatred?"

"Buddhists advocate mercy and seldom think of hatred. But since you ask me today, please allow me to dwell upon it." Master Tianxin started counting his prayer beads as he said in a relaxed, unhurried tone: "Usually, people don't harbour hatred. What they have on their mind is hope for a better life. But when their bodies, reputation or interest are hurt, particularly when they are innocent, and the perpetrator was viciously inclined, grievances arise. Among them, hatred is the severest kind. It emerges when a person feels that he or she has been deeply humiliated. But all sorts of grievances in a person's heart will gradually dwindle and fade away. However, it can be a protracted process for these hateful grievances to go away. And it always motivates people to act."

"To act?" Nuannuan gasped, her eyes wide open.

"Yes, to avenge oneself. A hurt person wants the one who hurts them to feel the same pain. If one can't harm the perpetrator, one tends to avenge oneself upon the perpetrator's kith and kin. Because of this, Buddhism considers vengeance to be the most terrible feeling and the most significant threat you worldly people pose to each other. There are prayers to the Buddha for the riddance of the hatred pent up in mundane people's minds in the Buddhist texts we chant every day."

"Can the Buddha rid hatred?" asked Nuannuan.

"He'll try his best. But Buddhism advocates the universal practice of his doctrines. Therefore, individuals can eradicate the root of hatred from their minds. Why do you suddenly ask me this question?"

"I just thought of it randomly. Would you please come and dine with us at our home?"

"No, thank you. I must return to the temple." Cupping his palm in his hand, Master Tianxin turned and departed.

The abbot had almost disappeared into the distance, but Nuannuan still stood where she was, with Dangen's hand in hers. "Respectful Buddha, I think hatred has arisen in my heart. Please help me to get rid of it…"

Nuannuan knew the meaning behind Zhan Shideng's words and, afraid that he really would forcefully intervene, she told Kaitian about it that night. Kaitian also reacted with shock and hurriedly asked Nuannuan: "What do we do?"

After a moment of hesitation, Nuannuan said: "I think he's trying different ways to force us to present him an offering. I've heard that every time Hu Datou brews a jar of yellow wine, he'll receive a flask. Every time Zhan Guoli slaughters a cow, he'll gift him with about ten *jin* of beef. Every time Black Bean sells a batch of Chinese medicine, he'll take a few cartons of cigarettes. We've admitted so many guests already – no wonder he's unhappy not to receive something from us. What the hell. Let's get rid of this problem and give him some money as a gift."

"How much?" Kaitian sounded distressed.

"I say five hundred because, with an appetite like his, I'm afraid that a smaller sum wouldn't solve anything."

Kaitian had no choice but to put five hundred yuan into a red envelope marked with Spring Couplets and carried it, alongside a case of Wolong liquor originally meant for guests, as he went to Zhan Shideng's house.

At that moment, Zhan Shideng had just finished his dinner and now sat beside his table picking his teeth. He had expected to see Kaitian arrive and, seeing him enter holding a box of alcohol, stood up with a smile. "Kaitian, a rare guest here, please take a seat. Why have you arrived carrying this alcohol? There's no need for these formalities with me. Nowadays, your house has many guests. It's only right to let them drink these gifts."

Kaitian was naturally uncomfortable to part with the things but kept a big smile on his face and said: "Leader, you supported us right from the beginning to build the lodging house, allowing us to earn money. How could we ever forget your kindness? I had said a long time ago I would come here, but tourists seem to be arriving in droves, and I've been as busy as ever, delaying me up till today. Well, take this change for your children to wear new clothing, as a token of regard from their uncle." While saying this, Kaitian stuffed the red envelope into Zhan Shideng's pocket.

Zhan Shideng did not refuse but instead picked up a cigarette and handed it to Kaitian, saying: "My wife's brother gave me these Hongtashan cigarettes a few days ago. This here is Yunnan tobacco. You know Yunnan, right? In the vast southwest, the mists are thick, and the tobacco leaves are moist, making for ideal flavours. They are more flavoursome and smooth than ours."

Kaitian pressed some under his nose and sniffed, exclaiming with much praise: "Fragrant! This tobacco really is fragrant. What a pity I don't smoke. Leader, it seems that if the stone wall tourists really did want to stay in other homes, we would have nothing to say about it. But for the sake of our guesthouse, please allow us to continue to have the tourists instead of distributing them to others. We really do need to earn some money at the end of the day, and of course we would give you a cut of this. I'm no fool you know – shouldn't I know how to thank you for looking after me all this time?"

Zhan Shideng took a long draw on his cigarette and then laughed. "Kaitian, this is all very conscientious of you, but from the beginning, wasn't it I who saved you? Do you think the township police station would let you out without me? From the beginning, wasn't it me who allowed you to build your housing, and then the Chu Di Ju guesthouse? If you're grateful, you should continue to do what you're doing now. I'll stop the villagers from grabbing your business. The only thing is, I want to see you for this at least once a month."

Kaitian's heart skipped a beat. *Oh fuck! I have to do this once a month?* However, he hurriedly agreed. "OK, OK…"

After making the commitment with Zhan Shideng, Nuannuan and Kaitian felt temporary respite, and Nuannuan was next occupied with how to keep visitors to the Great Wall of Chu staying longer at the guesthouse. Most of the guests had no genuine research interest in the wall – they would arrive in the afternoon, stay at the guesthouse, see the stone wall on the second day, spend another night and depart after breakfast on the third day – a total of two nights' accommodation and five meals. If every group of guests were to stay for four nights, it would double their earnings. Thus, Nuannuan thought long and hard for a way to keep guests for a longer period, with her first thought being to take them to Lingyan Temple. The temple was not far from Chu Wang Village. It was a large structure, with visible temple frescos, scenes of monks chanting Buddhist scriptures and conducting religious rituals, and a forest of pagodas constructed to worship eminent monks who had passed away. Besides, there were also the scenic spots of the Double-pearl Mountain Springs and Thousand-acre Bamboo Grove.

Kaitian had some doubts. "As temples are everywhere, who is willing to go and see another?"

Nuannuan replied: "We'll have to be convincing. We must inspire the guests to see it."

Kaitian waved his hand. "But I haven't the talent to do such a thing."

"I'll give it a try."

Not long after, another group of tourists arrived to see the Great Wall of Chu. While eating a meal after returning, Nuannuan said to them: "There's another place here you may find worth visiting. Only one and a half kilometres from Chu Wang Village is the Tang Dynasty Lingyan Temple. This temple was constructed in AD 700, more than a thousand years after the Great Wall of Chu. By first seeing the Great Wall of Chu and then Lingyan Temple, you will experience the true greatness of our ancestors, who could build such a long wall and multitude of buildings in a temple. You can discern boldness of vision from the Great Wall of Chu and exquisite craftsmanship from Lingyan Temple. The temple has gone through multiple building and rebuilding in its thousand-year history. But whenever it stands, pilgrims will come in droves. People find that the Buddha in this temple is the most responsive to their prayers. There's a popular saying among the people living on the west bank of Red Lake: 'Burn a bunch of incense sticks in Lingyan Temple, and your family will be populous and prosperous.'"

And so, the visitors were inspired by Nuannuan, and all expressed interest in going to the temple for a look. Even Kaitian was surprised by Nuannuan's marketing rhetoric. He whispered to her: "I didn't expect that you could be so silver-tongued. You were so eloquent and fluent."

Nuannuan smiled. "Now that we're business people, we must learn how to talk to our customers. Frankly, I did my homework for what I said. I've read several books."

After breakfast on the second day, Nuannuan brought the group of tourists to see the temple. At the gateway of the temple, Nuannuan and the visitors ran into Master Tianxin. Nuannuan went up and bowed to him, saying: "Reverend Abbot, would you mind a group of visitors bothering you and touring the temple?"

Master Tianxin greeted her back and responded: "No, not at all. Setting his mind to save everyone in the world from eternal misery, the Buddha expects people to come to him. Please come in."

On that day, the tourists were first fascinated by the immense structures and elegant murals, and then watched with curiosity the solemn scenes of monks conducting Buddhist rituals. Finally, they strolled with great interest through the ancient towering trees, the thousand-acre bamboo grove and the forest of a hundred pagodas around the temple. As they wandered, the cicada chirped, the birds twittered and the springs gurgled to form a background symphony. The visitors didn't return until dusk.

It was a good start.

But regrettably, a trip to the temple only took one day and would not keep the tourists for much longer. The only way would be to think of another idea. After the tourists left, Nuannuan was cleaning the yard and turning the thought over in her mind when she saw her father arriving with two carp.

Dad entered the yard and said to Dangen: "Gen, Grandma and Grandpa have some fish for you."

Nuannuan quickly went up to greet her dad. She took the fish, asked him to take a seat and said: "Keep the fish for yourself and Mum. I won't grudge Dangen good food."

The old man laughed. "Yesterday, I went down to the lake, and by the favourable wind cast out my net, but without realising it, the boat entered the triangular Soul-Bewildering Zone. Well, as soon as I saw the navigation mark, I hurried to get the boat out of there, and just when I least expected it, a mist, smelling like gunpowder, emerged, and blotted my view so that I couldn't even see the bow of the boat. I closed my eyes and sculled hard in the same direction. Luckily, nothing unexpected happened, and I rowed out of it fast enough. I caught these two fish after I got out of the foggy area, and I think they're not like the normal fish I catch every day, so I brought them back to treat Dangen."

Hearing Dad's story, Nuannuan had an idea. *Mists? The Soul-Bewildering Zone? Yes, we can bring the tourists to the lake's centre to see the strange phenomenon. It doesn't matter if we don't know its cause. As long as we can extend the stay of the tourists at our place, everything will be fine.*

Nuannuan told Dad of her new plan, and the old man grew interested as he listened. He said: "Yes, it takes about a day to see the mist in the lake if you delay a bit on your way to and from it. The old man naturally understood that the longer the guests stayed at Chu Di Ju, the more money his daughter and son-in-law could earn."

Nuannuan called Kaitian to her while Kaitian was busy in the backyard. With a thrilled expression, Nuannuan said: "After tourists see the Great Wall of Chu and Lingyan Temple, we'll tell them about the Soul-Bewildering Zone in Red Lake and that they can find whatever they want to see in the mist. I think most of them will go to see it after our promotion."

Kaitian scratched his head. "Now that's an idea to keep tourists, but whose boat will they go in? We don't have one?"

"They can just sit in Dad's boat, which we'll convert from a fishing boat into a tourist boat," Nuannuan said flatly.

The old man stopped them. "What? I won't be able to fish any more?"

"How much money can you earn by fishing? After one day, you are tired to death, and the most you could catch would be about twenty *jin* of fish. If we were to take tourists to the Soul-Bewildering Zone, we could get ten yuan per ticket per person, and our boat will sit twelve people without a problem. So twelve people on one trip is 120 yuan. When there are more tourists, how much do you think we can earn with two trips a day?"

The old man nodded his head. "That... makes a lot of sense. You do what you have to."

"Let's do it then. Kaitian, tomorrow you go to Juxiang Street and buy some lacquer, give the boat a fresh coat, clean it up and fix twelve small seats in. The boat will look as good as new, and when the next group of tourists come, we can give it a try. Sound OK?"

The old man hesitated a second and then nodded his head.

Still worried, Kaitian said: "But what if nobody goes to see it?"

"Isn't all of this success just based on risk? Didn't we take a risk when building the Chu Di Ju guesthouses?" With that, Nuannuan patted Kaitian on the shoulder, and the matter was decided. On the second day, she persuaded Kaitian to buy lacquer and some other things to tidy up the boat. After ten days, the boat, originally a tired old fishing vessel, had been lacquered with a fresh coat and turned into a reasonably convincing tourist boat, with twelve fixed chairs, each of which had its own safety belt.

A couple of weeks later, a group of tourists from Xuzhou, twenty-one in total, came to see the Great Wall of Chu. As usual, Nuannuan arranged for them to stay at the guesthouse on the first night, took them to see the stone wall on the second day, the temple on the third day, and on the third night told them about the mist of the Soul-Bewildering Zone. In order to get the tourists in the mood to see it, Nuannuan made her speech as tantalising as she could. "There's a place here that you'll regret missing. In our Red Lake, there's a small triangle, and at that place you may sometimes see a strange mist. To get there, you must take a boat, and in the mist you can see what you desire, and if you're not careful and enter the mist, you may become dizzy and enchanted, and a great peril may befall you…"

At first, some of the people didn't believe there could be such a place, and only through Nuannuan's sincere conviction did they, half doubting, finally express willingness to see it. After breakfast on the fourth day, Nuannuan and Kaitian took them to the lakeside. Everyone produced ten yuan. Shortly afterwards, Nuannuan took twelve people onto the boat.

That day, the wind was gentle on the calm lake, the sun shone bright in the sky, and the visibility on the lake was good. Nuannuan's dad sat by the stern of the boat, steering steadily. Nuannuan stood at the bow of the boat, introducing tourists to the names of the isles around them and fretting to herself. *What if the tourists aren't interested?*

Once the boat had stopped by the triangular area, Nuannuan said: "During the past two days we have seen the Great Wall of Chu and Lingyan Temple, both man-made wonders. Today we come to see a natural wonder…"

Her voice had barely faded when suddenly a white mist grew from the otherwise calm surface of the lake and spread to fill the air. The tourist's eyes opened wide, and they all cried out: "Wowww…"

Nuannuan had seen the mist more than once, but on this occasion it really had unexpectedly risen out of the lake without any warning. Nuannuan felt awe and astonishment spreading within her, and she stared unblinkingly at the mist as it rose, thickening and expanding. Finally, from deep within, she could make out rows of houses...

"Houses! It means that I am thinking of building more houses." Nuannuan murmured...

When the converted Chu family boat made it back to the lakeside, the tourists aboard were theorising, one after another, with each face full of surprise and excitement. As soon as the boat pulled up to the shore, the remaining tourists hurried to the waterside and asked the people aboard loudly: "Hey, did you see it?"

Some from the boat answered: "We saw it. The mist is so strange, rising straight from the water surface, clouds after clouds, and with all kinds of visions within."

Kaitian walked up to his father-in-law, who was smoking quietly on the bow. "Dad, what do you think?"

Nuannuan's dad nodded. "Good. The guests were pleased."

Kaitian stuffed a roll of cash into his father-in-law's pocket, a total of 120 yuan, the charge for the boat ride. The old man took the money out and placed it in Kaitian's hand, saying: "What if I fall into the water? Do you want to see me drop it into the water?"

The remaining trip to the Soul-Bewildering Zone was also a success, and the tourists were endlessly excited about the new experience. Even that evening, they were still discussing the boat trip, amazed by the mysteries of that part of Red Lake, and still guessing as to the reason behind the mist. With the addition of Lingyan Temple and the Soul-Bewildering Zone, tourists were staying at Chu Wang Village for two more days and two more nights, and Kaitian and Nuannuan earned a lot of money from accommodation fees.

After dinner that night, Kaitian stuffed 210 yuan from the twenty-one boat tickets into his father-in-law's hands. The old man felt some embarrassment, and with a red face, stuffed the money into Dangen's pocket, saying: "Is this money for me?"

Kaitian laughed. "Next, I'll install an engine, and we can split the earnings of the following trips between us."

After he said this, he looked at Nuannuan, who took the money and put it back into her dad's hands: "Take the money as yours. Isn't money in your hands the same as money in ours?"

The enchanted area in the lake quickly attracted the attention of tourists, and just about everyone who came for the Great Wall of Chu would go for a trip there. With more tourists, the single motorised boat belonging to Nuannuan's dad was not sufficient, so Nuannuan found Jiuding and said that the Kuang family would cover all the refitting expenses and that he could take tourists to and from the Soul-Bewildering Zone. Every round trip would earn him sixty yuan. Thinking of it as much easier than fishing, Jiuding immediately agreed to the arrangement.

The Kuang family's daily income was considerable now. Nuannuan and Kaitian had to spend lots of time counting the banknotes of different denominations – earnings from the accommodation, the Great Wall of Chu tour, the tour guides and the tickets for transporting the tourists by boat to the Soul-Bewildering Zone. But they gradually realised that some tourists would arrive from the eastern bank and, in order to save money, would not look for their guesthouse; instead, they would head directly to the Great Wall of Chu and Lingyan Temple, and some would even put up a small tent on the mountain and sleep outdoors. Nuannuan thought to herself: *We must earn some money from these tourists as well – as you have arrived at Chu Wang Village, you'll have to leave some money behind.* She thought about this for a night and came up with an idea.

Early the next morning, she asked Kaitian to find Red Belly and Big Mouth, the two local layabouts, to ask if they would be interested in a lazy way to earn a buck. The two men said of course they'd do it. Thus, Nuannuan made them follow her and Kaitian, carrying a plank.

The two walked and pouted. "This is no lazy way to earn money. Why are we carrying this wood about?"

Nuannuan ignored them, walking alongside Kaitian, axe and saw in hand. On they walked, all the way to the foot of the mountain and the road that led to the Great Wall of Chu. Here, the road was no more than five metres wide, with a precipice on either side. This was the only way up the mountain to see the Great Wall of Chu. Nuannuan and Kaitian put up a simple wooden gate, and on the side hung a small sign with ticket prices. Red Belly and Big Mouth were to guard the gate on each side and explain that, from this point on, anybody who was not from a Chu Wang Village family would have to purchase a ten-yuan entry ticket. No entry ticket, no way up the mountain.

Nuannuan said: "You two guard the gate, and we'll pay you ten yuan each day."

It was indeed a lazy way to earn a buck, and Red Belly and Big Mouth were delighted with the prospect. "Sure, sure."

Kaitian wrote the character *Chu* on a white banner and stamped it with a personal seal to qualify it as a mountain entry ticket. He would sell the tickets himself, and outsider tourists would believe this to be a governmental regulation, stick to the rules and buy a ticket to head up the mountain. Sure enough, after one day, Kaitian had earned 230 yuan. After paying Red Belly and Big Mouth, the earnings were 210 yuan. *Damn, this is easy money.* Kaitian was so happy that he almost jumped, regretting that he hadn't thought of this idea sooner. If he had sold tickets from the beginning until now, how much money would he have earned?

It grew warmer with each passing day. The tourists coming from the eastern banks by small boats continued to grow until finally the May 1st Labour Day holiday arrived. Kaitian was now a grown man and had never paid much attention to the Labour Day holiday, and he had certainly never experienced any benefit from the holiday itself. But now he suddenly understood this holiday's importance, because on that day, for the first time, 197 people came to Chu Wang Village from the city. The great number of colourfully dressed city people who stepped off the boat and onto the banks of the lake gave the people of Chu Wang Village a big shock. The young and old of the village rushed out to see what all the noise was about. The male villagers gaped with curiosity at the cameras, recording equipment and fantastically shaped water bottles the tourists held in their hands. Women looked with envy at their clothing and adornment.

Spotty Laosi's wife exclaimed: "Look at their skirts. They are showing so much thigh. If they were in our village, many men would be tempted to touch them."

Sister-in-Law Shallot whispered: "Look at that woman whose trousers are so tight that they even reveal her butt crack. Isn't she afraid of ripping them when she crouches down?"

Jiuding's wife laughed after hearing that. "They can seduce men with ripped trousers. That's called coquettish. Unlike them, we can only moan a little while lying in our men's arms."

Surprisingly, Zhan Shideng also walked out to take a look, thinking that people would ask who the leader was. He didn't expect that not a single person would ask for him, and nobody took any notice of him at all. They asked only: "Who is Chu Nuannuan? Which one is Kuang Kaitian?"

Zhan Shideng cursed silently: *It's stupid of the city dwellers to squander their money on the wretched stone wall. They must have too much of it.*

Nuannuan and Kaitian were both pleasantly surprised and a little flustered. *Wow, how can so many tourists all show up at once?* Nuannuan asked her sister Hehe to head to the mountain and replace Kaitian, who was selling entry tickets She also asked her to call in Spotty Laosi and a few tour guides she had hired beforehand to take the tourists up the mountain to see the Great Wall of Chu in different groups. She then asked Shallot to hire Jiuding's wife Huiyu to quickly steam buns and roll noodles in preparation for the return of the tourists from the mountain. She wondered where they could all stay. *Split them into different homes? As soon as that happens, it'll be difficult to keep them at the Chu guesthouse. There must be a way.* Nuannuan tapped on her forehead and thought hard while Kaitian pulled at his hair, pacing around in the yard. Nuannuan suddenly said: "I have an idea, but I don't know if it'll work."

"What idea?" Kaitian asked eagerly, his eyes wide open.

"We can use sorghum stalks to build shacks – a few dozen by the lakeside. Wouldn't that solve our problem? Some of our villagers did the same when they had too many guests at their weddings. Let's do it. I think it'll work since the weather is still warm."

"Yes, it's a great idea." Kaitian happily clapped his hands. "I'll go and get this done then."

They quickly hired two groups of people, sending one group to Juxiang Street to buy bedding and ship it back on flatbed carts, and the other group to the village with cash to collect sorghum stalks. Afterwards, seventy simple shacks were constructed on the open area by the lake, with every shack able to sleep two to three. Each shack was floored with reed mats and wheat straw spread with a set of bedding on them. At only fifty yuan per night, each shack opened out onto the lake, an authentic taste of the mountains and fields.

After seeing the Great Wall of Chu, the tourists all liked this accommodation, and before dinner was ready, every shack had already been taken.

On this day, Nuannuan and Kaitian earned a considerable sum. The money from the Great Wall of Chu mountain road entry tickets alone was 1,970 yuan. According to her elder sister's request, Hehe handed the entrance ticket income she had collected to her sister and brother-in-law. Kaitian laughed, unable to conceal his delight. Shallot, Jiuding's wife and a few other female neighbours, now temporary employees, were busy making noodles and steaming buns for dinner. Even at the price of one bowl of noodles for six yuan and one steamed bun for one yuan, the demand exceeded supply. Adding the income from the guesthouse accommodation, the tour guide fee for Lingyan Temple and the enchanted area boat tickets, Kaitian earned almost ten thousand yuan on that day. *Good gracious! When did we make so much money in a day?* Kaitian sighed with wonder that night as he sat on the bed, counting the day's income before going to sleep. He was so excited that he repeatedly slapped himself on his legs covered by the bedsheet.

Nuannuan laughed as she unbuttoned to undress herself. "I see someone is excited."

"Labour Day is fucking great. If only it continued," Kaitian said, rubbing his hands together.

"As far as I can see, earning so much in a day isn't necessarily a good thing."

"What do you mean?" Kaitian looked unhappy as he stared at Nuannuan.

"Be careful – someone's eyes are going green with envy..."

By then, Nuannuan had just taken off her top, and her ample breasts popped out from her vest and caught Kaitian's attention. His unhappiness instantly forgotten, he grabbed them.

"I'm exhausted. Today..." before Nuannuan could finish, Kaitian had already climbed on top of her. "We must guard against people's jealousy..."

Before Nuannuan could say another word, the bed started to shake violently...

There was cause for Nuannuan's concern. Just as the Labour Day holiday had passed and the tourists had departed, people from the township taxation office arrived, asking for Kaitian to pay tax from the business. Kaitian still had a lingering fear of the police from the last incarceration, and he was terrified to see the people in uniform. Naturally, he could not pluck up the courage to oppose them and simply handed over the tax.

Soon after, Zhan Shideng asked Zhan Datong to summon Kaitian to his home. It was just dusk, and Kaitian and Nuannuan were piling up the bedding used by the tourists when they heard the sound of Datong at the door.

Kaitian asked: "Why does he want me to go over?"

"He said he just wants to discuss something with you."

"Do you know what he wants to discuss?" Kaitian passed a cigarette to Datong, then poured a cup of alcohol and put it in his hands.

Datong, the alcohol glutton, didn't decline. He threw his head back, draining the cup into his belly at once. The alcohol softened him, and he said in a low voice: "From his tone, it seems he's not happy about the shacks you put up and the entry tickets you're selling. He says you're getting too greedy for your own good."

"You'd better take some money," Nuannuan said quietly.

After seeing Datong out, Kaitian spat with contempt and cursed under his breath: "Some leader. And still pressing for money." Kaitian put five hundred yuan in his pocket and said to Nuannuan: "I'm off to his place."

Nuannuan sighed. "That five hundred yuan won't be enough for him."

"How much more do you say?"

"One thousand," Nuannuan said.

"One thousand?" Kaitian opened his eyes wide in torment. "Without lifting a finger, he walks away with 1,500?" Seeing Nuannuan nodding, Kaitian had to put one thousand into his other pocket.

Zhan Shideng was standing by his big front door. Upon seeing Kaitian, he asked with an irritated look: "If I had not sent for you, you wouldn't have come to see me, would you?"

Kaitian stepped into the yard with a smile. "Of course I would. I thought yesterday, as soon as I had seen the tourists off, I would hurry to tell you about the progress of the business and bring you the money." While speaking, Kaitian took out five hundred yuan from one of his pockets to put into Zhan Shideng's hand.

Zhan Shideng shot a glance at the stack of notes in Kaitian's open hand and said: "I'm not a beggar, and you don't have to come here to simply pay me off. Today, I have called you here to formally talk about two issues as the village leader. The first issue is that visitors are paying for tickets to go up the northern hill and see the stone walls. This is something for the village to manage. An individual like you can't take all of the money into your own pocket. That hill is public property, and that stone wall was not built by the Kuang family. You understand me? The other issue is about where you put up the sorghum stalk shacks. That area also belongs to the public, and they pose a fire hazard so must be immediately torn down."

As soon as Kaitian heard this, he knew that the money he had offered was too little. Quickly producing the one thousand yuan from his other pocket, he said: "You see now, I should have made myself clear why I came here. Today, I brought along two payments – this five hundred yuan is half of the income from tickets sold for going up the mountain to see the stone wall, and this one thousand yuan is half the income of accommodation, food and tours. I have given myself a rule that no matter how much I earn, I keep half for myself and the other half for the leader, as the leader has given me the ability to earn money. If I forgot this, I would be ungrateful and unworthy of being a human being." While speaking, Kaitian stuffed both payments into Zhan Shideng's pocket.

Zhan Shideng's expression warmed slightly, and he accepted the money. Pointing to a seat in his yard, he said to Kaitian: "Take a seat. Now I spoke with you about the issues because the villagers have already reported you, so I have to talk with you about it... Well, let's just ignore them, and even if you do wish to continue, I'll turn a blind eye."

Kaitian was quick to express his gratitude, giving thanks while tormented over the 1,500 yuan. *My god! Not even lifting a finger, he's walked away with 1,500 yuan. He walks away with your money, and you must thank him. That's not something you see every day.* Rather than just resigning himself to it altogether, Kaitian made one request. "Leader, I'm worried that if afterwards more tourists arrive, we haven't currently got anywhere for them to stay. If we were to build more rooms in the vacant lot in front of our houses, would you be OK with it?"

"Do what you like. Build more if you want." Zhan Shideng waved his arms as a gesture of seeing his guest out.

Back home, Kaitian told Nuannuan about his meeting with Zhan Shideng and finished with an angry curse. "This bastard takes away our money without any financial or labour input."

Nuannuan had anticipated the result and remained silent. Finally, she said: "If you don't want him to push you around any more, you'd better compete for the village committee leader's post."

Kaitian was stunned. "Who would elect me as the leader? Can Zhan Shideng give the post up to me?"

Nuannuan said coldly: "No one has ever said that Zhan Shideng will be the committee leader of our Chu Wang Village forever. Isn't the leader elected every three years?"

Kaitian chuckled. "I think you're dreaming. Who'd elect me, a man with neither power nor influence? We're better off making honest money with our tourism business. I asked Zhan Shideng's permission just now, and he gave his consent to our building a few more houses."

Nuannuan nodded. "We do need to add more houses. Shacks are a one-time thing and can't be used for accommodating the tourists."

In the following days, Kaitian again rushed about buying bricks, tiles and cement, while Nuannuan and Shallot dealt with the small number of tourists. One afternoon, Nuannuan and Shallot were tidying up the guesthouse when they saw some city people entering the yard. They thought they had come to see the Great Wall of Chu and called them into the house, telling them to stay the night and climb up the mountain tomorrow.

They listened as though confused and said: "Why go up the mountain? We won't be climbing up the mountain. We're here to look at the lake."

Nuannuan then assumed they wanted to see the mist of the Soul-Bewildering Zone and quickly said: "It's too late to see the enchanted area. By the time you take a boat to the centre of the lake, it will be just about dark."

Again, they were confused. "What is this enchanted area? We aren't here for that."

Nuannuan did not expect this and asked: "So what are you here for?"

One of them answered: "We're here especially to look at the lake water."

Nuannuan was surprised. "What's the use in looking at the water? Didn't you go along the water when you arrived by boat from the eastern bank? You didn't see it then?"

This was met with laughter. "We have already seen the lake water with our eyes. In fact, our mission is not only to see the lake but also use some equipment to test the water from different areas."

Nuannuan finally understood, as she had seen some large boxes among their luggage. She was surprised but did not ask them why they were testing the water – only if she could help them with anything.

The leader among them said: "We heard on the east bank that your Chu guesthouse is the closest to the west bank, the cleanest and the tidiest. We plan to stay here in the guesthouse for ten days, to use as our dorm and office area, and will pay the standard rate. If possible, we'll hire a boat and head to the lake for some tests every day."

Nuannuan took this as good news and quickly nodded. "Sure, sure..."

Kaitian returned at dusk, and when Nuannuan told him about the situation with the new guests, he was quite surprised. "Especially here to test the lake water? Can it be that there's something wrong with the water of Red Lake?" Kaitian decided to find out what it was all about and, on the next day after breakfast, agreed on a price for renting a boat and took the people to the lake on his father-in-law's refitted boat.

They opened up a map, and Kaitian immediately saw at the top was written *Map of Red Lake*. They pointed and planned, and then explained to Kaitian the route to take: first a circuit around the lake, then a visit to each of the five areas of the lake marked as the north, south, east, west and centre. Kaitian was surprised but pleased. He was surprised that they chose to circle the lake, which would take a few days. *What would they be doing?* He was pleased that they would be renting a boat for a longer time so that he would be earning more money. In the following few days, Kaitian steered the boat according to their requests, and when arriving at each area, everybody was busy taking up water then using machines on racks to check it. Kaitian thought it was hilarious. *What's worth looking at in this water?* This went on, stopping and starting, for over a week.

After a week, the boat finally arrived back at Chu Wang Village. Kaitian had already grown well acquainted with them and chose a youngster in the group to ask about the trip to Red Lake and why the research was needed.

The youngster replied: "We're here to test the water quality. If it qualifies, a water diversion project could be started here."

"Oh?" Kaitian's eyes were wide. When he was young, he had heard that the lake water here would be transferred north, but he had never seen any activity and thought of it as merely grown-ups exaggerating. It seemed that what they talked about would come true indeed. "So after you test the water, do you think it will qualify?"

The youngster smiled. "The last data just came through – this water doesn't just qualify, it is actually high-grade mineral water. It can be directly consumed without purification, especially the water in the central area with the mist, which has a higher quality than mineral water. You and your people who live along the lakeside are truly blessed because you can probably live longer lives by drinking the water."

Kaitian laughed. "The folk and cattle here have always directly drunk this water, and just as you say, many of us have lived past the age of ninety. Old Grandma Liu can still eat stir-fried yellow beans with her teeth at 120 years of age."

The youngster laughed out loud. "After today, the water from Red Lake will be moved to the north, and I want to drink it every day so that I can eat stir-fried yellow beans at 120 years too. Kaitian, after the water irrigation plan opens, your village on the lakeside may become much more lively, you know."

"Lively? What do you mean?" Kaitian didn't understand.

"Many people will probably come to look at the water of this lake."

"Really?" Kaitian's heart skipped a beat. If that were the case, there would be many more opportunities for earning money.

"Yes, it's true. Northerners drinking Red Lake water will naturally have the thought to come and see the source of their water.

When that time is here, visitors from Tianjin and Beijing will be numerous…"

In bed that night, Kaitian told Nuannuan about all of his experiences of the last few days, and Nuannuan lay there pensive. She said: "It looks like another opportunity for us to increase our tourism operations. Don't you plan to construct more houses? This time, you need to build better ones to accommodate the people from the metropolises."

Kaitian nodded. "Right, we could install glass windows in the front and rear walls, and pave the floors with bricks. Then we'll install a colour-paper ceiling beneath the roof of each house. We can invite the best carpenters to build the finest tables, chairs and beds. Guests who enter these rooms will never want to leave them."

Nuannuan broke into a smile. "You're talking big again. No people will stay in the best house forever. Have you seen such a house in the world?"

Kaitian laughed. "Yes, I have. That's ours. Every time I enter our house and see you undressed in bed, I will find it impossible to tear myself away."

"Nonsense!" said Nuannuan. She blushed and turned her fine-complexioned back towards Kaitian.

This expansion of Chu Di Ju was different from the last two times; it was well known in the village that Kaitian and Nuannuan were now rich, so the construction went relatively smoothly as everyone was happy to help. A couple of young men took their trolley and went with Kaitian to buy bricks and tiles; timber came to their doorstep alongside tools. Jiuding and some other young men even went straight to them and said: "Big Brother Kaitian, Sister-in-Law Nuannuan, just name anything, and we'll make it work for you."

Nuannuan and Kaitian were surprised by their enthusiasm. Before, they would have to beg for help from people in the village; yet now people would come to them and offer their services. That assured Nuannuan's determination to get richer. *If we can earn more money, our life will get easier and easier. Zhan Shideng, one day you'll not dare to cross us.*

It was the Kuangs' fourth construction, including the renovation of the house where the couple lived. Kaitian had not made up his mind about the expected size of Chu Di Ju. Nuannuan said to him: "Since there will be construction anyway, let's make it a big one."

The couple decided to put thirteen new guest rooms in Chu Di Ju: five rooms as the main body of the construction with the one in the centre connected to the original Chu Di Ju; two rooms in the east wing; two others in the west wing; and two more on each side of the gate. The four main rooms, excluding the one used as a connecting hall, combined with the two wings, would be guest rooms; the two rooms on the right side of the gate would be kitchens; the two on the left would be used as dining halls.

Thanks to the materials they had prepared, the input of good handymen and favourable weather, the guesthouse compound was constructed well. After only ten days, over a dozen new houses were standing – uniform green bricks and white walls, a true sight to behold. There was nothing else like the two big compounds of Chu Di Ju in all of Chu Wang Village.

The day the extensions were completed, many of the villagers ran over to see. Uncle Black Bean joked to Kaitian: "I can tell from your courtyard that you're wealthy now. If I were a bandit, I would come to rob you."

Kaitian burst out laughing. "I've put all my money into building the houses. If you came, you could only take a few sheets. If I robbed you, I could get all your cash for all the medicinal herbs you've sold."

On that day, Zhan Shideng had business to attend to in the city of Nanfu, on the eastern lakeside. On returning to see Kaitian's Chu Di Ju, he stared at it for a long time with nothing else to say. He had permitted Kaitian to extend the compound but did not expect so many new blocks, each of which was not only larger than his own house but also more impressive. *It looks like this little prick has been earning some big money.* He was quietly shocked, and for the first time he felt that his position was being threatened. *Fuck! Are this couple going to become upstarts? It's time to humble their pride.*

After the Kuangs had finished the renovation, Nuannuan told Kaitian: "Such a large compound is awaiting guests, but the two of us alone couldn't manage to tidy it all up, so let's hire three women from the village specifically for this – otherwise, it may spoil the visit for the tourists."

Kaitian asked: "How much should we pay these workers?"

Nuannuan was silent for a moment. "Food included, two hundred yuan."

The expansion of Chu Di Ju showed the villagers the financial power of the Kuang family. Having heard that Nuannuan and Kaitian were hiring three girls to work there and offering them two hundred yuan a month and free meals, more than ten families brought their daughters over, asking Nuannuan and Kaitian for them to stay as employees. Nuannuan and Kaitian had thought it would be difficult to hire the employees and never expected that this would occur.

Afraid of offending the families, Kaitian whispered to Nuannuan: "What shall we do?"

Nuannuan was moved, as it was the first time since her marriage into the Kuangs that people had come to ask her for help. She said to the parents and daughters with a smile: "Your willingness to help us means you think highly of us. Although I only need three people, I'll record your names, and when I need more people I'll certainly hire those who I may not hire now." That day she picked three girls, with the rest leaving full of hope.

Not long after Chu Di Ju's extensions were completed and furnished with beds, tables and chairs, and before the chance to buy bedding, a group of guests arrived to see the North-South Water project. That afternoon, Nuannuan and Kaitian were in their room discussing what bedding to buy, when suddenly a great noise came from outside. They went outside to see what it was and saw at least fifty senior citizens from big cities, each wearing a red plastic badge on their chest.

The tour leader was a young chap. He walked over to Nuannuan and Kaitian and asked: "Are fifty-two people able to stay in Chu Di Ju? If so, we'll stay here on the west bank for one night, and if not, we can simply tour the west bank for a while, then take a boat back."

"Yes, of course you can stay," Nuannuan quickly replied. She calculated in her mind for a second: *Chu Di Ju has twenty-one rooms in total. The rooms that have been built as kitchens and dining halls can be furnished with beds. With ten rooms each holding three beds, and the other twelve holding two each, they can take in everyone.*

"How much do you charge for each room?" the young man asked again.

"One hundred yuan for accommodation and meals in a room with three beds, and 110 yuan for accommodation and meals in a room with two beds."

"OK, we'll stay here." The young man waved his little flag.

"Do you all want to have a rest in your rooms now, or wait until evening?" asked Nuannuan, worried that none of the rooms had bedding yet, so how could anybody relax in the rooms now?

Fortunately, the tour guide shook his head and said: "We won't go in yet. The group will first head to the lakeside for a look at the water. Did you know, our tour group exclusively consists of retired Beijing cadres. They've come here to comprehend whether or not this water is clean for transfer to the north and have especially taken this opportunity as a holiday to come and investigate…"

With the remaining time that afternoon, Nuannuan asked Kaitian to hire a walking tractor to buy bedding from Juxiang Street. She asked Shallot, Jiuding's wife and all of the other employees to prepare meals. Then she arranged for the three girls to lay out beds and tidy the rooms. She volunteered to accompany the tour group from Beijing to the lakeside, first to see the cogongrass, the poplin grass on the embankments, the Chinese ash trees, the tung trees and the magnolia grove on the hillside. After this, she persuaded them to split into two groups to visit the water in the crystal-clear lake. She made sure that they were confident about the water quality and then began to tell them about the three other sights worth seeing: the Great Wall of Chu, Lingyan Temple and the misty Soul-Bewildering Zone. She said: "You'll regret it forever if you don't see them."

Nuannuan introduced the Great Wall of Chu, Lingyan Temple and the Soul-Bewildering Zone with all the pleasing words she could recall from her lexicon. The Beijing group, who had initially planned only to see the lake water, became interested and asked the tour guide to stay a while longer on the west bank and see all three sights. Nuannuan's heart sang with happiness. *Another big sum to earn.*

As the older people had already retired, they were not in a hurry. Coupled with the difficulty in walking, they strolled at their own pace, so it took four days in total to see all three sights. Nuannuan was overjoyed. *This is the kind of business only God could gift us.* The income from four days' accommodation, touring fees, boat hire and the mountain pass tickets was twenty thousand yuan. Even subtracting the two thousand yuan expenses for buying ingredients for meat and vegetables, the remaining money all went into Nuannuan's pocket. This was the first group of tourists to stay at the renovated Chu Di Ju and the largest number ever to stay.

As the group left, the head of the tour company expressly walked over to Nuannuan and said: "Your Chu Di Ju, the compound for tourists within the village, is a good place, especially the meals, with all of the flavours of the wilderness. City folk who are used to eating bland fish and meat find them fresh. Everybody is delighted. From now on, my tourism agency may establish trips to Red Lake. How about if Chu Di Ju was to become our designated tourist accommodation?"

Nuannuan didn't understand. "What's a designated tourist accommodation?"

"It means that every time I bring tourists here, they'll stay at Chu Di Ju, and even if other tour groups want to stay, you must first grant accommodation to us".

As Nuannuan heard this, she broke out into a laugh and said: "Yes, yes, I'm just worried that my Chu Di Ju won't have room for everyone…"

Owing to this success, Nuannuan had a better grasp on what the days ahead would be, and it looked as though committing to the renovation of Chu Di Ju had been the right thing to do. With an income like this, they would earn back the money from the initial investment in no time.

The night after the tourists left, Nuannuan said to Kaitian with joy: "Let's throw a party with some rice wine to celebrate our first success in entertaining the guests in the newly expanded Chu Di Ju. We'll invite cooks Sister-in-Law Shallot and Huiyu, tour guide Spotty Laosi, boatman Jiuding and the three assistant girls."

Kaitian showed his reluctance. Scratching his head, he hemmed and hawed. "Since we've paid them their wages, do you think it's necessary to treat them with a drinking party?"

Nuannuan said with anger: "Why are you so miserly? Do you think I'm doing it for fun?"

Seeing Nuannuan mad, Kaitian nodded his consent. "OK, OK. I'm going to invite them."

The dishes to go with the wine were ready, and the wine was warmed up. After they were served, Nuannuan raised her bowl of wine and said: "Brothers and sisters, we wouldn't have achieved this success after the expansion of Chu Di Ju without you and your devoted service. Come, let me make a toast."

Gulping down his wine, Spotty Laosi broke into a smile. "Kaitian and Nuannuan, how did you pray to the Buddha to get so blessed? Please tell your Brother Laosi how to emulate you and make a fortune in the future and build a few dozen houses as you've done."

Before Kaitian and Nuannuan could respond, Sister-in-Law Shallot cut in with laughter. "How to be blessed? You must refrain from sleeping with your wife for 365 days a year and go to Lingyan Temple to burn incense and kowtow. If you do so, I guarantee that you'll have good luck."

"Why can't I sleep with my wife?" asked Spotty Laosi, the smile fading on his face.

"You've got to have a pure body and mind," responded Sister-in-Law Shallot.

Spotty Laosi turned to Kaitian, laughing. "Is that true with you? You two haven't slept with each other for the whole year indeed?"

Nuannuan blushed instantly. "Shame on you, Laosi," she joked.

After the party, Kaitian and Nuannuan saw Spotty Laosi, Sister-in-Law Shallot and the others off. The entire village was asleep as silence reigned all around. Nuannuan and Kaitian went to inspect Chu Di Ju to ensure all the doors were locked and windows shut. They parted at the gate and started checking, one on the left and the other on the right. When they met in the last room, Kaitian suddenly grabbed Nuannuan by her hands.

"What's wrong?" Nuannuan didn't get what he meant initially.

Kaitian chuckled. "We haven't slept here since its expansion. Let's have a new experience in the brand-new room."

"Look at you." Nuannuan rubbed a finger against the bridge of Kaitian's nose and followed him into the room. After Kaitian had closed the door, he carried Nuannuan to the bed and said: "Please don't stop me tonight, OK? I'll give free rein to myself and do what I like. When we do it in our residence, we have to be careful in case we startle our parents and Dangen. I've never fully enjoyed you."

Nuannuan giggled in the dark and, giving Kaitian a gentle pinch on his cheek, said affectionately: "Shame on you."

It was their most unrestrained lovemaking since Dangen's birth. Kaitian banged the hardest this time, and the noise he made was earth-shaking. But Nuannuan knew that the compound was so big that their noise would not be audible outside. Therefore, she didn't stop Kaitian. Instead, with her eyes closed, she let him enjoy himself and her to the fullest. Eventually, even she couldn't help but moan loudly.

With no guests to receive, Kaitian and Nuannuan felt at ease. Having exerted themselves in bed last night, they did not get up early and were still in bed when the sun had fully risen. The previous night, Kaitian had been too tired to move, so he stayed in Chu Di Ju. Nuannuan, on the other hand, went back to their residence because she had to take care of Dangen. Yet Dangen had already fallen asleep with his grandma by the time she got home. Nuannuan had slept on her own that night.

Usually, Dangen, a habitual early riser, would ask to wake up his parents at breakfast time. He complained that they had gone back on their word that people were not supposed to sleep in. His grandma would stop him, saying: "When we had guests staying in our houses, your parents had to get up early and go to bed late. They seldom have an opportunity to rest like this. Leave them alone, and let's have our breakfast first. We can set their portions aside so that they can eat them whenever they're up."

Unexpectedly, before the grandma and grandson's conversation had barely finished, the voice of Zhan Shideng, the leader, was heard outside the yard gate. "Is Kaitian home?"

Zhan Shideng was standing outside. Kaitian's mother rushed to let him in. "Mr Leader, come inside. Kaitian is not up yet. I'll wake him up now."

She gave a chair in the yard to the leader and rushed to Kaitian and Nuannuan's room. Nuannuan had been woken up by Zhan Shideng's loud voice, and she was getting up with a resentful look. Seeing her mother-in-law, she whispered: "I don't want to see him. Go and get Kaitian in Chu Di Ju – he stayed there last night."

Her mother-in-law nodded and rushed out to apologise. "Mr

Leader, sorry for the wait. Kaitian slept in the other house yesterday. I'm heading there now."

Nuannuan had dressed and got off the bed. She looked through the window at Zhan Shideng, who was sitting in the yard, smoking at leisure. The sight of him brought back the scenes of humiliation she had suffered, and evoked the hatred buried in her heart. *Son of a bitch! Why are you at our home? Asking for money? Haven't we just given you a large sum? Spending the money others have made with their blood, sweat and tears. Do you have peace of mind? You think we picked up our money so you can ask for it at will?* Nuannuan balled her hands into fists...

"Mr Leader, many apologies, I slept late," said Kaitian as he ran into the yard, his hands busy buttoning up his shirt. "Here, have a smoke." He offered a cigarette from his pocket.

"I'm fine, Kaitian. Now that you're the rich man in the village, you can sleep as long as you like."

"I'm nothing, Mr Leader. What can I do for you?" Kaitian asked carefully.

"Of course. I don't dare to intrude in your graceful house without any serious business."

"You shouldn't have come over yourself. If you need anything, just let me know, and I'll be there for you."

"This business I have today is quite some business. So I had to come over and tell you about it myself."

Kaitian was surprised. "What serious business? Does it concern us?"

"Yes, it does. According to regulations from above, in order to prevent water pollution in Red Lake, your Chu Di Ju must be closed to all tourism business. Moreover, the stone wall on the hill has been there since ancient times, so it does not belong to you. You do not have the right to sell tickets or to guide any viewing tours. As for Lingyan Temple, it's where the monks live, and there's no need to attract tourists there, either. Whoever wants to tour around here should go themselves. You should not be part of it. From today on, you should farm your fields, and your father-in-law should fish in the lake. No more nonsense."

"What is this?" Kaitian was stunned.

"I'm here to announce the decision made from above and by the village committee. If you dare violate it, you'll have to be careful."

Kaitian's face turned red. "We have a deal. You'll have half of our income."

"I'm not a man who can be bought with money," said Zhan Shideng with a cold smirk. "Half of your income? You think I'll believe you? You built yourself this big new house. But with the money you are willing to share with me, I can't even make a house half as big as yours. Forget about the deal. This is serious. Stop all that you've been doing. We shall live on as we used to."

Nuannuan walked out, her expression cold as ice. "I'm afraid that Mr Leader can't have his wish granted this time."

Zhan Shideng turned to her and said in a monotonous tone with his eyes narrowed. "Just when I thought the wife was not home. Why not?"

"I learned about it from TV – the regulation only prohibits factories alongside Red Lake. There's nothing about tourism and guesthouses in the village. What pollution can tourists cause apart from their piss and shit? That will be used as fertiliser for the fields. There's no pollution. People in the village piss and shit themselves. You're the leader, so you must understand how much the fertiliser has helped the crops and plants alongside the lake and purified the water."

"You and your sharp tongue," said Zhan Shideng, his eyes still narrowed. "You can talk all you like, but the regulation from above has already been formulated. I told you not to receive any more visitors, and you must abide."

Nuannuan glared back. "Even though the regulation from above is wrong? We ordinary people still have the right to argue, right? What should we do with so many houses we've built? You tell me."

Zhan Shideng chuckled gloatingly. "You can use them as storehouses to stow your grain and firewood. You can also pen your livestock and fowls in there."

Nuannuan gnashed her teeth and meant to curse loud: *You son of a bitch!* But she repressed her anger and calmed her tone. "It's apparent that tourists need places to stay. Do you want to watch them having difficulty looking for accommodation?"

"That's none of my business," said Zhan Shideng with a shrug. "They deserve the difficulty by coming from afar to see the water and stone wall, don't they? Why is the water worth viewing? What's the attraction of a wall made of stones? Temples are everywhere, so why do they have to make a long trip to see Lingyan Temple? And the mist in the middle of the lake – I don't believe it's more pleasant to the eye than the colourful lights in cities. To my mind, they're crazy and have too much time on their hands. If they have no place to stay, that's a problem they bring on themselves. We don't have to worry about it on their behalf."

"No matter what, I won't let my houses be empty." Nuannuan's response manifested anger, which she had failed to suppress.

"It looks like you're arrogant because you've got money. Fine. We'll wait and see." Zhan Shideng left his threat before stepping out of the courtyard.

Panicked, Kaitian went up to Nuannuan and said in a low voice: "He's mad. His underhand means are sure to hurt us. What shall we do?"

Nuannuan shot a glare at him. "What do you mean by 'what shall we do'? Can he eat us? I don't believe there's such regulation from above. We can't submit to his humiliation like before."

Anger churned in Nuannuan's heart for the rest of the day. *Zhan Shideng, you want us to beg you again? No way!*

Three days after Zhan Shideng's visit, Nuannuan heard some noise from the small pier in the afternoon. She knew it was from a new group of visitors. She stepped out and found dozens of people from the city walking towards her house. She called Kaitian out, and the couple walked quickly to receive the visitors. Nuannuan thought to herself: *I'll give them accommodation, and Zhan Shideng will have no way to stop us.*

Much to her surprise, before Kaitian and she could reach the pier, Zhan Shideng's voice, loud from the tin horn he had in his hand, was heard from the pier. "Dear visitors, according to the new regulation from above, no house in this village shall provide accommodation to you. Please return to the east bank before sunset – otherwise, you'll have nowhere to stay tonight."

Nuannuan and Kaitian stopped in surprise. They did not expect Zhan Shideng to do this. Hearing his words about no accommodation being available, the visitors quickly did a tour by the lake and, without seeing the Great Wall of Chu, returned to the boat on which they had arrived back to the east.

Spotty Laosi, who Kaitian had hired as a guide, rushed over with curiosity as he was unaware of what was happening. "Hey, Sister. Why does the leader forbid you to receive the guests?"

"The leader fears that we may tire ourselves too much, so he wants us to rest a few days," Nuannuan replied, gnashing her teeth.

"Yikes! He cares way too much. Because of his care, I'll have no money to make," mumbled Spotty Laosi as he walked away.

Zhan Shideng, who had been standing by the lake, walked towards the young couple with a smug smile. He said in a serious tone: "My apologies to you two. It's my responsibility to maintain stability in the village. I am the leader, and I must execute the decision made from above."

"We'll sue you for this," said Nuannuan in full resentment.

Zhan Shideng laughed with his eyes narrowed. "Go ahead. Sue me. Be it the township court or the county court, wherever you like to sue me, I'll be there. Chu Nuannuan, I know your boldness has increased along with the money in your pocket. Three years ago, you never dared to talk to me like this."

"Three years ago, I also believed you can't do whatever you want without being punished."

"We'll see."

"We will."

Nuannuan turned her back on him abruptly to hide her angry tears...

The moon had sunk into the lake early. The dogs in Chu Wang Village were fast asleep. Everywhere was quiet. Nuannuan sat on the steps of Chu Di Ju's main house, staring fixedly at the arch over the gate to the courtyard. Hatred still tormented her: if it were not for Zhan Shideng's obstruction, this compound could have earned her a lot of money. Each day, she would suffer significant loss with so many houses unoccupied.

The door to the yard squeaked, and from behind it came Kaitian. "Go to sleep, please," he said.

"I'm not sleepy," she responded.

"Do we have a case?" whispered Kaitian.

"We sure do. We can't helplessly watch the houses lie empty."

"That motherfucker," cursed Kaitian as he sat beside Nuannuan in the dark.

"How much money do we have?"

"Nineteen thousand yuan."

"I'll take ten thousand yuan tomorrow. I'll go to sue him in the township. If that doesn't work, I'll go to the county, and if that still doesn't work, I'll go to the city."

"OK."

"Ask Sister-in-Law Shallot to tell the three girls we hired to sleep in Chu Di Ju so that they can guard it. Tell Hehe to come and accompany your mum and take care of our parents and Dangen."

"OK..."

The next day at midday, Nuannuan and Kaitian arrived at the township office on Juxiang Street. Nuannuan had Kaitian buy two bottles of Red Lake liquor and two cartons of Fengyang cigarettes, and they went to the gatekeeper and called out at the guard: "Big Brother, how have you been? I have come to the township with my boy's father, and I want to see you too."

They gave the liquor and cigarettes to the gatekeeper. He was happily surprised and offered seats to the couple. "What are these presents about? I can't accept them."

During her last visit, Nuannuan looked so worried and in pain. However, this time she was calm and relaxed. She laughed loudly and said: "I haven't seen you for some time. Don't mention these small gifts. Without your help last time, we wouldn't have been successful."

After some small talk, Nuannuan got down to business. "Big Brother, I have something to ask you. In Chu Wang Village, we have houses with extra space, and there have been some visitors who came to see Red Lake. Do you think we could give them accommodation and earn some extra money?"

"Of course. You have the house, and they're willing to pay to stay. Just let them stay," said the guard. He sounded pretty confident.

"But I heard that the township office set up this new rule against receiving guests. Because their piss and shit may pollute the water in the lake."

The guard looked surprised. "What bullshit. I've been to your village, and it's not that close to the lake. People only piss and shit in the toilet, and you peasants get fertiliser from that. How can that pollute the water?"

Nuannuan felt reassured by his words. "Big Brother, can you please ask the leader who's in charge of this pollution rule? I must be sure about this."

"Sure, sure. I'll go and ask the township mayor now," said the guard as he pushed the gate leading to the courtyard outside the township office.

After a short while, the guard returned and said: "The leader of your village, Mr Zhan, is also in the office of Township Mayor Chen. The mayor is asking for you two so that he can talk about it with you."

Nuannuan's heart sank. She knew that things would not work out this way.

Zhan Shideng was sitting in the mayor's office with a smile. Mayor Chen spoke in a friendly tone. "Your leader has told me about your situation. Red Lake is included in the South-to-North Water Diversion Project, ensuring high-quality water in the lake. Your Chu Di Ju is indeed harming the lake, so you should stop receiving guests. Let us all think of the big picture. You can use the house for other purposes. Is that OK?"

Nuannuan argued with him for a while, but that did not change the mayor's mind. She knew that no words from her would change the result, as the mayor fully trusted the leader. She stopped talking and walked out of the office.

Kaitian looked upset. He asked: "What next?"

"We'll go to the county office."

"Seriously?"

"You think I'm bluffing?" Nuannuan could not hold back her anger any more.

On the third day at midday, the couple walked out of the long-distance bus station in the county seat. The busy streets and crowds thoroughly amazed Kaitian: it was his first visit to the county town.

"Where shall we go?" Kaitian asked with uncertainty.

Nuannuan, who had seen the world when she had worked in Beijing, said measuredly: "Let's locate the county government first."

The couple asked their way around and finally reached the county office late that day, but it was closed, and they had to stay for one night. The couple went to find accommodation, but the hotels in the county town were too expensive: they went to a couple of them, and every place would cost more than one hundred yuan without a meal or tour guide.

Kaitian, who begrudged spending the money, said: "If we stay in a hotel, a night's fee would be worth six or seven kilograms of pork. It's not worth it. We'd better put up for the night in the waiting hall of the bus station."

Nuannuan said: "We'll stay in this hotel that charges over a hundred yuan a night. We're doing hotel business, so we need to find out how hotels in cities operate and learn from them."

Seeing Nuannuan determined, Kaitian went into a hotel with her to check in. Nuannuan looked here and there as they walked into the hotel. She first asked the porters about their income. Then, she went to the sofas in the hall and started chatting with a man sitting on one of them. After that, she browsed the price list on the wall behind the reception desk. She visited the hotel shop to examine the commodities on the counters and in display cases. As they went into their guest room, she jotted down all the amenities in it on a piece of paper.

Kaitian had no idea what she was doing and asked: "Are you still in the mood to care about the trivial?"

Nuannuan responded: "This is by no means trivial. We don't come to the county seat often, so we must take the hard-earned opportunity to observe how the townspeople operate their hotel business. It's an opportunity for us to learn. Our Chu Di Ju may never be a match for a town's hotel, but we have lots of room to improve based on what we know about their hotels."

"But what's the use of learning if we aren't sure we can keep on doing our business?"

"You lack confidence and want to accept defeat. I don't believe that the higher authorities are so muddle-headed that they would stop people from doing things that are beneficial to others. You may rest assured."

"OK, I'll be assured. We'll see what you'll do after you lose the appeal tomorrow," mumbled Kaitian. He headed for the toilet to urinate, and there he accidentally touched the hot water tap when he washed his hands. He rushed out joyfully and said to Nuannuan: "Good gracious! They've got hot water here. Why do they pipe hot water when they have thermoses?"

Nuannuan smiled. "For bathing. Mix the hot water with cold water, and you can take a bath." As she said this, she demonstrated to Kaitian, who quickly turned on the tap.

"Wow! Townspeople know how to enjoy themselves – bathing with hot water mixed with cold water." When he had filled the bathtub with enough water, Kaitian undressed and got into it. As he doused water on his body, he shouted: "It's lukewarm and feels better than Red Lake's water in summer. Quick – take off your clothes and join me."

Standing there, Nuannuan murmured: "How nice it will be when we can also provide hot water to our customers in our Chu Di Ju guesthouse."

The following day, they got up at sunrise, bought some steamed buns from a small restaurant, and rushed to the county office with the buns in their hands. They spent a great deal of time asking about which office to go to and learned that they could only be seen in the office for petitioners. When they finally reached that office, it was already late in the afternoon. As they rushed inside to talk about their trouble to the official sitting behind the desk, they saw Zhan Shideng seated on the sofa and smoking a cigarette with his eyes narrowed, gazing upon the couple. Nuannuan's heart sank again. She looked at Kaitian. The couple could feel their hope vanish in the air: they simply could not win. Unsurprisingly, before Nuannuan could finish talking, the official said to her: "I've heard about this from your leader. You must understand that it is our priority to ensure the water quality in Red Lake. Please use your house for other purposes. Go home to farm your fields and fish in the lake."

Nuannuan did not say anything back. She knew that any word of hers would be in vain. She nodded at Kaitian and said: "Let's go."

The couple left. Kaitian sighed and said: "We can't go against Zhan Shideng. He's been the leader for all these years, and he knows everyone everywhere."

No sooner had Kaitian finished speaking than Zhan Shideng appeared behind them. They heard him chuckle coldly. "Are you going to the city or the province next? I'll gladly pay my own way to come with you, just in case you can't find the place to bring your complaint."

Nuannuan ignored him but said to Kaitian: "Let's go. We'll go to the train station and buy our tickets to the provincial seat. I don't believe there are no authorities that will listen to our complaints." With that, she took off, dragging Kaitian by the hand.

When they had shaken off Zhan Shideng, Kaitian asked again: "Are we going to the province for real? It'll take several days for us to get there and back. We must tell our parents about our itinerary."

"I said that for Zhan Shideng's consumption. We aren't going to the province. Not even the city. I thought about it. Zhan Shideng does have his connections in the government. We can't win as petitioners. We should go to court. Judges will listen to us – they only know of the law, not the leader. Have you thought about why he didn't stop me from marrying you? Because if he did, he'd be working against the Marriage Law. Certainly he's not afraid of us, but he will be afraid of the law. Let's go now."

The couple went to the county court and talked about their grievances to an old judge. The judge said to them: "If you want to sue your leader, you should talk to a lawyer, and he'll help you."

Nuannuan asked: "Will that cost us a fortune?"

The judge answered: "Lawyers normally charge some money. But with a case like yours, it won't cost much."

Nuannuan made the decision. She said to Kaitian: "Let's go and find a lawyer."

They went to a law firm with the help of the judge. A middle-aged lawyer with the surname of Sun listened to Nuannuan. He took out a book about construction and demolition regulations in areas alongside Red Lake, and a book about the regulations concerning the environment near Red Lake. Then, he took out a map of Red Lake and did some measurements. He said: "Your village, Chu Wang Village, is not one of those to be relocated further back from the lake. Therefore, the regulation only states that no factory shall be built in your village, but nothing was said about receiving visitors in your house. If what you told me is true, your leader is violating your right to operate a legal business. I will make the case in the court, and we have the game in our hands. I'll go to Chu Wang Village to find you once things are advancing."

Nuannuan looked at the lawyer and found herself slowly tearing up. She wiped her face and said: "Finally, a man of reason in a place of reason. Thank you so much. You must keep your word and come to find us."

The lawyer answered amicably: "Don't worry, I've taken your

case, and I will not abandon you. Otherwise, no one else will trust me any more."

It was dusk when Nuannuan and Kaitian walked out of the court. They found an eatery, where Kaitian said: "In a happy moment like this, let's not just eat buns. I'll order a big bowl of noodles with lamb for each of us to satisfy our palate and give ourselves a pat on our backs."

Nuannuan laughed and turned to the eatery owner. "Fix us a dish of pork slices with green pepper and a beer. We ran into a saviour, so we'll eat to our hearts' content..."

When Nuannuan and Kaitian returned to Chu Wang Village, Zhan Shideng wasn't there. Nuannuan believed that he had gone to the municipal or provincial government to find his connections and respond to their complaints. Nuannuan hugged herself with pleasure. *This time, you've made a wrong calculation.*

On the fourth day, Zhan Shideng came back, looking fatigued from a long journey. Kaitian was sweeping the ground in front of his residence. Seeing him, Zhan Shideng approached, carrying a handbag. He said to Kaitian sarcastically: "I was waiting for you guys in the municipal and provincial governments. Why didn't you show up?"

Before Kaitian could respond, Nuannuan strode over from the courtyard and said: "We surrender. You're an official while we're but ordinary people. We can't do any harm to you by complaints, so we admit defeat. We won't use these houses to receive tourists. Instead, we're going to raise scorpions in them. Are there any regulations from the higher authorities against raising scorpions?"

With a smug smile, Zhan Shideng said: "You can raise scorpions. But remember this – never fight me. In Chu Wang Village, I, not you, have the final say."

"Of course," Nuannuan said with a deliberate drawl.

Just then, a group of tourists walked towards them. They had just got off the boat. Zhan Shideng went up to them and shouted as he had done last time: "Chu Wang Village doesn't receive tourists with lodging and food. Please return to the east bank before dark."

Helplessly watching money fly away from their hands,

Nuannuan stamped her feet on the ground with anxiety. *Lawyer Sun, please come sooner rather than later.*

Prohibited to offer accommodation to visitors, Nuannuan and Kaitian had no choice but to return to farm work. Kaitian had always been a good farmer, so he undertook his work with efficiency, and there was not enough for the two of them to do. One day, they were mending the small ridges in the field for the sweet potatoes, which was not even necessary at that time, when Hehe ran over and told them that a man named Sun had just arrived. She said there were also some officials wearing police hats who were looking for them. Nuannuan knew it was the lawyer. She dropped the farming tools and hurried home. When they arrived, the lawyer was guiding two judges to inspect Chu Di Ju. Seeing her, the lawyer said: "The county court dispatched a circuit court to try your case today in your village. I've asked the two judges to learn about your case..."

Nuannuan was unable to talk, being both too tired from running and too excited.

Zhan Shideng did not expect the couple to sue him. When he arrived in the village committee office and saw the judges, he thought it was no more than another regular inspection from above. He did not realise what was happening until the judges bid him to talk about why the Kuangs should not receive visitors. He panicked and hemmed and hawed, trying to find some sensible words. The judges made the ruling: "By prohibiting the family of Kuang Kaitian from providing accommodation to visitors, Zhan Shideng, the leader of the village committee of Chu Wang Village, has violated the citizen's right to run a legal business. Therefore, Zhan must stop harassing the business of the Kuangs and offer apologies..."

Zhan Shideng's eyes were wide open in shock. Nuannuan, standing aside, burst into tears. She fainted with excitement...

The next day, Nuannuan read the letter of apology that Zhan Shideng had written under the judges' orders and supervision. Kaitian had kept the letter from her after she regained consciousness for fear of further exciting her. Not until she had fully recuperated did Kaitian show her the letter. After reading it, Nuannuan knitted her brows instead of smiling with happiness.

"Why aren't you happy?" asked Kaitian with bewilderment. "This is the first time the leader has ever apologised."

"Precisely because of that, he won't take it lying down," said Nuannuan feebly. "We've made him lose face, and he's a person who hates to lose face."

"What you said makes a lot of sense. What shall we do then?"

"Leave him alone. We wouldn't have waged this legal battle against him if we had been afraid of him. We only need to reopen our Chu Di Ju business and make our money. We can walk tall as long as we have money."

Chu Di Ju reopened that very day. The young girls they hired started cleaning. Shallot and Huiyu were also busy cleaning up the kitchen, while Jiuding and the other boatman the Kuangs had hired prepared for the journey on the lake.

The whole village heard about the Kuangs' victory over the leader. Uncle Da Geng, a pepper grower, whispered to Kaitian at the doorstep: "That's great! You're a real man. You dare argue for your rights with the emperor of the village. I admire your courage."

Wang Tiechui, the stonemason, put his thumbs up at Nuannuan and said: "You're a brave girl to fight the leader. Even I feel my justice is served. I didn't expect you to do that."

Sister-in-Law Shallot tugged at Nuannuan to call her aside and whispered: "Many woman villagers said that court should have sentenced Zhan Shideng to eat some shit to alleviate their anger."

From what the kind-hearted Shallot had said, Nuannuan concluded that she must have suffered from Zhan Shideng's despotism as well.

Huiyu overheard their conversation and echoed: "To my mind, the court should have had his trouser snake dangling from his crotch cut off."

Sister-in-Law Shallot broke into a smile. "How could he pee then?"

Huiyu's joke made Nuannuan's heart skip a beat. She thought Huiyu might have known about Zhan Shideng's atrocity against her. But Huiyu's teeth-gnashing expression led Nuannuan to the belief that she must have been violated as well. *Didn't Zhan Shideng claim that he could sleep with any woman he wanted?*

After she got up the following morning, Nuannuan found Dangen had a runny nose. Fearing that he might have caught a cold, she went to Mei's family pharmacy to buy some medicine. She had just walked a dozen steps when she saw Zhan Shideng coming her way. She intuitively wanted to shun him, but there were no alleys for her to turn into.

"Hi. Isn't this the owner of Chu Di Ju?" Zhan Shideng deliberately called out loud.

Nuannuan pretended not to hear him, knowing that he was still angry at her for losing the case.

As she headed forward, Zhan Shideng yelled: "Halt!"

Nuannuan stopped and turned to glare at him. "Were you speaking to me?"

"Yes, it was you." Zhan Shideng swallowed. "I want to let you know you did a good job bringing me to court."

"Really?" said Nuannuan with feigned joy. "It's rare to get the leader's compliment."

"But don't be glad too soon," said Zhan Shideng with gnashed teeth.

Nuannuan responded with the same smile. "All right, I'll remember the leader's advice and be happy in the future."

Zhan Shideng's twitching cheeks revealed his anger.

While turning to walk back home, Nuannuan said to herself: *Zhan Shideng, why can't we make you mad? We'll make you so furious that you'll die of your fury.*

During breakfast, Nuannuan made herself laugh heartily with any excuse she could find. First, she laughed when she saw a grain of rice stuck on the tip of her son's nose. Next, she laughed again when Kaitian passed wind. After that, she laughed at the dog gnawing at a bone with no meat attached to it. Kaitian became suspicious and, staring fixedly at her, said: "Your laugh was a bit weird. How can you laugh like this without taking a magic laughing potion?"

Nuannuan glared at Kaitian. "Why? What's the problem if I laughed? Why can't I laugh? Someone doesn't want me to, and you, Kaitian, want to deny me the pleasure, eh? Something pleasing happened to me today, and I want to enjoy myself. What can you do about me if I laugh? Ha-ha-ha."

Kaitian didn't dare make a sound. He only watched her with astonishment, wondering what in the world made her subject to capricious moods. Nuannuan laughed and laughed until tears rolled out from her eyes. As she wiped her face, she yelled: "I want to laugh and see who dares to stop me."

After breakfast, Kaitian picked up the hoe and headed out to the farmland. Nuannuan stopped him and said: "You're such a mule. There's no work left in the fields. What are you doing now?"

Kaitian answered: "There's no guest in the house. So I was thinking of finding something to do in the fields."

Nuannuan pouted in feigned anger. "Use your head. We can go and find the visitors."

Kaitian did not understand. "Where? The visitors are all from the city. How do we know who wants to come and visit the west bank of Red Lake?"

Nuannuan waved her hand. "We shall go to the east bank. I think some people are visiting the east bank. It's only that Zhan Shideng told them not to come over because there'll be no food or bed for them. We'll go to the east bank today to help the visitors come down here. We can't sit still waiting for our bankruptcy."

"Are you sure we can get tourists over?"

"Why not?"

"All right." Kaitian put down the hoe and told his mother about their plan. Later on, the couple started walking towards the pier by the lake.

They had just got on their tour boat and untied the mooring line when Ma Wu, a fishmonger, rushed over and said: "My good Brother and Sister-in-Law, you're going fishing with the tour boat, aren't you? Let's make a deal – please make sure you wholesale the fish you catch to me. I wish you, a wealthy couple, could bless me so that I can make a little fortune too."

"Sure, but you must be patient and wait." As she said this, Nuannuan started the engine.

There was no wind on the lake that day. The boat picked up speed on the peaceful lake towards the east bank. As Nuannuan watched the water part and retreat beneath the boat, she tried to remember the last time she visited the east bank. Because they could get almost everything needed around the house on Juxiang Street, Nuannuan had not paid a single visit to the east bank since her return from Beijing.

When the boat anchored, it was already midday. The busy pier surprised Nuannuan. A few years ago when she returned home, the scene had been entirely different. There were various boats for visitors on the pier in addition to fishing boats and small boats for the locals to travel. But there were now big passenger ships that would head to several major cities in Hubei Province; they were all big and beautiful. Many visitors were embarking and disembarking. Various vendors were selling snacks, beverages and small souvenirs alongside the pier.

Kaitian window-shopped with great interest. He stopped at a stall selling noodles with lamb, sniffed at the lamb slices and ordered two dishes.

Nuannuan heard him and stopped him with a glare before dragging him away. "You only remember eating. Are you a hungry ghost?"

Kaitian laughed. "The sun says it's afternoon. Isn't your stomach rumbling?"

"Let's go to the long-distance bus station and see if anyone wants to go and see the west bank."

There was a parking lot by the side of the main road where coaches and cars were parked. From their plates, it could be deduced that some were from cities in the province, while some others were from Beijing and Hebei; still others were from counties in Nanfu City, and two coaches had just arrived from the provincial capital. Seeing the visitors stepping off the coaches, Nuannuan dragged Kaitian and walked towards them in haste, preparing to ask whether or not some might want to visit the west bank. Suddenly, a familiar voice arose in the centre of the crowd: "Dear visitors, the west bank of Red Lake is not open for tourism. Please plan your trip accordingly."

Nuannuan and Kaitian looked at each other in surprise. They both squeezed into the crowd and found out it was the village hooligan Zhan Xiao'er, who had done nothing but snatch free meals. Kaitian gripped his collar in anger and slapped his face. "You son of a bitch, what bullshit are you yelling about? Who told you the west bank is closed?"

Zhan Xiao'er was shocked and upset. He was about to shout back when he realised it was Kaitian and Nuannuan. He looked defeated and tentatively asked: "Are you Brother Kaitian and… Sister-in-Law?"

Kaitian grabbed him by the ear and said with great anger: "I've been wondering why my Chu Di Ju has been vacant all these days. It was you who spoiled our business. You son of a bitch!

Come with me to the police station and see what they make of you."

"Please, please don't, Big Brother Kaitian," pleaded Zhan Xiao'er as he took a step back.

"What have I done to you to make you hate me so much?" Kaitian took out a knife that he used to peel radish and waved it in front of Zhan Xiao'er, threatening to cut his ear. He looked ferocious and shouted: "I'll cut your ears off and throw them to the dogs if you can't give me a good explanation today."

"I... I..."

Nuannuan, who had been standing aside and watching everything, suddenly asked: "Is there someone else behind this?"

"Yes... No..."

"How much does Leader Zhan pay you to do this?" Nuannuan asked in a calm voice.

Zhan Xiao'er did not expect the question. "How did you know it was the leader's idea?"

"Just answer my question. How much?" Nuannuan asked again, staring into his eyes.

"Three yuan – enough for a pepper soup and a steamed bun," Zhan Xiao'er answered. He sounded quite satisfied. "Six dimes for a pepper soup, and four for a steamed bun on the east side of the lake. A good meal."

Kaitian raised his knife again. "You bastard! You betrayed us for a meal?"

Nuannuan pushed Kaitian's hand away and looked at Xiao'er. "I have another job for you, six yuan per day. Are you in or not?"

Xiao'er showed some interest. "What am I supposed to do? Is it hard?"

"You work here. Same job, different words."

"What words shall I yell out, then?"

"Dear visitors, you are all welcome to visit the west bank, where the mysterious triangle, the Great Wall of Chu, Lingyan Temple and the beautiful lakeside are awaiting you. You are welcome to stay in Chu Di Ju in Chu Wang Village, where you can find all the convenience and hospitality."

"Just like that?" Xiao'er's eyes were wide in surprise.

Nuannuan nodded in confirmation. "Just like that."

"OK, I'll do it."

"Dangen's dad, give him the money for three days," said Nuannuan as she turned to Kaitian.

Kaitian hesitated, but eventually he gave eighteen yuan to Xiao'er.

"You must make sure at least one group of visitors goes to the west bank every three days. The group can be big or small, but there must be a guarantee of getting one group at least," said Nuannuan as she stared fixedly at Xiao'er again. "Of course, it's better if you can send some people over every day. Also, every three days, I'll send a boat here to pick up the visitors. When there's no boat from us, you can send them on someone else's boat. With every visitor who stays in Chu Di Ju, you'll earn one extra yuan. If you send over a group of more than twenty visitors, you'll earn an extra ten yuan."

"Are you serious?" Xiao'er was overtaken by amazement.

Nuannuan stared at him. "My words are as real as the money we just gave you. When have I lied to anyone?"

"Great. I'll show you what I can do." Xiao'er spoke with great excitement.

"Another thing – if you loaf on the job, I have ways to deal with you. I'll cut all your payment, and you'll go back to your days when you couldn't get regular meals to satisfy your stomach. We'll tell the leader you initiated the idea to work for us. He hates betrayal, and he will show you. Kaitian has an uncle living here by the east bank, and he has six sons – you don't want to upset them or they'll..."

Xiao'er panicked and said: "Please don't. Why would I want to loaf on such a good job?"

Having parted with Xiao'er, the couple went to the noodles-and-lamb eatery. While eating, Kaitian growled: "I didn't expect that son of a bitch Zhan Shideng to play such a low-down trick and stab us in the back. It's lucky we came over. Otherwise, we'd still be in the dark, thinking that no one was interested in crossing to the west bank."

"I told you Zhan Shideng wouldn't take his defeat lying down."

"I'll confront him tomorrow and ask him why."

Nuannuan stared at him. "What will you ask? Can your question stop him from giving us trouble and make him helpful? Leave him alone and see what other tricks are up his sleeve. Let him use all of them. From tomorrow on, our family's tour boat will come over here once a day to take visitors. The boat must come here every day with or without visitors so that everyone here will know about the regular shuttle to the west bank. We also need to find someone who can do good calligraphy and put up a sign to introduce the scenic spots on the west bank, including the Great Wall of Chu, Lingyan Temple and the Soul-Bewildering Zone. We'll have him write about the delicious food – green beans, sesame leaf noodles, mushrooms with free-range eggs, wild mushrooms with stewed chicken, fresh carp from Red Lake stewed with soy sauce and the special yellow rice wine. We'll carry the signs on the boat and put them up right here so that it attracts people's attention and their curiosity about the west bank."

"Sure, sure."

"One more thing – be smart and watchful. We must guard against Zhan Shideng and prevent him from stabbing us from the back."

"Sure, sure."

On the evening of the third day after they came back from the east bank, more than twenty visitors arrived on the Kuangs' boat and some other boats. Some heard about the west bank from Xiao'er, some saw the sign and others read the articles about the Great Wall of Chu. They were the first group of guests after Chu Di Ju reopened. Nuannuan was very happy about the fresh start. She occupied herself with the guests and hurried Shallot to start cooking the meals. Kaitian met Spotty Laosi, the tour guide, and the boatman, Jiuding, about the visitors' schedule. The couple did not go back to their room until the visitors finished their dinner. It was by then that they realised that they, too, needed to have some food. However, before they could make it to the kitchen, they heard Zhan Shideng's voice in the darkness not far away.

"You've got tourists again, eh? Congratulations."

Stunned, Nuannuan and Kaitian turned around. They saw Zhan Shideng strolling over from the nearby shadow, wearing a smiling, congratulatory expression. Nuannuan instantly knitted her brows and responded coldly: "Thank you, Leader, for your blessing."

"He-he." Zhan Shideng forced a smile and then turned to Kaitian. "Counting your money again. You're a lucky guy, Kaitian."

With Zhan Shideng's hiring of Zhan Xiao'er to sabotage the Chu Di Ju business in mind, Kaitian snorted with resentment.

"I've come over here to give you an announcement," said Zhan Shideng with a smile. "The road leading to the hill will be closed tomorrow. I sent someone up to do some maintenance. It will be open soon."

Kaitian was angry to hear his words. "Close the road? We've got visitors here, and they must go to see the Great Wall of Chu tomorrow."

"That's why I'm here tonight so that you can change their plan. Tell them to come next time. There's ample time, isn't there?"

"You!" Kaitian was too angry to talk back.

Nuannuan stared at Zhan Shideng with a smirk. She knew what he meant by blocking the road. She would have argued with him angrily and cursed him: *You bastard! How can you push people around like this?* But she was aware that debating with him would not make him relent but could only prompt him to conspire further against them with the power in his hands. "All right, we'll swallow the insult for another time," she said with the calmest possible tone. "Thank you, Leader, for groping in the dark to inform us and for thinking of us. We'll remember your kindness…" Seeing Zhan Shideng disappear in the darkness, Nuannuan spat on the ground and said with her teeth clenched: "Kaitian, one day, even with the slightest possibility, I'll make you the leader."

"Are you insane? Who will let me be the leader? My ancestors do not grant that type of wish."

"There'll be an election soon. We must think of some way to pull him off the position."

"Let's focus on tomorrow's plan. The visitors will not be satisfied if they can't go to see the Great Wall of Chu because we especially introduced that on the sign by the east bank. Most of them are here exactly for the wall."

"Who said we're not going? Zhan Shideng is closing one road, so we'll find another one leading to the wall."

"Another road? The hill is steep."

"A couple of years ago, they forbade us from getting firewood from the hill. But Dad and I sneaked to the hill and found a trail at the end of the cornfield belonging to the Fan family. If you split the grass and bushes, you'll see it. Part of that trail is steep, so we must find a good ladder."

Kaitian was not fully convinced. "Are you sure?"

"I am. Tomorrow, I'll take the visitors, and you should simply follow us. Bring a ladder with you."

The next morning after breakfast, Nuannuan gave Dangen to her mother-in-law and talked to Shallot and Huiyu about dinner preparation. Kaitian made some arrangements around the house too. Then the couple took the visitors out.

At the entrance to the village, they bumped into Zhan Shideng, who asked in a raised voice and with a smug smile: "Kaitian and Nuannuan, what scenic spots are you taking your guests to? Lingyan Temple? Why do you bring a ladder with you?"

Nuannuan ignored him and only hemmed and hawed as a response. Before they reached the small trail, Nuannuan raised her voice and said to the visitors: "In order to make our trip to the Great Wall of Chu more exciting, we're taking this dangerous trail into the hill. You can experience how steep the landscape is here in the domain of Chu."

The visitors were not angry at all. Instead, they were excited. "That's exactly what we're looking for."

Though they did not climb up the hill at a reasonable speed, the trip went smoothly. When the visitors, all covered in sweat, saw the Great Wall of Chu on top of the hill, they all shouted out in excitement and satisfaction…

Before dark, Nuannuan and Kaitian led the tourists down the hill and back to the village. The couple were about to wash their faces when Spotty Laosi came into the yard with joy. He said to the couple: "Good heavens, you drove Leader Zhan crazy today."

Kaitian was stumped. "What made him mad?"

But Nuannuan knew the reason. She asked: "How crazy was he?"

"He poured out a torrent of abuse on the youngsters who sold tickets at the end of the road leading up to the wall. He called them fools and blamed them for not having notified him about the other route to the Great Wall of Chu. He said if he had known the alternative way, he'd have sold you the tickets to earn over two hundred yuan himself. He was so mad that he slapped himself on his arse and repeatedly said he had let you off easily."

Spotty Laosi's account brought a smile to Nuannuan's face, which had been stern for the whole day. Raising her voice, she asked Sister-in-Law Shallot to heat a few bowls of rice wine and then said: "I'll drink to my heart's content and toast Brother Spotty Laosi."

The next group of visitors arrived two days later. There were a dozen of them. Zhan Shideng did not close the road this time. Instead, he asked them to buy tickets to enter the hill. Spotty Laosi was the tour guide, so Nuannuan only walked the group to the end of the road and turned back after they had entered the wooden gate with tickets. Nuannuan said to herself smugly: *Zhan Shideng, do you accept defeat? What other tricks can you play?*

Just then, she heard Zhan Shideng calling her from behind: "Is this the proprietress of Chu Di Ju?"

Nuannuan turned back and saw him walking out of the small ticket office. She calmed herself down and asked in a plain voice: "Can I help you?"

"It's nothing important," said Zhan Shideng with a smile. "Just so you know, for the sake of the protection of the wall and for the ecology around the hill, we'll be closing this whole hill very soon. After that, anyone who uses any trail and dares to enter the hill will be severely punished."

Nuannuan's face went stiff. She involuntarily shuddered at his words. She knew that there would be no way she could continue her business of taking visitors to the wall once the higher authorities issued an order to close the hill. *Zhan Shideng, now I know how ruthless you are.*

Zhan Shideng gloated while sounding considerate. "When you have tourists in the future, you can take them to tour Lingyan Temple and the mist in the middle of the lake."

"That's true." Nuannuan tried her best to sound as calm as possible, but she was upset. She knew that without the chance to see the wall, the number of tourists was bound to decrease dramatically. When she turned back to walk home, her legs were visibly shaking.

As soon as Nuannuan got home, she summoned Kaitian over to discuss the situation. Neither of them knew what to do. If the hill was closed to protect the environment, it would be a righteous reason that they could not challenge.

Eventually, Kaitian said: "How about we write a letter to Uncle Tan in Beijing and see if there's anything he can do?"

Nuannuan thought about it and nodded. "OK. You write the letter now and make sure to include the details. You must go to Juxiang Street to send it this afternoon."

There was no reply a dozen days after the letter was sent, and Nuannuan grew more anxious with each day that passed. During that time, Zhan Shideng had a dozen planks put in front of the village committee office, each with *Hill closed for environment protection* written with red paint. The hill would be closed when the planks were moved to the hill. "Uncle Tan, please hurry. Haven't you received our letter? Maybe you're feeling unwell?"

One afternoon during lunchtime, the Kuangs heard a familiar voice from outside the yard gate. "Kaitian and Nuannuan, are you home?"

The couple turned and saw Mr Tan Wenbo walking in with two men who looked like officials.

The couple walked up in excitement. "Uncle Tan!"

"Wow, look at your place. New houses. You've got a talent for business." Uncle Tan repeatedly complimented them as he looked around Chu Di Ju with a satisfied smile.

Nuannuan smiled and invited them to take a seat. "It's you who taught us to earn money from tourism."

"I shall introduce you," said Uncle Tan as he pointed at the two men who came with him. "This is Lao Cao from the Culture Bureau of the provincial government. This is Xiao Zhao from the Culture Bureau of the county office. They have both visited the wall secretly and offered support to my research." He then introduced Nuannuan and Kaitian. "This is the couple I talked about. I stayed with them every time I came here."

The two men shook hands with Nuannuan and Kaitian amicably. Lao Cao sat down and said: "Xiao Zhao and I both read the letter you wrote. We came here with Mr Tan to talk with you about the Great Wall of Chu. At the moment, the government does not have a spare budget for the renovation of the wall, but we must begin protection efforts at once. And how should we do that? Of course, closing the hill is one way, but it's also a silly way. Having visitors to the wall is not a bad thing. The wall is made of stone, and sightseeing won't easily harm it. Moreover, if the visitors could learn to adore the culture of Chu and increase their affections towards our nation, that will be a very satisfying result."

"You're right. But our Leader Zhan Shideng insisted on closing the hill," said Nuannuan angrily.

"We can't leave the Great Wall of Chu with no one to care for it at all," said Lao Cao. "If visitors climb up and down the wall causing the stones to fall and the wall to collapse, that would be very serious. We must think of the best way to protect the wall and promote tourism at once."

"I have an idea," said Uncle Tan. "We should establish a tourism company that will take charge of the Great Wall of Chu. The company will sell tickets and hand in half the income to the Culture Bureau for the sake of further renovation and protection. The company needs a manager, some tour guides, security guards, cleaners and ticket sellers."

Xiao Zhao, who had kept silent, nodded and said: "That's a good idea."

"Who shall be put in these posts?" asked Lao Cao. "Will the village committee run this company?"

"If they don't, we'll do it." Nuannuan hastened to answer while winking at Kaitian.

Kaitian hurriedly added: "Yes, we'll do it."

"It's good to hear you say that," said Lao Cao as he stood up. "We shall go and talk to your village Party secretary and the leader of the village committee."

"Our Party secretary has been sick for a long time. It's the leader who makes all decisions for the village," said Nuannuan.

"Then it's the leader we shall talk to."

Nuannuan took Uncle Tan, Lao Cao and Xiao Zhao to the village committee. She felt that would be her opportunity: if Zhan Shideng would not help with the company, she would do it. If he would, then she would settle with the money from the accommodation.

Much as Nuannuan had expected, Zhan Shideng was quite unhappy to hear that the hill should not be closed. Yet he could not lose his temper in front of officials such as Lao Cao and Xiao Zhao. He looked even more upset when he heard about the company and the handover of half the income. He rejected the offer coldly and said: "Do you think it's right to start up a company? With the mere income of ticket sales, how much can we have left if we give half to you? We never had many visitors to the west bank. What if we have only a hundred visitors every month? At ten yuan for one ticket, we could not earn more than a thousand yuan. Not to mention the salaries of the tour guides, cleaners, ticket salespeople and security guards. If we have to give half of the income to you, the village committee will be working in vain."

"This company is not set up for the sake of immediate profit – we're protecting the cultural heritage left by our ancestors," said Uncle Tan.

"You're only talking, but it's we who have to do the actual work. How can we farmers live without making a profit? If you didn't have the state retirement pension, how could you have this leisure time to come and study the wall?" Zhan Shideng was blunt as he thought he was talking to nobody but a retired researcher.

"If it's too difficult for the village committee, then forget it. We will find someone else." Lao Cao waved his hand, unhappy with Zhan Shideng's attitude.

"What fool would run such a loss-making business?" Zhan Shideng gave Lao Cao a hateful look.

Nuannuan suddenly spoke up. "We Kuangs will do it."

Zhan Shideng stared at her in anger and kept his silence. After a while, he laughed coldly and said: "Do it if you like."

"Xiao Zhao, we shall see this through, then," said Lao Cao as he turned to Xiao Zhao. "You should draft a contract of intent under the name of the bureau and have Nuannuan sign it. After the establishment of the company, you should sign a formal contract again."

"No problem."

On her way home that day, Nuannuan was filled with joy. Of course, she knew that little profit could be earned from the sale of tickets to the Great Wall of Chu. But with the support from the bureau to run this business, Zhan Shideng could no longer make trouble with her, and she could earn more money from Chu Di Ju with more visitors. The profit should be good combined with the money from tour guiding.

That night, Nuannuan warmed up some yellow rice wine and cooked a full dinner for Uncle Tan, Lao Cao and Xiao Zhao. Uncle Tan raised the bowl of wine and said solemnly: "Kaitian, Nuannuan, with this contract signed, we're putting this Great Wall of Chu into your protective hands. Though the origin of the wall is still of academic dispute, it's in effect one of the heritages left to us by our ancestors. This is the true value of the wall that makes your place worth visiting. You must remember to protect it from further harm while you earn money from visitors. Otherwise, you'll be the shame of your ancestors."

"Rest assured, Uncle Tan," said Nuannuan with full respect as she put down the bowl on the table. "The improvement of our family's life has much to do with the Great Wall of Chu left to us by our ancestors. So we feel quite attached to it as well."

The next day Lao Cao and Xiao Zhao left, while Uncle Tan stayed in the village for another five days. He went to see the wall every day. Nuannuan asked Kaitian to keep him company, but Uncle Tan rejected the offer – he told them he was quite familiar with the hill and that he could follow the visitors who would go there every day. He told the couple to work on the company.

Nuannuan occupied herself with the establishment of the company. Before Uncle Tan's departure, Nuannuan said to him: "Uncle Tan, we went to the township and the county office these last few days, and the establishment of the company is on its way. Since you named our Chu Di Ju, could you please name the company as well?"

Uncle Tan thought for a while and wrote down: *South Water Landscape Company*.

Kaitian did not understand. He asked: "What is South Water?"

Nuannuan smiled and answered: "Red Lake is involved in the South-to-North Water Diversion Project. Of course people from the north will call it 'south water'."

Kaitian nodded and said: "Yes, that's right. Our company runs the landscape near the south water. It's a perfect name."

Kaitian drove the boat to take Uncle Tan back to the east bank. Nuannuan saw them off at the pier. When bidding them farewell, Uncle Tan said to Nuannuan: "In Hebei, there's a village called Shou Ling, meaning 'to guard the mausoleum'. Nobody knew why the village had such a particular name until the discovery of the mausoleum of Liu Sheng, a prince of the Han Dynasty two thousand years ago. The name of your village, Chu Wang Village, seems like a similar mystery. I don't think it's because a family of the surname Wang lived here. I asked the seniors in the village, and no one talked about a Wang family. So I have my hypothesis."

Nuannuan was confused.

"Maybe there are some other secrets of the ancient Chu State hiding in this village."

"Secrets?" Nuannuan was amazed. "What type of secrets?"

Uncle Tan smiled. "It's just my hypothesis. I would surely tell you if I knew what the secrets were…"

Nuannuan looked at the boat sailing away. She turned to look at the lakeside, the village and the hill, and said to herself: *Are there really secrets of Chu hiding in my village?*

The Kuangs officially established South Water Landscape Company a couple of weeks later. The plate with the company's name was on the gate to Chu Di Ju. On the morning of the opening, Nuannuan said to Kaitian: "To celebrate this day with a big bang, you should buy some firecrackers and light them in front of the gate."

Kaitian nodded. "Sure."

The loud noise of firecrackers attracted both adults and children in the village. People looked with curiosity at the plate with red characters on a white background…

Leaning on a cane, Grandma Five, who was illiterate, said to Kaitian in bewilderment: "You rascal! What are you doing with that thing?"

Kaitian hurriedly explained: "We're running a company."

"What's the benefit of running a company?"

"Making money," replied Kaitian.

"Do you mean a company is a cucumber? And how can a cucumber make money?"

"No, a company and a cucumber are different things." Kaitian felt awkward as he found it hard to make himself understood by the uneducated grandma.

The pair triggered a burst of laughter in the crowd. Nuannuan rushed over and helped Grandma Five into the courtyard.

Kaitian was registered as the manager of the company. However, Nuannuan was the one in charge of the business. On the evening of the company's establishment, Nuannuan said with all seriousness to Kaitian in bed: "Now that you're the manager of the South Water Landscape Company, tell me – what shall we do next?"

Grabbing Nuannuan's breasts, Kaitian grinned cheekily. "I don't want to think too much. Except for lovemaking, you oversee everything, and I'll follow your instructions."

Nuannuan gently punched him on his forehead and said: "Shame on you."

She put the affairs of the company under four categories: tour guiding, where she put Spotty Laosi in charge of taking the visitors to see the wall, the lakeside and the temple; boat management, where Jiuding was in charge of taking visitors around in boats; accommodation and meals, where Shallot was the head of food, drinks and rooms; and finance, where Kaitian managed the sale of tickets to the wall and boats, tour guiding fees and accommodation fees. Nuannuan agreed with Spotty Laosi, Jiuding and Shallot that they would be paid 450 yuan every month, and the number would rise or fall according to their performance. Because of the clear division of work and the good pay, the three of them were highly motivated to make the company work.

Nuannuan had the village carpenter make a new wooden sign and painted it white. She had someone write on it with red paint: *South Water Landscape Company welcomes you to the beautiful west bank!* Jiuding and Black Bean shipped the sign across and put it up on the east bank. More visitors were willing to come to the west bank because there was a functional tourism company, and Chu Di Ju was fully booked every night. With more visitors, came more income for the company. Kaitian could not control his smiling face every night when counting the money.

The autumn harvest had arrived as the days passed in Chu Di Ju, where everyone was busy receiving guests. People in Chu Wang Village were happy to see their corn cobs bursting out of the husks, the green beans getting bigger and darker, the sweet potatoes fruiting out of the soil, the cotton flaunting their white flowers and the peppers in the fields turning as red as the setting sun. Everything was telling people to get ready for the harvest. Knowing that everyone working in the company had crops in their fields, Nuannuan had them rotate working hours so that some could go home to help with the harvest.

One morning shortly after the guests were just getting up, Kaitian and Nuannuan went to do their farm work, planning to harvest all the maize in the field by the side of the lake before lunch. Spotty Laosi was taking a group of more than twenty visitors to

Lingyan Temple when he passed by and stopped to joke with Kaitian. "Brother, be careful when you break the maize ears off. Don't let the ears hurt the thing in your crotch. Then, your labour would be worthless."

Upon hearing this, Kaitian threw a maize ear at Spotty Laosi's crotch and yelled: "Take this maize ear with your thing."

Spotty Laosi dodged it. Their boisterous antics enabled the visitors to recognise the company's manager Kaitian and his wife working in the fields and stop to watch them harvesting the corn. This group of visitors were all from an IT company in Zhongguancun, Beijing, and few had seen anyone working in a field. Out of curiosity and excitement, one visitor suggested that they take a picture of them breaking off maize ears. Nuannuan was glad and said: "Sure, take any picture you like."

The visitors all went into the field to take pictures as they harvested the maize. One visitor asked: "Can we take the maize we harvested home as a souvenir?"

Quick-thinking Nuannuan nodded. "Yes you can. But one yuan for every maize ear you take."

"OK." The visitors were more than happy to pay. They did not mind paying such a low price and began looking for the biggest corn to take. Finally, each took at least two corns with them. One even took six. Kaitian made close to one hundred yuan that morning simply by selling the corns. When the visitors left for the temple, Kaitian said to Nuannuan in satisfaction: "Now I understand why people always say that those who have money will earn more money. At the start, it was so difficult for us to even earn one yuan. But now we just got one hundred without doing anything."

Nuannuan thought about it for a while and said: "Do you see what I see from this?"

Kaitian did not understand. "What is it?"

"We can earn money from one more tourist activity just like this."

"Yes?"

"The harvest," said Nuannuan as she patted her thigh. "Local people like us only feel tired with the harvest work here in the village. But those city people, they feel excited about it. We'll take them to harvest green beans, red peppers, sweet potatoes, cotton and peppercorns in the fields. They can work there for as long as they want and take away as much as they like, as long as they pay us. They'll stay longer in the village, and we'll earn more money by providing them accommodation."

"Great! Another way of making money. My wife is a genius."

As he said this, he covered Nuannuan's lips with a kiss, but she hurriedly pushed him away with a glare. "People may see us." Then she thought for another while and said: "This reminds me of the orchards in Beijing."

"What orchards?"

"They open their orchards to visitors from the city so that they can pick their fruit. People in the suburbs of Beijing open the gardens up to earn money from the visitors."

Kaitian was amazed. "Making money just like that? What do they grow in the gardens?"

"I've never been there. I was working hard. But I guess vegetables and fruits – aubergines, cucumbers, pumpkins, tomatoes, grapes, peaches, pears, apples. People living in the city feel confined, so they easily get animated about farm work. I'm thinking that in the future, we can open similar gardens in the village and attract more visitors."

"Let's try it next spring in our contracted fields," said Kaitian as he rolled up his sleeves.

"Sure. Let's give it a try…"

The next day, a group of visitors arrived from the east bank. They were all from the city of Tianjin, and there were dozens of them. Nuannuan and Shallot came to the pier to welcome them. As Nuannuan was busy greeting the visitors stepping out of the boats, she heard a cynical voice behind her. "The proprietress of the company is busy with her business."

She turned and looked. The smile vanished from her face, and she said in a stern voice: "What can I do for you, Leader?"

"Your prosperous business tells me you're making a fortune. I'm here to ask if you want to hire someone to count your banknotes. I can be as fast and accurate as you want."

"Go home and count your own money!" rapped Nuannuan.

She had just turned to leave the lakeside when Zhan Shideng shouted: "Hold on!"

Nuannuan stopped, turned around and glared at him. "Spill it if you want to say anything."

"It's time to elect the leader," said Zhan Shideng, his voice suddenly turning soft. "According to the requirement of the township office, I must notify every family in the village about the election. If anyone from the township office comes here to ask, remember to tell them that I did this."

Nuannuan frowned and asked: "When is the election?"

"Next month. You need not prepare anything – just come over to vote."

Nuannuan stared at Zhan Shideng fixedly, smirking secretly. *Zhan, you think you can fool us into casting a ballot to keep you in your post, right? You're daydreaming. I'll do everything possible to keep you from being re-elected. You bastard! Your days are numbered. We needn't get prepared? We'll surely get everything prepared. We'll be ready to vote you out of your position. Let's wait and see.* Nuannuan was tight-lipped and walked away...

Nuannuan's was preoccupied as she ate dinner. She called out to Kaitian as she put her bowl down. "Dangen's dad! Come here a minute." Then, she went into the bedroom.

Kaitian believed Nuannuan was going to ask about the day's income, and he entered the room, saying excitedly: "Five thousand, five hundred – equal to a year and a half's income from farming."

"I'm not asking about money. I want to talk to you about our influence in the village."

Kaitian did not expect this. "Influence? What influence?"

"Do you want to be the village leader?"

Kaitian laughed. "Wanting is one thing. What man doesn't want to become an official? Every time I make a request to Zhan Shideng, he torments me. I think to myself that if I, Kaitian, were to become the leader, he would see my real strength. But do you think it would really be possible? And who would want me to be leader? Would Zhan Shideng even allow it?"

"Next month, there'll be another election to elect a new leader."

"But isn't the new election just to re-elect Zhan Shideng? Wasn't the last election just like this? His family has connections in all of the villages and the county, and these days you need connections high up to be an official."

"A village leader is elected by a vote from the entire village, and if the villagers don't vote for him, he won't get it, even if people high up want him in."

"The Zhan family outnumbers us Kuangs and your Chus put together. Do you think any Zhan would vote for us? Not only that, he'll keep his position by fighting tooth and nail. He has scared many into cowardice this way. Who is courageous enough to vote against him and trigger his anger? Let's not come up with such dreams."

"That's not entirely the case. As leader over the past few years, although Zhan Shideng hasn't harassed villagers with the Zhan surname, he hasn't brought much good fortune to them either, and many in the Zhan family are still so poor they can't even rub two coins together. And haven't a few of them borrowed money from us? The only Zhans who truly remain in touch with Zhan Shideng are his younger brother and sisters, and his male cousins."

Kaitian scratched his head. "You're right about that."

"So I think that our effort could decide the matter, and this is an opportunity that will never come our way again. If you really do become the village leader, Zhan Shideng can never give us trouble again. Also, it would bring much honour to the old Kuang family. Have the Kuangs ever had an official in the clan?"

"Nope. I've heard Dad say that we've worked in the fields for many generations, and our ancestors might never have had the blood of officialdom nor burned the imperial incense of official tombs."

"Let's not talk about all that superstitious nonsense. How about we just go for it?"

"But when I think of competing with Zhan Shideng for the position, I feel a little panicky."

"Bah, you good-for-nothing. What's there to be panicky about? Can he eat you like a tiger? Don't forget you're a man." Nuannuan deliberately pursed her lips. "Or we'll have Zhan Datong castrate you with a butcher's knife, so you don't have to be a man."

Kaitian smiled and pretended to untie his belt. "If you're willing to live a widow's life while I'm still alive, you can have my balls removed."

"No more joking. Let's get down to business," said Nuannuan as she gently punched Kaitian on the chest. "Stop laughing, OK? I've got something serious to discuss with you."

"OK, OK, let's get down to business. Let's do whatever you say. But if I can't get it, don't blame me and seethe with so much anger at night that you boycott me in bed."

"Well, each time we talk, you'll derail our conversation with your lustful thoughts."

"If we really are going to compete with him, we'll need an idea to go with it."

Nuannuan raised her hand and brought it down swiftly on the bedside frame. "I've already got one. Starting from tomorrow onwards, we must do more for the village folk, so they understand we are people who will bring them good fortune."

"Sounds like hot air to me. We don't have any authority, so what can we do?"

"We have some cash in our hands now, and money can make things happen."

"Like what? We use our own money?"

"We can start to do a few things for the present time. First, regardless of whether they are a Zhan or a Chu, we hire a son or daughter from each of the poorest families in the village to work in our company. We provide them with a working wage to subsidise their family expenses. Our Chu Di Ju needs a few more people to serve food, wash and change the bedding, and clean the rooms."

"Yes, this can be handled easily."

"Second, alongside the pier and by the village, we can put up some wood-board shacks with nice-looking shop fronts to sell general goods. This wouldn't cost much, and after they're put up, we can get the open-air stall traders selling alcohol, tobacco and local mountain products to move in for free. Then they won't need to deal with the whipping wind and burning sun all day – they'll probably thank us for it."

"Yes, this is a good idea too – we'll only need to spend a bit of money."

"Put in a bit, and you get out a lot. You get me? Also, this is a good way to attract more tourists for us. It allows them to see that everything here is neat and tidy, upright and honest."

"Got it."

"Third, don't the tourists like the scene of an autumn harvest?

Wouldn't they want to go and do it themselves? Go and tell Ma Sige to get a few tour guides to bring tourists into the fields of the poorest of the Zhans. They can allow them to help out by harvesting and, when possible, buying the family's produce. They'll probably thank us endlessly for that."

"That they would."

"Fourth, go and buy some pencils, erasers, pencil cases and homework books for primary school students, a couple of hundred yuan worth, and give them as gifts to each family with a primary student. Tell them that this will help the children to attend school, and show them that, as the Kuangs earn more money, we can expand our aid to subsidise one year's school fee for every middle school student."

"Who will go and give those gifts?"

"You, of course. This is your opportunity to be friendly with the village people."

"OK. Any other ideas?"

"One more. On the days that we have many guests, we'll introduce them to a few of the more hospitable families for accommodation and meals, and let those families earn a bit with a hosting fee. They, too, will probably thank us endlessly. Let's take the time to visit Lingyan Temple in a few days to burn incense and worship the Buddha. We can ask him to bless you so you can be elected."

Kaitian half-believed what Nuannuan said. "Does the Buddha understand things like elections and officialdom?"

"I think he does. Isn't the Buddha in charge of everything in the world?"

On the second day, Kaitian began working on the many ideas that Nuannuan had come up with. After a few weeks, the results were becoming evident.

As the villagers knew he had money in his pockets, on seeing Kaitian they used to speak to him with tones of jealousy or flattery. Nowadays, Kaitian could hear a difference; when the villagers saw him, they sounded genuinely respectful and thankful.

When Kaitian told Nuannuan about this change of tone, she laughed. "That's exactly what we want. I have also carefully taken note of it – in the past when people saw you, they would always start with a laugh and say: 'Kaitian, you fucker, you've earned more money again, have you?' And now, many people open with a warm-hearted question. 'Kaitian, busy lately?' Don't underestimate the difference between these two questions. It proves that, in the minds of the villagers, you're no longer just a wealthy man disconnected from them. This is a good start."

"Can a good start help us? I heard that the electoral commissioner has arrived, and he's staying in Zhan Shideng's house, eating and drinking with him every day. Zhan Shideng has also sent out the message that the township government has once again recommended him as the candidate."

"It doesn't matter who promotes a candidate or who himself is a candidate. Votes must come from the people in our Chu Wang Village, and no one from the township and county would dare to vote in our stead. Two days ago, I secretly called the big brother who guards the township government gates. According to him, electing a leader is based on the number of votes. Whoever gets the most votes is the leader. So you need not worry about Zhan Shideng. Let them recommend him as the candidate, and if more people vote for you, then you'll be the leader without any recommendation from above. What we need to worry about is letting more people know that once you do become the leader, you'll bring more benefits to the village folk than Zhan Shideng does."

Kaitian's eyes were wide open as he asked: "So apart from all of the ideas that we have now, what else should we do?"

"I've thought about it. Take a big sheet of white paper and write with a brush all of the things that you want to do after becoming the leader. Stick it on the village committee office wall so that the whole village knows what things you are willing to do after you step up to the position."

Kaitian scratched his head. "What things will we do for the villagers? I've never really thought about that."

"Well, you give it a good thought. If you're going to become the leader, you'll have to use your brains a bit more."

"To increase the yearly income of every household," Kaitian probed while tugging at his ear.

"Yes, it's better to have a figure so that every villager will understand at first sight. My thought is – if you really become the leader, you should increase the yearly household income by three hundred to five hundred yuan. Sound OK?" Nuannuan looked at Kaitian, smiling.

"Damn, we'll need a plan for it to be OK."

"I've heard from some of the tourists staying at Chu Di Ju that our locally produced sweet potato could be transported and sold to the east bank vermicelli factory for two cents more per jin. And if our local duck eggs, chilli peppers, hawthorn, fungus and Sichuan peppers are transported to the city on the east bank, they could all be sold for about twice the price. When the time comes, you should organise people to purchase goods here at a price higher than the west bank but lower than the east bank, then transport them by boat to the city on the east bank to sell. This way, the villagers can earn a bit more, and the buyers can benefit too. Isn't this a good idea? Also, I heard a tourist from Beijing say that the type of magnolia tree we plant on either side of our local houses not only looks pleasant but also has medicinal and fragrance properties. Inside its flower buds, you'll find eucalyptus oil, lily magnolia essence and much more. They can be used as a medicine to cure diseases and also as a perfume. I've heard that a factory has been built on the east bank to make perfume, specifically from collecting the flower buds of the magnolia. I remember Uncle Black Bean went to the east bank to sell the flowers, and Zhan Shideng relied on the sale of magnolia flower buds to earn lots of money. If you become the leader, you must go and find out, and make an agreement with the factory, and afterwards call on every family to plant magnolia trees on either side of their houses. As this kind of magnolia grows quickly, two to three years after planting, the flower buds will be ready to collect, and when that time comes, wouldn't every family be able to sell the buds to earn some money? I also heard somebody from Tianjin say that nowadays, city folk are interested in eating edible wild herbs. Now, don't we have lots of them growing on the other side of the mountain? When that time comes, and when all of the families have time, everybody can go up the mountain, collect the herbs, dry them in the sun and then sell them. This is another way to earn money, right?"

"Oh my, you certainly know more than I do."

"You need to use your ears and listen more when these city folk are here. They've seen more and have a wider range of knowledge, so while we provide them accommodation, we must also learn a little from them."

"Yes, from these ideas, I feel the courage to write a pledge down on paper. I'll write: 'Grandmas, grandpas, uncles, aunties, brothers and sisters. If you choose me, Kuang Kaitian, to become the village leader, I promise that each year, I will add three hundred to five hundred yuan more to the basic income in every household.'"

"To put it in this way makes you seem like a true man."

"I'll write it just like that. Now, off to buy a big sheet of paper and a brush."

Kaitian's campaign pledge was put up on the village committee's gable at high noon, and immediately Chu Wang Village exploded with the news. People came one after another, still carrying their food bowls to have a look. Some reacted with surprise, others with excitement, tapping on the rims of their bowls with chopsticks. "Goodness, that Kaitian has some guts. He's not afraid to go toe-to-toe with Leader Zhan." Yet others reacted with worry, going to the Kuang family household and whispering to Nuannuan: "Be careful now – you don't know what people will do to your family." Nuannuan only smiled and said nothing.

An older man named Baogui rushed over and whispered to Kaitian: "You have my vote because of the few hundred yuan alone."

Sister-in-Law Shallot didn't say anything but gave Nuannuan a thumbs-up.

That day, Zhan Shideng was entertaining cadres from the township, and it was already late afternoon by the time he learned about it all and came running to see. In shock, he did not move from that spot for a long time.

He had been re-elected as leader for years, but it was the first time anyone had run against him. Anger filled every cell in his lungs, and he squeezed out a slur from them. "You're fucking boasting. Can you keep your promise?"

With that, he was about to tear off the poster when Nuannuan passed by and saw his move. She stopped him by yelling: "I don't think it proper for you to tear off what we've posted up there, do you? What's written up there has nothing to do with you, and the wall on which it is pasted isn't yours. What grounds do you have to remove it?"

Zhan Shideng was at a loss for words. He knew that Kuang Kaitian wasn't violating the election regulations with what he had written, and it was unreasonable for him to tear it. So, he turned around and shouted viciously at Nuannuan: "Competing with me for the leader's position – who do you think you are? You're too fucking self-confident and conceited."

Nuannuan feigned a smile. "Then you don't even have to get rid of the poster. You can just treat it as a joke that Kaitian is playing on you, can't you."

Zhan Shideng had to walk to the village committee office in anger.

The election day was close now. After supper, Nuannuan dragged Dangen around, dropping by the most impoverished families in the village. She did not mention the election but instead drew out daily conversation, chatting about their children, the crops and poultry foul, and giving some advice on earning money, speaking with the families until she felt a genuine friendship growing. Nuannuan used this tactic to bring many people onside with Kaitian.

On the morning of the first day of formal voting, Nuannuan said to Kaitian: "We should go to Lingyan Temple to pray to the Buddha for getting elected."

Kaitian agreed readily. He bought some incense and offerings and went with Nuannuan. Upon entering the temple gate, Nuannuan caught sight of the ancient ginkgo and couldn't help remembering how she played hide-and-seek with Kaitian around it when she came to pray with her mum. Oh, so many years had passed in the blink of an eye. At that time, she was only a little girl knowing little of the world. But now, she was here to ask the Buddha to help Kaitian with his election. After setting the offerings upon the altar, burning incense and making a vow by kowtowing in the main hall, they walked out, only to see Master Tianxin, whose hair and beard had become white.

Nuannuan went up and bowed. "How are you, Master?"

Master Tianxin held his palms together in front of his chest, squinted his eyes, and tried to remember who they were. After a while, he beamed. "Long time no see. The way you both look, you must be free from hunger and cold now."

Nuannuan smiled and asked him about what she had on her mind. "Master, does the Buddha have a say in someone wanting to be an official?"

Twiddling his beard with a smile, Master Tianxin said: "So many people pray for officialdom, and they bring so many offerings that the Buddha can't satisfy everyone, even if he wants to. In my opinion, it's up to a person's luck if they can or can't become an official. But since luck often plays jokes on people, how do you know it's a good thing to be an official?"

Nuannuan didn't quite catch what the abbot said but felt too embarrassed to ask more questions. She consoled herself by thinking: *We've burned our incense anyway, so the Buddha should be intelligent enough to see through everything.*

She said goodbye to Master Tianxin, and they went home. As soon as they arrived, they learned that a meeting would convene in front of the village committee's office in the evening. The purpose of the meeting was to have a demonstration on how to cast a ballot to avoid voting mistakes the next day.

Nuannuan and Kaitian came to the meeting after supper and found the ground packed with villagers. Lao Tao, a polling monitor from the township government, presided over the meeting. He told the audience about the township government's recommendation of Zhan Shideng as the candidate before picking out fourteen villagers from the crowd. Lao Tao gave each of them a ballot and showed them how to mark them and cast their votes. He then let them rehearse the process. As it was a mere rehearsal, Zhan Shideng seemed composed, sitting there with a smile on his face. Nuannuan and Kaitian were nervous, worried that this demonstration would mislead the villagers and affect tomorrow's polling. After the fourteen villagers dropped their ballots in a box, Lao Tao had the ballot box opened and the votes counted. He then announced the result: Zhan Shideng got six votes, Kuang Kaitian got seven, and Chu Xingeng got one.

The audience abruptly fell silent. Nuannuan felt a sense of relief. Kaitian pressed her hand in secret, and the two looked at each other without saying a word. When she looked up at Zhan Shideng, she found his face had turned sullen in the dim light. He was slowly striking a match to light a cigarette. Lao Tao was still explaining to the audience: "What you saw is the whole process of polling. Just do what we've done tomorrow. One of the demonstrators did the right thing by writing a candidate on the ballot this evening. If you don't want to vote for a candidate, you can write the name of the person you prefer..."

When Nuannuan and Kaitian returned home, Dangen had gone to sleep in Kaitian's mother's arms. Nuannuan took Dangen over and, while undressing him, said to Kaitian: "We can't be happy too early. We only got one more vote from the fourteen voters. We have no idea what will happen when the actual polling takes place tomorrow. Besides, seeing a sign of disadvantage to him, he's bound to go to many villagers to canvass for himself tonight."

Kaitian panicked. "What shall we do, then?"

"I think Baiquan and Dongsheng and their families are likely to be swayed by Zhan Shideng. We should have visited them, but let's forget it. Rumours would fly around if Zhan Shideng saw us..."

Before Nuannuan's words died down, Zhan Shideng's voice flew from behind the courtyard door. "Kaitian, can you come out?" His call stunned the couple, and Kaitian cast a glance at Nuannuan. She signalled for him to go and meet Zhan Shideng, and then she followed out quietly.

"You want me, Leader?"

"Kaitian, I've got a question for you." Zhan Shideng was unusually gentle and suppressed. "Do you want to be the leader?"

"What? Well..." Kaitian scratched his head anxiously, evidently caught off guard by Zhan Shideng's candidness. It also took Nuannuan, who was eavesdropping behind the courtyard door, by surprise.

"If you're serious, I'll withdraw my candidacy, and I'll let you be the leader. It's petty for us brothers to compete. We'll scratch each other's back no matter who wins, won't we? I gave you my support when you built this Chu Di Ju guesthouse, right? If you're just running for the post for fun, you'd better tell the villagers tomorrow at the polling place that you don't want to become leader. Then, we won't dilute the ballots."

"Well..."

Behind the door, Nuannuan immediately realised what Zhan Shideng meant. She cursed in silence: *Zhan Shideng, how dare you still threaten us with your dirty trick.* Then she dashed out of the door, put on a smile, and said: "I see. It's Leader Zhan. Kaitian only cares for some fun. How can he dare to compete with you for the leader's position? He doesn't have the balls. Besides, since you're the township leaders' candidate, who has the guts not to vote for you? I overheard what you said just now. Sure. Kaitian will tell everyone that he doesn't want to be the leader before the voting starts tomorrow."

Kaitian threw a bewildered look at Nuannuan.

Zhan Shideng was pleased, and he chuckled. "That's good. After my re-election as the leader, I'll give your South Water Landscape Company my full support. You may rest assured. I'll feel honoured and take some credit as a leader if you become wealthy, right? OK, go back to your sleep. I've got to get going."

As soon as Zhan Shideng had turned around, Nuannuan gnashed her teeth and cursed in silence: *Arsehole! You still want to fool us at the last minute.*

Kaitian hurriedly dragged Nuannuan into the courtyard and asked in a small voice: "Are you sure we won't run any more?"

Nuannuan was speechless and just signalled Kaitian to bolt the door. She didn't speak until they were back in their bedroom. "If he can fool us, why can't we fool him?"

"You mean we'll run tomorrow?"

"Of course."

"What if he wins?"

"We'll sell the houses of Chu Di Ju at a discount price, leave the village, take our parents and Dangen with us, and do odd jobs somewhere else."

Kaitian fell silent. After a long while, he said in a low voice: "How about we drop out of the election? Now that we've tricked him, the consequence will be severe if he wins. Then we'll become his sworn enemies, and he'll try all he can to ruin us. Just think about it. If we do odd jobs somewhere else, we'll have to travel while helping our parents and carrying our son. Do you think it'll be easy? We've come a long way and have a reasonably deep pocket. Even if Zhang Shideng becomes leader again, he can't go so far as to come down hard on us, and he may not harbour too deep a grudge. The most he can do is make things difficult for us. I don't think he'll stop us from doing our business. As long as we have our company, what's to be afraid of?"

Nuannuan heaved a deep sigh. "You think I don't know it's a better option? But I don't want to suffer from his bullying any longer. Besides, he's been making a terrible mess of the village, making it so poor. I don't want to see our native place remain so impoverished. Now that we have the opportunity, why don't we jump on it? If we lose, we'll have to grin and bear it. But with the chance available, I can't reconcile myself to giving it up."

Kaitian nodded. "As you say."

"Let's fight for it for the last time."

Nuannuan had a restless night. She couldn't go to sleep at first as she kept asking herself: *Is it the right thing to do? What if Kaitian loses the election? Are we really going to sell Chu Di Ju? Are you really going to take the whole family with you and do odd jobs away from the village? Can our aged parents stand the long journey with bumpy roads? Will Kaitian blame me for all of this?*

Later, she finally drifted off to sleep, only to stumble into a nightmare in which she and Kaitian sat on a boat with her parents-in-law heading towards the east bank. Suddenly, a fierce gust of wind sprang up and tossed the boat up and down. The boards began to break off to allow the lake water to surge into the boat...

She was startled awake and sat up with a loud cry.

Kaitian, who had been snoring, also woke up with a start, but he soon lay back and fell fast asleep. Nuannuan wiped the sweat off her forehead and slowly lay down. But she could never go back to her sleep. Her eyes were wide open till daybreak.

The next day after breakfast, the bells to start the election rang in the village. As there had been few visitors staying at Chu Di Ju over the past few days, Nuannuan had yesterday given all of her workers the morning off so that everybody could vote. Hearing the bell, Big Sister Shallot called all of the workers to follow her to the assembly place. Nuannuan watched Shallot with much gratitude and believed that if these workers were to vote, they would surely vote for Kaitian.

Nuannuan and Kaitian went to the meeting place. Before they

stepped out, Nuannuan stared at Kaitian and found him nervous. She patted him on his shoulder and said in her usual tone: "Cheer up. You're not going to an execution ground." Only then did Kaitian gather himself and go out with Nuannuan.

A dozen steps away from the meeting place, Nuannuan heard someone calling her: "Auntie!" Initially, she thought it was addressed to someone else, so she didn't stop until she heard: "Aunt Nuannuan!"

She turned her head, only to see Zhan Shideng's eldest daughter Runrun, who was standing by the roadside with her eyes fixed at her. Surprised, Nuannuan asked: "Did you call me?" Runrun nodded, beaming, and waved at her. As she walked up to Runrun, she wondered why she had called her at this moment since the two had never had close contact before. Nuannuan remembered that she had merely nodded a bit at most when running into her in the village. Her only knowledge of the girl was that she was a boarding high-school student on Juxiang Street and the apple of Zhan Shideng's eye. "What's up, Runrun?"

"My dad is over there. He said he'd like to have a word with you," Runrun said as she pointed to a corner of some walls nearby.

Nuannuan's mouth twitched and barely let out an audible smirk. *Zhan Shideng, you're so pathetic that you even take advantage of your daughter.* But on second thoughts, she knew Runrun was innocent and would be hurt if she had seen her smirking. Therefore, Nuannuan suppressed it with great effort. With a wave of her hand, she asked Kaitian to go ahead. She then headed towards the corner. As soon as she saw Zhan Shideng, Runrun said: "Auntie, I'm going to the meeting. I'll leave you to Dad."

Nuannuan went straight up to Zhan Shideng.

"Nuannuan, my good sister. Will Kaitian and you change your minds?" Though dressed up, Zhan Shideng had a pitiful look in his eyes. His back stooped a little as well.

Nuannuan pretended not to have heard him. "What did you say?" She suddenly realised that Zhan Shideng had never spoken to her in such a courteous manner in recent years.

"About Kaitian dropping out of the election."

"No, we haven't changed our minds."

Zhan Shideng nodded. "That's great if you haven't. You must tell Kaitian again to make it clear he isn't going to be part of the election.

After I get elected, I'll pay you back and make sure that your South Water Landscape Company will grow tremendously."

"Can I go now?"

"Yes, yes, you can." Zhan Shideng waved politely, looking as if he feared offending her.

While heading to the meeting place, Nuannuan said to herself: *Zhan Shideng, I wish heaven would know how much you're obsessed with being a leader and prevent you from getting elected.*

"It was her father, eh?" Kaitian asked when Nuannuan joined him.

Nuannuan nodded and said in a small voice: "The same story – he doesn't want you to run against him."

"Son of a bitch!"

Nuannuan looked up towards the sky. The weather was good – a deep blue sky with only a few white clouds, which were quickly pulled into wisps by the wind, just as poplar cotton is tugged into the sky from the ground. *Buddha, gods, without the cover of cloud, you see clearly. We contend with the leader only to escape his torment. If only you uphold this justice, then the Zhans' wish will not be granted.*

Only when she heard the sound of Lao Tao, the township cadre, did her eyes fall back to the assembly place. Lao Tao again explained the significance of the election, the reason why the township had recommended Zhan Shideng as a candidate and the customary rules and regulations of an election. He then faced the assembly and asked: "Does anybody want to say anything?"

The noisy assembly suddenly fell quiet.

"Before I distribute the ballots, anybody who wants to speak up can say something," Lao Tao again emphasised.

Nuannuan immediately sensed the glance that Zhan Shideng, who was sitting by Lao Tao, cast over her and Kaitian. She felt it scratching her body all over as if it were his hand. Nuannuan feigned ignorance and directed her eyes towards Red Lake. She spotted a fishing boat slowly drifting on the water, surrounded by a few mallards swimming around it, leaving streaks of beautiful ripples behind them.

"Do you have anything to say? You can say whatever you want. Opinions and announcements are both welcome." Lao Tao was still encouraging the villagers to speak. Nuannuan had heard from his township that he was aware of Zhan Shideng's intention to keep Kaitian out of the election.

The assembly was silent. Nuannuan guessed that Zhan Shideng must be grinding his teeth in anger at her and Kaitian. Perhaps because he found it impossible to drag on like this without any reason, Lao Tao had to announce: "Well, if nobody has anything to say, then let's distribute the ballots…"

Nuannuan's chest grew tight. She understood that if Kaitian was not voted in after this act of utterly stamping on Zhan Shideng's face, the family would have to prepare to leave the village and become migrant labourers. After filling in the ballot and putting it in the box, she did not go to speak with Kaitian or anybody else. Instead, she went by herself for a walk to the lakeside. All that was left was to wait – wait for a result that she could not predict. She knew that Zhan Shideng was also waiting, and she hoped that he was waiting in vain.

More boats appeared on the blue lake. The people on one of them were hauling their net, with several dozen aquatic birds circling the boat and squawking. Some of the fish that the fishermen had caught were the birds' favourite; otherwise, they wouldn't have been so familiar with the fishermen.

There's nothing that doesn't have a reason for its existence or appearance, Nuannuan told herself. It was true with her: she had left the crowded assembly and come to this deserted lakeside because she was afraid of the election result. She feared that if the result wasn't what she wanted, she might burst into tears on the spot. Should that have happened, she would have made a spectacle of herself.

She gazed at the water while listening out for sounds of activity from the assembly. The noise had already died down, the votes had probably already been cast, and the ballots would be called out…

She crouched down by the lake and gazed at the cogongrass, her eyes raking over its stalks and roots and the nodes thereupon. She wanted to divert her attention from the assembly by doing so. She wanted and feared to hear the announcement. There was a splash in the water close to the bank. It was a fish of the kind accustomed to swimming on the edge of a lake. She craned her neck towards the source of the splashing while guessing what kind of a fish it was. Sure enough, it was a black-backed grass carp. While foraging, the grass carp didn't expect that someone would be watching it at this time of day. So it swam unhurriedly, with its fins and tail flexing back and forth. Nuannuan, a fisher, had the urge to find fishing gear to catch this aquatic vertebrate as soon as her eyes fell upon it. But at that moment, applause came from the assembly place behind her, and her whole body trembled.

Has the result arrived?

She couldn't help but turn and look. She saw Shallot running towards her very fast, clutching her chest.

"Nuannuan, Nuannuan…"

Nuannuan held her breath.

"Voted in… Kaitian was voted in…"

The words burst over her, and the heavy weight on her chest suddenly broke into a thousand pieces. It was as though she could see the pieces falling away, and she felt a calmness she had never experienced before. At first, her legs wanted to dance. Then they went limp, and she sat down. She could hear her tears splash onto the ground.

She didn't remember how she returned home – only how Lao Tao from the township office was sitting and speaking to Kaitian, with many villagers squeezed into the yard, and Spotty Laosi and Jiuding were raising glasses of alcohol…

PART TWO
land

METAL

The next day, Nuannuan woke very late. After many days of nervousness and anxiety, followed by repeated joyous lovemaking the previous night, she was now exhausted. She slept with complete indulgence till the sun was high in the sky. Her mother-in-law heated her breakfast in the wok and told her, while she was eating, that Kaitian had gone for a meeting with the village committee. She nodded, then continued eating and, suddenly aware that she was no longer to be tormented, thought to herself that she hadn't had such a delicious meal for a long time. *What a good feeling.*

Dangen had rarely seen his mother sitting at ease after a meal, wearing a smile on her face. Upon seeing her, he rushed over and threw himself into her arms. Then, he fumbled again for the breasts that his mum had long weaned him off.

Kaitian's mother caught sight of him and yelled at her grandson: "How old are you? Aren't you ashamed to ask for your mum's breastmilk?"

Nuannuan was in a perfect mood, so she didn't scold and reject her son like before. Instead, she smiled and watched Dangen lift her blouse and place a nipple into his mouth.

Her mother-in-law reprovingly said: "If you pamper him like this, he'll become unruly."

Nuannuan smiled at her mother-in-law. As she was feeling happy, she didn't mind any complaints.

When Kaitian arrived back at midday, he said that the township had notified him to go to the government for a meeting the day after tomorrow.

Nuannuan laughed. "You should go. A township meeting is such an honour to attend. Zhan Shideng used to go to those meetings with such a smug look on his face."

Kaitian tugged at his lapel and muttered: "What, go wearing these clothes?"

"What's wrong with your clothes?"

"You never saw when Zhan Shideng went to the township meetings, did you? His clothes were always prim and proper. If I arrive in these clothes, I'll surely be the laughing stock of the meeting."

Nuannuan realised that Kaitian wanted some presentable clothing. "Well, this won't be hard to manage, right? In the afternoon, we'll go to the Liu family tailor shop in the village – they have ready-made fabrics and do fine handiwork. Tailor Liu will make some presentable clothing for you, and if it's ready in time for the meeting, there shouldn't be a problem, right?"

Kaitian nodded and laughed. "Right!"

After lunch, Nuannuan gave Dangen to Grandma, then took Kaitian to the Liu family tailor shop. When Tailor Liu saw the newly appointed leader arriving, he very warmly offered a seat and poured tea. Hearing that Kaitian wanted some clothes made up, he hurriedly brought over fabrics that the family had stowed away for Kaitian and Nuannuan to choose from.

When Nuannuan chose a light-coloured fabric, Kaitian shook his head. "No, no. Haven't you seen on the television, every leader wears dark clothes?"

Nuannuan said: "Fine. Then we need a dark blue material."

Tailor Liu asked what the design of the clothing would be, and when Nuannuan said that a jacket would be fine, Kaitian again shook his head, saying: "It should be a suit. Suits are now the government dress. Don't the big leaders you watch on TV all wear suits?"

Nuannuan laughed. "OK, OK, have a suit then."

When the suit arrived on time, delivered by Tailor Liu before dark the next day, Nuannuan at once called for Kaitian to try it on. The suit was a good fit on Kaitian, and he strolled around the yard, chest out and chin raised, asking Nuannuan: "Do I look like a leader now?"

Nuannuan laughed. "Yes, yes…"

Kaitian had two days of meetings in the township and arrived back from Juxiang Street on his bike at dusk, just as Nuannuan was at the front of Chu Di Ju arranging things with some late-arrival guests. After the guests entered the yard, Nuannuan turned her head to see Kaitian pushing his bike along with a cigarette in his mouth. "Welcome back. I didn't know you were a smoker. Why are you smoking?"

Kaitian answered with a laugh: "During the township meeting, all of the other leaders were smoking. If we don't smoke, it'll be obvious that we're out of the loop, so I started smoking."

Nuannuan wasn't too happy about this. "You learn damn fast."

"It won't do not to learn. People only see you as a leader if you always appear as one," Kaitian exclaimed with his hands spread.

So that Kaitian could focus completely on his job as leader, Nuannuan shouldered the work of the company by herself. From advertising on the east bank to attract tourists, to arranging guest accommodation in Chu Di Ju, to guiding tourists to visit the Great Wall of Chu, Lingyan Temple and the lake, it was all down to her to coordinate and manage. She was busy every day, morning till night.

A couple of weeks after Kaitian took office, Nuannuan asked him how he felt being a leader.

Kaitian thought for a second and said he felt honoured because everyone in the village vied to greet him and talk with him. He had never felt so liked.

Nuannuan said: "What's important is that you must do something substantial for the villagers. You must fulfil your campaign promises one by one so that you can live up to the expectations of those who voted for you."

Kaitian nodded. "You may rest assured that I'll do an excellent job in my capacity. At present, I'll think about how to increase each household's income. I'm planning to send someone out to get in touch with buyers of Sichuan peppercorns and chilli peppers…"

One night just before bedtime, Nuannuan still had not seen Kaitian return to have dinner, and she was anxiously awaiting him, thinking that he must be busy with the village work. Her heart skipped a beat with the thought. *Even busy men must eat.* Just as she was thinking to leave Dangen at home and go to the village office to find Kaitian, Uncle Black Bean entered the yard, propping up Kaitian, as they both staggered in. At first, Nuannuan thought that Kaitian had come down with some kind of illness, but as she stepped forward to meet them, she sensed the thick scent of alcohol coming from him – only then did she realise he was drunk. "God, where have you been drinking so heavily?" Nuannuan asked with a start. She knew that Kaitian didn't usually indulge in alcohol, only drinking a few cups when the occasional opportunity arose to accompany guests, and she had never seen him drunk before.

"At my place. Today is a good day, so the two of us drank a little more than we should have," Uncle Black Bean hurriedly explained.

Nuannuan listened, hiding her surprise. She knew that with many children, Uncle Black Bean's family was far from the wealthiest in the village. Without any money to offer a drink, how could Kaitian get drunk at his house? Nuannuan did not ask more questions, and she held up Kaitian so that Uncle Black Bean could leave. Kaitian was so drunk that he kept on sliding off onto the ground and couldn't even get into bed. Nuannuan used all of her energy to put him back into bed. Lying there, he continued to mumble: "Drink up... drink up..."

It was not until the first light of day that Kaitian became conscious, and it was then, as Nuannuan gave him a bowl of boiled water, that she was able to ask him why he had gone to Uncle Black Bean's house to drink.

Kaitian said: "He wants extra land to build a new house so that his oldest son can get married. He's asking for such a big favour, so of course he offered me a banquet. He should have sent a present too. Didn't we also send a gift to Zhan Shideng with our land ownership?"

Nuannuan hadn't seen this side of Kaitian. "His family is so poor, yet you still have the mind to drink from his cups?"

Kaitian laughed. "So poor that they can't manage one banquet for me? Actually, Black Bean's wife isn't much good with stir-fry, and her meal was rubbish compared to the daily meals that you cook."

"From this day on, you must not drink like that." It was clear from Nuannuan's tone that she was unhappy.

"OK, but I'll have to drink from time to time – otherwise, everyone will think that the leader is a good-for-nothing, that he won't even accept a meal and a drink, and after a while they'll begin to look down on me."

This annoyed Nuannuan. "Where did all this bullshit come from?"

"You wouldn't know. I heard it at the township office. They say that even when going to the Commission for Discipline Inspection, you've got to drink…"

One day after finishing dinner, Shallot hurried in looking for Nuannuan, telling her that a male guest staying at Chu Di Ju was asking for the manager. Nuannuan didn't expect this. "Is he not satisfied with our service?"

Shallot shook her head. "I don't think it's about that."

"Is he requesting a special tour?"

Shallot shook her head again. "I don't think it's about that either."

Nuannuan said: "Let's go and check it out."

The man was about forty years old, wore a formal suit and had a smart and efficient look about him as he waited at the entrance to Chu Di Ju, his gaze directed towards a distant point on the surface of the lake. Hearing Nuannuan's footsteps, he turned around and, fixing his eyes on her, said: "You're the manager?"

Nuannuan nodded her head. "What can I do for you?" She vaguely recalled that this person had stayed at Chu Di Ju a few times before and had sometimes walked around in the village.

"Are you a high-school graduate?" He looked down at Nuannuan with an air of disdain, examining her closely.

Nuannuan did not like his tone. "Yes. Why do you want to know this?"

"I can't converse with people who are not educated through high school." He then laughed with a tone of leniency. "Do you realise that your village is currently in decline?"

"Decline?"

"I've done some investigation into your village and found that about forty young and middle-aged villagers have left for odd jobs elsewhere, and eleven blocks of fields on the hill-slopes have been left to rot. The population is shrinking, and the land is going to waste. If this isn't decline, then what is?"

Nuannuan sighed. "Oh, that decline. Everybody wants to go to the cities and earn money. What else is there for them to do?"

"You're right. Our country is currently entering a phase of urbanisation, and the phenomenon we see here is one inescapable outcome. But we must also understand that though the people of our nation are many, the land is still vast, and urbanisation can't replace rural life. Now suppose the day comes when rural life is no more, and the farms are left to waste – then there will be no such thing as this idyllic scenery. This will be the true loss of our nation."

Something stirred in Nuannuan, and she began to feel warmth towards this person spreading through her chest.

"Europe already feels such a regret."

"Europe?"

"You studied geography in high school, so you should know about Europe, shouldn't you?"

Nuannuan did not reply, though her face flushed with displeasure. *Why does this man always sound as though he is lecturing me? Coupled with his arrogance, it really makes him easy to dislike.*

"Europe's urbanisation has created the decay of rural life, and as a result the idyllic scenes are being lost, the farmer populations are ageing and shrinking, and the farmlands are quickly turning into a wilderness of waste. Many places have already reverted to wilderness, and now they're beginning to worry that such idyllic scenery will be but a memory in the near future."

Nuannuan watched him in silence and had no idea what he was getting at.

"On the surface, a return to wilderness is beneficial for the environment, but in fact precisely the opposite is true. In the Peloponnesian Mountains, east of an ancient Greek city, there's a village that once had a thousand people who all toiled in the fields, with lands of green grass, orchards spread throughout and livestock on the mountains. Now only a dozen or so older people are left behind, mud washes through when it rains, the grass doesn't grow, and all of the orchards have been left to spoil. The entire place is now full of dry shrubs, wildfires are common during summer, and the whole environment is dull and lifeless. An expert from the European Environment Agency said that 'as soon as shrubs cover the plains, the grassland ecology is all but lost'. All of the flowers, grassy plants, birds and butterflies also vanished, and forests will not grow there for a few hundred years, regardless of species. Therefore, Europe has awoken to the importance of such environments, and it has begun to subsidise farmers who cut the wild grasses on the uncultivated lands on a yearly basis, in order to prevent the area from reverting to a complete wasteland."

"Please just tell me exactly what you want to say." Nuannuan was feeling a bit impatient. She still had many things to do, and there was no time to worry about the troubles of Europe.

He carried on unhurriedly. "But it's important to first go through the theory. With the support of the theory, we can move on to the practicalities, understand?"

Nuannuan forced a smile. "Well, carry on then."

"There are some indications now that decline may be happening here, but it has not yet caused serious effects. At the same time, I'm aware that your village owes its existence to excellent natural abundance. With the clear lake, the green trees on the mountains, the abundant grasslands, and the cows, donkeys and sheep kept around the farmhouses, your quiet village, primitive agricultural techniques, cultural relics from the State of Chu, and ancient food stock practices, such as the village millstone, wood-fire clay cookers and the like, have some true value to visitors."

"A true value to visitors?"

"Yes. Nowadays, rural areas do not contribute much to the economy of the country. Whether or not a village can attract people's attention will depend on its true value to visitors – in other words, whether that village has a tourism value. If so, it can develop and prosper. If not, it will decline and decay."

"Oh?"

"But your Chu Wang Village is already a place where tourists come for relaxation and tourism."

Nuannuan forced a laugh this time. "The adults of this village have spent their whole lives here, and they are yet to see anything good about this place."

The man laughed. "You live among such fortunes, yet you do not see them. As a matter of fact, I'll tell you I've come to your Chu Wang Village three times now. The first time was to see the Great Wall of Chu, Lingyan Temple and the mists in the lake, and the other two times I came specially to do some investigations into your village. As I said, this time is much the same. I have come to investigate and understand why thirty-seven older people in your village are older than ninety years old. There's nothing special about their quality of life – that they live for such a long time is mainly due to the benefits of good water, good soil, good food and good air."

"Really?" Nuannuan grew more interested as she listened. "I've never specifically counted how many older people we have in the village, and you've gone and found out."

He nodded. "I've come to find you, specifically to tell you that this is a place where city folk will come for holiday relaxation. This will stem the trend of decline and decay, and in turn develop a popular tourist resort, allowing the local villagers to flourish through fast development."

"Really?"

"Your village needs a saviour."

"A saviour?"

"This saviour must understand the trends of development in the world, have a unique understanding of environments, possess plenty of knowledge of tourism, and be able to generate dynamism. In fact, this saviour is here right now."

"Where is he?" Nuannuan had to laugh at this man and his vague manner of speech.

"He is me. I am here to save your village."

Nuannuan controlled her laughter. "How will you save it?"

"I'll save your village through a rapid development of its tourism industry, a process that the Western nations have used to save their rural areas. The West started rural tourism in the 1960s, and it first originated in Spain. After the 1970s, rural tourism entered a period of rapid growth in the United States and Canada. Provence in France, Piedmont in Italy, and Kent in England have all thrived through tourism development in the rural areas that had begun to decline. In the village of Santo Stefano in Cesano, Italy, there were 1,700 villagers in the early twentieth century. However, because of the attractions of the city, the villagers gradually left, and in the end only 124 people remained. Fortunately, a Swedish investor was interested in the beauty of this place. He bought a lot in the hamlet and converted a group of medieval buildings into hotels, making this hamlet one of the main attractions in the province of Abruzzo. Many tourists come here every day. The village also attracted some people to settle there."

"We have already developed our tourism industry," said Nuannuan.

"This development is simply too small and slow. Look at your Chu Di Ju. It's built with the bare minimum, with no en-suite bathrooms, so guests have to get up and put on clothes before heading outside to use the toilet. You can't host wealthy guests and have no way of earning big money."

"These wealthy guests you speak of, would they really be willing to come to our small village?" Nuannuan asked, listening intently.

"Where else do you think they are willing to go? Abroad? They've gone everywhere and are fed up with it all. None of the places they go can be visited for long periods. And they've seen all of the famous scenery anyway. Right now, what they want most is a place to relax – a place with clear water, green mountains, few people and good air. Such places are not yet open to development. Here in your village, to the east is the boundless Red Lake, and to the north, south and west are endless, ever-stretching mountains. Livestock forage in the grass and between the trees, farmland spreads up to the sides of the mountains, the sails of the fishing boats reflect across the vast, clear water, and the environment even holds the beautiful imagery of ancient human activities. A most tranquil place for people."

"Well, with all of this in mind, what do you say we should do?" Nuannuan was slowly growing more and more interested in what this man was saying, although she did not like his preaching.

"Immediately build more high-grade holiday dormitories. These should have the same exterior as your houses, conserving the local-styled appearance, but the facilities inside will be modernised, with top-rated beds, flushing toilets, bathrooms, entertainment areas and reading rooms, all in order to bring the city folk here and give them the feeling that they never want to leave."

"Where would we get the money to build such houses?" Nuannuan said in surprise.

"What if someone was willing to give you an investment?"

"Are you saying that someone is willing to build such houses together with us?"

"Yes, the other party will provide money, and you'll build the houses. Then they can be jointly managed, with all of the profits split sixty-forty."

"Who? Who would give us the money to build these houses?"

"Me! What do you say?" The man laughed, his eyes again flashing with superiority.

"You? Really?" Nuannuan did not lose her temper but rather opened her eyes wide. This man, who clearly thought very highly of himself, didn't look wealthy. *Is he exaggerating?*

"I don't look like a wealthy man, right?" he said as he took out a business card and gave it to Nuannuan. "Here, allow me to introduce myself. My name is Xue Chuanxin. I'm responsible for directing new projects of Five Continents Travel Group in the provincial capital. And you are?"

"Chu Nuannuan. Our company is called the South Water Landscape Company. Our company director is the father of my baby, Kuang Kaitian."

"Should I speak with Director Kuang about our companies collaborating?"

"You can just talk with me." Nuannuan stared at him. "Director Xue, I would like to know something – if you're going to build holiday dormitories, what kind of money would you be investing?" She wanted to test the water with him.

"The first investment will probably not cover everything, as this is a new tourist route, and so we must work gradually. Building too many houses would leave some empty and idle."

"What about a hundred thousand yuan?" Nuannuan was hopeful. She knew that with a hundred thousand yuan, they could build a few good houses.

Xue Chuanxin laughed. "What could be done with a hundred thousand yuan? This afternoon I went behind the mountain near your village to look at a stony open space, and I estimated you could build fifty houses there."

"Fifty?" Nuannuan took a sharp breath. "How much money would that need?"

"Three million yuan. Building the houses, adding fittings, then renovating the landscape and the surroundings. In such a secluded area, that figure should do it…"

Nuannuan stared at his mouth and had already stopped listening to what he was saying. The amount of three million yuan had stunned her. In all her life, this was the first time she had known money could have such a big number. *Three million! How can this man possibly have so much? How can he be willing to invest this sum in our remote Chu Wang Village? Is it possible?* Nuannuan forgot how she bid farewell to the man or how she arrived back in her own bedroom. Her mind was filled with the figure of three million. *Would three million yuan of banknotes even fill our bedroom?*

Not until she awoke the next day was Nuannuan able to completely calm down and tell Kaitian in detail what had happened.

Kaitian had arrived back home very late the previous night, and Nuannuan had wanted to turn over the possibility of this matter thoroughly in her mind, so she had not told him immediately. After thinking about it all night, she concluded that even if this were a fraud, her own company would not lose anything. *If he doesn't give over the cash, we won't build the houses. Once the houses are built, if they don't continue to pay, we won't renovate them. Once they're renovated and they start earning money from guests, if we don't receive our shares, then we'll just seize the houses. After all, he's doing this on our land.*

Kaitian listened somewhat disbelievingly. *Who in their right mind would throw three million yuan into our remote land? There are lots of fraudsters about these days, so we must be careful and not make the same mistake that we did with the weedkiller.* But in the end, he said to Nuannuan: "I'll leave this business deal to you. Anyway, the open space on the back mountain of our village is deserted. I heard from the older generations that the big canteen in our village was popular when it was built. It's said that the cooks in the canteen often heard a woman's cry at night. People thought that the place was not suitable for building resident houses. After the canteen was closed, no one wanted to build a house there. Then the canteen collapsed, leaving the land wasted. You can talk to him and let him know that we'll only invest the land but nothing else. If he's willing to invest money, he can come. If he doesn't want to, he can leave."

A meeting to sign the letter of intent was agreed in the afternoon three days later. Nuannuan did not imagine Xue Chuanxin would be so fast with it all. It seemed as though he had decided that Chu Wang Village would be the place for him to make money. Once the letter of intent was agreed, Five Continents Travel Group and South Water Landscape Company began the management of the new holiday dormitories of Chu Wang Village. Five Continents would be responsible for investing three million yuan into building the new holiday dorms, including the cost of all room fittings, wooden furniture and electrical goods, while South Water Company would be responsible for building the blocks and the installation, as well as providing the land for the buildings. They would jointly manage them, splitting the profit, with sixty per cent to Five Continents and forty per cent to South Water. After signing the agreement, Nuannuan still did not truly believe that it was all real, and she comforted herself that it was a dream. None of this could have been truly happening. It was not until a couple of weeks later, when Xue Chuanxin brought the formal contract and a cheque for one million yuan along with two engineers to Chu Wang Village, and then placed an order for cement, sand and wood in Juxiang Street, that Nuannuan affirmed that this was really happening. She then began to busy herself with the management and formalities of the ownership of the land.

Kaitian said: "What formalities? First build, then manage the formalities. We can do what we like with Chu Wang Village now."

Nuannuan shook her head. "We're spending millions and building dozens of houses, and on village land too. With something as big as this, you're simply asking for trouble if you think you can manage it alone. First report it, receive the approval of the township, then hold a meeting with the villagers, explain how the land will be used, that we will buy the land for a fixed number of years at a fixed price with a legal right to use, and then our company can formally purchase the land."

Kaitian was impatient. "But I'm the leader. Can I not simply decide upon the legal right to some uncultivated land?"

Nuannuan stared at him. "You're beginning to sound very much the way Zhan Shideng did when he started. How can the land of the village be decided upon by one man?"

On hearing this, Kaitian changed his tone. "OK, we'll go with your idea. First to the township office to make a report."

Now that Kaitian had become the leader, when he and Nuannuan arrived at the township government office, it took no effort at all to meet with the newly appointed mayor. When Kaitian explained the situation, the mayor was quite surprised. "Your village attracting three million investment is a big thing, and a great opportunity to increase the income of the remaining workforce there too. Right. I agree that you may use this uncultivated land. According to the Environment Law, the distance of your village from the lake permits you to build such houses. As for the price of the land, according to current regulations concerning the public-owned land in the township, the standard cost is ten thousand yuan per acre, which can be used for fifty years, but the entire village must be told of this matter…"

The uncultivated land took up an area of 20.3 acres. When taking the land measurements, Nuannuan specifically invited the sick village Party secretary and several old cadres from the village committee, alongside some high-standing older locals to monitor them. Afterwards, Nuannuan took eighty-nine thousand yuan that she had prepared for the land purchase, and a credit note of thirty-four thousand yuan, and handed both to the village accountant with the whole village watching. The credit was clearly marked to be paid off within one year. The eighty-nine thousand yuan was just about the entire accumulated wealth of Kaitian and Nuannuan. Not until after handing over the credit surety and money did Nuannuan realise that this was the largest single investment that the family had ever made. It was also a gamble. This project had to succeed. If it failed, not only would all of her work come to nothing, but the squeezing pressure of debt would again be upon them.

Xue Chuanxin named the new project Shang Xin Yuan. Thanks to Xue Chuanxin's meticulous planning and Kaitian's support, the construction of Shang Xin Yuan commenced. Xue Chuanxin provided and arranged the blueprints, building materials and workers, and Nuannuan called in some unskilled labourers from the village. Excluding board and meals, she paid sixty yuan per day, a handsome wage in Chu Wang Village, and there was stiff competition for the job. Wages of the unskilled workers were calculated within the three million yuan. Nuannuan also provided a guesthouse free of charge for Xue Chuanxin to live in.

Although Xue Chuanxin spoke with much exaggeration, Nuannuan discovered that he was in fact very much down to earth. He worked clearly and logically, and had everything planned down to the last man and job. After the materials were prepared, the digging of the foundations began.

Who would have thought that, just as the digging began, an astonishing discovery would be made?

At Xue Chuanxin's request, the foundations were to be sturdy, and so holes were dug a little deeper than usual. When digging for the first row of houses, a young labourer's spade suddenly made a *ping* sound as it struck against a hard object. It was a noise unlike that made hitting a rock, and the youngster cleared away the earth to find a large green-rusted copper object buried beneath. He called out: "Come and check this out." A group quickly gathered around, and at first sight everybody was stunned. Together, they pulled the copperware from the ground. *Good heavens!* The object was at least half the height of a man and extremely heavy.

Xue Chuanxin and Nuannuan had both been discussing work not far away, and they turned their heads to see what was going on before running over. Xue Chuanxin took a look and said: "Wow, a copper *ding*! My god, a real treasure! How can such a thing be found here?"

Nuannuan didn't really understand, and she quietly asked: "Can it still be used?"

"It still has a use all right. This is a cultural relic – very precious."

The youngster who first discovered the *ding* heard this and hurriedly said: "But I dug it out."

Xue Chuanxin laughed. "No matter who dug it out, if it really is a cultural relic then it belongs to the country, and after they take it away, you'll be rewarded. Everybody, continue to dig at the second row of foundations. Nuannuan, go and give the county's Culture Bureau a phone call and ask them to send someone over to see."

The crowd hurriedly dispersed and went back to work.

Five Continents Group had paid to install a telephone line into Chu Di Ju. After Nuannuan had returned to call the county Culture Bureau to tell them about the discovery, she thought to herself that Uncle Tan would probably also be interested to hear, and so she gave him a call as well. Sure enough, he became unusually excited at the news and said: "I'm on my way now."

Three people from the county Culture Bureau arrived that same afternoon. They used small brushes to carefully remove the sticky mud from the *ding* and discovered that it was covered with decorative lines, and on two sides they could make out vague characters. With this, the three were without doubt: it was an ancient cultural relic but would require more steps to determine what age it had come from. Uncle Tan arrived in the afternoon of the next day, and by this time the *ding* had been carried into Chu Di Ju. Uncle Tan stood before the *ding* and inspected it carefully. "Strange. Strange," he said. Then he went to the site that it was dug from and said: "There may be more things in the area. You should keep digging and searching."

Xue Chuanxin was worried that this would delay the construction process, and he had some doubts. But Nuannuan was unable to refuse Uncle Tan, so she instructed the labourers to keep digging. Sure enough, after only a short time, another piece of copper, smaller this time, was dug up, and Uncle Tan held it up with utmost excitement, saying: "Bell chimes – extremely valuable." With all of their energy, the labourers dug across the whole area and ultimately had a collection of ancient jade musical instruments called *qing*, some *yong* chime bells, jars, pots, bowls and incense burners.

Everyone was shocked and mystified, asking Uncle Tan how he knew about these things. Uncle Tan carefully examined the dug-up items and said: "The inscriptions on the copper object confirm it as a Chu *ding*, and not any regular Chu *ding*, but an object used in the Chu imperial court. If you look closely at the four corners, there's an inscription that looks to be the symbol 'king' – not a word that was used casually back then. How could an object of the imperial court find itself here in such a remote area? This leads me to doubt that this had any ceremonial use in the king's quarters. There must be remaining objects apart from this one, so I suggest you keep on digging in the area. You see, the set of bell chimes also has a vaguely inscribed 'king' symbol."

Nuannuan and the crowd went to look at the bell chimes, and sure enough, every bell showed a raised symbol that looked like the ancient symbol 'king'. After Xue Chuanxin had come to see, he and Nuannuan exchanged an expression of amazement.

Nuannuan could not resist asking: "Uncle Tan, as you see it, what ceremony related to the imperial court would have been performed here in the time of Chu?"

Uncle Tan shook his head. "At this moment, it's hard to say. It will require more text-based analysis."

Xue Chuanxin suddenly exclaimed: "Expand the digging. There could still be more objects down there."

Upon hearing this, the labourers recommenced digging and just about dug up the entire 20.3 acres of land. Apart from a few areas of ashen black earth, nothing new was dug up.

Nuannuan urged Xue Chuanxin: "Let's seize the moment and continue with the building of the houses."

Xue Chuanxin was not at all concerned. "Don't worry, let's wait for Uncle Tan to conclude his research before we carry on."

People from the provincial Culture Bureau and the Nanfu City Culture Bureau arrived after dinner the next day. Uncle Tan spent three days in Chu Di Ju and at the excavation site researching, and although they all believed it to be an object from the Chu imperial court, they were unable to establish the exact time that the objects were cast in a kiln. As to why they were discovered here, nobody could conclude anything.

The next day after dinner, Xue Chuanxin asked Nuannuan to meet with them by the shore of Red Lake. He laughed and asked the old man: "Uncle Tan, I know you have not yet come to a conclusion about the cultural relics, but would you be able to first tell us what you personally think about them?"

"What I think about them..." Uncle Tan hesitated. "Why are you both so anxious to know what I think about them?"

Nuannuan looked at Xue Chuanxin. She didn't know the reason for this either.

"Because this concerns our plans. We originally decided to build holiday dormitories on this plot of land. If we know your opinion, we may be able to adjust some of our original designs."

"OK, I'll tell you what I think. But it's only a hypothesis, and at the moment, fact and fiction are as one, so in order to explain how these imperial court copperware came to be found here, we must make up a story that has no grounding in archaeology."

Xue Chuanxin couldn't hold himself back. "We're willing to hear your story."

"As I'm sure you already know, the earliest capital of Chu was in Danyang, though the seat of Danyang is still debated among archaeologists. Some say its location was in today's Zigui of Hubei Province, but I believe that the ancient Danyang can be found only a few kilometres from today's Danyang, at the confluence of the Xi and Dan rivers. There it stayed, until Chu's King Wen, who ruled after Chu's King Wu, moved the capital from Danyang to Ying, today's Jinan, north of Jiangling County. If my idea is correct, then the Early Chu capital Danyang is not far from your Chu Wang Village, and according to this hypothesis, Chu's King Wen, who lived in Danyang, was also called Chu's King Zi, which may have some connection to your Chu Wang Village."

"Oh?" Nuannuan's eyes opened wide.

"I have carried out an investigation. Chu is the last name of most people in your village. However, for generations there had not been any family with the surname Wang. Normally, a village like yours would be named Chu Village. Yet your village is named Chu Wang Village. That is very strange, but it also, to some extent, proves my hypothesis. Wang, as a character, also means king. Of course, there might be many other reasons for the naming. According to legends, King Zi was the son of the former king and a common-born woman. My guess is, during official work ruling the palace of Danyang, his father would take short holidays and go to different places. On a hot summer day, in search of cooler weather, he and some stewards might have arrived at this village, before it was named Chu Wang. In this quiet village by the side of the lake, he had not only found cooler weather and relaxation from the stress of ruling as a king but also, much to his surprise, a beautiful young woman. After spending many joyous nights with her, he returned to his palace in Danyang. He heard about her pregnancy and took her to the palace. The child she had was named Zi. When he grew up, he became King Zi of Chu. The people in the village who had raised the king's mother must have named their home Chu Wang Village – village of the King of Chu – to commemorate him."

Nuannuan smiled and said: "Uncle Tan, you're such a good storyteller."

"Let him finish," said Xue Chuanxin.

"That must have happened no earlier than 600 BCE. Due to internal and external crises, King Zi was forced to move the capital of Chu. Before his departure, he performed a solemn ceremony in front of his palace in Danyang. After that, he rode a southbound boat with his advisers and consorts. They had brought many goods from the royal palace. When they passed Chu Wang Village, King Zi thought about his mother, who had passed away by then, as well as her home village. He had been sorrowful since the decision to move the capital. Thoughts of his mother had an even more profound impact on him. Therefore, he ordered the boats to halt so that he could come to the village himself. He had a simple ceremony shack built and ordered people to decorate it with a *ding* from the palace and many other ceremonial vessels. He also sent for the court musicians with their chime bells because he needed to hold a small farewell ceremony there…"

Xue Chuanxin smiled. "You could write a novel with this story."

Uncle Tan sighed and said: "It's a shame that it's fiction. I'll be so happy if we can find archaeological evidence to prove it."

Xue Chuanxin was excited. "But fiction has its use too."

Both Nuannuan and Uncle Tan were confused. "What use?"

"You would understand me if you had been to Yangcheng in Shanxi and visited the former residence of Chen Tingjing, grand secretariat and minister of personnel under the reign of Emperor Kangxi during the Qing Dynasty," said Xue Chuanxin, still smiling. "In front of Chen's former house, there's a large performance every day. The show is based on one of the local legends. Emperor Kangxi used to frequent Chen's residence with his royal guards. Every time he made the visit, Chen would welcome him with his family outside the door. More than a hundred people in the village participated in the performance, wearing clothes in the style of the Qing Dynasty. Because of this performance, visitors from all over China swarmed there. My idea is that we can turn Uncle Tan's story into a similar performance to enhance tourism here."

"Wow!" Nuannuan started to understand.

Uncle Tan was still confused. "How do you plan to put on such a show?"

"We shall preserve the excavation site where they found Chu *ding*, chime bells and potteries, and build a shack above it for protection. Not far away from it, we'll build a ceremony shack according to the Chu culture and set up replicas of relics. We'll hire people in Chu Wang Village to dress up as King Zi, his advisers and royal consorts, and train them to act as if they are putting up a serious sacrifice and farewell ceremony before they ride the boats southwards. A show like this will surely attract visitors and bring us more opportunities."

"You're a good businessman," said Uncle Tan as he burst into laughter. "If you want to use my story, you'll have to pay me some royalties."

"Of course. Next time you visit, you can stay in this Shang Xin Yuan for free. And that will be your fee."

Nuannuan said in satisfaction: "If this can work, then people in the village will have some extra income outside of farm work."

"We work in tourism, so we must do everything to attract more visitors. We can have all kinds of ways to attract tourists. Do you understand? Brilliant. Let's get started," said Xue Chuanxin as he waved his hand. "I'll go now to the provincial capital and ask the architects to update the blueprint."

Nuannuan had developed respect for Xue Chuanxin after their last meeting. He was indeed a clever businessman prepared to make money, and he would not let any opportunity slip away from him.

One week later, Xue Chuanxin returned from the provincial capital Zhengzhou. The people from the Culture Bureau had already left with the relics from the excavation. Uncle Tan had returned to Beijing too. According to the updated blueprint that Xue Chuanxin had brought back, one row of guesthouses was omitted to make space for two shacks: one named Excavation Shack, where the archaeology research site was, and the other called Farewell Shack, which was to be built according to the style of buildings where people from ancient Chu would hold sacrifices and farewell ceremonies.

The construction resumed.

Every morning after breakfast, Nuannuan would inspect the tourism work in Chu Di Ju, then she would go to the construction site of Shang Xin Yuan. Though she did not have any knowledge about construction, she could tell whether or not the workers were loafing on the job or wasting unnecessary materials. Her observations were so accurate that Xue Chuanxin was surprised and praised her as "an excellent supervisor".

The construction of the shacks was not complicated, so they took no more than a month to finish. Looking at the pleasing result, Nuannuan felt relieved. Finally, she did not have to worry about the investment – it was now new houses in front of her. This was the point when she eventually put her full trust in Xue Chuanxin's determination to do business here.

After the completion of the principal part of the Shang Xin Yuan project, Nuannuan asked Kaitian to invite Xue Chuanxin to their home. She fixed a few dishes herself so that they could drink to their hearts' content. During the dinner, Nuannuan made a toast to Xue Chuanxin, saying with all sincerity: "Brother Xue, you're a real doer. You deserve our admiration."

"Wait and see. I said I'm here as a saviour. I'll turn your declining Chu Wang Village into a thriving town that's teeming with tourists one day." Xue Chuanxin sounded arrogant again, and a look of disdain crept back into his eyes. Nuannuan smiled, thinking that all people of genuine ability would behave like him.

Following the construction, the renovation, which was quite beyond Nuannuan's knowledge, had started. Boats carried tiles, floor planks, plaster mounds, boards, paint and lights from the east bank. Nuannuan had only seen those materials in Beijing, and she had never expected them to be useful in Chu Wang Village. The electronic goods and the furniture were purchased in Nanfu or the provincial capital. There were microwaves, electric irons, mini fridges, cabinets, swivel chairs, chaise longues, heaters, fitness equipment and carpets. Nuannuan found the decorations quite an eye-opener.

During the decoration, villagers came over to check the progress. They were all in shock at the sight. Spotty Laosi exclaimed: "My goodness! I didn't expect that we could have such a place in Chu Wang Village. Aren't these the yards and buildings we see in films?"

Jiuding also commented with alarm: "Compared with these yards and houses, my place is a doghouse."

Grandpa Tianfu blurted out: "Motherfucker! Older generations said that when people die, they go to heaven. I think the dead can just come here to stay. This is *the* heaven, the most beautiful place I've seen in my lifetime."

Before finishing the renovation, Xue Chuanxin came to see Nuannuan and Kaitian. He said to them: "We must now look to the preparations for the opening. One of the preparations is to pick twenty-five girls and fifteen boys and send them to the provincial capital for training."

Nuannuan did not understand. "That many people? What will they be trained for?"

"They'll learn how to receive guests properly."

Nuannuan laughed. "You don't need training for that. Offer them some water, bring them some tea, keep their rooms clean and make their beds. No one went through any training to do that in my Chu Di Ju."

"Chu Di Ju is for ordinary tourists, so your staff would suffice. But Shang Xin Yuan is built to receive VIPs, and we must have a high-standard service system. Three of the twenty-five girls will work at the reception – they must be able to check in guests through a computer system. Five will wait in the restaurant – they must learn to arrange the cutlery, help the guests with the menu and serve dishes properly. Twelve will work in housekeeping – they must understand how the electronics work in the rooms and how to protect the carpets and wooden furniture. Two will work in the laundry room – they must be familiar with the washing machine and ironing goods. One will work in the beauty salon and must learn how to wash, cut and dye. Two will work as cleaners and must keep the whole place in order. They must also make sure to learn about garbage sorting and processing. I acknowledge Red Lake's water protection – people from above are concerned with pollution, so any casual litter or even general waste will not be tolerated. As for the fifteen boys, ten will work as security guards – there will be one security officer, and the other nine will take turns to patrol in a team of three and make sure that our guests and properties are under protection in Shang Xin Yuan. Three will help the cooks in the kitchen – they must know the basics of cooking. One will be the electrician and must understand how to deal with regular problems such as a dead bulb. The last one will work in the garden and take care of the grass, flowers and trees. So tell me now, do you still think that training is unnecessary?"

Hearing his speech, Nuannuan was stunned. She had never thought about a clear division of labour. *Of course training is necessary.* She smiled and answered: "Big Brother Xue, I did not realise how different things are in Shang Xin Yuan and Chu Di Ju. We'll do as you say. I'll go and find people and send them to the provincial capital to study."

There were a few young people in Chu Wang Village and the neighbouring villages who had not left to work in the cities. They hastened to Nuannuan's house after hearing about the job opportunities with a promised monthly salary. The courtyard was filled with youngsters – some even came with their parents in the hope of getting hired. Nuannuan hired some good-looking ones who had been educated in high schools. However, wishing to offer the opportunity to the poorer families in Chu Wang Village, she also picked several quick-witted ones, despite their modest background and lesser education.

The next day, she took the forty young people to Xue Chuanxin. He was quite satisfied and said: "This place is indeed a good area – every one of them is easy on the eye. Now go home and prepare for the trip. We'll go to the provincial capital in three days and stay there for a twenty-day training. All fees are covered by Shang Xin Yuan."

The young people went home in great excitement.

Xue Chuanxin turned to Nuannuan and said: "You should prepare for the trip too."

Nuannuan blinked in surprise. "Me? What am I going to do there?"

"According to the contract, we're running the business in cooperation. Since your husband is working as the leader of the village, he will not have time to manage it. Therefore, my partner here is you. And you must go to the provincial capital and learn to work as a manager."

"I need training too?"

Kaitian cut in: "You need damn nothing. We've got a kid at home. Besides, a manager is a leader. I've never heard of a leader who needs training."

"You've signed the contract with Five Continents Travel Group, so you must work accordingly. If you, our business partner, are managing this place with no knowledge of budget, taxation, strategy and human resources, how can we expect to make any money at all?" Xue Chuanxin put on a grave expression. "You can hire a babysitter. How can you think of making money without making a little sacrifice?"

Kaitian was unhappy. "Well, you didn't make it clear initially. How can you send her to the provincial capital and separate my wife from our son? What if Dangen cries for her? What if I miss her? You want me to sleep alone at night? It's unreasonable."

Xue Chuanxin burst into laughter. "It's only twenty days. You can't stand the loneliness already?"

"All right. I'll go and get trained. And I'll learn how to work as a proper manager," said Nuannuan as she took Dangen in her arms. She kissed him on his cheek and lightly patted him on his backside. "You'll sleep with Grandma now…"

Nuannuan led the forty young people she had hired and lodged at Zhangyuan Hotel in the provincial capital. It was the time when all the brilliant lights in the city had just been turned on. With the colourful lights shining behind the shop windows, the never-ceasing stream of cars on the streets and the joyful noises of the crowds in the city, Nuannuan suddenly remembered the first time she saw Beijing. At that moment, once again, she felt the charm of it all. *Wouldn't it be lovely to live in the city?* She looked back at the young people behind her and noticed the amazement and fear in their eyes, not much different from herself when she first arrived in Beijing.

The guests in the main hall turned to look at this lot dressed like rural people. From their look, Nuannuan saw surprise, contempt and curiosity. *What are you looking at? We're people like you – only that heaven had us born in Chu Wang Village and made us different from you. If you'd been born in our village, you'd be the same as we are.*

Xue Chuanxin said to them: "This is a four-star hotel subsidiary of our Five Continents Travel Group. You'll get your training here."

Nuannuan nodded. She felt quite nervous, wondering if she and the young villagers could manage to stay here.

After dinner, Xue Chuanxin had his staff bring over forty-one navy-coloured uniforms and offered one to everyone. Nuannuan asked about where the hotel staff take showers. She took everyone over and said: "Each of you must take a shower and change into the uniform with clean underwear. I know many of you have lice. But from today on, we'll live as people in the city do, and shower once every two days. You'll soak your old underwear in boiled water to kill the lice. You must make sure that you are rid of lice before you put on the uniforms. The uniform will become your identity. You'll bring it back to Shang Xin Yuan and wear it at work. So everyone, take good care of your uniform."

Nuannuan became familiar with showers when working in Beijing, so she finished quickly and waited in her uniform for the others to finish.

She heard Xue Chuanxin exclaiming: "Wow, you're a different person now that you've changed into the uniform. You look like a young woman."

Nuannuan felt flattered and said: "Being a mother, I'm not young any more." But she said to herself: *Clothes make the woman, and fine feathers make delicate birds. We rural people can look good in fine clothes.*

After the young people came out in their uniforms, Nuannuan had them fall into two lines and stood in front of them. That was how she was trained in Beijing. She announced: "Now that we're in the provincial capital, no matter what work you do, you must not invite shame on yourself, or people will look down upon Chu Wang Village."

The next morning after breakfast, Xue Chuanxin arranged for a few departmental heads in charge of different jobs in the hotel to take the young people to start training. Afterwards, he led Nuannuan to the manager's office. Nuannuan felt nervous again, but she said to herself: *There's nothing to be afraid of. There's nothing that you can't learn once you put in the effort. You have run Chu Di Ju well. In here, the job will be similar, but with a higher standard.*

A female deputy manager was in charge of Nuannuan's training. Xue Chuanxin called her Big Sister Han, so Nuannuan did the same. Big Sister Han was quite friendly while Xue Chuanxin was there, but she revealed her impatience and scorn after he left. She said to Nuannuan: "Twenty days is not enough to learn how to manage a four-star hotel."

Nuannuan knew from her tone that she was one of those people who would only show respect to the rich. To deal with such people, you must at least pretend to be rich yourself. She had met many managers in Beijing, and she knew that most of them were merely employees rather than owners of a hotel. Therefore, she answered: "Big Sister Han, I'm not here to become a manager of a four-star hotel like you in twenty days. My family run a resort ourselves. Maybe one day I can get Big Sister Han to help us manage it." This response was quite humble yet also delivered the message of her ownership.

As expected, Big Sister Han did not answer quickly. However, after a short while, her attitude changed with a smile. "Hotel management is not rocket science. We just need to make sure that our guests have a good night's sleep, good meals and a good time during the day. Let's begin with the basics of managing work in the reception."

Nuannuan knew this was her opportunity to learn some useful skills. When she was working in Beijing, she wanted to find such an opportunity to learn but had failed. Therefore, she was determined to make the most out of the training. She listened to Big Sister Han's instructions and observed every detail of how she dealt with her job. She took all kinds of notes about things that she found worth remembering and went through every regulation, rule, procedure and assessment standard. She had never been exposed to such knowledge – despite her experience in Chu Di Ju, she found such a technical managing system here incomparable. For example, as a staff member in the hotel, one has to use two different languages: body language and spoken language. When using body language, one must demonstrate the energetic, modest and amicable style of working. As for the spoken language, special attention must be paid to perfect pronunciation, intonation, manner and speed. The phrasing must be carefully designed as well.

To Nuannuan, the training was intriguing, and she became more curious as it proceeded. Apart from what she learned from Big Sister Han, she bought a book titled *Modern Hotel Management* from a bookstore, and she regularly visited different departments in the hotel. She would go to the reception and ask about the concierge, luggage care, check-in/check-out and cashier. She would go to housekeeping and learn about procedures in dealing with everyday situations in the rooms. She would go to finance and familiarise herself with internal settlement, auditing and cash flow. She would go to security and try to understand how to deal with emergencies...

Big Sister Han was happy with Nuannuan's active learning, and she offered her sincere praise. "You're the best pupil I've ever seen. People from guesthouses and hotels all over the province come to study with me every year, but it's rare for anyone to learn as conscientiously as you have."

Nuannuan smiled and said: "I have no choice. If I can't do well here, I can't make money through the resort we run. The loss will be all mine."

Twenty days passed quickly. In the last two days of training, Xue Chuanxin led Big Sister Han, Nuannuan and the department heads into the hotel to hold an assessment session for the forty young people. The result was fine. Though some were still not good enough at their job, everyone passed. Xue Chuanxin was pleased. "Good. They can all start working once they are home."

Nuannuan was relieved. *At least they didn't disgrace the village.*

The night before leaving, Nuannuan was packing her things when Xue Chuanxin came with a bag. Nuannuan thought he was bringing some learning materials, but when she took it out she found it was a beautiful dress.

"Come on, try it on and see if it fits."

"Who? For me?" Nuannuan was taken aback.

Xue Chuanxin smiled. "Who else if it's not for you? It's for you only."

"No, no." Nuannuan shook her hand in haste. While working in Beijing, she learned that a woman couldn't accept a man's gift. If she did, she would invite trouble to herself. "Please take it home and give it to your wife."

"You're worried that I'm trying to woo you? Frankly, you've got a rustic charm that fascinated me when I first saw you. I'd have tried to make you my woman if we were not business partners. Now that we are, we can't do things like that any more. If we did, it would be impossible to reckon our accounts. Do you understand?"

Nuannuan blushed to the toes. She didn't expect he would have been so straightforward. *To make me your woman? That would've been easier said than done. Who do you think you are? Who do you think I am?* Nuannuan would have told him that, but she held back the words. She pardoned him as she was familiar with his arrogant behaviour.

She only smiled. "I don't need it. Please give it to your wife. I've got dresses."

"It's a bonus for your hard work in the training session. I bought it especially for you. It's not only a reward for your hard work and learning but also a bribe to you, the deputy general manager of Shang Xin Yuan. I say bribe because we two will often work together in the future. Working together, we'll inevitably have disagreements. I hope you'll give me more support for the sake of the big picture of making money. I hope you'll be on the same page as me. Come, take it, please."

Nuannuan had to accept the dress and smile. "You may rest assured, Brother Xue. You're the general manager and have seen more of the world than I have. I'll listen to you, of course."

On the pier of Chu Wang Village, as usual, not many people were around. When Nuannuan and the forty young people, all dressed up in their new uniforms, disembarked, Spotty Laosi did not recognise them. He stared at them in curiosity.

Nuannuan called out: "Big Brother!"

He cried out in complete surprise: "Yikes! It's you. I thought you were some troops."

Xichuan, who ran a small grocery by the pier, also shouted out: "Good heavens, how you have all changed in such a short time outside of the village."

Nuannuan had everyone fall into two lines. They walked towards Shang Xin Yuan with perfect synchronisation. The villagers, old and young, all went out to look at them in curiosity. At that moment, Nuannuan suddenly had an epiphany: *Changes are possible through training. Twenty days ago, I took away a group of young peasants. After the training in Zhongyuan Hotel, they have turned into professional young staff. For the next step, I should take the training to those already working in Chu Di Ju.*

In front of Shang Xin Yuan, Nuannuan announced Xue Chuanxin's requirements: "At eight o'clock tomorrow after breakfast, you must all report to work here. Now you can go home."

After the forty young people left, amazed laughter and praise could be heard everywhere in the village. As she walked home, Nuannuan felt proud: *It is us Kuangs who have brought such happiness to the village.*

When she arrived at the courtyard, her mother-in-law was

trimming vegetables. Dangen was leaning against her knees. He was playing with the long-eared rabbit they kept in the yard with a piece of pak choi leaf. Hearing Nuannuan's steps, her mother-in-law raised her head and asked who the visitor was. Dangen was the first to recognise her. He ran towards her, calling: "Mummy, Mummy!" Nuannuan opened her arms and held her son as tight as possible.

It was suppertime when Kaitian returned from the village committee office. Nuannuan was still in uniform because she wanted him to see how she looked in it. Sure enough, Kaitian was dazed at first and soon went up to her, whispering: "I thought a young lady had entered the wrong house. It turned out to be you. Wow, the thing down there is reacting. I wish I could carry you to bed right now."

"Watch your mouth!" Nuannuan blushed and gave him a gentle punch on his chest.

In order to devote all her attention to the business in Shang Xin Yuan, Nuannuan had put Shallot in charge of Chu Di Ju and raised her monthly salary to eight hundred yuan. Shallot was very grateful. She said to Nuannuan: "My sister, you have never treated me as the silly peasant's wife that I am, who knows of nothing but sorghums. Even if you do not raise my payment, I'll do my best to work for you. Without your Chu Di Ju, I'd be trapped in my fields, and I'd never have heard of a hostel. Go and do what you have to do in Shang Xin Yuan. I'll spare no effort in Chu Di Ju."

The third day after Nuannuan and her forty young staff started working in Shang Xin Yuan, the first group of guests sent by the PR department of Five Continents Travel Group arrived – six families in total. Their manners and styles were the most exquisite that Nuannuan had ever seen. Each family took up five rooms: the couple stayed in two main bedrooms and one living room, while the child and the nanny each took one bedroom. Three of the six families brought their dogs, so each asked for one more bedroom for the dog. Xue Chuanxin set up the price of five hundred yuan for one room so each family would be paying two to three thousand yuan every day. *What an extravagant life!* Nuannuan asked Xue Chuanxin if he had informed them fully about the accommodation fee. Xue

Chuanxin laughed and said: "Don't you worry about whether or not they can afford this. The truth is they're all big-time bosses. They earn tens of thousands every day. What's a thousand or two yuan to them? Be assured, Shang Xin Yuan is built to make money from these rich people."

The guests were quite selective about food, and they specifically asked for delicacies from the mountain and fresh produce from the lake. Xue Chuanxin set up an unbelievably high price for the food: 80 yuan for steamed local chicken with fiddleheads, 90 yuan for red pepper and carp from Red Lake, 108 yuan for a plate of lake shrimps and 280 yuan for wild mushrooms with softshell turtles. But their guests were not hesitant about ordering: each family had at least five or six dishes for every meal. The profit from food was considerable. As the partner of Shang Xin Yuan, Nuannuan was of course happy about making the extra money. However, she felt slightly guilty because the dishes were not worth as much in the village. Sensing her guilt, Xue Chuanxin smiled and said to her: "With your kind heart, you can never do real business. Remember, the quality of a good businessman does not lie in his heart but in the revenue he makes. We have provided them food from natural, unpolluted sources, and such food does not even exist in the cities. Of course they should pay us more."

The six families were going to the Great Wall of Chu the next day and asked if they could have a picnic on the hill. Xue Chuanxin said he could arrange it, but the charge would be high because it would be challenging to get it up there. The six families asked how much, and Xue's answer was three hundred yuan. They smiled. "Go ahead and fix it for us. Three hundred yuan is fine."

Nuannuan decided that to make the guests satisfied and prevent possible accidents, she and Spotty Laosi would serve as the guides because the family was among the first batch of tourists to Shang Xin Yuan to make the sightseeing trip. Now that he was already a seasoned guide, Spotty Laosi could speak fluently about the Great Wall of Chu's origin and legends. One following the other, Nuannuan and Spotty Laosi took the guests up the hill slowly. On the hillside, a man from the family struck up a conversation with Nuannuan and asked her about the wall's discovery. Nuannuan then told him about Uncle Tan's exploration. As they chatted, they lagged behind the crowd. All of a sudden, the man broke into a peal of laughter. He interrupted Nuannuan's description and whispered to her: "Sister, you look charming, especially with your breasts. I dare say that no film stars can match yours in size."

His flirtation caught Nuannuan off guard. She was in such a daze that she was lost for words. She could only say: "You…"

"You've got an excellent natural environment here. Look at your complexion – it's so fine that it finds no match among city women. Frankly, I want to have a chance to touch it. And your lips are so dainty, tender and moist that they make my mouth water. I want to put mine against them very much. Your buttocks are so ample that I want to enjoy their elastic feel."

Nuannuan was so mad that she felt her blood surging into her face. *Why is there such a shameless man in the world?* Only then did she realise that the man had lured her away from the crowd and accosted her.

"If you like, I can arrange for us to be somewhere alone. I'll pay you handsomely."

Nuannuan was seething with fury and wanted to berate him loudly: *You swine! Do you think you can do anything with your money, like insulting a woman?* But she was aware that he was among the first group of tourists to Shang Xin Yuan. She couldn't lose their business by venting her grievances, so she swallowed her anger and forced a smile. "Aren't you afraid of your wife if she finds out about this? Aren't you worried that I'll tell her?" Without awaiting his response, she rushed forward to catch up with the group. For the rest of the day and the remaining days of the man's stay, she never gave him any chance to be alone with her. When the people ate the picnic the cooks had brought up the hill that noon – three hundred yuan a person – Nuannuan no longer felt guilty about the price hiked up by Xue Chuanxin. They were supposed to pay that much money because the more money they had, the more wantonly they would behave.

In order to extend the guests' stay in Shang Xin Yuan, Xue Chuanxin carefully planned their visit. On the first day, they went to see the Great Wall of Chu. On the second day, they visited Lingyan Temple. On the third day, they discovered the Excavation Shack and the Farewell Shack with Xue Chuanxin's two-hour-long introduction to the progress of archaeological research, and then they examined the replicas of the relics one by one. On the fourth day, they saw the mysterious mist in the centre of the lake. On the fifth day, the male guests went fishing by the lake while the females went to pick mushrooms on the hills. On the sixth day, they experienced farm life in the fields and purchased vegetables. The six families stayed for six full days in Shang Xin Yuan. Nuannuan could not help admiring Xue Chuanxin's outstanding skills of retaining and pleasing his guests. Upon their departure, the six families all seemed more than satisfied.

Nuannuan had the finance office calculate the rough income, and the number was close to eighty thousand yuan. What a success, and in just six days! At this rate, they would earn their investment back in no time. Moreover, to Nuannuan's surprise, shortly after the departure of the first group, a second group of more than twenty guests arrived. It was a group of younger wealthy people. All of them worked as mid-level executives in a big company. There were no children in the group, and none of the men or women seemed to have been married, since they asked for one room each. This new group of guests enjoyed singing, dancing and other entertainments. They stayed up almost every night to sing and dance. They spent much time playing poker, Chinese chess and mahjong as well. Therefore, they would not start sightseeing until one o'clock in the afternoon. Apart from all the scenic spots, they asked to do many other activities: adventures in the Old Elephant Ridge in the South Mountain, tours into the forest in the North Mountain to see ancient trees, hiking on the hill to pick up rocks with strange marks, fishing trips in Red Lake, a cooking experience with local sweet potatoes and maize, photography with children and seniors in the village. Anything they could think of, they would make sure to enjoy. Xue Chuanxin asked Nuannuan to do everything she could to satisfy their demands, as long as the efforts would extend their stay. Of course, Nuannuan understood what he meant.

The second group stayed for seven days. It was not long before their departure that Nuannuan realised they were here for a special holiday arranged by their company for mid-level executives. The group brought in an income of close to ninety thousand yuan. Nuannuan was pleased and said to Xue Chuanxin: "You're such a brilliant businessman. You have sent so many rich guests here."

Xue Chuanxin laughed and answered: "I'm not the brilliant one here. It's my company and its brilliant sales department. They are highly professional. They analysed the market and identified our target clients. Then, they sent letters and visited them in person to make sure they became our clients."

Though the third group consisted of only two guests, Xue Chuanxin paid much more attention to them than to the previous groups. He took a boat to the east bank to welcome them himself. Moreover, he gave Nuannuan a special instruction: "You must make sure the security is perfect. We will not receive any other guests. Tell people that the place is being renovated. The two guests will check in without registration of name or any payment. No one except for the staff of Shang Xin Yuan should be allowed inside."

Nuannuan did not understand. "No payment even for food? Won't we lose money?"

Xue Chuanxin smiled as he looked at her. "We're doing business here. Will a good business lose money?"

How can we make money by not charging? Nuannuan found herself more than confused.

Their guests arrived late in the afternoon. The man was in his late fifties. He wore a large pair of sunglasses that covered his face. The woman was in her twenties. She was very attractive in her fine clothes, with an exquisite hairstyle. Xue Chuanxin himself took them to a suite: one living room in the centre with two bedrooms on each side. He even poured them water himself. Nuannuan guessed that they were a father and daughter. During dinner, Xue Chuanxin had Nuannuan offer them the menu herself. Much to her surprise, the man did not take off his sunglasses, even when eating.

Nuannuan told Kaitian about the guests at home that night. Kaitian found it quite strange as well: *How can they let two guests occupy the whole of Shang Xin Yuan?* But he was not bothered. "Follow Mr Xue's instructions, and he'll bring us money." Kaitian rarely went to Shang Xin Yuan because of his work in the village committee.

The two guests were very quiet. Most of the time, they would stay in the suite, and occasionally they would take a walk in the courtyard. But they always went back to the room after a short while. Nuannuan asked whether or not they would like to see the Great Wall of Chu. The young woman thanked her and said that they would rather take a good rest and relax. One evening after dinner, the young woman told Xue Chuanxin that they wanted to take a stroll by the lakeside. Xue Chuanxin hastened Nuannuan to follow them with two security guards: they must walk behind them, yet they must also keep a fair distance. Nuannuan nodded and took the two security guards out. At that time, everyone in the village had gone to sleep, so it was very quiet around. The crescent moon was hanging in the night sky, rendering a moist, dim light over the misty lake. The man and the woman walked alongside the lake slowly as the water lightly touched the bank from time to time, resonating with their soft words. Nuannuan could not hear what they were talking about, but once in a while she could hear the young woman giggle. She could tell the two had an intimate relationship. She thought to herself: *They're not like other fathers and daughters.*

It did not take long for the crescent to descend and reveal the stars that filled the whole night sky. The young woman, discovering the change, happily cried out: "Look at all those stars."

The man seemed quite pleased too. He spoke out loudly: "What great beauty. This is what an unpolluted sky looks like. It offers you peace and clarity. It makes you forget about your gains and losses."

The two spent some time looking at the night sky. After a while, they sat down by the side of the lake. The man waved a hand at Nuannuan, asking her to come close. She realised that he had finally taken off his sunglasses. It was too dark to see his face. The man asked Nuannuan in a kind voice: "Young lady, do you have any legends here about Qu Yuan?"

"Qu Yuan?" Nuannuan hesitated for a moment.

"Qu Yuan, the one we commemorate on Dragon Boat Festival, where everyone eats *zongzi*."

Nuannuan suddenly remembered Qu Yuan's story told by Jiuding and Uncle Tan. She answered: "They say that Qu Yuan visited this area."

The man seemed to be speaking to himself. "Yes, I believe so. This is the birthplace of the Chu people. When Qin invaded this place, Qu Yuan must have come to the frontline here. He was an important minister. He might have even written some of his poems here."

Nuannuan remembered that other tourists told her about Qu Yuan's 'The Lament'. She wanted to share it with him, but she did not speak up, worrying that she would make a mistake.

"Suppose that this area really had not changed since ancient times. When Qu Yuan took a walk here by the side of the lake, his mind half on the war and half on the political affairs at home, what would he have felt?" mumbled the man.

The young woman patted his head and said: "All right, all right. Stop talking about a dead man. Let's think of something nice and fun."

It was past midnight when the guests returned to Shang Xin Yuan. Xue Chuanxin was waiting in front of the gate. Nuannuan did not go home until she saw Xue Chuanxin take them back to their suite. When she got home, both Kaitian and Dangen were asleep. She went to bed but could not close her eyes for a long time. She could not help but think of how the young woman had patted the man on his head – that was not what a daughter would do to her father…

After the two guests left, another group arrived and took up all forty rooms. Everyone in the group seemed to be an official: they called each other by the name of their high positions and acted in a perfect manner. The schedule was well defined, and everyone followed it strictly. They stayed for five days and brought Shang Xin Yuan an income of more than twenty thousand yuan from the accommodation fee alone. On the day of their departure, Xue Chuanxin asked Nuannuan quietly: "See? Are we losing money at all?"

Nuannuan suddenly started to understand what he meant. She asked him: "Do you mean that without the two guests from last time, we would not have had this group of guests? Without the free stay of those two, these guests wouldn't be paying us all this money?"

Xue Chuanxin laughed and said: "Great! Our boss Ms Chu here has learned to use her head and see things as an interrelated system."

The group of guests that followed surprised Nuannuan even more. One afternoon, Xue Chuanxin asked Nuannuan to go with him to the pier and welcome a new group of visitors. He gave her a mysterious smile and said: "We must be very careful with this group."

Nuannuan at first thought that they were receiving another group of discrete VIPs. Nevertheless, she was highly surprised when the boat disembarked because all the guests were foreigners. Nuannuan did not know what to do. *Our Chu Wang Village is attracting foreign visitors?* Xue Chuanxin stepped up calmly and said in English: "Hello!"

A tall man in the group walked over and nodded at Nuannuan. He said to her in Chinese: "Dear lady, how do you do?"

Nuannuan answered with a blush: "How do you do?"

The news of foreign visitors in Chu Wang Village spread fast. People in the village all came over to see the foreigners, including some seniors with their walking canes. By the side of the road from the pier to Shang Xin Yuan, villagers filled every space. It was the first time that Chu Wang Village had foreign visitors, so everyone was curious and excited.

Spotty Laosi squeezed himself through the crowd and gazed fixedly at a foreign woman's breasts. When she walked away, he exclaimed loudly: "Look at the foreigner's boobs. They're eye-catching indeed, large and bouncing like a chicken trying to pick up grain on the ground. One is equal to both my wife's. They must feel good too."

"Feel your mother's tits!" His wife pinched his ear before his slurs died down. It hurt so much that he screamed like a squealing pig seeing a butcher's knife. The villagers burst out laughing.

Nuannuan learned later that their new guests were Europeans teaching in several Chinese universities in the provincial capital. They were invited by Five Continents Travel Group to visit the Great Wall of Chu. The next day, when leading them on a tour of the hill, Nuannuan was worried that they would not understand anything about Chu. However, after several lines she made about the construction and engineering techniques of the wall, one of the guests, a Mr Hart, spoke up in Chinese with a slight accent. "Chu's techniques in construction were not as impressive as those in bronze manufacturing, silk weaving and lacquer decoration."

Nuannuan did not expect a foreigner to acquire such detailed knowledge about Chu. Later on, she asked him with a smile: "What else do you know about Chu?"

Hart answered solemnly: "I know of the religion and customs of Chu. They believed that they were descendants of the God of Sun and the God of Fire. Therefore, they adored red clothing, worshipped towards the East and paid much respect to witchery.

I'm also familiar with its history. The State of Chu lasted for more than five hundred years, between the rise of Chu Xiao'ao and the defeat of King Huai. Many outstanding figures were nurtured in Chu, the most famous being Qu Yuan under the reign of King Huai. But during Qu Yuan's time, Chu had already been in decline. I have read Qu Yuan's long poem 'Heavenly Questions'. I still remember the first few lines:

> *Who could tell us at the last when did begin the past?*
> *How could anyone know the formless high and low?*
> *Who knows where darkness did end when light and shade did blend?*
> *How to imagine things in the air but not on wings?*
> *How could darkness turn bright?*
> *When was day divided from night?*
> *How did light and shade combine, originate and change?*

Nuannuan could only understand half of what he said, but she had developed a certain respect for the man. At the same time, she felt embarrassed as the descendant of Chu: she did not even know half as much about her ancestors as this foreigner did. She felt the necessity to read more; otherwise, if other visitors were to ask her about the history of Chu or the poetry of Qu Yuan, she would be more embarrassed without a good answer. Before the foreign visitors left, Nuannuan went to the bookstore on Juxiang Street and bought *A Brief History of China* and *Translation of Selected Qu Yuan's Chu Ci*.

The success of Shang Xin Yuan shortly after its opening was beyond Nuannuan's expectations. In less than a month, they had achieved an income of close to three hundred thousand yuan. Nuannuan did some calculation and realised that it would take less than a year for her family and Five Continents Travel Group to earn back their initial investment. The next year they would be making profits. The business was so different from running Chu Di Ju with the help of a professional company. Nuannuan felt quite fortunate to have found the cooperation with Five Continents and the leadership of Xue Chuanxin, a man with a true gift for business. Thinking of the bright future of her business, Nuannuan could not hold back her happy laughter. *Finally, we Kuangs have found a way of getting rich. If we keep working like this, Dangen will not grow up with the difficulties we had.* In the following days, Nuannuan even started walking with a spring in her step.

It was raining. The raindrops, blown into an angle by the breeze, were making a gentle sound as they fell on top of the tiles, the leaves and the road. They were like rice falling into a jar. There were four guests in Shang Xin Yuan. Nuannuan was anxious because they could not visit the tourist sites in that weather. She could not leave them trapped in their rooms, but the hill, the temple, the lake and the fields would not be as nice in the rain. To her relief, the guests asked to see Red Lake in the rain after breakfast. Nuannuan hurried to find four umbrellas for them and took them to the lake herself.

Nuannuan rarely had the time and wasn't often in the mood to simply watch the lake in silence in the rain. When she actually stood beside it, she realised why Red Lake in the rain was worth the visitors' attention: thousands of raindrops were splashing into the water, making various patterns and waves on the surface, similar to the sight of fish competing for food. The lake became blurred, hidden behind the mist of water with one or two occasional boats, the shape of which became blurred as well, rendering an illusory sense that one gets when looking in the moonlight. Several birds detained by the rain were flying against the wind on top of the water, looking anxious and helpless. The four guests strolled alongside the lake with their umbrellas. They were talking about something. Walking behind them, Nuannuan was worried that they would be disappointed by the lake in the rain. Luckily, she heard their laughter as they talked about a poetry competition titled 'The Red Lake in the Rain'. Nuannuan was happy to hear that.

Before midday, Xue Chuanxin had someone fetch Nuannuan. He said to her: "Now we should start the second project."

Nuannuan did not understand. "The second project?"

Xue Chuanxin smiled. "Have you forgotten about the shack we built earlier?" He pointed at the Farewell Shack in front of Shang Xin Yuan.

Nuannuan started to remember what they had discussed. She asked again: "What shall we do?"

"The first step is to decide what will be on display in the Farewell Shack. I have thought about it, and I think we should make a sacrificial table with planks. The style must be simple and archaic. We'll put several replicas of the excavated Chu *ding*, chime bells and pottery. In addition, there'll be a lit incense burner and several wax goods made in the shapes of food used for sacrifice."

Nuannuan nodded. "Consider it done."

"The next step is to decide on the performance. I have thought about it too. There'll be four acts. Act One 'Arrival of the Boats' – King Wen of Chu, also known as King Zi, rides the boats with his queen and his stewards. The boats will arrive in a line with background music of bugles and bamboo whistles. Boats in the time of Chu were not grand or extravagant, but we must give them an imposing manner. The decoration must look as Chu as possible so that the visitors will find it unique. Act Two 'Disembark' – After the fleet docked, the samurai first came ashore and guarded the road from the lake to the Farewell Shack. King Zi steps out of the boats in the music of Chu and walks towards the Farewell Shack with his queen, his stewards following them. The group must look majestic to impress the visitors. Act Three 'Ceremony' – King Zi walks into the Farewell Shack with his queen to offer incense and kneel. All of his stewards will kneel too. King Zi will quietly speak words of the farewell ceremony and cast a solemn ambience. Act Four 'Departure' – King Zi will start walking back towards the lake with his queen and stewards. He looks back with every step he takes. After they are on board, they will again kneel on the boats and bid farewell to their birthplace. The ships will slowly start to leave at that moment. The visitors must feel the sorrow of their departure."

Nuannuan looked at Xue Chuanxin in amazement and said: "You and your intricate plans. You're as professional as a film director. OK, we'll do as you said."

"For the third step, we must decide the cast members. Again, I have thought about it. This performance requires no lines, so people need to do nothing but put on clothes in the style of Chu and make movements according to the script. There is no need to hire professional actors. We shall hire people in your village, boys and girls, men and women. Young men can play the soldiers and generals, and older men can be the king's advisers. Young women can play the queen and the consorts, while the older ones can be their ladies-in-waiting. How about this – we shall not pay them too much for every performance, but they'll still get some extra income by doing this. The performance will not last more than one hour, so they can arrange their other work well. Also, we will not put on a daily performance. Once a week is enough. You will choose the cast members."

Nuannuan asked: "How many in total?"

"Eighty. The more people, the grander the performance will look."

"OK."

"For the next step, we prepare the clothes, props and ships for the performance. You choose the cast members, and I'll take care of the rest."

Nuannuan was relieved to hear those words...

People in the village did not sign up for the performance of Shang Xin Yuan when they first heard about the job opportunity. Zhan Datong laughed. "When have we castrators and farmers done things like this? We'd make a laughing stock of ourselves."

However, after they found out about the ten yuan per person for acting in one performance, many were eager to try. Ten yuan can buy one *jin* of pork – quite enough for a good meal of dumplings.

Later on, Xue Chuanxin had the security guards in Shang Xin Yuan put on a rehearsal and showed the people that the job required no more than putting on clothes and caps, carrying the sword of a general or a soldier, and walking between the lake and the shack – nothing difficult at all.

After that, people started signing up. The first ones to do so were the youngsters who were already working in Chu Di Ju and Shang Xin Yuan. Following them were the middle-aged male and female villagers. Spotty Laosi never liked to be left behind when it came to making money, so he asked Nuannuan to sign up both him and his wife. When Jiuding asked him jokingly what role he wanted to play, Spotty Laosi replied: "How about the King of Chu? I fancy living the life of a king. I've dreamed of being one but never had a chance. Now it comes even though it's just pretend."

Jiuding and Xue Chuanxin both laughed. The latter said: "I'm afraid you won't fit the role."

Jiuding was more straightforward. "You've got to look at

yourself in the reflection of your pee and see if a man with pockmarks can play a king or not. Can a king be pockmarked?"

"Then I'll play a courtier, such as a prime minister, so that I can become majestic and domineering."

"OK, OK, we'll assign you the role of the highest-ranking civil official, standing in the forefront of the other courtiers," Nuannuan promised him with a smile.

Jiuding then asked Laosi's wife with feigned seriousness: "What role do you prefer, Sister-in-Law Spotty Laosi?"

Laosi's wife responded: "I'll still play his wife, whatever official he'll act."

Spotty Laosi was unhappy upon hearing that and protested loudly: "That won't do. A high-ranking official's wife is called her excellency and must be young and pretty. How can she play the role of such a lady? She'd be all right as a lady-in-waiting. My role's wife must look more beautiful than she is."

His wife got angry and kicked his backside. "You swine! How dare you abandon me as soon as you become an official."

Chu Wang Village seemed busier as the hiring and role distribution began. Shallot went to Nuannuan, looking embarrassed, and asked: "Could you perhaps put Changlin in a small role so that he can earn ten yuan himself?"

Nuannuan knew of Changlin's limp arm and his struggle to do any work. But she could not refuse. She bowed her head and thought for a while before asking Shallot: "Can he row a boat with one arm?"

Shallot responded: "He does everything with one arm."

Nuannuan said: "Then he can row King Zi's boat."

After several days of auditions and planning, the cast members were finally chosen. But who would play King Zi? Nuannuan could not make the decision. Xue Chuanxin said to her: "It'll be best if Kaitian plays the role. He's the leader, so people will listen to his instructions as the king."

Nuannuan thought about it and consented. She told Kaitian about the role at the dinner table.

Upon hearing it, Kaitian quickly waved his hand and stepped back, yelling: "You've got to be joking! When did you see me perform before? Do you want to make a fool out of me?"

"You may not have performed before, but why can't you do it now?"

"No, I won't do it." Kaitian resolutely waved his hand.

Nuannuan stared into Kaitian's eyes. "Do you want our South Water Landscape Company to make money? If you do, pluck up your courage. In fact, there's not much in performing. It's only walking back and forth a little in the robe of King Zi of Chu. It's nothing more than playing house as we did in our childhood. The only purpose of the performance is to attract more tourists to Shang Xin Yuan and Chu Di Ju. It's just fun, so don't be afraid. The South Water Landscape Company isn't my business alone. How can you be indifferent to it? You refuse to do it while so many other villagers offer to help. Why?"

"It's not that I don't want to," Kaitian hurriedly explained as he sensed anger in Nuannuan's tone. "As I've never heard of King Zi of Chu, how can I play him?"

"King Zi was the last king of the Chu State, with the imperial honorific title of King Wen of Chu. He was a man who meant what he said, and everyone listened to him. Don't worry about how to act. Xue Chuanxin said he would invite a director from the provincial capital to coach us. We won't put on a show publicly before we're well-rehearsed."

"Do you have to put on the show?" asked Kaitian with displeasure.

"The performance is meant for further developing our tourism resources. Sure, we don't have to, but then we won't be able to attract more tourists and make more money. Besides, this is not just our South Water Landscape Company's business. Xue Chuanxin from Five Continents Group put forward the proposal."

"Wow! I've never dreamed of acting as King Wen of Chu. It's as good as forcing a hen to crow *cock-a-doodle-doo*."

Nuannuan giggled. "Please crow then."

A couple of weeks later, all of the clothes and props had been prepared in the provincial capital. When Xue Chuanxin came back to Chu Wang Village with the goods, he also brought back a TV director. The boats, on the other hand, were bought from other lakeside villages. The decorations were changed to the style of Chu afterwards. Despite their modest size, the boats looked quite impressive when put together. After breakfast on the morning when the preparations were ready, Xue Chuanxin asked Nuannuan to gather all the cast members in front of Shang Xin Yuan so that the director could give each of them their clothes and teach them how to put them on. The scene was quite interesting, with eighty people all dressed as people of Chu. They looked at each other and burst into laughter. The birds in the trees were driven away by the noise.

Nuannuan helped Kaitian put on the costume and hats of the role assigned to him: the King of Chu. Kaitian said with a bitter expression: "It's so hot. I can't stand it. You're making me suffer."

Nuannuan warned him in a low voice: "You're doing it for your own family. It's better than farming under the sun."

King Zi's well-designed coat looked truly majestic. After Kaitian put it on, Nuannuan couldn't help but shout with laughter: "He-he-he, he. You look like an emperor indeed."

Spotty Laosi, who was wearing the coat of a civil official, came over and said enviously: "Kaitian, how great it would be if we changed our costumes. I'd definitely make others look at me differently in your outfit. But I'm not as lucky as you are. I have to be your subject and submit to you even on stage."

Later on, the director started the rehearsal with the aid of Xue Chuanxin and Nuannuan. Thanks to Nuannuan's precaution that no payment would be made if anyone was to loaf on the rehearsal or work against the director, everyone paid good attention. The performance was not difficult, so the show was good enough after three run-throughs. The director was pleased and said: "We'll do a couple of rehearsals like this, and the show will be presentable next week."

Coincidentally, two groups of visitors from Wuhan and Shanxi arrived at Shang Xin Yuan. There were also some other guests staying in Chu Di Ju. Wishing to extend their stay by one more day, Nuannuan suggested to Xue Chuanxin that the performance of *Farewell* debut on the day of the guests' departure so that they could offer some opinions and ideas. Xue Chuanxin agreed after a discussion with the director.

The night before the debut, Nuannuan had all the staff notify the guests about the "wonderful situational show *Farewell* set in the time of Chu". Some guests left after breakfast with no interest in the performance. The next morning, before the boats started to let people on board, according to the director's instructions, Nuannuan waved the yellow flag tied to a long bamboo pole in front of Shang Xin Yuan. At that moment, a line of Chu boats emerged from a bed of reeds close to the riverbank in the shape of a long snake. People dressed up and stood on each boat decorated in the style of Chu, with men playing an instrument made of either pottery or horns, making touching music that sounded quite like weeping. Some others played bamboo whistles. In no time, the weeping music and the sound of the whistles filled the air and greatly attracted the attention of the visitors. Those who were ready to get on board with their luggage all ran close to see the show. With the sound of music, the people on the Chu boats disembarked. Thirty soldiers, with bronze swords in their hands, jumped onto the pier and ran towards the Farewell Shack in two lines. In the blink of an eye, the soldiers had formed two rows by the sides of the road, with the exact same distance between each of them. Suddenly, the weeping music and the whistling noise stopped. Taking its place, the beautiful music of Chu played from the loudspeakers on top of several trees. At the same time, King Zi, his queen and their stewards began to step out of their boats and walked slowly towards the shack. Advisers and stewards, in their various costumes, attracted praise from the crowd. The solemn movement of the majestic group made the visitors open their eyes wide in awe and curiosity. In front of the Farewell Shack, King Zi and his followers knelt towards the north. "My mother, my ancestors – thy son, thy descendants, had to move to a new capital today. Though my body will be on another soil, this soul will stay with thee. One day this body will return and offer the sacrifice again to thee..." In the loudspeaker, the voice of King Zi sounded sorrowful...

The visitors and the locals found the performance fascinating. As the group finished the ceremony and started towards the boats, loud applause burst out in the crowd.

Many visitors missed their boats and had to stay for an extra day.

The performance was a big success.

It seemed that this idea of attracting tourists was right. Nuannuan, Xue Chuanxin and the director glanced at each other, and all looked satisfied.

Nuannuan walked up to Kaitian, patted him on his shoulder and complimented him. "Good job."

Her voice had barely died down when Spotty Laosi shouted in an affected tone: "Who's this rustic woman? How dare you pat His Majesty King of Chu on the shoulder? Is anybody there? Place her under arrest!"

Jiuding, who was also in his official costume, chuckled. "You treacherous court official, are you blind? How can you misidentify the queen?"

At this moment, Spotty Laosi pointed to Youyou, the young married woman who acted as the queen, and said: "The queen is standing next to the King of Chu. How can you be so audacious to talk nonsense? Is anybody there? Come and arrest them all!"

Their banter made the crowd bend over with laughter. Youyou laughed so much that she leaned on Kaitian...

At first, Kaitian was reluctant to join the show. However, as time went by, he became more and more active. During the first performances, Nuannuan had to push him onto the set. He was not comfortable as an actor; sometimes, he might even refuse to go with the excuse of meetings in the village committee. After a couple of performances, he became more and more interested. On the days of the show, he would put on the clothes of King Zi early and wait for the others to arrive at the venue. He would arrange his schedule well so that meetings in the village committee would take place on days when there wasn't a show. He was quite serious about the job: he not only paid much attention to his own acting but would also be upset if someone was not performing to a certain standard. He would scold them: "If you want to do it, do it well."

Kaitian's performance greatly satisfied Nuannuan, Xue Chuanxin and the director. The director asked him how he felt about playing the king. He thought for a while and answered: "It just feels so good. To have so many people surrounding you, paying respect to you and afraid to say no to you. They're all your subjects. You can do whatever you like to them. That feels good."

Seeing that all the performers had got their feet wet, the director took his payment and left. After that, Nuannuan and Xue Chuanxin became the stage managers whenever there was a show. One day during the performance, Spotty Laosi stood in the wrong position, and in the panic of correcting the mistake, he accidentally bumped against Kaitian. Typically, Kaitian would have ignored it, and nothing would have happened. But out of the blue, he flew into a rage, yelling with his eyes wide open: "Is anybody there? Take him!" Everyone was stunned because this was not part of the plot. Even Nuannuan and Xue Chuanxin were flabbergasted. The soldiers initially planted their feet on the ground in a daze and then, under Kaitian's glare, had to escort Spotty Laosi off the scene, their swords and spears pointing at him.

As soon as the performance concluded, Nuannuan reprimanded Kaitian: "How can you change the plot at random?"

She had expected Kaitian to apologise but was surprised by his response. Putting on a fierce face, he retorted: "Why can't I order him to be taken away? A subject struck me."

Xue Chuanxin, who had followed Nuannuan, laughed. "Great! The leader got inside the character he was playing. It's called 'living the part' in the theatrical language. It's hard to come by, and we should commend him instead of blaming him."

Spotty Laosi came over and cut in jokingly. "Looks like I'll have to be careful in the future. I might get him so angry that he decides to cut off my head."

Everyone around burst into laughter except Kaitian, who was still wearing a long face.

With the increase in the number of shows, Kaitian started to perform more naturally. His every move, including his facial expressions, made him resemble a monarch with the power of granting life or death. Xue Chuanxin and the tourists also spoke highly of his true-to-life characterisation of the King of Chu. Nuannuan initially was pleased with the praise and joked with Kaitian at home: "I didn't expect you to be such a talented actor."

But what came to pass later gave Nuannuan a strange feeling. It was one night when a man came to Kaitian for help. The man had been fined for having a baby out of the one-child quota. Kaitian was cold and indifferent and sent the man away with sarcastic remarks.

After the man left, Nuannuan said: "You shouldn't have treated him like that. Being so sarcastic is out of character for a village committee leader."

Nuannuan's words kindled the flames of Kaitian's rage, and he yelled: "How dare you criticise me?"

Nuannuan was also angry. "Why can't I criticise you? Why can't anybody criticise you? Who do you think you are? A king?"

Kaitian yelled again: "I am the leader of Chu Wang Village, the supreme leader! I am the king!"

The last word gave Nuannuan a shudder. He had never talked to her in such a raised voice before he had started acting the part of King Zi of Chu. *What's happened to him?*

After the dispute that night, Nuannuan would never be happy when she saw Kaitian dressed in King Zi's costume and walking with a majestic and smug look. But she forced herself to feel pleased with the performance's result as it attracted more and more tourists.

One day at sunset, the head of each family was gathered by the village committee to discuss the donation for the construction of an elementary school nearby. Nuannuan was walking past the committee office on her way home from Shang Xin Yuan, so she stopped to listen. Most people had agreed to donate 120 yuan per household if there was a child going to school. Some others proposed 100 yuan or 130 yuan per household. In the end, Kaitian spoke out: "Listen to me, we'll go with 166 yuan per family. This is an auspicious number."

The crowd fell silent for a while. Then, two men stood up and said: "Mr Leader, 166 yuan is a little too much. The extra thirty yuan means a lot to us."

Nuannuan thought Kaitian would explain why he had decided on 166 yuan. On the contrary, he simply glared at the two men and asked in a cold voice: "Who makes the decisions in Chu Wang Village? You or me?"

The two men could not answer. Seeing Kaitian's angry face and cold attitude, the crowd dared not speak. Nuannuan looked at Kaitian. She felt as if she were looking at a stranger.

One afternoon several days later, Nuannuan was finishing cooking at home when she saw Kaitian ride a brand-new motorcycle into the courtyard. She was surprised. "You can ride a motorcycle now?"

Kaitian got off it and skilfully parked. "This thing is easy to learn. If you can ride a bicycle, it takes only half an hour."

"Whose new motorcycle is this?" asked Nuannuan as she stepped forward to touch the shining paint.

"Mine!"

Nuannuan was more surprised. "Yours? When did you buy it?"

"I was the only one riding a bike to the meetings in the township office. The chief secretaries and leaders from other villages all ride motorcycles. I was embarrassed to show up like that, so I had a discussion with the chief secretary, and we bought two of these – one for him, one for me."

"With the money of the village committee?"

"Of course I didn't spend our own money. I'm the leader, and I'm working for the welfare of the village. Why can't I ride a motorcycle like the other leaders do?"

Nuannuan did not speak for a short while. Then she said: "The money of the village committee holds funds from each household in the village. Everyone is watching where it goes. How can you spend it like that? Aren't you afraid of people talking behind your back? If you truly want a motorcycle, we can buy one with our own money. It's not like we can't afford it."

"Come on, you nag at everything I do," said Kaitian as he glared at Nuannuan. "Who's the leader of the village, you or me? Who knows how to make a decision, you or me? Do you think you're better than me?"

Nuannuan was stunned by his questions. After some time, she sighed and finally said: "It seems that my words don't matter in this house any more…"

The situational performance of Chu enjoyed a wider reputation and attracted more and more visitors into Chu Wang Village. Due to the growth of tourism, merchants from Juxiang Street and the neighbouring villages all went to Chu Wang Village too. Some even came all the way from the city of Nanfu. A few put up small stands near the entrance to the village, the pier, Shang Xin Yuan or Chu Di Ju to sell goods, while others rented local houses to open shops. At first, most of the merchants were selling things like water chestnuts, dried lake shrimps, wild mushrooms, black fungus, reed roots, day-lilies, fiddleheads, fried bean jellies, pepper and chilli soup, and steamed buns. These were followed by merchants offering toys and other everyday products: jade toys from Du Mountain, silk tapestries from Zhenping, silverware from Xichuan, Six-Flavour

Dihuang bolus, rare rocks, bandages, wicker baskets, dried wildflowers, paintings and calligraphies, and traditional Chinese Viagra under the name of "The Never Falling Gold Spear". The last to arrive were entertainers: traditional He'nan Zhuizi storytellers, Yu Opera singers, monkey trainers, acrobats, *suona* players and fiddlers...

Chu Wang Village had suddenly become a busy place, with an enormous number of people. Xue Chuanxin said to Nuannuan proudly: "What do you say – have I or have I not stopped the decline of Chu Wang Village and saved you all?"

Nuannuan was more than pleased to see the village in its busy state. She laughed and answered: "Yes, yes. You're the saviour of Chu Wang Village."

"It won't take long for Chu Wang Village to develop into a small town. Maybe in the future, there'll be a new micro city of Chu Wang Village," Xue Chuanxin said as he waved his arms.

"I hope so," Nuannuan replied jokingly. "I'll have the villagers erect a stone statue of you at the village entrance for people to view."

"How about we borrow the term 'Father of the Nation' and name me 'Father of the Village'?"

Nuannuan was displeased with his remark and changed the subject. "Mr Xue, I have another idea. When we've earned all the investment back, maybe we can invest in the construction of several shops in the style of Chu by the side of the main road heading from south to north in the village. We can ask experts in the history of the Chu, such as Uncle Tan, to participate in the design so that we can perfectly reproduce the lifestyle in the State of Chu. We can also encourage the villagers to participate and gradually transform the road into a Chu Street. When that's done, visitors could stay in Shang Xin Yuan and Chu Di Ju, visit the Great Wall of Chu, Lingyan Temple and the mysterious triangle in the lake, experience farm work in the fields to pick crops and vegetables, and watch *Farewell*, all of which will enhance their enjoyment in Chu Wang Village and extend their stay. Moreover, on Chu Street, we'll need more people to dress up like Chu people and take care of the shops. More people in the village can participate in the tourism business and earn extra income outside of farm work. This will be something I can do for the village."

"You do care for your village," said Xue Chuanxin as he burst into laughter. "Even if we have enough money in the future, your idea is not realistic, since it brings a lot of trouble and not enough revenue. If you want to expand the business, I'll build a dozen European-style guest houses, with a courtyard attached to each so that guests will have their own space for activities. They'll be VIP houses specially designed for higher officials and celebrities. We'll charge more than two thousand yuan a day each."

"Really?"

"Of course! The houses must look elegant so we should hire famous architects from Europe. They must attract everyone's attention at first sight."

"But where will you find the land to build them on?" said Nuannuan in shock. "The village has used up all land ownerships, and there is nothing left but farmland. You can't build houses in the sky."

"Things will work out when the time comes. You and I should not worry about that now. We must focus on our work..."

One day at sunset, Nuannuan was picking up a group of visitors by the side of the lake as Jiuding steered the boat to the pier. He had been hired by Shang Xin Yuan to take guests to see the mysterious triangle in the lake. He cried out: "Big Sister, I have something to report to you."

Nuannuan smiled and said: "What is it? You seem serious."

"I want to open a fish restaurant and hire people to help me out. Red Lake is famous for its fish, and the visitors love them. So I just want a small restaurant that sells fish dishes. I don't even need a chef – my wife Huiyu can cook the fish well enough. We can fix all kinds of fish dishes to cater to people with different tastes. We can steam fish heads, deep-fry fish fillets, stew fish maw with five-flavour spices, make sweet-and-sour fish soup, braise fishtails, dry-braise crucian carp, boil striped catfish in hot sauce and crisp-fry whitefish. We can prepare any fish dishes the customers prefer. Do you think it can work?"

Nuannuan nodded and happily responded: "That's good. You're utilising the advantages of our lake. You can find all kinds of fish in Red Lake. And we village people can find all kinds of good ways to cook them. It is indeed an idea worth good money. You should do it, and I'll help you. What can I do?"

Jiuding smiled and said: "I don't really need you to help with setting up the restaurant. We can use our house and cooking utensils. We'll make a few wooden tables and chairs. But can you talk to the leader and get his permission? Of course, I will not abandon this boat. Huiyu will take care of the restaurant, and her little brother will work as an assistant."

"Sure, I'll talk to Kaitian. But remember, you don't need the leader's permission to open a business. Start your work, and I'll congratulate you upon the opening."

Jiuding's small Fish Feast did good business after its opening. Visitors would go to taste the dishes in groups, and they filled up all four tables. Nuannuan went over several times, and each time she saw Huiyu and her brother covered in sweat, busy at work. Whenever there was no need for boats to Shang Xin Yuan and no farm work in the fields, Jiuding would work in the restaurant.

One day, Nuannuan joked with Jiuding: "You've diverted the guests from the dining facilities of both Chu Di Ju and Shang Xin Yuan to your restaurant. You've got to pay us some compensation."

Jiuding hurriedly begged her: "You and Brother Kaitian's body hair is thicker than our waist. The money we're earning is no match for yours. Please allow us to scrape only a few grains from your rice bowl."

Spotty Laosi laughed at Jiuding's ambition with Fish Feast when it first opened. He said: "How can city people eat your wife's fish? What fish dishes haven't they eaten? Do you want to attract them with the scent of your wife's hands or breasts?" However, when he saw the visitors constantly walking in and out of the restaurant, as well as Jiuding and his wife's busy hands taking in the cash, he became jealous and regretful. *Damn, why didn't I think of such a way to make money?* When he saw Jiuding buy a colour TV with the money he had made, Spotty Laosi grew even more jealous. He went to Nuannuan and said to her: "I'd like to open a fish restaurant for my wife too. Is that OK?"

Nuannuan laughed at his words. "There are so many different ways to make money. Why do you want to take the same road that others took? If you do open another fish restaurant, it'll be impossible to avoid arguments with Jiuding because you'll be fighting for customers. If you ask me, you should open a dessert shop for her to sell sweet soup with lotus seeds. Red Lake is famous for its lotus. She could buy some local white fungus and cook the soup with crystal sugar and powder of lotus seeds. If you sell one bowl at two yuan, I'm sure the visitors will fight for a taste. They travel a lot and need some dessert to reduce internal heat. Your soup will sell well."

Spotty Laosi listened and nodded. "That makes sense, good sense. Nuannuan, you're so smart. This is worth a try."

Shortly after their conversation, Spotty Laosi's dessert shop opened in the house opposite his. Spotty Laosi's wife made the soup, and his niece served them to the customers. There were no tables in the shop; instead, there were a dozen stools in front of the door. Spotty Laosi continued his tour guide job with South Water Landscape during the day. In the evening, he would return to help his wife out. Exactly as Nuannuan had expected, before they went to have dinner in Chu Di Ju and Shang Xin Yuan, many visitors loved the taste of a soothing lotus seed soup after a day of sightseeing. On a good day, Spotty Laosi's wife could sell more than fifty bowls of soup and earn a net profit of more than thirty yuan. The income kept a smile on the couple's faces.

Spotty Laosi tried to invite Nuannuan over to treat her to his lotus soup as a token of gratitude for her brilliant idea. Knowing that their money was hard-earned, Nuannuan declined each time, saying: "I'll leave it for now and eat my fill when I suffer from internal heat."

Uncle Black Bean had never earned much from picking and selling herbal medicine and, seeing how quickly Jiuding and Spotty Laosi were able to earn a buck, he too grew determined to earn some. He found Nuannuan and asked: "Hey Nuannuan, now that everyone is making money, can you think of a way for this old uncle to make some too? How about if I open a shop to earn some cash?"

Nuannuan laughed. "I'm afraid running a shop wouldn't work to your advantage. In fact, I do have an idea for you to make money, but I don't know if you'd be interested or not."

"What is it?" Uncle Black Bean asked hurriedly.

"If you were to plant cucumbers, tomatoes, string beans, aubergine, gourds and other vegetables that can be harvested, along with those that you normally plant – red sage, magnolia, papaya, knotweed and other herbal medicines – all in your own plot of land, you could turn it into a plant-picking garden."

"A plant-picking garden?" Uncle Black Bean was puzzled.

Nuannuan explained by telling him how folk in Beijing's outskirts made money with their gardens. She said: "Kaitian and I had planned to do this. But we gave it up after Kaitian became the village committee leader. All you need to do is manage the growing of the garden itself, and then I can guarantee to bring tourists in. A sure way to make money."

"Great! I trust you. You've got vision since you can run Chu Di Ju and Shang Xin Yuan so well. I'll open up the garden next spring as you say."

Before people knew it, it was getting chilly. The number of tourists who came to the west bank dwindled. One day, Nuannuan laundered clothes in her residence as there was nothing to do in the vacant Shang Xin Yuan. She also cleaned her parents-in-law's bedroom and other rooms. Then, she strolled to Chu Di Ju. She had learned from Sister-in-Law Shallot that about a dozen visitors from Kaifeng were coming to stay in Chu Di Ju, so she went to make some arrangements. Sister-in-Law Shallot had become the manager of Chu Di Ju after Nuannuan started working in Shang Xin Yuan. She wanted to ask if Sister-in-Law Shallot had any difficulty and needed her help. She had stepped a few metres away from her residence when she heard a gruff voice. "Chu Nuannuan!"

This unusual voice startled her, and she abruptly turned around to look in the direction of the call. She caught sight of a skinny older man leaning on a walking cane. He was standing there glaring at her with anger written on his face. A perplexed Nuannuan asked: "You called me?"

"Phew. Did I call a dog?" the older man said with venom while stamping his cane on the ground.

It was the "phew" that betrayed Zhan Shideng's identity. She was taken aback the moment she recognised him. *How could Zhan Shideng have changed so much? How could he have so transformed?* He looked like a different person – a senile man. His prowess and majesty had suddenly vaporised. It was the first time Nuannuan had seen him since his downfall. She had heard he was sick. Of course, she didn't care what disease was nagging him. Nor did she care how long he had suffered from it. He looked seriously sick to her, which was beyond her wildest imagination. *Wow, people can change so fast!*

"Do you have something on your mind?" Nuannuan found it hard to leave immediately, wondering if he got sick because he got voted out of his office. If so, she felt a bit responsible for it.

"If I didn't, then why would I have to come to see a slut like you?" Zhan Shideng squeezed the words from his teeth.

These harsh words blew away the little pity she had for him. She quickly turned around, ready to leave. She didn't have to fear him because he was now an ordinary person like her. He didn't have the power to call and stop her. But she quickly changed her mind and slowed her steps to a standstill. Then she slowly turned around to glare at him. She wanted to know what in the world he would do to her.

"You slut! You fooled me. You promised to stop Kaitian from running against me." Zhan Shideng walked up towards Nuannuan, his wide-open eyes bloodshot with a ferocious look.

Nuannuan broke into a smile of triumph mixed with pity, thinking: *Your anger is still lingering.* But she calmly said: "Why did you try to keep him out of the election? Who gave you the right? Why did we have to do whatever you told us?" Staring into Zhan Shideng's vicious eyes, she added: "You should be open-minded. Just think why you have to remain in the post forever."

"Slut! I didn't see through you. I didn't expect you were so cunning."

"Now have a good look. Do you think all those who you bullied before were stupid, that they would take your bullying lying down?"

"Don't be happy too soon."

His threat enraged Nuannuan. "If I'm happy, what can you do about it? Do you still want me to cry before you? Do you still want to see me humbly beg before you? You're dreaming. Things like that will never happen."

"Wait and see. The day when you cry will come."

"Don't even think about it."

"Don't think about it?" A cold smirk flickered in Zhan Shideng's eyes. "Let me ask you. Have you told Kaitian about my sleeping with you? Did he know I cuckolded him?"

"You swine!" The sudden onslaught of humiliation dazed Nuannuan.

"I calculated that you hadn't told him about it. I guess you've kept him in the dark all this time. Please allow me to divulge it to him myself, would you?" Zhan Shideng's face twitched with excitement. "Let me see how you react. Don't you want to be happy?"

"You beast!" Nuannuan shivered with wrath.

"It's time to tell Leader Kuang how willingly and happily his wife slept with the then Leader Zhan. It's time to let Kaitian know how much his wife enjoyed herself in Zhan Shideng's bed."

"You swine!" Furious, Nuannuan bent down to look for a rock or brick so that she could whack Zhan Shideng on his head with it. Unfortunately, there was nothing under her nose. She had to look around her. She had just stood up with a stone when she found Zhan Shideng gone.

"Son of a bitch!" Nuannuan yelled with indignation and tears. Just then, Sister-in-Law Shallot passed by, and Nuannuan quickly wiped the tears off her face.

"Nuannuan, what are you doing with that stone in your hand?" asked Sister-in-Law Shallot with a smile.

"I saw a bitch," said Nuannuan as she cast away the rock with anger. She turned around and asked: "Are you prepared for receiving the tourists?"

"We're pretty much ready. But I've got something I wanted to check with you." Sister-in-Law Shallot unhurriedly explained what was on her mind, but Nuannuan couldn't hear a single word. Zhan Shideng's outburst had ruined her excellent mood and brought back the memory of her past misery, plunging her into a new wave of anxiety. *If Zhan Shideng does what he threatened to do, how will Kaitian react?* It seemed that she had to tell him everything instead of hiding it from him. Now her misery had turned against herself. *Zhan Shideng, I've never imagined that there should be such a shameless person like you in the world. You violated me, and now use it as a weapon against me...*

Nuannuan couldn't accomplish anything for the rest of that afternoon. Zhan Shideng's threat weighed heavy on her mind. *What shall I do? Shall I tell him first? But if I did, he would ask why I had waited for so long. Shall I wait till Kaitian asks me? That would be even worse. Good heavens! I just thought life had turned for the better. I didn't expect that Zhan Shideng would bring up the old scores again. You son of a bitch! I'll kill you! I'll kill you!*

When Kaitian came back for lunch, Nuannuan carefully looked at his face. Fortunately, everything was as usual. It seemed that Zhan Shideng had not had time to tell him.

After the meal, Nuannuan summoned the courage to say: "Kaitian, I want to tell you something."

Kaitian obviously thought she would talk about the company, so he waved his hand. "I'm going to the township to have a meeting in the afternoon. I hope you'll take more of the responsibility for looking after our family and the company."

The next day, a dozen or so tourists arrived at Shang Xin Yuan. These guests had not been introduced to Shang Xin Yuan by the marketing team of Five Continents Group; instead, they had arranged the trip themselves, arriving as walk-ins. Although they were few in number, it was quite a task to arrange everything for them. Some only wanted to see the Great Wall of Chu, some only to see the lake, some only the *Farewell* performance, and others just Lingyan Temple. In order to accommodate everybody, Nuannuan exerted all of her energy, ultimately arranging the details of every tour. As she arrived home before dinnertime, Dangen raced towards her, laughing. Kaitian arrived next, his face darkened with anger. Believing it to be trouble from the village meeting, Nuannuan, still laughing with Dangen, said to him: "Look at your dad with dark clouds over his face. Quickly go and wipe them away."

Dangen rushed over to his dad's leg, saying: "Dad…"

"Fuck off!" Kaitian shoved his son away violently, and little Dangen, unable to react in time, fell flat on his bottom and began crying loudly.

Kaitian was now in the bedroom and struck out again, breaking something else – maybe Dangen's drinking cup. Kaitian's mum heard the commotion and came in to stare at her daughter-in-law in shock, muttering to herself: "What the hell is up with him?"

Nuannuan didn't say a word but stood up and walked slowly into the bedroom.

"Don't you want to ask me what the fuck is up?" Kaitian asked quietly, his hands gripping at the chair armrest with such anger that blue veins were protruding.

Nuannuan said nothing. She stood silently and stared at Kaitian, waiting for him to speak again.

Kaitian turned around and threw a piece of crumpled-up

notepaper at her. Nuannuan slowly opened it and read what was written on it:

Kuang Kaitian, I know you enjoy being the leader, so let me tell you something else to enjoy: I slept with your wife, and she stripped before me with pleasure! You can go and ask her yourself how it felt!

Zhan Shideng's name was signed at the bottom.

Stars appeared before Nuannuan's eyes, and she swayed on the spot.

"Is this true?" Kaitian turned to face her, his eyes wide open in fury, his teeth clenched.

"What do you think?" Nuannuan said angrily as Kaitian glared at her with a stabbing gaze.

"Just tell me if you did it. Be straight with me."

Nuannuan broke the silence. "I did."

Kaitian whipped his palm across her face, snarling out: "You slut! I knew it was true. Otherwise, how could Zhan Shideng be so brave as to sign his name."

Nuannuan staggered back from the vicious attack but quickly righted herself. As blood oozed from the corner of her mouth, she smirked and said: "That was pretty hard. Do you want to hit me a few more times?"

Nuannuan's challenge inflamed Kaitian. He lunged towards her, grabbed her by her side, and brought his punches down upon her. As he pounded, he screamed: "How dare you make me lose face like this!"

Nuannuan made no attempt to protect herself or fight back by raising her hands. She only endured his beating.

"Why are you so mad? Why did you hit her? Nuannuan has worked the whole day and just got back home…" As she scolded Kaitian, his mother picked up a shoe behind the door and whammed her son on his shoulder. Kaitian had to leave, seething.

Kaitian's mum, cuddling Dangen to calm him down, had heard the noises and ran into the bedroom, holding Dangen as she yelled out in shock: "What the fuck is this? Have you gone mad?" Then she rushed to protect her daughter-in-law. Only then did Kaitian stop his attack.

Nuannuan's face was now covered with blood. Held up by the

wall, she did not cry or respond. She forced herself to stand upright, with eyes open wide in bitter shock, teeth clenched tight.

Kaitian's mum stepped in front of Nuannuan and consoled her. "Nuannuan, don't lower yourself to the level of this brainless animal. Mum knows he is wrong. Please vent your anger out on me." She tried to wipe the blood off Nuannuan's face.

Nuannuan still said nothing and, pushing her mother-in-law's hand away, she walked to the bed and clutched some clothes to her chest before turning to walk out of the house.

"Nuannuan, where are you going?" Kaitian's mum lunged and grabbed her by her sleeve. "Supper is ready. Since you've worked the whole day, please eat something first. Please don't be angry with him any more. He's got a hot temper like his dad. If you pardon him, I'll ask him to apologise to your later."

Nuannuan struggled from her mother-in-law's grasp silently and strode towards the courtyard door without looking back. Hearing Dangen crying in the yard, she only looked back once before stepping out. *Kuang Kaitian, I let you hit me. Come and hit me again. Now I finally know who you are. You arsehole!*

That night, she slept in one of the rooms of Chu Di Ju. Barricading the door, she lay quietly on the bed, listening to Kaitian's mum calling out and Dangen continually crying. She lay completely still, oblivious to it all, feeling the pain in her face, reliving the painful images of Kaitian beating her. This was the first time she had been physically beaten. She would have never imagined her abuser to be Kuang Kaitian...

The next morning before it was light, Nuannuan had already set off to Shang Xin Yuan.

The on-duty security guard did not expect her arrival. "Ms Nuannuan, an early start?"

Nuannuan nodded, saying vaguely: "Something urgent."

Xue Chuanxin had given Nuannuan an office room to use, and she rarely went there except for short meetings. Now she entered it to clean herself up so as to present herself as normal. She joined the staff as they ate breakfast. They did not expect her and glanced at her periodically.

Eventually, Xue Chuanxin asked: "Not eating at home today?"

Nuannuan forced a smile. "The food at home is too oily. I'm just here for a new flavour."

Later that morning, a new group of tourists arrived. Just before lunchtime when Nuannuan was busy receiving them, Kaitian's mum arrived with Dangen. The security guard let the grandma and her grandson into Nuannuan's office, and as soon as the old lady saw Nuannuan, she said: "I've already cursed that fucker Kaitian till I was blue in the face, and really let him have it for you. You need not lower yourself to his level. Come home and have some lunch."

Nuannuan simply said: "Mum, take Dangen home. I have things to do and will eat lunch here."

Kaitian's mum heard the calmness in Nuannuan's voice and believed that Nuannuan had already let everything go. But at dinnertime, Nuannuan again had dinner with the on-duty staff, eating very little, her anger held in her chest. *Kuang Kaitian, how could you attack me? Attack your wife? Why didn't you ask me why I had to do it? Why not ask me? Zhan Shideng, you're not a human being any more. You're a beast. You raped me and continue to harm me. Do you have any conscience? I wish I could kill you. Heaven, the Buddha, and the lake god, if you're omniscient, please punish him.* After darkness fell, she asked a housekeeper to get a set of bedding from Sister-in-Law Shallot in Chu Di Ju. Nuannuan decided that she would sleep in her office.

Soon after she got the bedding, Kaitian's mother rushed over again. She tried to talk her into going back home in a whisper: "How can you not sleep at home? What if Dangen asks for you in the night?"

Nuannuan said: "Mum, please go back. I'll sleep here to think about what has happened. If Dangen cries and asks for me, doesn't he have his dad who knows how to beat people?"

Unable to persuade her daughter-in-law to go with her, the mother-in-law slowly walked back home herself. Seeing Nuannuan was staying the night in Shang Xin Yuan, Xue Chuanxin went over beaming. "You must be angry with Leader Kaitian, I guess. I think Leader Kaitian is a fool, offending such a gorgeous wife. Isn't he afraid that she would elope with another man?"

"Go away." His joke brought a smile to her face.

The following day after breakfast was the scheduled time for the *Farewell* show. Nuannuan wasn't planning to go out to wave the yellow flag to signal the beginning of the show. But she didn't want others to find out that she was at odds with Kaitian. So, she had to do what she was supposed to do. After the performance, Nuannuan spotted Kaitian coming from the lakeside, surrounded by a crowd. His face was cold, with a murderous look. Nuannuan shuddered at the sight. *Son of a bitch! You're more like a formidable King of Chu than when you're acting the role.*

Nuannuan did not return home to sleep or eat for several days. Shallot and Jiuding's wife Huiyu did not know why Kaitian and Nuannuan were angry. They took turns to try to persuade her to return home and said: "As the saying goes, 'A husband and wife never hate each other after they fight.' You'll reconcile when you hold each other at night."

But she did not respond to their urgings. *How can I forgive Kaitian for beating me? If I went back home now, I would encourage his arrogance. I can't let him think he can beat someone without consequences.* But, having been away from home for days, she began to miss it. She was worried about Dangen, wondering if he could eat and sleep well. Her parents-in-law also concerned her. She feared that the family chores might overwhelm them. And she couldn't leave the management of Chu Di Ji to Sister-in-Law Shallot alone. Some things required her to make the decisions. Nuannuan thought at this moment that she would return home if Kaitian came to apologise and promise not to physically abuse her any more. But Kaitian never showed up. In the following days, she was especially weary of people's footsteps, beginning to yearn for Kaitian's in particular. But she never heard them. *Kuang Kaitian, you're ruthless indeed. You won't say sorry even after you struck me?* At this point in time, Nuannuan began to think that she did in fact hold some responsibility in the matter. If she had told Kaitian how Zhan Shideng forced her to sleep with him, maybe he would not have lost his temper. To have heard it from Zhan Shideng must have been a stab right into Kaitian's heart. As a man, he has every right to lose his temper at such a thing. With these thoughts, the burning anger in her chest slowly died down, and she wished to return home.

At noon on that day, Nuannuan returned to Chu Di Ju with the excuse to find Shallot to discuss something. There, she thought that no matter who she bumped into, she could simply give in and head home without causing any more trouble once they urged her to return home.

Only a few steps from entering Chu Di Ju, Nuannuan did not

expect to hear Kaitian's happy voice drifting in from the courtyard. "Haha! Little Youyou, you do flatter me." Nuannuan froze on the spot. *What's Youyou doing here?* She knew the young girl Youyou was a right lazy glutton and was often on the hunt for men to fool around and flirt with. It was said that before she was married into Chu Wang Village, she had already had two abortions. When the director initially cast Youyou as the Chu king's queen in *Farewell*, Nuannuan felt a bit uncomfortable, but the performance was just a show for the guests, and she didn't think much of it. Now hearing her laughing with Kaitian, she couldn't help but feel a bit shocked.

"How was I flattering you? I'm being serious." Youyou was obviously pandering to him. "Ever since you became the leader of Chu Wang Village, the sky is bluer, the water is clearer and money rattles loudly in the pockets of every family. Even the dogs bark with more gusto. Everybody says that without you, there would be no bright future for Chu Wang Village."

"All right, all right, that'll do. What can I help you with?" Kaitian's voice was full of pleasure.

"We want to build another three-room house..." Nuannuan could not listen any longer, and just as she turned to leave, Shallot appeared. Seeing Nuannuan, she hurriedly grabbed her by the arm and said: "Oh, good sister, you're back. Wouldn't it be best to hurry back home to see Dangen? Every time I see your little baby, I hear him crying for you." She then turned and shouted: "Kuang Kaitian, come and take Nuannuan home."

The laughter in the courtyard stopped. Nuannuan turned to glance at Kaitian, only to see the smile still lingering on his face. She felt a bit miserable seeing that he had been so happy while she was away from home. But she didn't want to give up the opportunity to come back. So, half dragged behind Shallot, she headed back to her house. On entering the courtyard, Dangen rushed forward, tears welling from his eyes...

With the trouble having settled down, the Kuang household appeared to return to its daily routine. But Nuannuan knew that things had changed, and the past and the present were no longer the same. As Kaitian did not admit what he had done, Nuannuan constantly felt a knot in her chest. Kaitian stopped speaking to Nuannuan, and his temper continued to shorten. At an instant, he would break into a rage, sometimes at other villagers, sometimes at the actors in *Farewell*, and sometimes at little Dangen. Nuannuan ignored it and spent most of her time at Shang Xin Yuan or helping Shallot manage Chu Di Ju. When things needed doing at home or in the fields, Nuannuan and Kaitian would go one at a time – Nuannuan would manage things by herself, whereas Kaitian would call peasants over to help out while spending his time inspecting other fields.

In the evenings, Kaitian would often return very late, always being hosted for a meal at this house and that house. He would get into bed and fall asleep immediately. They scarcely made love as Kaitian would seldom touch Nuannuan. One night, he came back and climbed into bed, smelling like a distillery. Without saying a word, he reached for Nuannuan's body. Though unhappy, Nuannuan didn't express her disapproval, allowing him to do whatever he wanted. But it was as if she were doing a dreary routine job, and it made her feel worse. Nuannuan thought her life was without flavour. But regardless, the days wouldn't stop coming just for her sake. She was still determined to work every day, but she no longer felt happy or trusting. People seldom heard her laughter any more, and even the sound of her voice grew rare.

Fortunately, the first snows arrived, and with that the tourists vanished. As they had done the year before, Nuannuan shut Chu Di Ju. Xue Chuanxin also closed Shang Xin Yuan and began to balance the accounts. Before Xue Chuanxin left for the provincial capital to spend the New Year, he put the Kuangs' initial investment to Shang Xin Yuan, 123,000 yuan in cash, into Nuannuan's hands and said, laughing: "You've made your investment back. Next year we can start earning profit. And if the year is good, we'll make a big amount."

With the money in her hand, Nuannuan felt a brief consolation. A year of hard work had paid off. She returned thirty-four thousand yuan of the village money to the village accountant, signing off the loan receipt. Combining the remaining eighty-nine thousand yuan with the thirty thousand yuan earned this year from Chu Di Ju, she piled the cash together underneath her mattress. When Kaitian returned home that night to get into bed, Nuannuan held up her hand to stop him and, without a word, she lifted the mattress up for him to see. Kaitian looked at the pile of cash for a moment and then said: "Sleep."

They lay together over the money. Kaitian was snoring soon, but Nuannuan did not fall asleep for a long time...

On the morning of New Year's Day, Kaitian asked Nuannuan for Shang Xin Yuan's keys. Nuannuan couldn't help but ask: "What do you want them for?"

"I want to put on a show of *Farewell* to add to the celebratory atmosphere."

Nuannuan asked with surprise: "As we don't have a single tourist, who's your audience?"

"Myself. Performance doesn't have to involve an audience." As he spoke, Kaitian took the keys and called Spotty Laosi next door, demanding that he get the cast together.

Calling back over the courtyard wall with reluctance, Spotty Laosi mocked: "My Leader Kaitian, are you addicted to acting as the king? Why do you want to put on the show *Farewell* instead of having a good time with your family at home?"

"You ignorant man. People feel happy when they perform, and the village will be livelier. Go and call them together," said Kaitian with displeasure.

"Who will pay for the performers? General Manager Xue went back home for the New Year season," Spotty Laosi reminded Kaitian.

"Are you demanding money for working a little? To put on the show is my order – the village leader's order. So, everyone must participate without pay. Whoever dares not come, I'll increase his apportioned tax in the future."

Hearing his threat, Spotty Laosi nodded submissively. "OK, OK. I'll call them together. You're my leader, boss and king. I'm your fellow villager, employee and subordinate. So, I obey."

How could a *Farewell* show on New Year's Day have an audience? Which villager would still be interested after watching it a million times? Even the children who liked the excitement barely came to watch because they were fascinated with lighting firecrackers. All the performers were listless except Kaitian, who was in high spirits. Watching them from some distance, Nuannuan wondered why Kaitian was so thrilled.

First, the ice on Red Lake began to slowly disappear. Then, the snow piles on the mountainside gradually melted. The first sprouts of grass appeared by the shore, followed by red mountain peach blossoms, and then the migratory birds returned to the mountain forests. The season could wait no longer as spring arrived at the west bank of Red Lake.

The inhabitants of Chu Wang Village again became busy with the spring sowing. On the lower reaches of the mountains, they were planting sweet potato, chilli peppers, aubergines and chives, as well as seeding corn, putting down pumpkin seeds and spreading rapeseed. For farmers, the year would depend on the work of spring, and as the annual Spring Festival was a time of crucial importance for the crops, they slept late and rose early to tend the fields.

While the other families of the village were at their busiest, the Kuang family carried on at the same pace as before, awakening at the same time for breakfast, without haste or hindrance. The reason for this was that Kaitian and Nuannuan had leased their plot of land to Zhan Tongfang in order to grow crops. The idea was Nuannuan's. She said they had to attend to the business of Chu Di Ju and Shang Xin Yuan and often neglected the work in the fields. Besides, farming yielded very little income. Therefore, it would be better to lease the land to other farmers so that they could devote themselves to tourism wholeheartedly. Anyway, with money, they could always buy grain and vegetables, which weren't expensive nowadays and didn't sell well. The income from a few more guests would cover the expenditure on food. Kaitian hadn't been interested in farming and had to do it under the pressure of making a living. Now that he had become the village committee leader, he didn't want to farm any more, and he readily consented to Nuannuan's suggestion. Nuannuan signed a contract: the Kuangs would lease their land to Zhan Tongfang for his use, with all harvests belonging to Zhan Tongfang, with all taxes in proportion to the size of the land being paid by Zhan, and at any time the Kuangs could claim the land back for their own usage.

Without a plot of land, Nuannuan felt at ease and no longer needed to worry about unpredictable weather. Nor would she have to wake up early and return home late, burned by the sun, stung by the wind and soaked by rain. It seemed that she didn't have to leave Chu Wang Village to escape from toiling in the fields.

While the villagers were busying themselves sowing, Nuannuan gently pushed open the gates of Chu Di Ju and Shang Xin Yuan. She asked staff to clean up the rooms in preparation for tourists.

The first group of tourists this spring comprised two affluent businessmen from southern China and their families. It was the first time Nuannuan had witnessed the life lived by people of immense wealth. One of the rich men had the surname Chu, who Xue Chuanxin called Boss Chu. The other was Gou, who Xue Chuanxin referred to as Boss Gou. Both were in their forties, but their wives were young women in their twenties. Their children were but one or two years of age. Each of the three-member families had four bodyguards and housemaids, and they came with escorts from Five Continents Group.

The first question that Boss Chu asked upon entering Shang Xin Yuan was if they had delicacies to satisfy their palates. Xue Chuanxin signalled Nuannuan to give them an introduction.

Nuannuan said: "Our place is a transitional belt from the south to the north in terms of its climate, so we have lots of delicacies. We grow all the fruit and vegetables that can be found in southern China but unavailable to our north. We also produce all the fruit and vegetables found in northern China that won't grow in the south. Therefore, we can satisfy all your fruit and veg needs."

Boss Chu shook his head. "We can have what you told us everywhere – none of it is rare. What I meant are the things we can eat nowhere else but here."

Nuannuan beamed. "Since we've got the lake and the hills, the delicacies are all hidden in them. Our people call them 'delicacies from land and water'."

These words aroused Boss Chu's interest, and he asked: "What's the rarest of the delicacies from land and water?"

"The fungus known as the spotted lion's mane is the rarest. And as for aquatic delicacies, the black-bellied catfish from the lake is the most precious."

Boss Chu nodded. "We'll have some spotted lion's mane and black-bellied catfish for our dinner today."

Nuannuan was about to ask the chefs to fix the two dishes when Boss Chu's wife unexpectedly asked: "How will you prepare the dishes? Dry-braising them or making them into soups? If you make us soups, you must simmer them for four hours. You can't rush it. In addition, we'll have six cold dishes and eight hot dishes..."

Nuannuan asked the chefs to fix them accordingly. Before they served the dishes, Boss Gou asked where they would eat. Stumped briefly, Nuannuan answered: "In the dining hall."

"That's not in good taste," said Boss Gou, shaking his head. "We'd prefer to eat by the lake. It's more intriguing if we can eat while enjoying the lake view and the fishing boats. We're here because we want to smell the mountain breeze and the lake water."

Xue Chuanxin ordered that a temporary shack be built by the lakeside at once, with the dinner table set up in it...

They ate until the moon climbed up the treetops. The two families were chatting and laughing and even had their housemaids sing for them, attracting many villagers. All the Shang Xin Yuan staff were hustling and bustling. But when the time came to pay the bill, Xue Chuanxin didn't relent and asked for 18,800 yuan for food and service, a figure that made Nuannuan's jaw drop with surprise. She had thought the two families would protest against the price hike, but without hesitation, Boss Chu snapped his fingers to signal one of his bodyguards to pay the bill.

On the third day, the two families said that they had had enough of the "delicacies from the land and water" and asked for something new for a change. When Xue Chuanxin asked what they wanted to eat, Boss Gou responded: "We've done an investigation into what to eat here in the past few days. Your chestnut white-bellied rats are pretty big. We can have a taste of them. Besides, the giant Chinese salamanders in the brooks of South Mountain are very famous. We want to have a taste of them as well."

His request stunned Nuannuan, who hurriedly told Boss Gou that the villagers here had never eaten the rats, thinking of them as filthy, and even the chefs didn't know how to cook them. The salamanders were a protected species that the government forbade eating, and none of the villagers dared eat them.

Surprisingly, the man chuckled and said: "We like to taste things that no one else has ever had. If an animal is forbidden, that means it's more worth eating. It's a cinch to fix the rats. You only need to skin and gut them and braise them with soy sauce as you do with rabbits. If you can't catch the salamanders openly, you can send people out in secret. We'll pay you handsomely, OK?"

"We'll catch the chestnut white-bellied rats for you if you insist on eating them. But we can't get you the giant Chinese salamanders. The government has banned their capture by decree. We'd break the law if we caught them," explained Nuannuan patiently. She hadn't expected that the two families would rack their brains to find delicacies to eat.

Boss Chu chuckled. "Don't be so serious. Everything depends on human resourcefulness. Any law has its loophole. Businessmen like us deal with legal stuff every day, and laws have never got us. Take taxation, for example – has any businessman not evaded taxes? They couldn't make money if they didn't. You can catch the salamanders stealthily. Doesn't this kind of fish call at night? You can catch them easily then. You should send two villagers to get them at night without anyone seeing. Who would go to the creek in the mountain at night? How about this – I'll pay fifteen thousand yuan for each of the salamanders so that you'll have some profit. What do you think?"

Nuannuan was about to shake her head to reject the offer when Xue Chuanxin responded: "OK, how many do you want?"

"At least four. It's better if you can get us six." Boss Gou stuck his fingers up.

"You pay fifty thousand yuan first, and the rest after we catch the salamanders."

Nuannuan was flabbergasted, fixing her eyes on the money in Xue Chuanxin's hands. As soon as the two bosses went out, Nuannuan shouted at Xue Chuanxin: "How could you comply with their request? How could you accept their money?"

Xue Chuanxin didn't say anything. He dialled a number on the phone and called: "Leader Kuang, please come over." Then, he turned around and whispered: "Don't yell like that. Why don't we make the available money? Are we stupid? Six salamanders will yield ninety thousand yuan for us. Is it easy to make ninety thousand?"

"But do you know that it's against the law to make this money?" Before her voice died down, Kaitian entered the room. Xue Chuanxin briefed him on what was going on, threw the fifty thousand yuan into his hand and said: "You decide if we're going to make this ninety thousand or not. You're the village committee leader."

"We'll do it. Why not?" said Kaitian without the slightest hesitation as he put the money back on Xue Chuanxin's desk. "I'll get people to catch the salamanders."

Nuannuan dragged Kaitian by his arm. "Kaitian, you're going to break the law."

"All right, all right. You can stay away from the deal. General Manager Xue and I will be in charge," said Kaitian as he pulled Nuannuan out of Xue Chuanxin's room.

Nuannuan was so angry that she shook off Kaitian's hand and went back home. As she walked, she said: "Kuang Kaitian, if something happens, you'll be accountable for it. Let me be clear with you – never bring this salamander money home. It'll sicken me if I see it."

Nuannuan went to sleep as soon as she returned home, and she refused to go to Shang Xin Yuan to work for the next two days. When she went back to work, the two bosses and their entourage had gone. The girl at the front desk told Nuannuan that Boss Chu was extremely pleased when he left. He said he enjoyed Shang Xin Yuan's food very much and even tipped the chefs three hundred yuan. Nuannuan didn't say anything but sighed deeply…

As the weather slowly became warmer, tourist arrivals began to grow on a daily basis. Some were individuals, while some were group tourists; some had contacts beforehand, while some came on the day without previous communications. Tourists with more money went to stay at Shang Xin Yuan, while those with less money stayed at Chu Di Ju.

On one particular day, eight young and middle-aged men arrived at Shang Xin Yuan. After arranging their accommodation and dinner, one of them called over to Nuannuan: "Hey boss, we've spent the whole day in our cars and on the boat, and we're exhausted. Can you arrange for eight masseuses to serve us in each of our rooms?"

Nuannuan was confused. "Massage?"

"Yes, we'll pay the standard price."

Nuannuan answered matter-of-factly. "We don't do massages here."

"No massages? During dinner, I noticed your female staff are all gorgeous, just like beautiful birds from the remote mountains. I never expected your women here to be such beauties."

Nuannuan was taken aback. "What does their beauty have to do with a massage? They have not trained in massage and wouldn't know how to perform it."

"Hey, check out this boss. Do you really not get my meaning, or are you pretending?" the man said with an unusual laugh. As he said this, his voice dropped to a whisper, and the men around roared with laughter.

Nuannuan didn't know what to make of it. *Have I made a mistake?* She stood there dumbfounded.

The man laughed again. "I know you're pretending to avoid negotiating the price. So name the price then. How much for one hour with one girl? And how much for one night? We're straight-talking people, so let's be clear with the price."

Only then did Nuannuan realise what they wanted, and the blood rushed to her face. She had never encountered this before. *Do such men exist?*

"Don't be shy. I'll name a price to get started. How about fifty yuan for an hour? Three hundred yuan for the night? That's about the current rate in the city. It wouldn't be hospitable to charge more."

"Fuckers!" Nuannuan's face was twisted. "Go and negotiate with your own sisters!"

The man and his friends were shocked by Nuannuan's reaction, and their smiles vanished immediately – none of them had encountered such a manager before.

"And if you don't want to stay here, you can fuck off!" Nuannuan called out in a stern voice that was audible outside.

Having heard the noise, Xue Chuanxin entered the room and escorted Nuannuan out while laughing and nodding his apologies. "Sorry, so sorry. Our manager seems to have had a bit too much to drink..."

"I'm not drunk," Nuannuan called back as she was pushed outside the room.

Xue Chuanxin pushed Nuannuan into the office and said with a severe expression: "You think that you can behave in such a way to guests just because you're the deputy manager? We're running a holiday resort business here. Don't you know that our customers are our bosses? Speaking to guests in such a way, with all that shouting and cursing, who would want to come and stay at our Shang Xin Yuan after such an outburst? The reputation of a resort relies mostly on word of mouth, and after your rudeness to those eight people, their eight mouths will get to work telling everyone what a bad place this is. That would be even more serious than a bad review in the newspaper. Got it?"

"But how can they dare to ask me for a woman like that?" Nuannuan was still brimming with rage, although her voice was lower now because she knew Xue Chuanxin was right. All of the hotel management books she had read told managers that above all else, you should never lose your temper with a customer.

"Guests have the right to make any request, and you also have the right to refuse their requests, but you have no right to shout unreasonably. Instead, you should simply explain that we have no massage service and no female company. Is that not reasonable? The way you just acted in no way resembled the way a deputy manager of Shang Xin Yuan should act – it was more like a quarrelling rural wife."

"OK, OK, I made a mistake." Nuannuan began to feel embarrassed.

"Let's go. Come with me. Let's apologise to them." Xue Chuanxin raised his hand to gesture in their direction.

"An apology?" Nuannuan did not particularly want to apologise.

"An apology now will quickly prevent any hard feelings. Otherwise, whatever would we do if tomorrow those guests decided to leave? In the tourism hotel management industry, this is known as the 'zero leavers policy'. If you're not careful and let one guest go today, a wave of ten will leave tomorrow. Have you completely forgotten your studies at the provincial capital hotel?"

"OK, I'll go." Nuannuan could only nod her head in agreement and follow Xue Chuanxin as they headed out to the room where the eight guests were. They were still together when Xue Chuanxin and Nuannuan entered. They stopped talking and gazed at Xue Chuanxin and Nuannuan with surprise. Xue Chuanxin broke the silence. "Our Deputy Manager Chu had something else on her mind and was in a bad mood. That was why she behaved a bit rudely. Now she's here to apologise to you."

Nuannuan echoed him in a small voice. "I'm sorry for the way I spoke to you. Please excuse me."

One of them laughed lustfully and said: "No problem. Don't mention it. Actually, it was quite a turn on to see Manager Chu so mad, opening her big eyes wide, throwing her ample breasts out and swaying her arse. She had the charm of a shrewd rustic woman."

Hearing the man's obscenity, Nuannuan began to glare again, but before she did, Xue Chuanxin hurriedly pulled her out.

Not long after this event, something very similar occurred. After dinner one night, three young men staying in Shang Xin Yuan called down to reception and asked for three women to accompany them for a drink. They would pay one hundred yuan per woman. The on-duty staff reported this to Nuannuan, who was immediately unhappy to hear about it. *If you want to drink, just do it by yourself in your own damn room. Since when did women have to come and accompany men?* She wanted to refuse the request but was afraid that Xue Chuanxin would again complain that she was disrespecting the guests. So she reluctantly said: "Tell them to wait."

Nuannuan called the female staff together and asked who among them had the stomach for alcohol. Only a girl named Xiang Xiang said she did; when she was little, her parents would wet a chopstick in alcohol and give her a taste. She said she could drink and that alcohol was no big deal for her. Nuannuan said: "OK, Xiang Xiang, take two others to accompany them to drink. The money they pay for this is yours, but resist offers to drink as much as possible. If you have no other choice but to drink a little, you absolutely must not become drunk – otherwise, you'll bring great shame to the people of Chu Wang Village."

Xiang Xiang said that would be fine, and along with two other women, she followed Nuannuan to the rooms of the three young men. On entering, they saw alcohol and snacks already arranged on a small table.

Nuannuan spoke first. "The girls of our village are under the strict supervision of their parents and do not drink alcohol. Certainly they are not used to drinking alcohol with strangers. On your request, I have brought these three girls, but please do not pour drinks for them."

One of the three men replied happily: "Relax, relax. As for girls like these, we'll care for them as much as you do."

Nuannuan left the room and went off to manage some other things. Just as she was preparing to go home and relax, Xiang Xiang and the other two girls ran out of the rooms shouting, their hair dishevelled and clothes all out of order. Nuannuan quickly pulled them aside, asking them quietly what had happened.

Xiang Xiang replied in tears: "They are bad men. They forced us to drink and tried to kiss us. They put their hands into our clothes and pushed us onto the beds."

On hearing this, Nuannuan exploded with rage. *OK, you wild animals, you think you can get away with such despicable acts in our Chu Wang Village. If this isn't indecency, then what is it?* Running with heavy steps, she kicked open the door to find the young men still drinking and laughing. She roared: "You despicable louts! Think you can bully my girls? Fuck off! Right now, get the fuck out of Shang Xin Yuan! We don't accept animals as our guests!"

The three men were stunned. One explained quietly: "We had already paid, so they should let us have a bit of fun."

"Bullshit!" Nuannuan was becoming more and more irate.

Just as she was about to let fly another outburst, Xue Chuanxin, who had heard the commotion, hurried in and pulled her into the office again. With a severe expression, he said: "How can this recklessness be the proper way for any manager to behave? Haven't we been over this already? You must smile when dealing with guests. Go and look in a mirror. You call that a smile on your face? And to kick out guests so late in the night. There's no precedent in all of China for such action. After turning them out, who would be brave enough to stay at Shang Xin Yuan ever again? Do you want our Shang Xin Yuan to collapse? I tell you, the boss of Five Continents is calling me every day on the phone, asking about the management here. Do you want us both to be finished here?"

This time, Nuannuan did not back down. "So, as far as you're concerned, just let them commit despicable acts on our girls?"

"Of course not. This whole alcohol accompaniment is only acceptable if agreed by both parties. If the girls do not agree, then they are wrong to force anything. It seems that nowadays, in order to bring in more guests and to keep them for longer stays at our Shang Xin Yuan, we must think of ways to supply such services."

"Like what? Are you going to find girls to be drinking companions?" Nuannuan's eyes were wide open.

Xue Chuanxin sighed. "Don't worry about this. I'll work it out."

Hearing Xue Chuanxin's words, Nuannuan secretly smirked. *Can you find the girls without me? Do you know there are far more people who believe in me than you in Chu Wang Village?*

Several days had passed, but Nuannuan hadn't heard anything from Xue Chuanxin. Therefore, she thought he was all talk.

At the end of each month, Xue Chuanxin would always return to the provincial capital to manage business and visit his family, as arranged by Five Continents Group. Who would have expected that this time on his return from the city, he would bring back six gorgeously dressed girls with him? There could not have been a bigger difference between the clothes of these six and those of the local village girls. When they arrived at the village lakeside pier, every villager who spotted them stared in shock, mouths gaping. The six girls were wearing bright-coloured miniskirts that exposed long white legs, with low-buttoned blouses baring cleavage for all to see. Each one wore make-up, with red lips. One pulled along a suitcase while another had a leather bag on her shoulder. The girls followed Xue Chuanxin with much excitement and laughter, like some old theatre troupe. The men who had been attracted by the scene fixed their eyes on them.

At that moment, Nuannuan was by the reception desk of Shang Xin Yuan, briefing some of the staff, and was quite startled to see Xue Chuanxin entering with all of these strange girls. At first, she thought they were a female tour group, and only when Xue Chuanxin had arranged for them to stay in the staff quarters did she begin to understand. She first asked: "They are…?"

Xue Chuanxin laughed. "I have found these girls specially from the city. They'll be responsible for massage and drink accompaniment, and will receive the same pay as our room service staff. Any additional payments the guests make outside of this are theirs to keep. Every time they serve one customer, we'll earn one hundred yuan."

Nuannuan replied: "Oh…" And then she said no more. *I didn't know there were girls out there willing to do such things. Yet they do exist, and here they are.*

Xue Chuanxin stared into Nuannuan's eyes. "In today's

increasingly modern society, if we're engaged in the tourism industry, and if we want to make money quickly, we must develop more humanised service projects. Understand?"

Nuannuan's brows wrinkled slightly. She was a little tired of listening to him talk this way. It sounded too much like lecturing...

From that day on, things changed dramatically at Shang Xin Yuan.

The first change was the noticeable increase in daily income. In the past, the main income came from accommodation, meals and tours. Now, service income from the six girls was added. In the beginning, Nuannuan took no notice of this income, thinking that it wouldn't bring much in. What she did not expect, however, was how quickly this service would develop. On average, each of the six women would serve guests twice a day with massage or drink accompaniment, and each service would provide a hundred yuan. Each day, that would be twelve hundred yuan; after one month, about thirty-six thousand yuan. Once the salaries of the six girls – five hundred yuan per person per month, or three thousand yuan in total – had been deducted, this service alone was bringing in over thirty thousand yuan a month to Shang Xin Yuan.

Nuannuan secretly refreshed her admiration for Xue Chuanxin. *After all, it takes talent to bring in money without new investment.*

The second change that occurred at Shang Xin Yuan was that the male guests almost completely stopped complaining. In the past, Nuannuan would spend every effort to ensure that staff were providing the best service possible, yet every evening there were always male guests who would be unsatisfied with this or that, and lodge various complaints. After the six girls arrived, the complaints were rarely heard, and instead, laughter was often heard from the rooms. Nuannuan did not expect this.

Yet another change was that on hearing Shang Xin Yuan offered massage and drink accompaniment girls, some of the male tourists staying at Chu Di Ju moved over to Shang Xin Yuan, happily spending more on accommodation. Nuannuan thought this inexplicable. *Is massage and being accompanied to drink really that important?*

Another change occurred in Kaitian. In the past, after the *Farewell* performance finished, Kaitian would drink a cup of tea at Shang Xin Yuan and then leave. Sometimes he would ask about the income and expenditure, but always only stay for a little while, as Nuannuan and Xue Chuanxin were managing everything in Shang Xin Yuan. After Zhan Shideng's letter, Kaitian spoke much less to Nuannuan and spent very little time at Shang Xin Yuan, sometimes leaving right after *Farewell* had finished. But after the six girls arrived, Kaitian's visits to Shang Xin Yuan gradually increased, sometimes coming twice in a day, asking Xue Chuanxin about the service of the girls, sometimes occupying a room with Xue Chuanxin and joking with him for half of the day. Nuannuan was happy about this. It was good that Kaitian, the village leader and head of the family, was here at Shang Xin Yuan.

Another significant change occurred in the local Chu Wang Village girls working at Shang Xin Yuan. They initially regarded the six girls from the provincial capital with curiosity, thinking they wore unique clothing and provided an exceptional service. One or two even looked down on them, thinking that what they did was hardly a regular job. But slowly, feelings of envy crept in. The reason for this was that the six girls collected a very high income. Although they received the same monthly salary as the others, they would also receive tips from their clients. In the beginning, the Chu Wang Village girls thought nothing of these tips – probably just a few yuan and nothing more. But on asking one of the six, a girl called Blossom, how much she would receive per service, she replied with a laugh: "There's no standard price, and it depends on whether the client is happy or not. I've taken one hundred yuan before, but it's usually about thirty yuan, and never less than twenty yuan." The girls who asked were shocked and quickly calculated on the lowest figure that if every customer gave twenty yuan, and they provided the service twice a day, that would be forty yuan. And after one month, it would be over a thousand yuan. Adding the salary on top of that, it would be almost two thousand yuan. *God, for doing practically nothing they collect such a high sum?* The women felt it unfair. With more income, the six girls spent more on food and clothing, and would often go into the small shop within Shang Xin Yuan and buy snacks like plum candy, chocolates and custard tarts. Initially sold to the guests of Shang Xin Yuan, the six girls were now buying and eating them instead. They would also take turns riding with Chef Bo on his three-wheeled motorbike to Juxiang Street among the meat and vegetables. Once they arrived, they would buy colourful clothing and leather high-heels. This attracted the envy of all of the female staff at Shang Xin Yuan...

One day, Xiang Xiang quietly asked Leilei: "Could you teach me how to massage so that I can make some more money?"

Leilei smiled and whispered: "It's a cinch. It depends on whether you have the guts."

"Guts?" Xiang Xiang became interested. "I do. I'm afraid of nothing."

Leilei said: "If so, you can stand aside and watch me next time. I guarantee you'll learn how to do it just by watching me once."

"Really? I'll owe you, then," said Xiang Xiang.

After dinner the following evening before she was going to service a guest, Leilei whispered to Xiang Xiang: "Follow me."

Xiang Xiang was off work at the time, so she nodded and followed Leilei into the guest's room. The guest was a man with receding hair. He was surprised to see two girls and said: "I only asked for one."

Leilei responded: "This is my buddy. She's here to learn the skill of massage. Just pretend she's not here, OK?"

The man was unhappy but still lay back on the bed while mumbling. Leilei opened her hands and pressed the man on his head and face casually. Then, she moved her hands down to his chest and stomach. The man then raised his hand to touch Leilei's face, but Leilei didn't dodge. She only smiled and said: "Brother, you're pretty fit! Are you an official or a boss?"

The man laughed and moved his hand down to rub Leilei's neck and shoulder. He asked, beaming: "What do you prefer, an official or a boss?"

Leilei giggled. "Either! An official has power while a boss has money. Power can be exchanged for money, and money can buy power. Both are better than us masseuses."

"You're a smart girl!" As he said this, he shifted his hand to Leilei's chest and grabbed one of her breasts.

The move stunned Xiang Xiang. She wondered why this man was such a jerk. She expected to see Leilei become angry, only to hear her laugh and say: "Brother, you can't touch my breasts without payment. Touch one, and you must pay me fifteen yuan." With that, she jolted her upper body away from the man's hand.

"OK, fifteen is fine. Do you think I can't afford it?" After he finished, the man fished a fifty yuan bill from his wallet and stuffed it into Leilei's hand. Leilei smiled faintly and put the cash in her pocket. She then bent over the man, thrusting both her breasts above his eyes. The man quickly raised both his hands and grasped Leilei by her breasts. Xiang Xiang quaked with terror, her face reddening to the ears. Leilei continued massaging as if nothing were happening. The man began to breathe more heavily and faster and tried to pull Leilei upon his body. But Leilei pushed him away and said: "Done! The session is over." After that, she went towards the door.

Xiang Xiang pulled the door open and rushed out first. Leilei pulled Xiang Xiang to a corner and asked in a small voice: "What do you think? Now you understand, right? You don't have to learn how to massage because what you do is make a man happy so that he will pay you voluntarily. It's the same with accompanying men when they drink. After they drink alcohol, men like to touch you here and there. Let them, and they'll have to give you tips."

Before Leilei had finished, Xiang Xiang could feel herself boiling with shame...

What she saw caused Xiang Xiang to lose sleep, her heart thumping loud for a long time. She had never thought that a woman could make money in this way. *Isn't their conduct shameless? What would their parents think if they learned about what they're doing? Would their fiancés marry them? Would something worse happen if one worked in this trade for long?* She contemplated the work of massage for several days but still failed to straighten things up. One evening at dinner time, she quietly called Nuannuan aside and told her what she had learned about the massage business. Nuannuan was taken aback when she heard it. She never thought that the six girls would serve the guests in this way. Since they came to Shang Xin Yuan, Nuannuan had never seen them delivering their service to the guests. She always felt that Xue Chuanxin recruited them, and the girls, having come from the provincial capital where they had seen the world, would never do anything out of line. Besides, Xue Chuanxin didn't ask her to take charge of their work. Xue Chuanxin was Shang Xin Yuan's general manager, and he didn't need his deputy to mind his business. Besides, Nuannuan was very busy. In addition to Shang Xin Yuan, she also had Chu Di Ju to worry about. As a result, she had been kept in the dark. Now she became anxious when she heard what Xiang Xiang told her. She made up her mind to get to the bottom of their services. She had to stop it if she could verify Xiang Xiang's claim.

Nuannuan would normally go home for dinner, with no need to return to Shang Xin Yuan afterwards, as Xue Chuanxin would manage things during the night. After dinner one night, Nuannuan made an excuse to go to Shang Xin Yuan. After finding out which of the rooms the six girls were providing service to guests in, she grabbed a universal key and opened one of the doors that connected with a service room into the guest's apartment. Nuannuan looked through a slit in the door and saw that the guest was lying on the bed with a girl massaging him. She was about to retreat from the room and go to find Xue Chuanxin when the man suddenly turned over and pressed the massage girl down beneath him. Nuannuan felt her heart skip a beat, expecting the girl to cry for help. She was determined to storm into the room to her rescue if she called out, and she would ask a security guard to grab the man and escort him to the public security station. But to her surprise, the girl giggled instead and whispered: "Brother, why are you in such a rush? We haven't negotiated a deal yet..." What she saw made her jump with fright and then fill with indignant rage. *So this is what those girls were up to. A massage indeed! They're clearly selling sex.*

Nuannuan stepped out of the service room into the corridor with her face red and teeth clenched, and she quickly marched to Xue Chuanxin's room, pushing open the door.

"You're still here?" Xue Chuanxin asked, putting a book down that he was reading under the light.

Nuannuan glared at Xue Chuanxin. "Do you know exactly how the six girls from the provincial capital are serving the guests?"

Xue Chuanxin fixed his eyes at her. "What do you mean? It's not just massage and drink accompaniment?"

"Do you know how they give the men massage?"

Xue Chuanxin laughed. "As a general manager, how can I attend to every detail? Massage is a craft, mainly to dredge people's meridians and promote blood circulation. You and I don't have to learn, and you don't need to worry about it."

"Would you like me to show you?" Nuannuan continued to stare at him. She wanted to find out if he was in the dark like she had been.

"What's the need to see what they're doing? As long as the guests pay us according to the regulations and have no complaints, we don't have to interfere. Do you think we have too few things to do? We should devote our energy to attracting more tourists."

"I think we have to interfere with this matter. Do you know what they're doing? They're losing the face of our Shang Xin Yuan. They're corrupting Chu Wang Village's public morals."

"Is it so serious?" Xue Chuanxin was still smiling, but his eyes showed disagreement with Nuannuan. "Don't make a mountain out of a molehill and ask for trouble."

"If you don't believe me, you can find a room where they're massaging. I never thought the girls would do it like this. I always thought they were supplying real massage services for the guests according to your request."

"You're taking it a bit too seriously. There are some things we can't be so meticulous about. We opened Shang Xin Yuan to make money. As long as there's money to make, we can do anything. As for the consensual things, what's to be worried about? Do we have too much time on our hands? We have to turn a blind eye to some things. Understand?"

"You mean you already knew what they did?" There was a flame in Nuannuan's eyes as his words confirmed her suspicion.

"How could I possibly know?" Xue Chuanxin quickly opened his hands. "OK, if you think they're massaging incorrectly, I'll go and see what it's all about. You go and take the night off, and we'll talk about it tomorrow, OK?"

Nuannuan left without saying goodbye. When she got home, Kaitian had already undressed in bed. Seeing Nuannuan entering the room, he didn't greet her, turned aside and went to sleep. The couple had been like this since Zhan Shideng wrote that note. Seeing Kaitian so indifferent, Nuannuan would have ignored him, but what she had found today was so grave that she couldn't bear it herself without sharing it with Kaitian. Nuannuan pushed Kaitian and snarled: "Something horrible is going on in Shang Xin Yuan."

"What?" Kaitian turned over, watched her, and waited for her to continue.

"Do you know how the six girls that Xue Chuanxin brought here massage the guests?"

Kaitian was silent. He was still staring at her, but his eyes showed no interest. He opened his mouth and yawned.

"It's simply shameful to lure a man into paying for sex." There was anger in Nuannuan's words.

Kaitian had a dry cough and asked in a plain tone: "Are there fewer or more customers in Shang Xin Yuan since the girls came? Is it making more money or less? Has the economic performance improved or not?"

"Of course, we're making more money, but…"

"But what?" Kaitian's tone suddenly became cold. "As long as you make more money, it's OK. If Shang Xin Yuan makes more money, we'll have more dividends. Why do we have to worry so much? Do we have nothing else to do? Our purpose of opening Shang Xin Yuan is nothing but to make money, isn't it? Is there any other purpose for the operation?"

"But you can't make money like this. If this thing leaks out, don't you think it's disgraceful? What would the villagers say?"

"Don't worry about grace or disgrace. Go to sleep first, and we'll talk about it later." After that, Kaitian turned over and quickly went to sleep.

Nuannuan didn't expect Kaitian to have the same attitude. She sat leaning against the headboard, seething with anger for a while. Then, she slowly undressed and lay down…

At first light the next day, as Nuannuan was dressing Dangen, a security guard from Shang Xin Yuan arrived calling for Kaitian, saying that Boss Xue was calling for the leader. Kaitian left with the security guard. Usually, when Xue Chuanxin called on them, it was for Nuannuan. She did not expect him to be calling for Kaitian directly, and she suspected it had something to do with the massage incident. *Whatever, you two talk. But sooner or later, you'll have to deal with me. In order to preserve the good name of Shang Xin Yuan, those six girls must leave. If we guarantee to keep Red Lake clean, we must also guarantee to keep Shang Xin Yuan free of filth.*

As Nuannuan arrived for work after breakfast the next day, Xue Chuanxin called her into his office. Kaitian was still there, sitting and smoking a cigarette slowly. Xue Chuanxin started with a laugh. "Due to our combined efforts, and especially because of Nuannuan's detailed plans, Shang Xin Yuan has developed well since the business opened. One could say Nuannuan has given herself entirely to Shang Xin Yuan."

Nuannuan said nothing and waited for him to continue. She did not think he had called her over simply to compliment her.

"Nuannuan, there's something we must discuss. Our company director has requested that every business reach the next level in building up the management. As for our project of cooperative management, the request is made that the next management cooperative must be held with the leading stakeholder. In view of this, we have asked for Leader Kuang Kaitian to participate as the manager of Shang Xin Yuan." Xue Chuanxin spoke with the greatest of caution.

Nuannuan laughed. "Fine! With him as the manager, I can relax."

"So it's decided. From today onwards, you need not come to Shang Xin Yuan any more for work. Understand?" Xue Chuanxin said, followed by a laugh.

On hearing this, Nuannuan's heart dropped. The implicit meaning of it was clear now – she was no longer required to work there. *How can he do this? Did I make a mistake? Or was it because of the incident with the six girls? It's probably due to them because last night, he in no way indicated that he wanted me out. Only recently, he was saying how satisfied he was with my management. I was thinking only of Shang Xin Yuan. How can this man be so narrow-minded? Fine, I'm done at Shang Xin Yuan. I don't need to worry about it any more.*

Kaitian spoke up as though to comfort her. "Well, Chu Di Ju will need your help, so you can continue to work there. As for Shang Xin Yuan, I'll come as and when requested. It's good that nowadays I can sort out everything at the village committee, and there'll be no need to worry about anything much there."

"Fine, I'll go then." Nuannuan turned after she spoke, and for fear that this injustice and indignant treatment would bring on her tears, she walked quickly. She did not want to let Xue Chuanxin see her cry. Having thought that Xue Chuanxin was a good man, she never expected him capable of such hurt. *Just over those six girls. Oh, you despicable man!*

Nuannuan didn't immediately go home to Chu Di Ju that day. Instead, she went to Red Lake to stroll along the shore. She wanted to calm herself down. She glanced back at the houses in Shang Xin

Yuan from time to time. From the initial negotiation of its contract to its current prosperity, she had devoted much of herself to it. Now that she had suddenly left, she felt a deep sense of loss. However, it still belonged to the Kuang family – she just wasn't managing it for the time being. *Isn't it the same whether Kaitian or I am in charge of it? Didn't I feel tired all the time and now finally have a chance to take a break?*

"Sister-in-Law Nuannuan, how come you have time to hang out here today?" A greeting coming from nearby startled her out of her thinking. Nuannuan looked up and realised that she had reached Jiuding's household responsibility fields, where Jiuding was spreading manure from a flatbed cart.

"Why didn't you go to work in the company?" asked Nuannuan.

Jiuding smiled. "It's my day off today. That's why I came to work in the fields. You're so busy that it's rare to see you stroll by the lake."

Nuannuan forced a smile. "Something's worrying me, so I'm here to collect myself."

"What can worry you? You earn several hundred yuan every day. I think you're living a life of heaven. What do you have to worry about? You've got to enjoy yourself eating baked cakes, drinking rice wine and humming some light tunes."

"Each family has a skeleton in the cupboard, Jiuding."

"Sister-in-Law, I've been wondering why heaven blesses your family only? Kaitian has become the village committee leader, and your tourism business is thriving. Yours is the wealthiest household in our Chu Wang Village."

"What do you mean? We've only made pocket money. Please let me know what I can do for you if you have something on your mind, Jiuding."

"Of course! Well, Sister-in-Law, if you don't mind my asking..." Jiuding showed hesitancy on his face.

"What is it? Go ahead and tell me. Don't hem and haw with me," urged Nuannuan. She didn't forget that she owed Jiuding because he had helped her when she was in the most difficult situation. She also knew that Jiuding, being repeatedly fined for having a child born outside the family planning quota, lived a hard life. She had always wanted to lend some help. Arranging for his wife Huiyu to work as a cook in Chu Di Ju was part of her effort to repay their kindness.

"I heard that Shang Xin Yuan has a few masseuses?"

"Yes. You already knew?" Nuannuan wasn't surprised. Who wouldn't be aware of a bunch of fancily dressed girls wandering into the village.

"People say they are whores, selling their flesh for money."

Nuannuan blushed from ear to ear. She felt as if she were suffering humiliation. "Jiuding, stop your nonsense. They only provide massage and drink accompaniment services. This is common in cities. Why have the services become such a filthy and unpleasant subject from your mouth?"

Seeing Nuannuan drawing a long face with anger, Jiuding hurriedly put on an apologetic smile. "Sorry, Sister-in-Law. If there's no such a thing, let's forget it. Don't be angry, please. Just pretend that I didn't ask you anything. You're the village committee leader's wife. If I angered you too much, the leader would punish me. Then what would I do?"

Though she was bluffing when she spoke with Jiuding and overwhelmed him with fear, she was panicky herself. It seemed that some villagers had learned about the girls' business. It would be terrible if it spread throughout the village. "Tell me, Jiuding, who told you about it?"

"He-he, forget it. I didn't say anything, OK?" begged Jiuding, who was still apologetic.

"Be frank with me. Who told you? I want to have a handle on this thing." Nuannuan forced herself to speak in a calm tone.

"Chuizi told me about it. He works as a security guard in your Shang Xin Yuan. When it was time to sleep one night, he suddenly heard a male guest arguing with a woman in a room. He knocked on the door and went in to ask what was going on. Only then did he see the woman who was in dispute with the guest was a massage girl. He tried to persuade the masseuse to leave as soon as possible to avoid disturbing other guests. He hadn't expected that the woman would burst into tears, complaining that the man only paid fifty yuan after having sex with her and accused him of bullying her. As she cried, she took out a fifty-yuan bill and a used condom to show to Chuizi. The guard was shocked. Only then did he realise what the masseuses had been doing…"

Nuannuan felt her face get hotter and hotter with embarrassment. Without checking it out, she knew what Jiuding told her was true. She could barely raise her head to look at Jiuding. If there had been a crack in the ground, she would have hopped into it. *My god! Shame on you, Nuannuan. Such infamy comes to pass right under your nose.*

She had no memory afterwards of how she excused herself from Jiuding. She only remembered going to bed as soon as she returned from the lakeside. She was as angry as she was self-reproaching. *Why did I trust them? Why didn't I try to learn about what had been going on? What will the villagers say about me when the whole thing comes to light?*

Kaitian came home at lunchtime. Nuannuan got out of bed as soon as she heard his footsteps. She said to Dangen: "Ask your dad to come in." Dangen rushed out and dragged Kaitian into the bedroom. The first thing she said to Kaitian upon his entrance was: "Drive them away."

"Drive who away?" Kaitian was puzzled.

"The six masseuses."

Kaitian knitted his brows. "Didn't we decide that you don't have to worry about the business of Shang Xin Yuan?"

"But they're still ruining our reputation. People will hold us accountable as long as we have a stake in Shang Xin Yuan. Otherwise, we won't be able to wash off the smirch no matter how we try."

"I think you're worrying too much. Everyone knows it's Five Continents Group that built Shang Xin Yuan and has a manager here. We're just helpers with the chores and get some dividends. Why do we have to worry so much? Manager Xue brought those girls here from the provincial capital. If we drove them away, what would Manager Xue think of it? Is it sensible to do so? If we offended Five Continents Group, what would the consequence be for us? Just pretend to be ignorant of things like this. Why take it so seriously?"

Nuannuan stared into Kaitian's eyes. "If you think this way, what shall we do if the law punishes us?"

"What law? One likes to offer the massage service, and the other wants to enjoy the service. It's consensual, so there's no law being broken. If they don't tell anybody after they get physical, who will know? If something happens, we have Xue Chuanxin from Five Continents Group and me from Chu Wang Village. There's nothing for you to make a fuss about. You just take care of Chu Di Ju from now on. All right, let's have our dinner." After saying this, Kaitian hurried to the kitchen.

Nuannuan grew angrier and yelled: "OK, OK. I'm poking my nose into your business. From now on, I won't concern myself with it even if a crowning calamity befalls Shang Xin Yuan." With that, she lay down on the bed, seething with anger as she covered her head with the bedsheet.

FIRE

Nuannuan did not go to Chu Di Ju until after breakfast the next day. When Shallot heard that Nuannuan would not be working at Shang Xin Yuan any more and instead managing Chu Di Ju, she said very happily: "Good, I feel so much better on hearing this. What you don't know is that there are some guests here who, having originally checked into Chu Di Ju, will then move to Shang Xin Yuan after hearing about the masseuses. You've allowed me to manage Chu Di Ju, and I'm always worrying about what to do when the guests are leaving. I feel as though this burden is pushing down on my chest."

Nuannuan said: "Don't worry, let's not think about it. With fewer guests, we earn less, but we can still feed ourselves."

Nuannuan was used to working in the city-hotel standard Shang Xin Yuan, so when she arrived back at Chu Di Ju, she immediately felt that the conditions were poor. Before Shang Xin Yuan, she thought that Chu Di Ju looked quite nice. Now, comparing the two together, the differences were obvious. It seemed that, in order to attract tourists, Chu Di Ju would have to undertake some renovations and changes. At least the family had some money, and Nuannuan was thinking of using some of it for the work ahead.

The first thing Nuannuan did was to add a bathroom to every guest room. In the past, when guests wanted to use the toilet, they would have to put on clothes and run out to the yard – not something that city visitors were accustomed to. As Chu Di Ju was a single floor, adding bathrooms was not too difficult. Nuannuan had the workers bury piping outside the yard and then build small bathrooms behind the bedrooms. The two rooms were connected with a simple door.

The second task was to build a shack in Chu Di Ju's yard. She put tables, chairs and sofas inside and then designed a counter. She would hire a girl to work behind it, selling daily items and tea supplies. She would also install a television so that the guests could eat snacks, drink tea and chat while watching some TV.

The third task was to plant flowers and grass all around the empty perimeters of the buildings of Chu Di Ju, just like in Shang Xin Yuan. Once this was completed, Chu Di Ju would look much more presentable.

Nuannuan did not increase the price – a room, tour and meals still cost a hundred yuan a day. Tourists who stayed all said that, in such a remote land on the western bank, a hundred yuan for this kind of accommodation and food was a real bargain...

Nuannuan was now only managing Chu Di Ju, and she no longer paid any attention to Shang Xin Yuan. Even during the performance of *Farewell*, she would not allow herself a look. Xue Chuanxin's actions had hurt her. They had started the business together, but just because they did not see eye to eye on one small issue, she was immediately pushed aside. Only a truly ruthless man could do such a thing.

After lunch one day, Nuannuan was intending to take a quick lunchtime nap when Shallot suddenly ran into the yard frantically asking: "Nuannuan, do you know about the extension Shang Xin Yuan is planning?"

Nuannuan shook her head. "No, nobody has told me. And like I would care? You needn't worry over it either – it has even less to do with you."

Shallot patted Nuannuan's thigh anxiously. "Hah! It has everything to do with me. Do you know how they plan to extend? They plan to extend through my yard and my yellow bean field, as well as those belonging to Jiuding, Zhankun and Zhan Tongfang. All of our houses and our plots of land."

Nuannuan was shocked. "What? Extending over such a big area?"

"Yes, this morning Xue Chuanxin and Kaitian spoke with Brother Changlin, saying that we must prepare to pull down the house and move, and that each house will be subsidised six hundred yuan, and that there is planning-approved land in the south of the village to build new houses on. Who could build a new house with only six hundred yuan? Isn't it impossible? We've had our land for who knows how many generations. Can someone just come in and get us to move? Not only that, but the field by our yard is also over three *mu* in area, and the crops grow well in this soil as we have continually put down fertiliser over the years. After this land is taken, what can we do? They say they can subsidise us five thousand yuan per *mu*. But after the subsidy has been used up, what can we do? That land has been our only source of income for years."

Nuannuan listened in shock. "Shallot, don't worry. This really is the first time I've heard anything about an extension of Shang Xin Yuan. I'm going to go now to get some answers for you." Nuannuan got up, put Dangen into Shallot's arms and quickly walked out.

At that moment, Kaitian and Xue Chuanxin were in a small VIP room drinking alcohol. As Nuannuan opened the door, they were clinking their glasses together, faces full of satisfaction. On hearing the door open, they assumed that it was a service woman bringing in food, and without turning to look, Xue Chuanxin said: "Come now, for the expanding Shang Xin Yuan, let's drink another glass."

Kaitian said: "Don't worry about the land. I have everything under—"

"Fuck your 'don't worry'!" Nuannuan shouted.

Xue Chuanxin and Kaitian turned their heads. Xue Chuanxin hurriedly got up and asked Nuannuan to join them. "Come, come, Nuannuan. We can drink together because we'd just begun when you came. Come, sit down and have a drink, please."

Kaitian's face was sullen. He was probably seething because Nuannuan had interrupted his toast.

She didn't sit but instead stood facing them both as she asked: "Shang Xin Yuan is really extending?"

"This decision has been made between Leader Kuang and me," Xue Chuanxin said, an implicit smile on the edge of his mouth. "You must have seen that tourists from all directions are coming, and that Chu Wang Village is becoming a new tourist attraction. Its remains of Chu culture, its temple buildings, its mysterious lake smoke, its clear waters and green mountains, and its farm life scenery have all aroused people's interest in the city. It can be said that the development prospects of Chu Wang Village are unlimited. There will be a large amount of money waiting for us to hold in our arms in the future. And our current reception capacity is not enough. There are too few high-end rooms and not many consumption items. Many tourists leave before spending their money. Therefore, we must expand Shang Xin Yuan as soon as possible. In addition to increasing the number of guest rooms, we also need to build a tennis court and a large ballroom. It's in line with the development strategy of our Five Continents Group. At present, many tourism companies are working hard in the city, but our Five Continents Group has turned its attention to the countryside. We believe that the value of urban sightseeing is gradually becoming smaller due to the homogenisation of cities. The construction of cities across China tends to be the same. Various houses in cities look the same. Looking at one city, you can roughly know the pattern of other cities. As the changes in the rural areas have been slow, they have retained their unique charm. A large amount of gold was buried under the soil in the countryside, waiting for us to excavate it. I submitted the plan to expand Shang Xin Yuan to the president of Five Continents Group, and the board approved it immediately. The expansion is also meant to save the declining Chu Wang Village for the people..."

Nuannuan had a cold expression as she said: "You can expand, but how can you pull down the homes of villagers, not to mention occupying their fields? It wasn't easy for the farmers to build their houses – it was usually done through the accumulation of a lifetime. To give six hundred to pull them down and build a new one, how could they manage? And not to mention the fields, their source of livelihood. You only give a few thousand to take it away? After they spend that money, how can they realistically go on? I told you in the past that if you really want to expand your investment, you can build a small Chu street. You can build your houses along both sides of the north-south road in the village. Then you don't have to demolish the villagers' homes and take over their land. Everything has a limit. Shang Xin Yuan and Chu Di Ju's current scale is just about right because we can profit from tourism without affecting the villagers' lives. It benefits everyone. If we overdevelop our business, we'll throw the villagers' lives into utter confusion. What good is that? Do you think you can be sure about increasing the number of tourists? With constant changes, there are more and more newly developed attractions in cities. After all, the transportation in our place isn't able to cope. You have to be realistic."

Kaitian broke off Nuannuan's speech coldly. "OK, OK, I get it. I get it. So you think you understand more about the tourism industry than Boss Xue? It's obvious that more and more tourists are coming. Why can't we pull the money right there into our arms? Expand it."

On hearing this, Nuannuan's face dropped. "I don't care about the extension. But to pull down the houses of Shallot, Jiuding and others, and occupy their fields, that's not right."

Xue Chuanxin shrugged. "Nuannuan, you're siding with the others. We'll make more money after the expansion, and we'll divide it between our two companies. We Five Continents Group won't take it all. You aren't as smart as you used to be."

"I'm not siding with anyone – I'm trying to help them survive. Of course, I also like money, and I'm also happy if I make more money, but I can't stop others from earning a living just because we make money. We'll be scorned and stigmatised. Sister-in-Law Shallot's family is so poor that she can't possibly tear down her house and build a new one."

"All right, all right." Kaitian waved to Nuannuan impatiently.

"Anyway, you can't demolish people's houses and occupy their farmland," Nuannuan emphasised again.

Xue Chuanxin became a little anxious. "It doesn't make sense. How can I expand without demolishing the houses and occupying the farmland? Is this how you treat me as the saviour of Chu Wang Village? Let me tell you, saviours in the past and present and at home and abroad all have weapons in their hands. In a sense, saving means occupation. If you want to be saved, you must accept my occupation. Of course, my weaponry is not guns, but money – capital. Understand?"

Kaitian motioned to Xue Chuanxin to sit down and said: "Why are you worried? She's not the decision-maker in Chu Wang Village. Proceed according to our original plan."

Glaring at Kaitian, Nuannuan yelled: "Kuang Kaitian, you mustn't take offence at my frankness, but I won't let you off if you bulldoze their houses and take away their land."

Kaitian said nothing. Instead, he poured a glass of alcohol and emptied it...

That same day, Nuannuan went back to Chu Di Ju and told Shallot: "Don't you worry – whoever thinks they can make you pull down your house, you need not answer. I bet nobody would have the courage to come and forcibly pull your house down."

Shallot relaxed on hearing this and said: "I'll head home and tell Brother Changlin so that he can relax too. On hearing the news about the demolition at midday, he was so angry he couldn't even eat anything."

After Sister-in-Law Shallot left, Nuannuan sat down to rest for a while. She was about to go to the courtyard to launder Dangen's clothes when Spotty Laosi's wife came in sobbing. Surprised, Nuannuan rose and went up to greet her, asking: "What's going on, Sister-in-Law Laosi?"

"That swine! Swine!" Spotty Laosi's wife burst into tears.

"Which household's swine? What happened to it?" asked Nuannuan in bewilderment.

"Spotty Laosi is the swine!" Finally, Spotty Laosi's wife made herself understood.

"How did he make you angry?" asked Nuannuan with a smile. She knew that the two often quarrelled over trifles. She hurriedly seated her in a chair.

"He tried to find all kinds of excuses to prevent me from getting access to his wage he earned this month as a tour guide. When I got angry, he gave me only 360 yuan, saying that was how much he got for the month. I didn't believe him because you told me before that you gave him 500 yuan a month. You can't give him only 360 and withhold the rest. I knew he kept the 140 yuan, but I stopped arguing with him. I wanted to find out secretly how he spent the money. So, I kept an eye on his whereabouts. Guess what I found out."

Her serious look caused Nuannuan to laugh. "What? It's only 140 yuan – not worth quarrelling over. You've got to let him have some pocket money to buy things like cigarettes."

"I found that he went to Shang Xin Yuan very often."

"What's the big deal about going to Shang Xin Yuan? Tour guides take tourists to both Chu Di Ju and Shang Xin Yuan. When I was the deputy manager there, I asked him to bring some guests.

Besides, acting as a key minister in the *Farewell* show, he has quite a few acquaintances over there. Perhaps he went to chat with them," Nuannuan explained with a smile.

"I thought like you at first, believing he was having fun with his friends. But after supper yesterday, I saw him go to Shang Xin Yuan again. As it happened, his uncle cycled over and had something to consult him about. I went to Shang Xin Yuan to get him. Guess where I found him in the end?"

"Where?" The smile faded on Nuannuan's face as she realised something.

"In a room where there were no guests. I asked the girl on duty if she had seen my children's father. She shook her head and said she hadn't. I searched every room until I came to the non-occupied number nineteen room. I was surprised when I heard him laughing with a girl in it. Which family's girl was she? Why was she laughing with him here? I pushed the door and found it bolted. My heart skipped a beat. What could a man and a woman do as they laughed in a room with the door locked? I went around to the rear window and peeped through the crack in the curtain. Guess what I saw."

Without saying anything, Nuannuan began to flush. She had already figured out what Spotty Laosi's wife had seen.

"A girl not from our village was riding on him half-naked. He was rocking her, smiling. That swine! Swine!" Spotty Laosi's wife burst into tears again.

Nuannuan patted her on the shoulder.

Spotty Laosi's wife continued to sob. "I didn't dare to disturb them at the time. I fear if I had called someone, people would have crowded over, and then I would have lost face. I found a place in the shade outside the Shang Xin Yuan compound and waited until he came out. Do you know how smug he sounded when he came out humming a tune? I lunged forward, grabbed him by his collar and slapped him on the face. He thought I didn't know what he had done, so he fiercely yelled at me: 'You shrew! What are you doing?' I yelled back with gnashed teeth: 'You bastard! Let's go and see your uncle. You can tell him what you've done.' He was still talking tough and said: 'I'm not afraid of seeing him because I did nothing wrong.' I ignored him until we got back home and saw his uncle. I said to his uncle: 'Let your nephew tell you what he did in Shang Xin Yuan's number nineteen room. If he doesn't want to tell you, I will.' The bastard now realised that I had seen through his tricks. He hurriedly begged me with his winks to save him from losing face, and I relented. He dropped to his knees to admit his misdeed after his uncle left. He had spent the 140 yuan on that girl. He said she had lured him by telling him that she could do anything if he gave her the money. He said the girl was so horny that he had a physical reaction. He said he had always wanted to experience a massage. He said he had discussed with the girl before he paid the front desk a hundred yuan and gave the girl forty as her tip. That was 140 yuan. Enough to buy lots of sesame oil. But he spent it all on that slut. Nuannuan, you must help me and drive all the sluts away from Shang Xin Yuan. Otherwise, Spotty Laosi may go and hang around with the girls again. When a cat knows what a mouse tastes like, it can't quit catching and eating it any more. You know the financial condition of our family. We don't have the money to squander like that."

As a tearful Spotty Laosi's wife made these accusations about her husband, Nuannuan felt ashamed. *Wow! What a scandal. And I'm responsible for it. I should have found out what they were doing earlier. I'm such a fool. What shall I do now? Since Xue Chuanxin has stopped me from handling Shang Xin Yuan's business, I can't drive them away. Only Kaitian can do it.*

After seeing Spotty Laosi's wife off, Nuannuan sat there seething with anger. She sighed and blamed herself for discovering what had been going on too late. She regretted not having figured out what those girls were doing and getting rid of them in time.

Kaitian had still not returned at dinnertime. Nuannuan grew a little worried, thinking he was again at Shang Xin Yuan eating, so she called over to ask him to come home for dinner and to tell him to force Xue Chuanxin to get rid of the masseuses. She didn't expect the girl on reception to tell her: "Leader Kuang has gone to a village meeting." Nuannuan was anxious and headed out for the village office.

Night enshrouded the building, and there was nobody at the village offices. Apart from the sound of the odd crow returning to roost, there was silence in the yard. Nuannuan saw a door had the word *Leader* written on it, and she immediately felt sad. It reminded her of what Zhan Shideng had done to her before. But she felt relieved when she thought that the occupier of the office now was Kaitian. It was unlocked, but on pushing at it, she unexpectedly found it to be jammed shut from the inside. "Kaitian, it's me. Open the door!" Nuannuan shouted out. She couldn't help but feel that the whole situation was bizarre: *Why would the door be jammed shut at this hour?* Then a noise came from within the room, and the door gradually swung open. Nuannuan pushed her way in and found Kaitian and Youyou together. Nuannuan's eyes opened wide.

"My sister, what a coincidence. I was here to talk about the land ownership with the leader. He had a headache and lay in bed so that I could massage him better, and now that you've arrived you can massage him in my place."

Kaitian laughed unnaturally. "And who would have known that Youyou here had learned massage from the girls of Shang Xin Yuan with such skill that the moment she began, my headache went away."

"Really? Well, please go ahead and continue massaging him, Youyou." Nuannuan put on a happy expression and did not expose any suspicion from the tone of her voice. But of course, Nuannuan was smart enough to know what was going on. *A man and a woman together behind a locked door giving massages?* Moreover, Youyou had hastily buttoned up her shirt incorrectly. Nuannuan felt hatred in her chest and wanted to curse and shout her lungs out: *Kuang Kaitian, you dare to commit such acts. You son of a bitch!* But she also knew that what she had seen was not clear evidence of what she assumed. They would probably both deny everything. *I will not make a move in haste – instead, I'll learn from Spotty Laosi's wife and wait for the right time.*

"Sister, I have things to do at home, so I'll head off now," Youyou said in a fluster as she headed out. She tripped on the doorstep as she went, and stumbled forward a few steps. Nuannuan closed her eyes for a minute and forced her curses deep down into her belly.

"What's up? Why are you looking for me?" Kaitian asked Nuannuan, more natural now as he watched Youyou leave.

"Nothing. I was just passing by and thought I would come in for a look." Nuannuan said casually. She was so filled with anger and confusion that she was in no mood to talk with Kaitian about the girls in Shang Xin Yuan. Compared with her, Spotty Laosi's wife was in a much better situation – her husband had just been massaged by a girl. But Kuang Kaitian's relationship with Youyou couldn't be explained away by massaging only.

After returning home, she pretended that she had seen nothing, and managed things at home and Chu Di Ju just as normal. Kaitian's parents had no idea that Nuannuan's thoughts were raging, like a strong wind whipping up the waves on Red Lake's surface. *I have to find out the truth. If she were really just giving a massage, I will caution them and nothing more. But if they have really moved onto more than that, then they better not complain about what I might do.* Although Nuannuan was already eighty to ninety per cent certain that they had moved onto more, deep in her heart she wished that this was not so.

From this day on, there was no change in Nuannuan on the surface, though she was watching every move that Kaitian made. Whenever Kaitian would go to a village meeting or have work to do, Nuannuan would quietly take a look. During the performance of *Farewell*, she would also go and quietly inspect. She now knew that they were slowly growing inseparable during the performance, and as Kaitian played the Chu King Zi, and Youyou the Chu Queen Zi, they were often together, pretending that their fiction was fact.

Oh dear, why did I allow Xue Chuanxin to put on this rotten show to attract the tourists in the first place? Yet, after many shows, Nuannuan still had not noticed anything, and even during the performance she hadn't seen any second looks between the two of them. But this did not eliminate her doubts, and having guessed that they were startled by what had happened, she decided to give them a chance and allow everything to carry on as usual; and if they were normal, Nuannuan would drop her suspicions entirely.

One morning during breakfast, Nuannuan said to Kaitian: "There are a couple of researchers on Qu Yuan staying in our Chu Di Ju, and they want to go to the hill and see the Great Wall of Chu the day after tomorrow. They also want to see if they can find a site where Qu Yuan used to live in this area. So they specifically asked me to accompany them. It will be dark when I'm home."

Kaitian nodded and said: "Go and pay attention to what they talk about. We can use that knowledge on tour guiding other visitors."

Nuannuan nodded and left.

The truth was, Nuannuan only sent the Qu Yuan researchers to the hill and returned to the village. She went to the small teahouse owned by Uncle Zhankun. It was Nuannuan's idea to open the teahouse. She said: "Uncle Zhankun, most of the visitors to our Chu Wang Village will want some local tea. If you open a teahouse, you'll be sure to make good money. You should use the water from Red Lake and tea leaves from the South Mountain. You have enough firewood in your own house, so the cost of running the teahouse will not be too high."

Uncle Zhankun found her words made good sense, and he started his business accordingly. It was no surprise when he quickly achieved a daily income of no less than thirty yuan. Therefore, when seeing Nuannuan enter the teahouse, Uncle Zhankun hastened to greet her. "Wow, Nuannuan – what an honour to have you as a rare guest."

Nuannuan smiled and said: "Uncle, I have always wanted to come to your teahouse, but I was too busy. You see, I just returned from sending a group of visitors to the hill. I can only come here to take a rest while they're sightseeing on the hill."

"Take a seat. I'll make some tea for you so that you can take your time sipping," said Uncle Zhankun as he fetched the water and the tea leaves. "Nuannuan, you are the most capable person in this village. You have Chu Di Ju and Shang Xin Yuan. All that money you earn every month. I'm jealous."

Nuannuan smiled and answered: "My uncle is good at complimenting others. I only earn enough to make my days easier." Her eyes, however, were glancing at the courtyard gate of the village committee. Her seat provided her with a clear view.

Nuannuan kept sipping her tea and mindlessly answered Zhankun as she waited. She was waiting for closure. She did not care what the result would be. It was almost midday when Kaitian casually walked by from a distance. Nuannuan did not move. She watched him take the keys to open the courtyard gate. She was feeling quite nervous. *Will Youyou come?* Deep inside, she had hoped that Youyou would not show up and that her suspicion was groundless. To her disappointment, it did not take long for Youyou to emerge. The first sight of her made Nuannuan's heart sink. She felt an oppression caused by anxiety and anger in her chest.

Nuannuan wanted to pay, but Zhankun refused to take the money, so she did not insist and left for the village committee.

Feeling her body shaking, she silently said to herself: *What are you afraid of? It's not you who made a mistake. You can't run away from the truth.*

She quietly walked towards the door that had *Leader* written on it as she took the key that she had someone make earlier. She carefully pushed the door to make sure that it was locked and then opened it so quickly that anyone trying to hide something inside would not have the time to react. She yanked the door open with a loud noise and saw what she had expected to see. She was surprised by how calm she was and did not rush over to tear the two apart. Instead, she stood by the door and sneered. The two in the bed were stunned. Youyou even kept her two legs pointing straight up to the ceiling. It took them a while to react and reach for their clothes. They were so embarrassed that they could not put their clothes on properly. "Imbeciles!" Nuannuan spat on the floor in disgust.

"Sister Nuannuan, I..." Youyou wanted to explain. She sounded like she was weeping.

"Get out!" Nuannuan shouted out in anger.

Youyou almost fell as she rushed outside.

"Kuang Kaitian, what do you have to say about this?" asked Nuannuan, her teeth clenched.

"What do you want me to say? You've seen everything." Kaitian had put on his clothes, but he did not look ashamed or nervous.

"Don't you remember our wedding vows?"

Kaitian scratched his head and seemed deep in thought.

"Have you forgotten?" Nuannuan's eyes were spitting fire.

"How many birthdays has our son had? Those words are too old to remember." Kaitian wanted to laugh at his joke, but he couldn't even put up a smile due to the shock of being caught.

"You're a pig! You bastard!" Nuannuan could not endure any more. She picked up a broom behind the door and threw it at Kaitian.

Kaitian ducked. The broom hit the wall and made a loud noise.

"You swore that you would take care of me for a lifetime and that you wouldn't even look at another woman. You..." Nuannuan choked in sorrow.

"Mr Xue told me everything. He said an affair is nothing new in the city. He also said that we're living in an age of passion..."

"Bullshit!"

"Seriously. He told me that powerful men in the city all keep their own lovers."

"So you want to learn from them. Will you eat shit if they do? You bastard!"

"You agreed to Shang Xin Yuan's *Farewell* show. Doesn't King Zi of Chu have lots of women?" Kaitian began to feel justified.

Kaitian's argument stunned Nuannuan. "Are you comparing yourself to King Zi of Chu?"

"King Zi of Chu is the monarch of a state, and I'm the leader of a village. The only difference between us is the size of the area we rule over. But we're both kings."

"Fuck your king!" Nuannuan picked up a washing basin behind the wall and threw it at Kaitian. The basin ended up on the floor with a bang. "You're still bragging without knowing your shamelessness. Are you a king? Do you think you can be a king? Tell me now what you're going to do."

"What else am I going to do? I won't see Youyou again."

"Just like that?" Nuannuan stepped up.

"What else do you want from me?" Kaitian shrugged.

"I want a divorce. You have put shame on my face, and you want me to keep living with you? No way." Nuannuan turned to leave.

Kaitian raised his voice. "Don't you threaten me with divorce. I'm not the only one who betrayed the marriage."

Nuannuan suddenly turned back. "What do you want to say? Who betrayed the marriage?"

Kaitian did not look at her. "You know who I'm talking about."

"Why don't you just say the name? Kuang Kaitian, let's be clear about it." Nuannuan rushed in front of Kaitian. "Who betrayed the marriage?"

"You did. There. You made me say it."

"What did I do to betray the marriage? Speak! If you can't make your case, I'll call everyone in the village, and we shall continue this in front of them all."

"Do you think you have put honour on your ancestors by sleeping with Zhan Shideng? Do you think I should reward you for doing that? Didn't you put shame on my face? Don't you play the virtuous wife in front of me. I didn't do anything to you that you don't deserve. Now we're even."

"You! That bastard Zhan Shideng! You bastard!" Nuannuan

wanted to hit Kaitian, but she could not catch her breath. She was overtaken by a spell of dizziness. Before she could move, she suddenly dropped down...

Nuannuan woke up. She was lying in bed at home. Her mother-in-law was looking at her sympathetically. Dangen was sitting beside the headboard, his eyes filled with tears. Old Doctor Mei from Mei's Pharmacy was taking her pulse. Shallot, Spotty Laosi's wife and Huiyu were standing in the room. Nuannuan blinked. It took her a while to remember what had happened in the office of the village committee; and the thought brought her to tears.

"She was in temporary shock due to overbearing sorrow. Some rest will help her calm down and get better. I wouldn't recommend any medicine," said Dr Mei as he stood up.

Kaitian's mother cried out for her son: "Kaitian, come and see your Uncle Mei off."

Hearing his name, Nuannuan closed her eyes. She had no intention to see him again; even the sound of his name put her to despair.

Shallot stepped up and wiped Nuannuan's tears away with her handkerchief. Though confused about the situation, Shallot knew that something serious must have happened, and it must have had something to do with Kaitian; otherwise, Nuannuan would not be so upset. "Nuannuan, you must eat. You haven't even had your dinner yet," she said.

Nuannuan shook her head, turned to face the wall and wept. "You should go home."

Shallot, Spotty Laosi's wife and Huiyu looked at each other and walked out in silence. Her mother-in-law stood in the room for a while. Since Nuannuan did not speak, she only tucked her in and said: "Dangen's mum, sleep some more." Then she left with Dangen.

Seeing the room empty, Nuannuan struggled up and started looking for her clothes in the closet next to the bed.

Her mother-in-law heard the sound from the room and hurried inside. She said: "Nuannuan, lie down and get some rest. I can find your clothes for you. Tell me which ones you want to wear."

Nuannuan answered: "Mum, I'm not getting changed. I'm going to my parents' home. I can't live another day with your son. I'm divorcing him."

"My child, what nonsense are you talking about? What divorce? What happened between you two? Tell your mum – I'm on your side."

"You should ask him. He knows best what he's done."

Kaitian's mother turned and shouted out: "Kaitian, come inside."

It took a while for Kaitian to slowly walk inside with the steps of an old gentleman in a Chinese Opera. With a cigarette in his hand, he seemed calm.

Kaitian's mother stared at her son and asked: "What have you done to upset Nuannuan again?"

Kaitian seemed unhappy. He snapped the cigarette off on the table with his fingers, making a loud noise. Afterwards, he threw the cigarette to the corner of the room and squinted at Nuannuan as he said: "What's this? Are you not done?"

Nuannuan didn't say anything. She only gripped the clothes under her arm, used all her force to get out of bed, and stumbled towards the door.

Her mother-in-law ran up and held her. "Nuannuan, calm down. Kaitian, are you blind? Come here and help Nuannuan."

But Kaitian did not move. He crossed his arms and stood there. He made sure that his glance did not fall upon Nuannuan. Dangen walked in with a glass of water. Seeing his mother leaving, he dropped the glass on the floor and ran to grab his mother's leg. He cried out: "Mum! I'm not leaving you!"

"Mum, don't stop me. You won't stop me," said Nuannuan in a calm voice. "I will divorce your son, and it's for his own good. He can't live with Youyou until I divorce him. How difficult his life is, having to sneak around with his affair."

"What? Youyou?" The old woman was in shock. "Kaitian, is it true? How dare you do this. Entangled with that Youyou? Oh my! Everyone in the village will feel ashamed of you! You imbecile!"

"Let it out! Keep yelling!" Kaitian stamped his feet and turned to the door. Suddenly, he stopped. His father, Kuang Kaigu, was standing outside the door with his walking sticks.

"Dad?"

Kuang Kaigu looked cold as ice. Ignoring his son, he struggled inside and asked Nuannuan: "Dangen's mum, life in this house has just got good. You must not ask for trouble, or our neighbours will laugh. You talked about the affair between Kaitian and Youyou – did you hear of it from someone's gossip, or did you make a wild guess? How can you believe in such a thing?"

"I didn't hear any gossip or make any guess. I saw it with my own eyes in the village committee office. I caught them in bed. Why don't you ask him if it's true?"

Kaitian's father turned his gaze to his son, but he did not ask anything. Kaitian did not look back at his father. He just kept staring at a spider's web in the corner of the room.

With a *whoosh*, the old man suddenly raised his walking stick and brought it down on his son. The blow was too heavy and sudden to avoid, and Kaitian fell to the floor. At the same time, the old man was falling on his face due to the momentum. Kaitian's mother could not react, and she burst into tears with her hands in the air. Eventually, she chose to help her husband. Dangen started crying loudly as well, and he clutched tighter to his mother's leg.

Kaitian quickly stood up and walked outside as his mother was crying.

As a result, Nuannuan did not leave as she planned. Seeing her in-laws in despair, she could not leave them. She knew that they would fall ill if she left. Moreover, she had Dangen. The boy held tight to her leg and pushed her towards the bed. He gazed at her with his eyes full of tears, not letting her go anywhere. She stood in the room for a short while, then sighed and plopped on the bed behind her, feeling exhausted...

Kaitian didn't return to sleep at home that night. Nuannuan scarcely got any sleep either. Lying in bed, she gazed at the ceiling and saw frame after frame of the past flashing in front of her mind's eye: the first encounter with Kaitian at Lingyan Temple; the fun they had by the village lake; the mutual care on their way to the elementary school; the neither-close-nor-distant relationship of their high-school years; the separation after Kaitian dropped out of the senior high; the courtship; the marriage; the birth of Dangen; the weedkiller incident; the backbreaking effort to pay off their debt; the construction of Chu Di Ju; the planning for Shang Xin Yuan... Each frame pricked her like a needle and simultaneously softened her up a bit. *How can we break off like that? But if I don't break off with him, what shall I do? Shall I forgive him? Just for this incident of infidelity? It's human to err. If only he could mend his ways. But if I forgave him, what about the humiliation he has inflicted upon me? Would I be willing to sleep with him in the future?*

The next day, Nuannuan stayed in bed for the whole day, deep in thought. *Should I divorce him? Should I leave?* She kept asking herself these questions. The thought of leaving this courtyard, every corner of which she had grown so familiar with, and this home that she had spared no effort in looking after since her wedding, made her heart ache. *Should I be patient? Maybe he'll stop seeing Youyou. If so, I could forgive him, and we could live our life.*

On the third morning, Nuannuan, extremely tired, finally made up her mind: she would suspend the divorce and see what happened.

After breakfast on the same day, though her legs were still feeling limp, Nuannuan went to Chu Di Ju anyway. Seeing her coming over, Sister-in-Law Shallot hastened to help her sit down. Nuannuan said: "Sister-in-Law, do you know what that bastard Kaitian did?"

Sister-in-Law Shallot nodded and sighed. She had learned about the affair from other villagers.

"What have I done wrong since I got married to him? I work so hard to take care of the family, and he repays my hard work like this. Does he have any conscience?"

Patting her on her shoulder, Sister-in-Law Shallot said: "To be honest, I didn't expect it. Well, we can never gauge a man's mind. The truth is, what life would Kaitian live today without your help? He's too greedy. But you don't have to be so angry. My grandma told me all married men think other men's wives are better. They're never satisfied – fond of the new, and tired of the old…"

Kaitian did not come home for the next few days. Spotty Laosi's wife said that he had been staying in the office of Shang Xin Yuan. Nuannuan thought to herself: *Don't come home – we'll see how long you can stay in the office.* She believed that Kaitian was thinking of a solution. *Think about it, and we'll see what you have to offer.*

Kaitian returned home one evening after dinner when Nuannuan was washing the dishes in the kitchen. He did not say anything and walked straight into the bedroom. His mother glared at him, but he did not say a word. When Nuannuan came inside after working in the kitchen, he had already gone to bed. Nuannuan stood beside the bed for a long time. The sight of Kaitian lying in bed facing the wall gave her the desire to storm out. However, despite several attempts, she could not move even one step. Eventually, she quietly sighed to herself and turned off the light. She got into bed, but she made sure their bodies did not touch.

Life in the Kuang house went back to normal after that night.

Nuannuan kept herself busy in Chu Di Ju every day as usual, yet she was always keeping an eye on Kaitian and Youyou. To her relief, Youyou had quit her role in the performance of Shang Xin Yuan and went to work in Nanfu with her husband. Nuannuan slowly started to feel assured and found her mood back to normal. After several days, Kaitian brought back a blouse for Nuannuan when he returned from a meeting in the township office. Neither the style nor the colour of the blouse was to Nuannuan's taste, but she put it on to show her gratitude, knowing that it was a gesture of Kaitian's willingness to reconcile. It reminded her of her excitement of getting the blouse he gave her shortly after their wedding. Nuannuan thought to herself: *The world was different then.*

Red Lake was at the peak of its beauty in the middle of spring: all the flowers were blossoming, the grass had grown to a proper height, the trees had covered themselves with fresh green, the birds had started singing, the butterflies were flying around, the bees were busy working, the dragonflies were flying through the clusters of reeds, the grasshoppers were jumping on top of the leaves, the ladybugs were dancing and the frogs were croaking all night long...

Dangen woke up and asked his mother to take him to see the frogs by the side of the lake. Nuannuan made a light-hearted promise because she wanted him to quickly put on his clothes. However, after breakfast, Dangen gripped her hand and insisted on going to the lakeside, so Nuannuan had no choice but to follow him after first speaking to Shallot about work for the morning. She thought to herself as she walked: *I was too busy to play with my son – this morning should be my break from work, and we shall have good fun.* Scared of accidents, Nuannuan gave a warning to Dangen: "Without an adult watching you, you must never play by the lakeside, or I'll whip your bottom with a cane."

Dangen, who rarely had the opportunity to play next to Red Lake, jumped up and cried in excitement like a foal seeing a meadow for the first time.

Mother and son had been playing by the lake for quite a while when Dangen suddenly remembered to ask her mother for a frog. Holding his mother by her hand, he walked gently, searching the grass on the lakeside for frogs. But it was not the time for frogs to party; instead, they were all hiding in the grass, motionless. Only a few let themselves go and croaked in a small voice. But they were all on high alert, and they jumped into the water and swam to the deep section of the pond one by one as soon as they heard the mother and son's faintest footsteps. Seeing this, Dangen, who had yearned to have one, expressed his frustration repeatedly.

Only when they had walked a few hundred metres did they see a frog that remained still. Dangen reached his hand out and was about to catch it when Nuannuan held him by his hand and stopped him. She said softly: "That's a mother frog." With that, she pointed at the pool of water beside it filled with tiny tadpoles swimming up and down.

Dangen was in a daze and gazed at the tadpoles with wide-open eyes. He asked his mother softly: "Are they the big frog's children?"

Nuannuan beamed. "Yes."

"But why do you only have me?" asked Dangen. "Why don't you have more children like the frog? Then I would have many brothers and sisters, wouldn't I?"

Her son's question made Nuannuan laugh. The frog jumped far away but still watched the mother and son warily.

"What are you laughing about?"

Hearing her mother's voice, Nuannuan turned and saw her standing behind them with Grandma. Nuannuan was surprised and hastened to take Dangen to them. She asked: "What are you two doing here?"

Mum said with a smile: "Grandma is missing Grandpa today. She insisted on coming here to burn some paper money in front of his tomb. I can't let her go out on her own."

Nuannuan said to Dangen: "Come and greet your great-grandma."

Dangen looked at Grandma and fell silent for a short while, feeling shy. Then, he spoke up. "Great-Grandma."

Hearing this, Grandma smiled, and Nuannuan could see that she had lost another tooth. She said: "Good, good. I've lived to see four generations together in this family. Even if I die, I know that I'll have a great-grandson burning paper money at my tomb, and I'll be satisfied."

"Don't talk about inauspicious things. Dangen will want you to attend his wedding, and you'll hold his baby in your arms." Nuannuan stepped out to support Grandma and called out to Dangen: "Come here to hold your great-grandma, and we'll all go to burn paper money for your great-grandpa."

The four, old and young, slowly walked towards the ancestral tombs. Through the clear air, the sun cast its warmth on the five grave mounds. A breeze caressed the grass on the grave tops, circled by a few butterflies.

"Are these insects the ancestors' souls? Dear ancestors, Nuannuan has been busy with her life every day and seldom comes to see you. Please pardon her." Nuannuan lit a stack of paper money in front of her grandpa's tomb and then distributed it to each of the ancestors, who she had never met. Their grave mounds reminded her that her roots were by Red Lake and that she was the descendant of this land.

Grandma sat down in front of Grandpa's tomb. She looked at the ashes and smoke from the paper money and lightly padded down the soil on top of the tomb. Mum stood aside silently with Dangen in her arms. It was very quiet, and they could hear the sound of the waves on the lake as if it were breathing. Nuannuan looked at Grandma's half-closed eyes; it was her own way of communicating with Grandpa. Years had gone by since Grandpa's death, yet Grandma would still walk all the way in her small steps to see him. *They must have had a wonderful relationship and been deeply in love.* Nuannuan tried to imagine a young Grandma walking on the bank of Red Lake with a young Grandpa, but she could not see clearly. She and Kaitian would be old one day. *If I were to leave the world before Kaitian, would he come to see me at my tomb?* The thought gave Nuannuan a shudder. *Maybe people today do not know how to love like they used to...*

On their way home, Nuannuan could not help but ask Grandma: "Was Grandpa good to you?"

Grandma laughed. "Your grandpa had a bad temper, and the smallest thing would set him to yell at me. But he had a good heart, and he cared for me. We weren't a rich couple. We knew how to take care of each other."

"Did Grandpa ever... do something behind your back?"

"Do what?" Grandma turned to look at Nuannuan.

"Did he ever have an affair with another woman?" It took all her courage to ask this question.

"You silly girl. How can you ask Grandma such a question?" Mum, who was walking by the side, glared at Nuannuan. "Do you want to upset your grandma?"

Grandma was still smiling. "Of course she can ask. What are you afraid of? As far as I know, your grandpa never did such a thing. To have another woman outside of the family, a man must have some power, some money, some good background or some idle time. But he had none of that. So how on earth is he going to find another woman? All day long, he had to worry about our food and clothing, and his family gave him so much to worry about that he could not spare any mind, money, emotion or energy to think about anything else. If a family has that kind of problem, then they must have a good life."

Nuannuan felt enlightened. *We do have a good life.*

"Why did you ask me this?" It was Grandma's turn to ask questions.

"Nothing. I was just curious." Nuannuan did not expect Grandma's question. Her face went red, and she could not hide the anxiety in her eyes.

"Are you worried about Kaitian? I can tell – you're my granddaughter after all. But you do have a reason to worry now that he has some power in his hand. Though it's not big, power is power. I've never played that game before, but I've seen others with power. Power is most likely to entangle with women because it burns like a flame. It's not only men who love having that flame in their hands – women also fly towards its heat like moths. You should be more careful. I heard from the seniors that power shakes a man's soul. No matter who you are, power will dazzle you. This is especially the case with Kaitian, who has little experience with power. You must be careful. Don't let him forget who he is."

Nuannuan's heart started beating faster as she heard Grandma's words.

The days had grown warmer since the harvesting of summer wheat and autumn crops. More visitors came to Chu Wang Village to hide from the heat of the city. One afternoon, Nuannuan was putting up mosquito nets in the guest rooms with Shallot and three other staff when Daming, Shallot's daughter, ran into the room and said: "Mum, Dad is asking for you at home. They're driving us out of our house."

Shallot dropped everything and ran out after saying to Nuannuan: "I have to go home."

Nuannuan knew that it must be caused by the expansion of Shang Xin Yuan, which would have to do with herself. So she followed Shallot.

When Nuannuan arrived at Shallot's house, she found Shallot, Changlin, Jiuding and several other people in the village were arguing in Shang Xin Yuan with the accountant Mr Han, who Xue Chuanxin had brought from the provincial capital. Jiuding was speaking. "You want us to leave our home for this amount of money? You're killing us. Don't even think about it."

Mr Han was smirking. "You want to raise the amount? Aren't you a greedy lot? Here's the deal – when the time comes, you'll have to leave."

Nuannuan's face clouded. She stepped up and said to Mr Han: "Mr Han, who gave you the right to threaten people here? They have lived in these houses and worked in these fields for generations. You don't have the right to take that away from them."

Seeing Nuannuan, Mr Han put on a bitter smile and said: "My boss Mr Xue and your husband Leader Kuang made the decision. I'm only here to deliver the news and hurry people up. If you have anything to say, say it to those two. The ownership of this land is ours according to the order from above."

Nuannuan answered motionlessly: "I don't care whose order it is. People in this village did not agree with that, so you can't force them."

Mr Han shrugged and left. Shallot, Jiuding and the others walked next to Nuannuan and said: "If it wasn't for you, he would have kept threatening us."

Nuannuan tried to offer them some comfort. "Don't be afraid. Officials from above have forbidden random acquisition of farmland. If they push you any more, we'll sue them."

The crowd felt more assured. Shallot said: "Nuannuan, I'm afraid that you'll have to talk to Kaitian and Mr Xue. Otherwise, they'll still send people to drive us away."

Nuannuan nodded and agreed.

Nuannuan planned to talk to Kaitian about the farmlands in the village during lunch, but he did not come home. She guessed that he was eating in Shang Xin Yuan and decided to delay the talk until that evening. After lunch, several guests arrived, and she sent them to their rooms. All of a sudden, she heard people crying and shouting outside. She walked out and saw Luoluo, daughter of Uncle Black Bean, running towards Red Lake in tears with her mother running behind her while crying in panic: "Luo... Luo..."

"What happened?" Nuannuan asked.

Luoluo's mother did not stop running. She kept saying: "Luoluo, stop! Stop for your mother!"

Shallot came out too. She looked at Luoluo and said in fear: "Oh no, that girl's going to throw herself in the lake!"

Nuannuan's heart skipped a beat when she heard the warning. Luoluo was indeed running in such a way that made others feel as if they were never going to see her again. Nuannuan turned and started running towards the lake.

Shallot was right. Nuannuan had only started running when Luoluo reached the lakeside. She jumped into the lake. Her mother burst into a desperate cry behind Nuannuan and fell to the ground. Nuannuan's heart sank, and she muttered under her breath: "What a silly girl." She paused for an instant and then resumed running towards the lake as fast as she could.

It seemed that Luoluo was determined to kill herself. She picked the most dangerous spot to jump – the water was deep, and there were many rocks underneath. Nuannuan reached the lakeside, tore off her blouse, looked at the water ripples and dived in. She was the best swimmer among all the women in Chu Wang Village, so it only took a her a second to pull Luoluo out of the water by her collar. Shallot, Huiyu and several others who had come to help all jumped in to pull Luoluo back. Luckily, she had not swallowed too much water. Nuannuan laid her down flat on the ground and shook her body. Slowly, Luoluo woke up. Seeing people surrounding her, she burst into tears.

Nuannuan and Shallot helped Luoluo into Chu Di Ju and changed her wet clothes. They laid Luoluo down to take a rest and then found her mother, who could not stop crying. They went into another room to ask about the situation. Luoluo's mother hesitated before she said while still weeping: "I can tell that both of you have a good heart. But I'll be honest with you – it's all Shang Xin Yuan's fault."

Nuannuan did not expect her to say this.

Luoluo's mother stopped crying and sighed. "Isn't Shang Xin Yuan paying the girls for the massage job? Girls in the village all know about it, and some of them were persuaded. They changed into clean clothes and went to massage the guests there during the night in secret. But they had to share the income with Shang Xin Yuan. My Luoluo could not earn much working in the city. She knew that her dad wanted to refurbish the house, so she went to work in Shang Xin Yuan behind our back. I knew that she had been sneaking out during the night in new clothes after dinner, but I didn't pay much attention. Now that she's a big girl, she should be dating, and we don't meddle in her business. But things went bad. A few days ago, she started throwing up a lot, and her dad told me to take her to Mei's Pharmacy. Old Doctor Mei tested her pulse and dragged me aside. He whispered to me that Luoluo is pregnant. I was stunned. She's only eighteen years old, and she's not seeing anyone at all. Can't you see how bad this news is? Back at home, I pinched her and asked her what happened. She cried and told me about the massage job in Shang Xin Yuan. She also gave me all the money she had earned. Those people from the city – what bastards! They took advantage of my innocent daughter. What am I supposed to do? With her dad's temper, he'll explode if he finds out. I thought about it for one day and one night and decided that I couldn't hide it from him. Of course, his face turned cold like steel, and he picked up a wooden stick to hit her. I tried to stop him but I couldn't. He beat her so hard that she had to roll over on the floor to hide. Luoluo did not ask for this, but what can she do? She chose to kill herself…"

Nuannuan was too stunned to react. *Xue Chuanxin, Kuang Kaitian, look what you've done.*

Shallot sighed and said: "Bad karma."

"Auntie, don't be afraid," Nuannuan said. "I'm on your side. I'll go and talk some sense into those people in Shang Xin Yuan, and I'll stop them from poisoning our girls. You should take Luoluo home and secretly talk about her abortion with Uncle Black Bean so that no one else will know about it."

Luoluo's mother held Nuannuan's hand and said: "Your auntie trusts you on this. We must not let another person know about Luoluo's situation. Shallot, you're a sister to her. You must also keep the secret, or no one will ever marry her in the future."

Nuannuan went to see Luoluo after discussing it with her mother. Luoluo was still crying as she said: "Sister Nuannuan, you should not have saved me. I'd rather die."

Nuannuan answered with a soft, comforting voice: "Silly girl! Your parents have raised you, so how can you kill yourself before paying them back? They will not stop being sad if you die. You're not as brave as I thought you were, thinking of death whenever there's a problem…"

Nuannuan found out from Luoluo that five or six girls in the village were doing the massage work in secret. Like Luoluo, they would make excuses to leave home after dinner and run to Shang Xin Yuan. They'd ask the receptionists to find clients for them, and they shared the income with Shang Xin Yuan. At first, they really offered massages to the clients with the simple skills they had learned. However, in order to earn more money, they gradually accepted whatever the clients asked of them. Luoluo told her that Xuehua, another girl in the village, had been infected with some venereal disease from the clients. She had constantly felt an itchiness around her groin, and she had to sneak to Juxiang Street to buy some ointment.

Nuannuan was overwhelmed by anger. She wanted to run to Shang Xin Yuan and make Xue Chuanxin and Kaitian understand how bad things had become and stop whatever they were doing. However, she knew that she must talk with Kaitian first because Xue Chuanxin would not even see her without Kaitian's consent.

While making supper, Nuannuan felt two flames of anger surging in her: one was at the land expropriation and the other at Luoluo's tragedy. Therefore, she was unusually heavy-handed when she chopped the vegetables on the board. From the thudding sound, her mother-in-law could detect her anger. She mistook it for a complaint against her for not cooking earlier. Therefore, she said to Nuannuan: "Let me do it. Since you've been busy the whole day, go and have a rest now."

Nuannuan realised her mother-in-law's misunderstanding and sighed. "I'm not angry with you. I'm anxious about Shang Xin Yuan's reputation."

Nuannuan made dinner for her in-laws and Dangen. But Kaitian had not returned home, and Nuannuan became anxious. She was about to phone him when a neighbour came over and said that the leader asked him to tell Nuannuan that he would not be home for dinner due to some business matter that he had to discuss with Mr Xue. Nuannuan was so furious that she kicked the chair in front of him, but she stubbed her toes, and the pain caused her to gasp. At bedtime, Kaitian had still not returned, and Nuannuan was worried that he would not come home that night. He had spent many nights out recently. Nuannuan decided to go to Shang Xin Yuan herself to find Kaitian. *No matter how big your business is, you should have finished the discussion by now.*

Nuannuan knew her way around Shang Xin Yuan. The security guard nodded to salute her, and the girl working in the reception hastened to greet her.

"I'm looking for Dangen's dad." She walked straight towards her old office, knowing that Kaitian used it as an office and a bedroom.

The receptionist tried to stop her. "Madam Nuannuan!"

"What is it?"

"No, no, nothing at all. Please take a seat, and I'll bring the leader to you."

"I don't need you to bring him to me." Nuannuan was suspicious of the girl's nervous attitude. *Is Kaitian hiding something from me?* She did not stop but instead quickened her pace before reaching in her pocket for the key and thrusting the office door open.

It was dark in the room, but the darkness did not prevent Nuannuan from seeing two people sit up in a rush on the single bed that she used to sleep in. Kaitian called out in surprise: "Who is it?"

Nuannuan did not answer; she only turned the light on. Seeing her, Kaitian hastened to reach for his clothes. Nuannuan recognised the girl next to him – she was apparently taking her time putting on her clothes. She was one of the six girls that Xue Chuanxin had brought from the provincial capital. Nuannuan neither cried nor cursed Kaitian. She did not even say a word. She stood there and watched the two getting dressed. Kaitian, who had finished covering himself, did not know what to say. He stood aside in embarrassment.

After the girl had walked out, Nuannuan said in an indifferent tone: "King of Chu, which of your women is this?"

"I... eh... hehe..." chuckled Kaitian in embarrassment.

"Don't worry. I don't want to make it difficult for you," said Nuannuan calmly. "Theoretically, you don't have too many. A king has three palaces and six harems of concubines totalling seventy-two, right?"

"Hehe, well..." Kaitian could only respond with a smirk.

"Tomorrow, we should go to Juxiang Street and get an official divorce. In future, you won't have to worry about me showing up when you sleep with other women. You may rest assured that I'm open-minded enough. I've seen lots of TV dramas, and I know that a king can sleep with whatever woman he likes."

As Nuannuan turned to leave, Kaitian opened his mouth as if he was about to call her back. Yet he did not. He followed her out of Shang Xin Yuan, stood beside the gate and stared at her figure disappearing in the night.

Nuannuan tried to walk calmly, sensing his gaze at her back. She was determined not to let him see her suffer. Not until she reached the shore of Red Lake and made sure there was not a soul around did she crouch down and burst into suppressed sobs and wails. *This is the man you dated. This is the love in which you once believed with conviction. This is how you've ended up. And this is your reward for what you've done. Chu Nuannuan, who else can you blame? Who? You've made all the choices yourself...*

It was midnight by the time Nuannuan stopped crying and picked herself up. The clouds weighed heavily in the sky, blotting all the stars and plunging everything around Nuannuan into complete darkness. Nuannuan sat immobile in the dark. The unrestrained crying vented all the grievances and anger pent up in her heart. She felt much relieved. She sat silently by the lake for a long time, contemplating her relationship with Kaitian before and after their marriage. Finally, she thought of the divorce the next day and heaved a deep sigh of relief. *Enough is enough. I'd rather suffer an acute pain for a short while than a mild one for a prolonged time. I can't hesitate any more. Let the break off be final.*

The next day during breakfast, Kaitian came home. Nuannuan did not say anything, and the family ate their breakfast in peace. After breakfast, Nuannuan had Dangen lead Kaitian to her room, and then she sent Dangen out. She said to Kaitian without emotion: "I have thought about the divorce agreement. We will halve the deposit. I won't take any part of the old house. Shang Xin Yuan, which we invested in, will be yours, and Chu Di Ju, which we built ourselves, will be mine. I will not participate in South Water Landscape Company either, and you shall have all the other incomes. Dangen can eat and sleep with either of us, but we will each pay half of his future tuition fee. What do you think?"

Kaitian seemed hesitant. He nodded and said: "Sure."

Nuannuan wrote down the agreement on the papers. Each of them took one and signed. Nuannuan said: "Now we should go through the formalities."

Kaitian coughed to clear his throat. Clearly, he meant to say something, but the words didn't come out. The two of them went out, one after another, without Kaitian's parents knowing what was in store for the family. Kaitian's mother even rushed out of the courtyard door and told Nuannuan to buy a kilogram of salt. Nuannuan nodded while thinking: *Mum, you'll have to ask your son to buy salt when you need it in the future.*

Things went well on Juxiang Street. The staff at the registration office were satisfied to see the divorcing couple with an agreement and no emotional dispute. They all knew of Kaitian, the leader and famous entrepreneur. When one of the staff gave Kaitian the divorce certificate, he smiled and said: "Mr Leader, you are the third divorce I have handled this year. I heard that today in the city, people have stopped wishing newlyweds a long and prosperous life together because marriages are not supposed to last. I think it's time that we do so here too…"

Nuannuan and Kaitian went back out to the street. Nuannuan said: "I need to go and buy something." She left on her own, without even a glance back at Kaitian.

On her way back to Chu Wang Village, four and a half kilometres away, Nuannuan silently walked while pushing her bicycle. This quiet lakeshore path awakened many of her memories. When she decided to date Kaitian, they cycled to Juxiang Street together to go shopping. The memories were still vivid, and the Kaitian of that time was still trustworthy and reliable. At that time, she wanted to be with him for the rest of their lifetimes, as her parents had done. But unexpectedly, their relationship had soured in the blink of an eye...

Nuannuan sat next to a cluster of reeds by the side of Red Lake until sunset. She did not want to go back to the village when the day was bright because people might want to ask about her business on Juxiang Street. To her relief, she did not run into anyone on the road from the village entrance to the courtyard of the Kuangs. It had saved her the pain of answering questions. She gave the two *jin* of salt to her mother-in-law and went to her room to pack. When her mother-in-law called her to have dinner, she sat down and ate a little. Her mother-in-law then asked her for the whereabouts of Kaitian. She did her best to smile as she said: "Mum, you'll have to ask him. I officially divorced him today. From now on, I have nothing to do with him and no right to ask about his business."

Kaitian's mother dropped her chopsticks in shock. She stared at Nuannuan and asked in a shaky voice: "Is it true?"

Nuannuan took the certificate out of her pocket and showed it to her.

Nuannuan walked out of the courtyard gate with her things in her hands amid the cries of Kaitian's parents. Dangen walked behind her in confusion. He knew that his mother was going to spend the night in Chu Di Ju, but he did not understand why his grandparents were in tears – his parents had not been fighting, and it was not the first time that his mother had gone out after dinner. He turned and shouted towards the courtyard: "Grandpa, Grandma, I'll wake up early tomorrow and come back to see you."

Nuannuan put Dangen to sleep in a guest room in Chu Di Ju. She sat in the dark and gazed upon the night sky from the window. The sky was empty that night – neither the moon nor the stars could be seen; instead, the thick clouds lingered in the darkness. Nuannuan suddenly felt unbearably empty inside. The home to which she had been devoted had just vanished in an instant. From now on, she would be a divorced woman on her own. *What's happened to my life? Where did I go wrong?*

Shallot came to work the next morning, and the staff told her that Nuannuan had stayed in a guest room. She thought that the couple had been fighting again and rushed over. Nuannuan had just washed her face, though her eyes were still red as she helped Dangen dress. Shallot said with a smile: "Did the happiest young couple fight again?"

Nuannuan faked a smile and waved the divorce certificate in front of Shallot. "There's no couple here. From today on, it'll be Leader Kuang and Chu Nuannuan."

Shallot took the certificate and said in surprise: "That's silly. How can you divorce Kaitian now? He's the leader and the vice president of Shang Xin Yuan. He has power and money. Do you know how many women want to be with him? You just gave away your position as his wife. They must be so happy to know that."

"Let them be happy. Whoever wants him can take him. I don't want him any more." Nuannuan was about to continue when the familiar music drifted over from Shang Xin Yuan. She looked up at the calendar and remembered that it was the day for the Shang Xin Yuan *Farewell* show.

Sister-in-Law Shallot said: "I've informed the guests staying in Chu Di Ju at dinner time yesterday of the show today in Shang Xin Yuan. I told them that they could go and watch if they like." Then she asked: "With your divorce, who will act as King Zi of Chu today? I don't think Kaitian will be in the mood to do so." With that, she glanced through the window and suddenly screamed: "He is still in the mood!"

Nuannuan also took a look, and sure enough, she saw Kaitian walking jubilantly in his King Zi of Chu costume, surrounded by many people. *Kuang Kaitian, be a good King of Chu and try to have more women...*

After lunch, Nuannuan went to her parents' home with Dangen. She had decided to inform them of the divorce because she knew that she could not hide it, and it would be better if they heard about it from her instead of the gossip from other seniors in the village.

When she arrived, Dad, Mum, Grandma and her sister were all at home, and they were happy to see her with Dangen. Mum was doing some needlework by the gate. She stopped and held Nuannuan's hand. "Have you been too busy? You don't look well."

Nuannuan felt tears in her eyes hearing Mum's loving words, and she did her best to stop them from falling. She gave an ambiguous answer. "We've had many tourists in Chu Di Ju recently – I was so busy that I didn't sleep well."

"Kaitian has vision and ability," said Nuannuan's father. "After he built Chu Di Ju and Shang Xin Yuan, you guys can have people send money to you, even when you sit at home. I didn't expect him to have the qualities and didn't want him to be my son-in-law. It looks like Nuannuan knew him better."

His remark made Nuannuan's heart ache. *Did I know him so well? If I wasn't so determined to marry him, what life am I living now? Why did I choose the path I took? Why?*

Nuannuan's sister picked up the topic and continued: "Sis, I didn't expect that my brother-in-law would be so talented. He pretty much lived the part of King Wen of Chu. I've seen the show several times. He looks like a king indeed with his gait, look and facial expressions that show the king's majesty and arrogance."

Previously, the compliment would have made Nuannuan happy and proud, but it now gave her pain and agony.

"Your dad lived in Chu Wang Village like a contemptible pushover for all those years until my son-in-law Kaitian became the village committee leader. Now I can stand up with my head held high. I don't have a son in my generation, but I have a son-in-law…"

Nuannuan hurriedly cut in to stop him further singing Kaitian's praises, embarrassing her more and making it harder for her to speak up. "Grandma, Dad, Mum, I have something to tell you."

"What is it? Do you want us to take care of Dangen?"

Mum turned and held Dangen in her arms to kiss him. "You've grown taller again. Do you miss Grandma? How are your father's parents doing? Your father…"

"Please don't be mad at me when I tell you," said Nuannuan.

Grandma raised her cane and tapped Nuannuan on her calf. "Say it, you brat! What are you hemming and hawing like this? How can you, a manager, speak so awkwardly like a rich family's daughter of the past confined in her lady's chamber?"

"I just divorced Kaitian."

"What?" Dad, Mum and her sister all cried out. Grandma kept silent, but her grey hair shook as she shivered. She stared at Nuannuan with her hands shaking on her knees.

Mum's face turned pale in shock. "What nonsense are you talking about? You have a child together. How can you divorce?"

"Was he the one who wanted a divorce?" Dad asked, his teeth clenched. "Because he's the leader? Because he's rich now?"

"No, it was me," said Nuannuan, lowering her head.

"Are you crazy? How can a girl want a divorce? Do you think it honourable? Have we had a divorcee in our family for generations?" roared Dad.

"I can't live with him any more, so I thought I might as well…"

"What do you mean you can't live with him any more? Do you think you can live as a divorced woman? Don't you feel any shame at all? No woman in Chu Wang Village dares divorce her husband," said Dad. He was furious and kept hitting the chair next to him.

Grandma knocked her cane on the ground and interrupted Dad's scolding. "Let Nuannuan explain."

Nuannuan flushed. She bowed her head even more and mumbled: "He cheated on me."

Grandma coughed and said: "I guessed so. That kid has been the king in Chu Wang Village since he was elected leader. He's been the richest man since you started making money. He's been the man with all the time in the world since you stopped working in the fields. Of course he can mess around with women. I guessed so. But I didn't know it would happen this soon."

"Did you hear about it from other's gossip or…" Mum flushed too. She could not ask her directly. It was not something that a mother could simply talk about with her daughter.

"I caught him." Nuannuan bowed her head even more.

"You should bear it," said Grandma with a sigh.

"All those kings and emperors in old times, they all had many women, didn't they? In that performance in Shang Xin Yuan, the King of Chu also had a group of women following him, right? His queen bore it, didn't she? Do you think she liked it?"

"But I don't want to bear it. I simply can't bear it."

Dad was still angry. "Now that you're divorced, how can I face anyone in Chu Wang Village?"

Nuannuan replied: "Divorce is nothing to be ashamed of."

"Bullshit!" shouted Chu Changshun as he got up. "It may not be a shame on you, but it's certainly a shame on me. Are you proud to be a divorced woman? Get out! Get out now!" He pointed at the courtyard gate.

Dangen was scared and burst into a loud cry. Nuannuan understood that it would not be easy for the older people to accept her divorce, so she stood up and walked towards the gate with Dangen in her hand.

WATER

Nuannuan's peaceful divorce from Kaitian was not only a shock to her parents but also to the residents of Chu Wang Village. Almost everyone thought that Nuannuan had made a silly decision. After learning about the divorce, Spotty Laosi came to Nuannuan and said in all seriousness: "Sister, I'm grateful to you. You've helped me through my poverty to earn some pocket money by hiring me as a tour guide. At this critical moment, I naturally side with you. Please think of a way to get reunited with Kaitian. He has power and money. If you weren't divorced, your position in Chu Wang Village would be like the first lady of a foreign president or the queen of an ancient Chinese emperor."

Nuannuan forced a smile. "Brother Laosi, I thank you for your concern, but everyone has his or her aspirations. I don't want to be a queen – I just want to live a normal life…"

Like their wedding, the divorce of Nuannuan and Kaitian was the talk of the village for a long while. However, as time went by, the gossip dissipated in the air.

Nuannuan's life went back to normal. She stayed in Chu Di Ju, and her daily work consisted of arranging the accommodation and sightseeing for her guests. In order to improve its surroundings, she had Shallot and several staff members work in front of Chu Di Ju. They dug open a pit that used to contain fertiliser and borrowed a pump to put water into it. There, they made a pond. They planted some lotus flowers in the pond and arranged some stools and tables around it so that their busy guests could sit there and relax after dinner.

Though Chu Di Ju was in front of Kaitian's house, Nuannuan never stepped inside his courtyard again. She knew that everything inside that house would bring back memories. She was afraid of the sorrow. Dangen had learned about his parents' divorce from the adults, but he could not understand what divorce meant. He would go to his grandparents as usual, and Nuannuan would not stop him. Every time he ran out of the Kuangs' courtyard with snacks from his grandma in his hand, Nuannuan would quietly sigh. One afternoon, Kaitian's mother made some dumplings. She came over to invite Nuannuan to join them after feeding Dangen. Nuannuan refused to go. But the old woman brought a bowl full of dumplings to her, so she had to accept and ate them in Chu Di Ju. Kaitian's mother said to her: "Dangen's mother, in the eyes of us two old people, you're still our daughter-in-law."

Tears spilled down Nuannuan's face as she heard those words.

Nuannuan had not talked to Kaitian since their divorce, and she had avoided any opportunity to meet him. She would only stand at a distance and look at him hosting the village's meeting with his arms waving in the air as he spoke. She would see him riding his motorcycle to the meetings in the township office with a cigarette in his mouth, looking relaxed and proud. She would look at him talking with Xue Chuanxin in front of Shang Xin Yuan, the two of them laughing so hard that they couldn't stand straight. She would look at him wearing the clothes of King Zi and playing his role in *Farewell* in a serious manner. She had heard from Shallot that Kaitian had been intimate with a woman who had recently married into Chu Wang Village. Nuannuan smiled. *They can be as intimate as they like – it has nothing to do with me any more.*

One afternoon, Nuannuan went to buy cold medicine from Mei's Pharmacy. At the doorstep, she ran into Zhan Shideng, who was walking out on a cane. Nuannuan instinctively made way for him and didn't want to speak to him. To her surprise, Zhan Shideng stopped and, squinting his eyes, smirked with heavy breaths. "Isn't that Leader Kuang's wife? Wow, you're prettier than before."

Nuannuan ignored him and continued to make her way into the pharmacy. But Zhan Shideng wouldn't give up. Glaring at her back, he smirked and called out: "Slut! Bent on being a leader's wife, but do you have the luck to enjoy it? Did he dump you? Are you happy now? You're a fucking living widow, watching others sleeping with the leader and pining with anger."

These slurs filled Nuannuan with flames of fury. She would have charged at him and given him a sound telling-off, but that would have attracted many onlookers. Therefore, she swallowed the insult. The veteran physician Mei in the pharmacy understood who was the object of Zhan Shideng's abuse and discerned the anger in Nuannuan's eyes. He said to Nuannuan in a low voice: "Don't be angry with a sick man. He's suffering from a minor stroke and can't walk steadily. I'm worried that he'll get worse. Please forgive him."

Nuannuan didn't say anything but instead slowly exhaled a long breath. She said silently: *Zhan Shideng, I won't quarrel with you. Heaven knows what you've done.*

While getting the medicine for Nuannuan, Physician Mei said: "It's not worth getting angry for the sake of power. How long is a lifetime? We've got to think of ourselves lying buried in the earth. After a few decades or centuries, the elements will level the tombs of two competing people. Later generations will unwittingly mix them up when ploughing the fields for farming. Who will be able to tell who is who?"

Nuannuan exhaled with a smile and said: "You're so right, Uncle."

On her way home that day, she already felt mollified. She hoped that she would live with peace of mind. Being irritated all the time would make a person sick sooner or later. However, she didn't expect another event to arise that would outrage her.

One evening after dinner, Nuannuan was talking to a guest in front of Chu Di Ju when she saw Luoluo walking from the pier, supported by her mother. She remembered what happened to her and ran towards them to ask in a quiet voice: "Has everything been resolved now?"

Luoluo's mother sighed and whispered: "It's resolved indeed. But Luoluo had to go through all that danger. She almost didn't make it. Just look how skinny she is."

Nuannuan looked at Luoluo in the dim daylight. The girl was now very slim, her face looking pale blue. She was leaning on her mother and looked as if she was about to faint at any time. Nuannuan's heart ached. "What happened to her?"

Luoluo's mother answered slowly: "We found a doctor through some connection. But he was not very skilful, and Luoluo bled too much. She almost died. It's all Shang Xin Yuan's fault."

Nuannuan listened to her and thought about how everything started when Xue Chuanxin brought back those masseuses. As she thought about it, she grew unbearably angry. After sending Luoluo and her mother off, she walked to Shang Xin Yuan and went straight into Xue Chuanxin's office. Xue Chuanxin was watching TV. Seeing Nuannuan standing outside with an angry face, he smiled and said politely: "Hi, Nuannuan, what a rare guest. Come on in."

Nuannuan went inside and said: "Do you know that you almost killed a girl?"

Xue Chuanxin's smile vanished. "What are you talking about?"

Nuannuan told him what happened to Luoluo. Xue Chuanxin put on a jeering expression and said: "Nuannuan, you can't simply put the responsibility of this silly business on Shang Xin Yuan. First of all, we didn't even know that she had worked here and offered services to the clients. Second, we don't think she got pregnant in Shang Xin Yuan. You know there are many ways that a girl can get knocked up – she can't blame Shang Xin Yuan for that."

Nuannuan's eyes widened. "You think she's lying? Do you want me to find a testimonial?"

Xue Chuanxin laughed. "What testimonial? Just tell me what you want from me."

"You must stop all that hideous business and return to work on tourism."

"You and your silly obstinacy. Shang Xin Yuan is doing well at the moment. What if we lose money because we change what's working?" Xue Chuanxin picked up the phone, dialled a number and then said to the person on the line: "Come over for a moment."

Nuannuan thought he was calling his employees to talk about the suspension of the massage services. However, it was Kuang Kaitian who showed up at the door. Nuannuan's face turned rigid. Kaitian did not expect to see Nuannuan in Xue Chuanxin's office, either. He stood there in surprise.

"I don't think I need to introduce you two, right?" Xue Chuanxin was still smiling. "Leader Kuang, Nuannuan just told me that this

Luoluo girl had an accident in our Shang Xin Yuan. She asked me to change the business model."

Kaitian had recovered from the surprise. He stepped aside to sit on the sofa in a relaxed manner and lit up a cigarette. "What happened?"

"She got pregnant," said Xue Chuanxin in Nuannuan's stead. "But I believe a girl can get pregnant anywhere. How can she prove she got pregnant by working in Shang Xin Yuan? She could get knocked up in the fields or on the hillside."

Kaitian turned to Nuannuan and said: "Exactly. You shouldn't be meddling with this."

Nuannuan did not look at Kaitian. She stared at Xue Chuanxin and said: "I think I need to have a say in this."

"How about this – I have some other business to attend to, so please talk about it with Leader Kuang. He's the leader in Chu Wang Village as well as our vice president. He has every right to settle any problems in Shang Xin Yuan." With that, Xue Chuanxin left.

"Hey! You!" Nuannuan tried to stop Xue Chuanxin, but he had already gone.

Kaitian said again: "Don't meddle with these small things. Go and take care of Chu Di Ju."

Nuannuan turned and glared at Kaitian. "What do you mean by small things? Do you know Luoluo almost lost her life? Her mother took her somewhere else to abort the child, and she bled profusely."

"That's because she wasn't careful. If she had asked the man to wear a condom, she wouldn't have to go through this ordeal."

"Wow! You have the nerve to mention condoms. If you didn't do such heinous business in Shang Xin Yuan, how could such a mishap occur with an eighteen-year-old girl like Luoluo? Where's your conscience when you blame her for it?"

"She didn't have to come. No one invited her." Kaitian's face became cold, and he cast the cigarette onto the floor.

"But you started it, and she wanted to make some money."

"You're right. So she has herself to blame."

"You guys enticed her to become a bad girl."

"I think you'd better not meddle in the matter. You have nothing to do with Shang Xin Yuan. Make your money in Chu Di Ju while we make ours here. Why are you poking your nose into other people's business? Go away!" Kaitian stood up with impatience.

Nuannuan was angered by his attitude. "Kuang Kaitian, I will solve this with you."

"How will you solve this? Who will listen to you?" said Kaitian with a smirk. "Who do you think you are? Just go and take care of your own business."

"Do you think no one can tell you what to do because you're the leader?" Nuannuan gave him a cold laugh. "Don't forget that you were elected by people in the village. If people can vote you in, they can vote you out. Count your days – the election is not far away."

"Don't threaten me with the election. I'm not Zhan Shideng. You can't drive me away like you did with him. The truth is, since I've had a taste of power as the leader, I will not stop being the leader. If you want to stay in Chu Wang Village and run your business here, you should not cross me. Or I'll make you pay."

Nuannuan laughed with irony. "Kuang Kaitian, when did you learn to threaten people? You have certainly learned fast."

"I'm not threatening you. I'm notifying you that, in Chu Wang Village, everyone must speak to me with respect and caution. You are the only one who dares to talk to me like this. I allowed you to do this because you're the mother of my son. But don't test my patience and cross me."

"What can I do to avoid offending you? Do you want me to tag after you like the maids of honour around King Zi of Chu, adjusting my behaviour in response to your facial expressions, paying my ritual respects, and yelling the slogan 'Long live the king' all the time?"

"You can do whatever you want. But since you aren't my wife any more, you aren't entitled to my protection."

"Good. Thank you for notifying me. I really want to know what you're going to do with me if I do cross you. Are you going to send your royal guards to arrest me? Or kill me? Or do you want to throw me, one of your out-of-favour concubines, into the cold palace and poison me?"

"We'll see."

"Yes, we'll see." Nuannuan turned and angrily walked out.

Nuannuan learned a lot from her previous encounter with Kaitian. Without taking power away from Leader Kuang Kaitian, it would be very difficult to change the business model in Shang Xin Yuan and stop them from driving Shallot and the others away from their farmland and homes. Xue Chuanxin was only unafraid of doing anything because Kuang Kaitian, the leader, was supporting him. Nuannuan began to feel regret. She should not have made Kuang Kaitian the leader; otherwise, her life would not be turning out so bad. She thought she must have been cursed. That night, Nuannuan made up her mind: she was going to bring Kuang Kaitian down.

Nuannuan knew that many women in the village were not happy about the masseuses in Shang Xin Yuan. Many parents were also angry, worrying that their daughters may be seduced because of them. She was certain that those people would not vote for Kuang Kaitian in the next election. Yet she was concerned who they would vote for? Without a competing candidate, Kuang Kaitian might still end up with the most votes. Therefore, one month before the election, Nuannuan secretly went to persuade Jiuding to run for the position. She told him that the only way to stop Shang Xin Yuan was by becoming the leader himself. Jiuding did not agree at first, feeling frightened of the possibility of Kaitian's revenge. Nuannuan had to talk sense into him by stating the motivation and reasons for it, as well as her certainty of his victory. Eventually, she persuaded him to agree to run for the position. She then advised him to visit each house in the village and explain to people his reasons for running.

A few days before the election, Nuannuan sent Shallot off to persuade several families in the village to vote for Jiuding. She also had Jiuding write down his election pledges on some red paper and put it up on the wall next to the village committee, just as she had told Kaitian last time. One of the pledges was most eye-catching: *I will restore the innocence and dignity of Chu Wang Village, and I will not allow anyone to put shame on us.*

Nuannuan knew that people would understand what it meant.

On the morning of the election day, Nuannuan, Shallot and Jiuding gathered together and estimated the result. The three calculated Jiuding's possible winning votes and were convinced of Kaitian's upcoming defeat. As she walked towards the election venue, Nuannuan could even anticipate Kaitian's upset face on hearing the result. *Kuang Kaitian, accept it – you should have come down a long time ago. You should resume your place as a farmer in the village, and I sincerely wish that you will not get a serious disease like Zhan Shideng did...*

Nevertheless, the result shocked Nuannuan, Jiuding and Shallot: Kuang Kaitian got close to ninety-five per cent of the votes and was re-elected as the leader. Applause rose after the official from the township office announced the result. Yet Nuannuan could not hide her stunned expression. *How is this possible?*

Kuang Kaitian looked satisfied as he walked over to Nuannuan, who was getting up to leave. "How did that go? You didn't expect it, did you?"

Nuannuan turned and glared at him. She did not answer.

"You lost, and you must accept it. Don't look upset like this. Do you know the reason for your failure? Let me tell you. You lost because you underestimated how much power is entangled with money. You and I only beat Zhan Shideng three years ago because he had only power and no money. This time, you lost to me because I have Five Continents Group, with all the money it holds, standing right behind me. Do you get it? As long as I have Five Continents, you will not win, even after three years. Understand? All right, let's stop talking about the election. Tell me something about Jiuding and you."

"What about Jiuding and me?" Nuannuan glared at him.

"Don't pretend in front of me. Why did you spend so much effort trying to get Jiuding elected as the village leader? Are you dating him? Time has changed. I would understand if you were. Besides, he's so young."

Nuannuan reached her hand to scratch Kaitian, who quickly stepped back with fright.

"Kuang Kaitian, I'll tear your mouth if you go on with this nonsense!" yelled Nuannuan with wrath. "Don't think I'll bring myself as low as you are!"

"OK, OK, let's change the subject and talk about the future," said Kaitian. "I think you should mind your Chu Di Ju business instead of meddling with other people's. Who doesn't think of making money these days? With cash, you can buy what you want and enjoy it as you wish. Everything will be OK. Let me know if you need any help from me."

"Do you want me to ignore the dirty business you and Xue Chuanxin are doing?" There was sarcasm in Nuannuan's eyes.

"What do you mean by dirty business? Isn't it only a massage service? Isn't it only the expansion of Shang Xin Yuan that will take over a few families' houses and farmland? Mr Xue said that there are schools in cities that specialise in training masseuses. City residents believe that muscle tension is the primary symptom of mental stress. Nervous tension begins with muscle tension. Therefore, a full-body massage is helpful to prevent illness. Besides, the expansion of Shang Xin Yuan is related to Chu Wang Village's future development. The township has enthusiastically supported and approved it. Can you stop it? Who are you? Do I have to remind you of your identity?"

"The kind of massage service you mentioned is not the same as the massage you are doing now at Shang Xin Yuan. The development you referred to is not the development that the people in the village want. It's a development that hurts others and benefits you."

"Even if the massage service is slightly different, Mr Xue said that this practice is common in hotels and restaurants in cities. Everyone looks the other way. Why are you so serious? Besides, even if you continue to be inquisitive and meddlesome, what will the result be? Who will listen to you? You should understand that in Chu Wang Village, nothing can change without my permission."

"Do you think you, a village leader, can dominate everything?"

"Even if I can't dominate everything, I can control most of it." Kaitian chuckled with pride.

"Don't forget there are still mayors of the township and county above you."

"That's rubbish. Haven't you heard the saying, 'The official sitting in the county seat can't order the official around like the one sitting right here'? I have influence here in Chu Wang Village. When the township or county mayor comes, I'll do what he tells me. But he will leave eventually. Then, I can still boss people around here, can't I? So don't try to fight me. You're bound to suffer if you do. Believe it or not."

"I don't believe in this vicious saying."

"Then you can put your belief to the test. You can go to the township or county mayor and see what they can do to me. The villagers chose me, not them. Besides, if you can go to them, Five Continents and I can too. And we can be more persuasive than you because Five Continents Group has money. Don't you understand?"

Nuannuan was too angry to eat her lunch and dinner that day. After sunset, she was sitting alone in disappointment when she heard sharp cries coming from Shang Xin Yuan, followed by the sound of people running. Just as the village had fallen quiet after a busy day, the noises set it back to life: pigs, dogs and donkeys were all bawling out while people shouted. Nuannuan walked out in surprise and asked Shallot, who had not gone home from work: "What happened?"

Shallot was not quite sure herself. "I don't know. A lot of people are running to Shang Xin Yuan. Something must have happened. Do you smell it? There's a bad smell coming from there."

Nuannuan sniffed. It was indeed a horrible smell. She asked: "What odour is this?"

A sudden shout rose from Shang Xin Yuan. "Call the police!"

"Let's go and see."

Nuannuan and Shallot walked quickly towards Shang Xin Yuan. The closer they got, the worse the smell was. They were curious, but they could not see clearly until they reached the wall of Shang Xin Yuan's courtyard. Someone had dumped manure around the walls of Shang Xin Yuan. Many people in the village were standing around looking with their hands covering their noses. Xue Chuanxin was covering his nose too, as he instructed the security guards to get rid of the manure with spades. Kuang Kaitian was cursing: "What son of a bitch did this? How dare he pollute my place? The police will be here any minute, and we shall see where the little prick can run to."

Nuannuan stopped a security guard from Shang Xin Yuan, who was running by. She asked him what was going on. The guard gasped. "Before we found out about the incident, a security guard on patrol smelt a stench. He also caught sight of a few human figures pouring something from the baskets they were carrying. He was about to check when a tourist who returned from strolling by the lake stepped on this stuff. It was so stinky that they screamed..."

Nuannuan almost laughed out loud. *Needless to say, someone with a grievance against Shang Xin Yuan must have done this prank. It's some idea. Xue Chuanxin and Kuang Kaitian, you should ask yourselves why others would treat you like this.*

Just as everyone was busy talking about the situation, three motorcycles arrived. On them were several police officers and one patrol dog. The police officers jumped off the motorcycles and taped off the area to stop people from entering the site of the dump. Shallot pulled Nuannuan by her hand and said: "Let's go home."

Nuannuan stayed awake for a long time. The faeces on and beneath Shang Xin Yuan's wall lingered before her mind's eye. When it was first built, many villagers went to visit and admire it. No one expected that such a thing would happen. It was disgraceful indeed.

The following morning, Nuannuan heard a woman's wailing voice before she got out of bed. *That's strange – who would start a family fight this early in the morning?* She got out of bed and went out to see what had happened. Two police officers had put handcuffs on Wei Liang, the young mason in the village, as well as two other young men. They were forcing them onto the motorcycles. Wei Liang's mother followed the police officers and cried: "My boy! Have pity! Mercy on my boy!"

Nuannuan was surprised. She asked her neighbour, Spotty Laosi's wife: "What are they taking the young mason for?"

Spotty Laosi's wife walked over and whispered: "Didn't the police bring a watchdog with them last night? The thing has a good nose all right."

Nuannuan corrected her. "You mean the K-9."

"Ah yes, the K-9," said Spotty Laosi's wife in a lower voice. "I heard that thing can smell everything on a man. It took one sniff and then another, and then it went straight to the mason's house, all the way into his courtyard. The police took him, but he didn't confess at first. Then the police found the basket that shipped the manure to the site, and he admitted what he did and told them about his helpers. My goodness, who would have thought such a bad thing could be done by these honest young men?"

"What for? Why did they do it?" asked Nuannuan. She remembered Wei Liang the mason as a good boy with a nice temperament, and he had never fought with anyone for anything.

Spotty Laosi's wife said with an even lower voice: "None of the three said anything. The police did all the interrogations, and in the end, Wei Liang said one thing – 'It was for the three wronged girls.'"

"Oh yes?" said Nuannuan as her heart skipped a beat. "The three wronged girls?"

"You know Luoluo, Black Bean's daughter, right? I only heard this from other people – the mason has been seeing her for some time. Maybe he did it for her. But I don't know what Shang Xin Yuan had done to wrong her, and I don't know which other two girls the two boys were dating."

Nuannuan suddenly understood. She was no longer listening to Spotty Laosi's wife. Instead, she turned to look at the mason and the other two young men. They were cuffed to the motorcycle face up, unable to move.

Just then, Kaitian came up and scolded them. "You bastards! You're so young, yet so evil too, eh? Let me tell you – you've violated the law." As he said this, he lunged forward and slapped the young mason on his face. The police officers dragged Kaitian from the mason and drove away on the motorcycles. "You still have the nerve to cry?" said Kaitian after he turned to the young mason's mother, who had plopped to the ground wailing loudly. Kaitian continued to roar. "See what a son you brought up! One who did something unspeakable! Dumping shit on our doorstep! Don't you think that's a crime?"

Seeing this, Nuannuan quietly went to the young mason's mother and helped her go back to her home. She tried to comfort the woman, who was crying desperately. "The police will only be detaining him for a couple of days to educate him. They're not going to punish him. Don't you worry."

As she was speaking, Shallot hurried over and said: "Nuannuan, I don't know what to do. Kaitian is taking revenge on Jiuding. He forbids him from rowing the boat for the visitors in the lake because his boat has safety issues. He drove him out of the cast of *Farewell*, saying his attitude was bad. Now Jiuding has lost both incomes."

Nuannuan's eyes flashed with hatred. Her face turned cold as she said: "Tell Jiuding that visitors staying in Chu Di Ju will still take his boat to the lake."

"There's more. Mr Han, the accountant in Shang Xin Yuan, went to our house and told us to move out by the end of next month, or he will forcibly demolish our houses. He also said we can't work on the farmlands after the autumn harvest because they're going to expand Shang Xin Yuan very soon."

Nuannuan clenched her teeth. "I'm going to call the township office and report what they're doing."

She went back to her room in Chu Di Ju and picked up the phone. She dialled for the reception in the township government and asked for the guard. Then she dialled the number of the chief's office that she got from the guard. When the call was picked up, she said: "Mr Chief, I am Chu Nuannuan, from Chu Wang Village..."

Before she could finish, the phone hung up. She called again, but no one picked up. She knew that the phone calls would do her no more good, so she decided that she would go herself to report to the chief. *Kuang Kaitian, someone from above will teach you a lesson.*

Nuannuan rode her bicycle to the township the next morning after breakfast. On her arrival at the township office, she could not help remembering how she had come here to see the chief in order to save Kaitian. *Who'd have known? It only took a few years, and everything has changed. Who'd have thought I would be here again to report Kaitian's fraud?*

Nuannuan was well known here due to the success of her tourism business. Therefore, with several acquaintances in the township office, she did not need to go through all the difficulties she experienced last time she came to see the chief. She stood in front of the township office for a short while. Before the guard noticed her, someone from inside called out: "Hey! Isn't that Manager Chu from South Water Landscape? Come in. Come on in."

Nuannuan walked inside and explained that her intention was to see the chief. She was immediately led to the chief's office.

There was a new chief in the position. He was very amicable and asked Nuannuan about her business: "Are there many tourists? What is the profit?" Nuannuan gave him a brief introduction to Chu Di Ju before changing the topic to her purpose of visiting. She told the chief about everything that Xue Chuanxin and Kuang Kaitian had done in Shang Xin Yuan. Nuannuan thought the chief would be so angry that he would send people to investigate them. However, he only sighed after hearing her words. "Nuannuan, my comrade.

You and Kaitian, your leader, established Chu Di Ju and Shang Xin Yuan, and you made good use of the tourism resources on the west bank of Red Lake. You did a good thing. You gained wealth for both yourselves and your village, and I support you. On the other hand, Kaitian is expanding Shang Xin Yuan to strengthen entrepreneurship here. Therefore, the township government agreed and offered him more land. Your competition with him is normal in the course of developing a free market. But you have to remember, your competition in business should not aim at bringing each other down."

Nuannuan listened to him carefully and frowned. "Mr Chief, what do you mean?"

The chief smiled and said: "I'll tell you the truth. A few days ago, your Leader Kuang and Mr Xue from Five Continents came here and told me that due to the competition between your Chu Di Ju and their Shang Xin Yuan, you would come to me and report their 'fraud'."

"Did they? And you believe them?" Nuannuan raised her eyebrow.

The chief held his smile. "I, your chief, hope that you'll only spend your efforts on your work instead of making up frauds to report. All these reports on each other will only be a waste of time and energy."

"So you think that I've wasted my time and energy on making things up?"

The chief's face turned rigid for an instant. It seemed he had seldom been questioned in such a manner. Yet he answered in the same tone: "It's not easy to create wealth in a rural area like ours. Even though some things may go wrong, you should not be too sensitive. Your Chu Wang Village suffered enough from poverty in the past. Now you have Shang Xin Yuan. You should cherish such a functional business."

Nuannuan's face went cold. She rose abruptly and said: "Mr Chief, as you think my actions show that I don't cherish the opportunities from Shang Xin Yuan, I'll leave you to your business."

She walked out without glancing back at the chief, who was stunned and left standing in his office. She realised that the "sense" Kuang Kaitian and Xue Chuanxin had talked into the chief meant her words would not do any good. She stood angrily outside the township office. In her mind, she was shouting: *Then I'll go to the county.*

A motorcycle pulled up beside her. She did not notice it, as she was planning her next move. Suddenly, she heard someone beside her saying: "Madam Chu, are you going to the county?"

She turned her face and saw Mr Han, the accountant who Xue Chuanxin had brought to Shang Xin Yuan from the provincial capital, sitting on the motorcycle.

"Han, how do you know that I'm going to the county?" Nuannuan was surprised.

"Leader Kuang and Mr Xue expected you to go to the county after you failed to report them in the township office. So they sent me here to take care of you. Do you want to take my motorcycle or a coach there? If you want to take the motorcycle, we can go now. You might be able to see the county officials before sunset."

"Fuck off!" Nuannuan shouted out in anger. She did not expect them to send someone to follow her. They must have made sure that she would fail in the township office and dealt with people in the county office too. *What do I do? Should I go? I will go. You can't have the county officials on your side too.*

The next day, Nuannuan took a coach and arrived at the county town at midday. She bolted down some noodles for lunch in a local restaurant and rushed to the county government office. She planned to stop the mayor outside, but she could not recognise either him or his car. So she had to go to the reception and expressed her wish to see the mayor to the porter. The porter replied coldly: "The mayor is very busy. He can't possibly see everyone who wants to see him, or he wouldn't be able to work at all. If you have something to talk to him about, you can go to the anteroom and talk to them. They'll bring it up in front of the mayor."

Nuannuan knew that according to the way things normally worked, she could never see the mayor, so she had to think of another way. She stood in front of the reception and thought for a long time. Suddenly, she remembered Xiao Cao from the Culture Bureau, who she had met once because of the Great Wall of Chu and another time for the protection of the relics. She decided that she would go straight to him.

It did not take her long to see Xiao Cao. He was a helpful man. After she talked about her intention to see the mayor, he immediately said: "No problem, I'll make the contact for you. However, cases like yours will be more efficiently solved by the vice mayor in charge of the sub-division of tourism. Even if you do bring the case to the mayor, you'll be sent to him."

Nuannuan nodded and agreed to see the vice mayor. Xiao Cao made a good effort and took Nuannuan to several offices himself. They found the vice mayor in one of the conference rooms. The vice mayor seemed quite busy, and he did not hide his impatience when listening to Nuannuan as she talked about her issue. He inspected her for a short while before responding: "Someone has already passed me the information that you and Leader Kuang Kaitian were married. Divorced couples always have a problem with each other, but you should not bring such personal problems into your business. Otherwise, your competition will not be fair…"

Nuannuan was offended by his words. "What does the vice mayor mean by saying this? Do you think that I'm making up the problems in Shang Xin Yuan because I have a personal issue with Kuang Kaitian?"

With an upset expression, the vice mayor replied: "I'm only giving you a kind piece of advice. All right, I'll remember what you said, and I'll look into it. Go home now."

Nuannuan now understood. Xue Chuanxin and Kuang Kaitian had already cast their influence on the vice mayor. It seemed that she would not have a satisfactory answer from the county office. Xiao Cao comforted her on their way back. "Since the vice mayor has said that he'll look into it, you should go home and wait."

She nodded and gave her gratitude to Xiao Cao. Then she went to a hotel to spend the night, with the plan to head to the provincial capital the next day with the same issue. *He can't have bought off every official.*

After dinner in the hotel, Nuannuan made a phone call to Shallot. She wanted to know about the business at home, and she was also thinking of Dangen. Before she left, she asked Shallot to take care of Dangen, and she wondered whether or not he had been troublesome. Much to her surprise, once the call went through, Shallot cried out in anxiety: "Nuannuan, you must come back now. Something serious has happened in our Chu Di Ju."

Nuannuan was shocked, and she asked what had happened.

Shallot answered: "Two of the guests in our Chu Di Ju were

diagnosed with diarrhoea last night. Leader Kuang came to check the kitchen and said that our Chu Di Ju did not meet the standard of food hygiene. Then he ordered that business be suspended immediately. This morning, all of the guests in our Chu Di Ju moved to Shang Xin Yuan. The leader even sent someone down to seal our kitchen."

Nuannuan's face clouded in anger. *That bastard, how dare he frame me like this.* She answered in a solemn voice: "You should go home and wait there. I'll be back tomorrow morning."

The next morning, Nuannuan was leaving the hotel for the bus station when she caught a glimpse of Mr Han, the accountant, on his motorcycle across the street. She knew that he was still following her. She strode towards him and said in a jeering tone, her teeth clenched: "Mr Han, how hard you've worked. You must follow me close – be careful you don't lose me."

Mr Han smiled in embarrassment and quickly started his motorcycle to leave...

It was after midday when Nuannuan returned to Chu Wang Village. Unusually, there was nobody around Chu Di Ju. Dangen was playing on his own in the empty courtyard. Hearing her steps, Shallot walked out of the house and said: "The leader has just had the seals torn off the kitchen. He said his investigation showed that it was not food poisoning that had given the two guests diarrhoea, so we can reopen the business now. But what business do we have left? The guests were all too scared to check in, and now they're all staying in Shang Xin Yuan."

Overwhelmed with anger, Nuannuan turned and headed straight to Shang Xin Yuan.

Kaitian and Xue Chuanxin were chatting over tea in Xue Chuanxin's office. When Nuannuan barged in through the door, neither seemed too surprised, as if they had already known that she would be coming. Kaitian turned to face Nuannuan and asked: "Can I help you?"

"Why did you seal off my kitchen?" asked Nuannuan as she tried her best to contain her anger.

"Well, it's for your own good," said Kaitian unhurriedly. "We suspected food poisoning when two customers suddenly had loose stools in Chu Di Ju. People in the tourism business like us fear things like this the most. I had the kitchen sealed to facilitate an investigation into a potential food poisoning case. As you see, I had the seal lifted after the Mei Pharmacy confirmed that the guests didn't suffer from diarrhoea."

"You meant to tarnish my Chu Di Ju's reputation and ruin its business," roared Nuannuan.

"Your accusation is unfounded."

Kuang Kaitian was not upset by her tone. He said with a phoney smile: "I'm the leader, and I have a responsibility to ensure the food hygiene in the village. If I simply let you have food poisoning cases, trouble from above will surely come to me, right? We must take care of the guests and satisfy those from above."

"Your true motivation is to stop me from reporting you to those above. You planned all this to drag me home. I was such a fool because I didn't know that you're full of craft and cunning," said Nuannuan in full resentment as she glared at Kaitian.

"Let me remind you that you're talking to a village leader. You must watch your mouth," reprimanded Kaitian with a sullen face.

Xue Chuanxin offered Nuannuan a glass. "Have some water. Have some water."

Nuannuan didn't take it. She continued with a look of contempt. "Wow, Leader, how important is your post? If you want me to watch my mouth, why don't you watch your conduct?"

"I warned you not to ask for trouble with me. You seem to have ignored what I said. I'll tell you again – if you continue trying to report us and bringing trouble to the village committee and me, something really bad may happen to you. Just try and cross me again. I didn't give you what you deserve because I care for Dangen's mother."

"Hah! So you care for me? Go to hell! I don't need your care. Do whatever you like. You think you can threaten me like this? Show me all your tricks – I'd love to deal with them."

Pahh! Kaitian kicked a chair over.

Bang! Nuannuan knocked down a stool...

The food poisoning incident stopped guests from checking into Chu Di Ju for a couple of weeks. It was during the peak season of tourism, and much profit was lost. Since Nuannuan had quit farm work, all of her income now came from Chu Di Ju, and she had to pay Shallot and the other employees. Therefore, she couldn't afford to be careless, and she spared no effort in saving the reputation of Chu Di Ju.

She instructed Shallot and the other staff members to carry out a thorough cleaning, and they paid particular attention to spots that had not been covered before. Then, they set up a billboard in front of the courtyard that read: *Daily sterilisation of tableware and cookware to ensure your food hygiene; daily change and cleaning of bedding and room to ensure your comfort.*

Nuannuan also went to the pier herself to take the visitors on a tour of Chu Di Ju before they checked in. After several days, people eventually did regain trust in Chu Di Ju.

Nuannuan realised that the tourism business was quite vulnerable: without a good reputation, no profit could be generated. It was also the first time that she felt the fear of sabotage from Shang Xin Yuan. If Kuang Kaitian and Xue Chuanxin did something that could seriously impair the reputation of Chu Di Ju, what could she do if she lost her business? Furthermore, without the profit from Chu Di Ju, how could she live with Dangen, her parents and her grandma? What would Shallot do without a job? Maybe she should not be so penny-wise and pound-foolish. Maybe she should stop reporting Xue Chuanxin and Kuang Kaitian and let them run their dodgy business. After all, it was not her business.

Once Nuannuan no longer left the village to report them, Kuang Kaitian and Xue Chuanxin stopped making trouble for Chu Di Ju. Shang Xin Yuan and Chu Di Ju were at peace with each other for the time being. As usual, Shang Xin Yuan was very popular, performing *Farewell* once every three days. More young women came to work as masseuses, which attracted more rich men to stay there. Xue Chuanxin built a pub and a nightclub in the neighbourhood and brought over several young girls from the provincial capital to work as waitresses, on the condition that they all wore miniskirts. The loud music every night seemed to flaunt the great business of Shang Xin Yuan.

Yet Chu Di Ju still maintained its own style. They targeted familiar visitors and organised guided tours. In order to attract more people, Nuannuan invited several street artists on Juxiang Street to perform He'nan Zhuizi storytelling and sing Yu opera after dinner in front of the lotus pond of Chu Di Ju. The guests were quite fond of the performances, and many of them would sit and watch with a cup of tea. Though not as upmarket as Shang Xin Yuan, Chu Di Ju generated a good profit from the large number of common visitors.

One evening after dinner, Nuannuan was watching a performance of Henan Zhuizi music with some guests by the lotus pond when she saw Xiang Xiang, the girl who worked in housekeeping in Shang Xin Yuan, walking towards her in tears. Nuannuan quickly stood up and asked in a soft voice: "Xiang Xiang, what's wrong?"

Tears ran down Xiang Xiang's face as she heard Nuannuan's caring whisper. Nuannuan knew that she must have been ill-treated. She took Xiang Xiang into her room in Chu Di Ju to sit her down and poured a glass of water before asking again: "Tell your sister what happened."

Xiang Xiang cursed as she wept. "They're pigs."

"Who?"

"That Xue guy and Leader Kuang."

Nuannuan's heart sank. "Them again? What did they do to you? Did they cheat your salary?"

"No," said Xiang Xiang as she shook her head, her voice low and anxious. "This afternoon, an old man under the name of Liang checked into Room Number Eight in Shang Xin Yuan. He seemed to be an official because Xue Chuanxin and Kuang Kaitian treated him with much respect. I took water to Liang's room, and he stared at me, checking me out. Then he asked me how old I am and whether or not I'm married. I told him I'm nineteen and I don't even have a boyfriend yet. He smiled and said 'good'. I didn't know what he meant, so I didn't pay more attention to him. After dinner, Xue Chuanxin asked me to go to his office because he had some work for me. I hurried over and saw Leader Kuang there. I asked about the work, and Xue Chuanxin smiled. He said: 'Xiang Xiang, do you want to earn some big money?' I hesitated, then said: 'Of course. What do I need to do?' Leader Kuang said: 'You don't need to go elsewhere. You can earn the money right here in our Shang Xin Yuan.' I thought it was something that needed my strength, so I said: 'Sure, as long as I can help.' Xue Chuanxin said: 'It's not hard work. We just need you to keep the guest company in Room Eight.' I asked him what kind of company he meant, and Leader Kuang said:

'Just chat with him and introduce the local specialities to him. Whatever the guest asks you to do, do it. Afterwards, you can come to Mr Xue and claim your five thousand yuan.' I was surprised to hear such a big amount. Five thousand! I thought they were making fun of me, so I said to them that I didn't believe something like this could happen to me. Xue Chuanxin then took a lot of cash out of one of the drawers and handed it to me. He said: 'If you don't trust me, take the money now.' I said: 'OK, OK, I'll work first. Then, I'll take the money.' How happy I was. I thought of my parents. They would be so proud knowing how much money their daughter could earn. I almost bounced my way to Room Eight, and I asked the guest: 'Whatever you need from me, just say it.' He smiled and asked: 'So they have made an agreement with you?' I nodded. Before I could answer, he pointed at the bed and said: 'Now get on the bed and take them off.' I was shocked and said: 'Take off what?' 'Your clothes. Let me have a good look at you. I grew attracted to you when I first saw you. I have never seen such an innocent girl. Let me have a good look at you, then we can–'

"I suddenly understood how I must earn five thousand yuan from this. I was so angry. How could they trick me into such a nasty business? How blind are they to see me like this? I turned and tried to leave, but when I pulled the door, I found it had been locked from the outside. I pulled so hard, but it simply wouldn't open. That man walked over to me and took me in his arms. He touched me and kissed me. He even pulled my blouse down to suck on my breasts. I couldn't push him away, so I cried out for help. I cried really loud, and Xue Chuanxin had to open the door from outside. That man let me go, and I ran out as I fixed my clothing. I saw Leader Kuang and Xue Chuanxin standing outside. They looked miserable. Leader Kuang said to me: 'You are so disobedient. You can't work in Shang Xin Yuan any more. Go home to farm your field.'"

"The way they treated you, they aren't humans." Nuannuan felt her gut flaming with anger.

"I hate them." Xiang Xiang started weeping again.

"I'll call the police now. They'll take care of them," said Nuannuan as she reached for the phone.

Xiang Xiang saw her move and pushed the phone down. She begged through tears: "Big Sister Nuannuan, the police will only make it worse. They'll definitely want my testimony, and everyone will know about what happened. I can't take that much shame. If my parents knew that someone touched me, kissed me and sucked my breasts, they would not survive the anger and disappointment."

Hearing her words, Nuannuan put down the phone and asked: "What do you want, then?"

"I just want to work for you here. Even if they let me work there, I dare not go."

Nuannuan sighed and nodded. "You can come to work in Chu Di Ju tomorrow."

After sending Xiang Xiang home, Nuannuan could not stop the angry feelings churning around inside of her. *Kuang Kaitian, what leader are you to dishonour girls from your own village?* Several times she wanted to go to Shang Xin Yuan and curse Kuang Kaitian and Xue Chuanxin face to face. But in the end, she stopped herself, worried for Xiang Xiang.

Spotty Laosi was the only full-time tour guide at Chu Di Ju. When it was too busy, Nuannuan and Sister-in-Law Shallot would work as guides temporarily. When Nuannuan left Shang Xin Yuan, she asked Spotty Laosi if he would remain or go with her even though it would involve a drop in salary. But after hesitating a little, Spotty Laosi said: "I'd better go to Chu Di Ju. I worked in Chu Di Ju first, and it was you who taught me the skill to make money. I must be grateful."

Nuannuan smiled. "Let's keep gratitude out of this. You earn your money through your intelligent work." Of course, when Chu Di Ju's business was slack, Nuannuan would allow him to work in Shang Xin Yuan and earn the ten yuan from performing in the *Farewell* show.

After breakfast one morning, all the guests in Chu Di Ju had got ready to watch the Great Wall of Chu, when Spotty Laosi, the only tour guide, was nowhere to be found. Nuannuan was anxious because she had informed him the night before. She hurriedly went to Spotty Laosi's house and shouted: "Brother Laosi, hurry!"

Spotty Laosi's wife came out wearing a long face and said: "He's dead! He's dead!"

Nuannuan was stunned at first, but his wife's behaviour told her that the couple were quarrelling. She whispered: "Can he take the tourists to the hill?"

"To the hill? He can't even go to the toilet," replied Spotty Laosi's wife with anger.

Nuannuan now realised that Spotty Laosi must be severely sick. She went away to ask Sister-in-Law Shallot to take the guests to the hill before she rushed back to get to the bottom of Spotty Laosi's illness. She asked: "Have you sent for Physician Mei?"

Only then did a tearful Spotty Laosi's wife tell her the truth. "Sister Nuannuan, I trust you, so I'll be frank – Spotty Laosi is a beast. Remember I reprimanded him when I discovered him fooling around with a masseuse last time? He swore on his knees that he wouldn't do it again. I believed him. I didn't expect that he would carry on doing it in secret. You see, heaven is punishing him by giving him this sexually transmitted disease. He didn't dare tell me, nor did he dare see a doctor after he got it. He secretly found some traditional medicine to treat himself, and now he's getting worse and worse. That thing is badly swollen. He could walk a bit a few days ago, but he had to bend both his legs and back. He still lied to me even when I asked him why he had to walk this way. His symptoms got worse last night, and he screamed like a pig to be butchered when he peed. Now he can't walk at all, and even his balls are bloating. He's currently lying in bed."

Her words reminded Nuannuan of Spotty Laosi's strange gait with a slightly hunched back. *You're doing evil, Shang Xin Yuan.* Anger filled Nuannuan's heart again, but she knew she couldn't vent it now because it was more important to get Spotty Laosi treatment. She said to Spotty Laosi through the window: "Brother Laosi, as things stand now, it's useless to hide it. I'll send for Physician Mei."

From the window came Spotty Laosi's voice heavy with shame. "Sister, the disease is disgraceful. Please don't tell anyone else. Please tell Physician Mei to keep it a secret for me. I'll repay your kindness in the future."

His wife said with contempt hanging from the corner of her mouth: "This bastard can beg people with sweet words when he's in difficulty but will forget about it when he recovers." Then she turned and yelled into the window: "When you're cured, go and find the girls again."

Spotty Laosi's voice came from the window again, but this time it sounded teary. "My children's mother, could you please lower your voice? Do you want the entire village to know my condition? Please keep some dignity for me."

Patting his wife's hand, Nuannuan said: "Please don't be angry any more. Our priority is to get him the treatment. I'll send for Physician Mei."

Physician Mei came that day. Shaking his head, he said Spotty Laosi would be in serious trouble if he had delayed two more days – that is, he would have lost the function of his genitals.

Spotty Laosi asked while gasping with pain: "What do you mean by genitals?"

Physician Mei sighed. "I mean that your dick would never be able to get hard. It would be useless."

"My god!" Spotty Laosi was flabbergasted.

Standing outside with Nuannuan, Spotty Laosi's wife said with resentment: "That wouldn't be so bad – then he wouldn't be able to fool around with the girls in Shang Xin Yuan."

Nuannuan tried to calm her down in a low voice. "Don't lose your head. If it became useless, you're the one that would suffer."

Spotty Laosi's wife started sobbing. "Good heavens! How has he ended up like this?"

After seeing Spotty Laosi, Physician Mei came out and told his wife what to do. First, she had to wash his genitals and apply ointment regularly. Second, the couple had to sleep separately and avoid mixing their bedding, and never let their children's clothes and bedding touch his. He continued: "Third, you must go to the clinic, where my wife will check you. If you need medication, you'll have to take it as early as possible." Then, he said to Nuannuan as he shook his head: "There are already three people with the same disease in the village. Could you ask Leader Kaitian to intervene? Otherwise, when the infection spreads widely, there'll be lots of quarrelling among husbands and wives. What's more, it will affect people's fertility."

Gnashing her teeth, Nuannuan said: "Uncle Mei, you may rest assured that someone will take care of this."

Nuannuan was so upset that she wanted to go to the provincial capital to report Kuang Kaitian and Xue Chuanxin again. However, she understood that they would immediately send someone to follow her and deal with the officials. Moreover, they may sabotage Chu Di Ju again. She must think of another way that would not trigger them. She thought for a whole night and decided to write a letter of accusation. This would be the only way to conceal her plan so that they could not do anything to stop her. She spent the next night writing eight letters to officials in the city office, the provincial office, the Security Bureau, the People's Procurator and the People's Court. She asked Shallot to go to Juxiang Street with the excuse of grocery shopping for Chu Di Ju and then send them as registered letters in the post office.

After sending the letters, Nuannuan paid all her attention to work around Chu Di Ju and waited for a reply. She believed that if even one letter made it, it would bring about enough attention to help her.

One evening when Nuannuan was putting Dangen to bed, she heard a siren as police cars entered the village. She did not know what had happened and ran out. Three police cars were parked in front of Shang Xin Yuan, and several police officers jumped out and ran inside. Nuannuan felt a sudden joy: she was sure that her letters of accusation had done their job. *Kuang Kaitian, Xue Chuanxin, do you really think that no one can punish you for what you did? Just you wait!* She walked closer with quiet steps and kept her gaze locked on the gate of Shang Xin Yuan. The neighbours had all been woken up by the siren. They stood quietly in front of their houses and looked at what was happening.

Spotty Laosi's wife walked out and saw Nuannuan under the distant light. She stepped up and whispered to her: "Finally, someone has answered us."

Nuannuan thought that at least one of the pair would be arrested that night. However, much to her surprise, the police officers emerged after a short while, and they did not have anyone with them. Kuang Kaitian and Xue Chuanxin walked out after them. They did not look panicked. On the contrary, they were both smiling with cigarettes in their mouths. Nuannuan felt her heart sinking slowly. One of the police officers shook the hands of Kuang Kaitian and Xue Chuanxin and said in a friendly tone: "My apologies for disturbing your normal business and your guests. Please excuse us."

Nuannuan was left standing in the dark in shock. *What is this? How can they not find a problem at all?* The joy that had just filled her heart had dispersed. Instead, she was paralysed by an enormous feeling of disappointment.

"Are they blind? Where can they hide the masseuses?" mumbled Spotty Laosi's wife.

Nuannuan watched in silence as the police cars exited the village and bumped along the dirt road by the side of Red Lake towards Juxiang Street. She did not move, holding her breath in angst until a flashlight shone on her. She turned to look.

"I thought you'd still be up." Kuang Kaitian's voice rose behind the light from the torch.

Spotty Laosi's wife and the other neighbours all hastened to leave when they heard the voice of their leader. Nuannuan did not answer him. She turned to leave when Kuang Kaitian suddenly shouted out: "Don't move!"

"What do you want?" said Nuannuan in a cold voice.

"You've seen it all, haven't you? The police came in to search and found nothing. They even apologised to us."

"Bah!"

"We all know that the police came over because of your great work. But what did you get? We won again. You should understand from what happened tonight that you'll never win by reporting us. The truth is, Five Continents Group has connections at every level, everywhere. We'll know in advance about everything, be it good or bad."

Nuannuan did not say anything. She turned and left.

"This is my last warning," Kaitian called out behind her.

Nuannuan did not sleep well that night. She could hear Kaitian's warning in her ears: "Five Continents Group has connections at every level, everywhere."

She knew he was not lying. *It's likely that a successful company would have important people in the government. What sense will it make if I continue trying to report them? Should I continue at all?*

Nuannuan did not get up to have breakfast. She allowed herself to lie in bed with vague thoughts. She could not feel the slightest strength in her. Shallot came over and said to her from outside the window: "Uncle Tan from Beijing is here."

She hurried to get up and put on her clothes. This was a surprise. "I didn't know that he was coming," she replied.

Uncle Tan was as skinny as she remembered. All of his hair had turned grey, but he still looked full of energy. He laughed happily when he saw Nuannuan. "A guest has invited himself. Have I brought you trouble?"

Nuannuan stepped up and helped him sit down. "We're more than happy to see you. How can you be trouble?" She poured him some tea.

"I travelled south for an academic conference, and I thought I should drop by to see you on my way back. A few days ago, I saw an article in the newspaper about the discovery of the Chu citizens' burial complex in the forest valley nearby. I want to see that too. It's been some time since my last visit to this ancient land of Chu, and I really miss it. How is everything? Have you had many visitors come to see the Great Wall of Chu?"

"Yes, a lot. Everyone visiting the west bank of Red Lake wants to see the wall. I'll accompany you if you want to go up the hill today," said Nuannuan with a smile. The arrival of the old man had driven away her bad mood for the moment. She had always felt grateful to Uncle Tan: it was he who had discovered the Great Wall of Chu, and the discovery had changed her life.

"Great! Let's go and see my old pal the wall first. We'll go to the burial complex later." Uncle Tan stood up to show his satisfaction.

As they walked to the Great Wall of Chu, Uncle Tan learned about Nuannuan's divorce through their casual conversation. The old man was astonished. He said to her: "Hmm, they say that divorce has become a trend in the capital city, but I didn't realise that the wind had blown this trend to your west bank of Red Lake. May I ask for the reason for your divorce?"

Nuannuan blushed and briefly told him the reason. The old man walked in silence for a while, then sighed and said: "Nothing is impossible in one's life. To experience something may not always be so bad. What Kaitian did, if you ask me, is the result of getting drunk on power. There are many things in this world that a man can get drunk on, but nothing compares with power. Power causes many mysterious things to occur. It demands obedience, brings enormous economic advantages and allows mastery of social resources. Once a man gets drunk on it, he knows no limit and will become indulgent in his life. Without desire, a man is not a man. However, indulgence of all desires will turn a man into a monster. If a man forbids himself from getting drunk, he'll also learn to adjust his desires to the degree that the society tolerates."

Nuannuan listened quietly – she knew that Uncle Tan was trying to comfort her.

"I study history, so I know how various men in all the dynasties in China have been drunk on power. I also know that many people wanted to regulate and constrain power. However, to constrain power is never an easy job. First, it requires the man in power to acquire a vision beyond material benefits so that he can be willing to create a system that restricts his own power. What a shame it has…"

Seeing Uncle Tan upset for the sake of her situation, Nuannuan quickly put on a smile and interrupted him. "Uncle, let's not talk about it now. We should talk about happier things. I heard that you're writing a book about the Great Wall of Chu. Is it true?"

"I'm in the process of writing, yes. But I don't know when I can finish it. Right, I have another task here. I need to tell you another folk tale that I learned recently about the reason why King Zi transferred the capital of Chu. I hope this will be included in the introductions that your tour guides are giving."

"What folk tale is that then?" Nuannuan was quite interested.

"Most academics hold two theories about the transfer of the capital. The first states that the southeast expansion of Chu opened up a large distance between the original capital and the centre of the state. The other theory states that King Zi felt threatened because the original capital was too close to the royal capital of Zhou. However, I have recently read about another story in a book of folk tales – King Zi lived an obscene life. In one of his jaunts, he had his eye on a beautiful woman who belonged to one of his generals. He used many excuses to call the woman to his court and indulged his proclivities with her. The general concealed his grudge and even voluntarily sent the woman to the king's court. However, he had been secretly planning a revolt in collaboration with various officials and generals who held the same grudge. He even brought over many others who served in the King's palace. Yet he did not expect the leak of his plan before he raised the banner of revolt. King Zi was shocked and furious, and he sent out his guards to arrest and murder those involved. Hundreds were killed. Though the revolt was crushed, King Zi knew that he had roused hatred in the capital city due to the enormous number of people killed and the connections they had with those still alive. Therefore, he no longer felt secure, and he suspected that everyone in the city was planning to murder him. He couldn't sleep at night because of the fear. The fear also drove him to take the decision to transfer the capital."

"I didn't know that."

"It's a story about a man drunk with power. If King Zi had not indulged himself, he would not have seized the woman from his general. Of course, the story might not be consistent with the historical facts, but I'm sure it will interest the visitors as a tour guide's tale."

"It's true. I've had so many visitors here. Every time we told them one of your stories about the site, they became more than happy to explore more."

It was dark when they came back from the Great Wall of Chu. Nuannuan sent Uncle Tan to rest in his room after dinner. Before she could wash herself and go to bed, Shallot came over and passed a scarf and a hat to her. She said: "Your sister Hehe came with these in the afternoon. The scarf is for you, and the hat is for Dangen. Hehe told me that your dad bought both of them."

Nuannuan knew that Dad had decided to make peace with her divorce, and she wanted to go straight to his house to see them. She missed her family so much. She fetched the beef and pork that she had prepared for the visitors from the kitchen and put them in a basket. She scooped up a chicken and then held Dangen's hand to leave for home.

Nuannuan's parents were both at home. Her mum was mending the bamboo pot lid while Dad was smoking. But Grandma had gone to bed. Mum looked healthy, and she hurriedly put the bamboo down when she saw her daughter and grandson. Mum took two kiwis from a basket and gave them to Dangen. She said: "The kiwis are presents from your Seventh Grandma from the east courtyard. Your arrival is well timed. Go ahead and enjoy them."

Dangen munched without standing on ceremony. Dad laughed. "Look at the way you eat – you'll grow up with a big belly."

Dad's conciliatory tone gave Nuannuan relief. She sat down and chatted with her parents. Though they changed the subject constantly, their conversation was agreeable.

Mum said: "You can't be single with a child like this all the time. If you see someone you like, you can start another family."

Nuannuan knew that this was a sensitive topic that might provoke Dad, so she skated around her answer. "I don't want to consider the matter for now…"

It was late at night when they left her parents' house. Dangen could not stop yawning as he walked beside his mother. He did not walk far before he had to close his eyes. Nuannuan smiled and said: "Who is this sleepy kitty?" She bent her knees to lift him and carried him on her back. As she walked and rocked her son on her back, two people suddenly emerged. They were carrying a small bed made of bamboo. Nuannuan asked: "Who is it?"

"It's us, Sister Nuannuan," answered the two as they walked closer. Nuannuan saw their faces under the moonlight. They were two security guards from Shang Xin Yuan. Nuannuan had once sent them to the capital city for training.

"Who are you carrying on this bed?"

"Zhan Shideng."

"Zhan Shideng?" said Nuannuan in astonishment. She lowered her head to have a better look. Sure enough, it was Zhan Shideng. Under the pale moonlight, he was lying on his back on the small bamboo bed. His eyes were wide open, and he was staring at her.

"What's wrong with him?" Nuannuan hadn't seen him since he cursed her on his cane at Mei Pharmacy.

One of the guards explained to Nuannuan: "He's had a stroke. He can only move his right hand. His legs and left arm are of no use now. He can't talk, either. He has to eat, drink, piss and shit in bed. Caring for him has used up all his savings. But his brain is still working. He can understand everything we say."

"Well!" Nuannuan took a closer look at Zhan Shideng. It was true that his wide-open eyes were filled with contempt and hatred. Nuannuan growled in silence: *You bastard, you still hate people even when you're so sick.* "Where are you taking him?"

"Leader Kuang asked us to take him to Shang Xin Yuan," answered the other man.

Nuannuan didn't understand. "What's he going to do in Shang Xin Yuan this late?"

"I don't know. I heard he's invited to a show."

"A show? What show?" Nuannuan was even more confused. She

did not know that Kuang Kaitian could be kind enough to entertain him.

"I don't know. The leader only told us to carry him there."

"Does he want to go?" Nuannuan took another look at Zhan Shideng. He seemed furious, as if he blamed Nuannuan for stopping him.

"The leader said he would give Zhan Shideng a hundred yuan as long as he came to see the show. We gave him the money, and he used his only good hand to write down a 'yes' on a piece of paper. He really needs money now that everything in his house was sold to pay for his medical fees. His wife has returned to her parents and his son. His daughter Runrun is the only one taking care of him now."

Nuannuan returned to Chu Di Ju and tucked Dangen in bed. As she lay beside him, she could not help thinking about Zhan Shideng again. The sight of him lying on the bamboo bed under the moonlight was still vivid in her mind. She did not know that time could change a person so much. *Zhan Shideng, you must never have imagined that you would end up like this.* The thought of Zhan Shideng reminded her of Kuang Kaitian. *What show could he possibly have for Zhan Shideng at this time of night? No one talked about a show company in Shang Xin Yuan either. Even if they had hired one, for what reason could Kuang Kaitian be generous enough to pay a hundred yuan to treat Zhan Shideng?* Nuannuan knew that Kuang Kaitian had always held his resentment since Zhan Shideng told him how he tainted her. As she thought about it, she felt herself more in doubt. *What on earth is Kuang Kaitian planning by sending the security guards to fetch Zhan Shideng?*

Nuannuan found herself walking out of Chu Di Ju as she could not withhold her doubt. Chu Wang Village, which was lively during the day, appeared extremely quiet now. Only a cat or dog made some noise in the distance. When Nuannuan realised that she was going towards Shang Xin Yuan, she paused, asking herself: *What are you doing? Are you still interested in what's going on between Kuang Kaitian and Zhan Shideng? Are you still willing to meddle in their affairs? But it's so strange, isn't it? Otherwise, why did Kuang Kaitian dole out a hundred yuan to invite his foe to a show on a silent night?* The intense curiosity to find out the truth drove her to move forward. Shang Xin Yuan was lit up glamorously as usual. The security guard on duty knew Nuannuan. He asked her in a soft voice as she approached: "How can I help my Big Sister Nuannuan?"

"Did they carry Zhan Shideng inside just now?"

The guard nodded and said: "They took him into one of the far houses. He's in number three now."

"Are they really treating him to a show?" asked Nuannuan.

The guard looked around and made sure that no one was listening. He lowered his voice and said: "I just heard about it. You mustn't tell anyone else, or I'll get fired. You know that Zhan Shideng is very sick and he needs money to treat his illness. But he has no money left, and his wife has left him in despair. His daughter Runrun is indeed a pious girl. She came here to give the guests a foot massage every night to earn money for her dad. She's a good foot masseuse, and she can earn three yuan per person. But that girl, she really is a masseuse. She doesn't provide any service other than foot massage. Last night, a rich boss guy came from the south, and he saw Runrun enter during dinner. He found her very pretty and told her that she would make some big money if she was willing to massage him tonight. By massage, the man meant dirty business. I heard that Runrun flushed and refused. But after some thought today, she went to inform the receptionist after dinner that she agreed to the man's conditions. Do you think Leader Kuang sent for Zhan Shideng because of sympathy so that he can ask for more money from that man? I don't really understand."

Nuannuan gasped.

"I heard that Runrun is engaged. It'll be seriously bad if they know."

"Does Runrun know that her dad is here?"

"No, she doesn't. She came in first. She must be giving a foot massage to some other guests now. That rich man likes his mahjong, and he won't miss a game after every dinner. The receptionist told Runrun to go to his room at eleven."

Nuannuan checked her watch and turned to enter Shang Xin Yuan. She knew her way around, and it took no time for her to find number three among the houses. She knocked on the door, and it took a short while before it was opened. Nuannuan pushed the door to enter and found it was Kaitian who opened from inside. Kaitian did not expect to see Nuannuan, and he said in surprise: "You?"

Nuannuan ignored his question and looked around the room.

There was no one else except for Zhan Shideng, who was placed in a round chair. He looked confused. The room was dimly lit by a step light on the wall.

"What do you want, having him here?" asked Nuannuan. She did not look at Kaitian. Her instinct told her that he would never mean well towards Zhan Shideng. Yet she could not figure out his true intention.

Kaitian lowered his voice as he sneered: "Why do you ask? Do you still care for him? I'm treating him to a good show."

"What show?"

"If you want to see it too, you can stay. It's indeed a good show, and I'm sure you'll like it," said Kaitian as he turned off the step light. The room fell completely dark.

"Kuang Kaitian, Zhan Shideng did hurt us in the past. But now he is frail, you shouldn't be ruthless and act out of spite."

"What? Do you think I'll pinch his arm and twist his ankle? I'm not stupid. I won't do anything illegal. I'm treating him to a show, that's all. Plus, he agreed to come here himself – he even wrote it down." He took a look at his watch before he turned and whispered to Zhan Shideng: "Zhan Shideng, you slept with my wife, and you felt so good about it. Today I'm going to show you how someone sleeps with your daughter, your precious Runrun. Isn't she the apple of your eye? Isn't she your last hope in life? Now watch."

Before he finished, he pulled off the curtain in front of Zhan Shideng. Nuannuan realised that the wall dividing this room and its neighbouring one was made of glass. The glass wall was covered with a black film, which turned the wall into a one-way mirror.

Nuannuan looked at Kaitian in shock. Zhan Shideng was stunned too. At the same time in the room next door, Zhan Shideng's daughter Runrun was talking to a middle-aged man under a bright light. The man gave a roll of cash to Runrun. She took the money and put it away before she reached to undo the buttons on the top she was wearing. They could see that she was crying as she did so. The man seemed quite impatient with her, and he eagerly stepped up to pull her top off. Zhan Shideng started making weak noises. He tried his best to twist his body in the round chair with his right hand, the only part of his body that he could move, patting on the chair to make noise. Nuannuan realised Kuang Kaitian's true intention. She made a wailing sound and said:

"Kuang Kaitian, how can you think of such a way to torture him? You're such a–"

"Calm down and keep watching the show. You must see this man take the clothes off your daughter," said Kaitian into Zhan Shideng's ear with a smile. "Did you take the clothes off my wife in the same style?"

"Kuang Kaitian!" Nuannuan yelled with a growl. "Do you still call yourself a human?"

Runrun and the man next door seemed to have heard her shout as both of them looked in Nuannuan's direction. However, they did not realise that they were being watched. The man suddenly stepped up and pulled off Runrun's top. He then forced her onto the bed.

Zhan Shideng wailed and closed his eyes.

"Why did you close your eyes? Keep watching," said Kaitian as he sneered in front of Zhan Shideng. "When you–"

Bang!

Kaitian was interrupted by the noise of shattering glass. He turned and saw Nuannuan smashing at the glass wall with a stool. She used one arm to reach to the room next door through the hole she had made, and she shouted at the man who was forcing Runrun: "You bastard! Let go of her!"

The sudden turn of events astonished the man and Runrun. They both turned to face her. Nuannuan opened the door and ran out. In an instant, she was in the neighbouring room, still holding the stool.

"What... what do you want?" said the man, who was wearing nothing but underpants as he stepped back in fear. "She... she consented to this. I talked about a price with her. I'll pay her six thousand yuan once I make sure she's a virgin."

"Fuck off, you piece of shit! You think you can do anything to anyone with your money? Do you know how sick her dad is? How can you force her like this?" shouted Nuannuan as she covered Runrun with a coat. She helped her off the bed and said: "Let's go. I'll lend you the money to treat your dad..."

Runrun cried all the way back to Chu Di Ju as Nuannuan supported her. She spent the night in Nuannuan's bed. She wept all night as she told Nuannuan about her father's illness, about her helpless situation trying to get him treated, about the pain she went through to make such a decision. She told her that she had talked to her fiancé about the deal to sell her body and told him to find another girl...

Nuannuan listened in silence. She waited for Runrun to finish before she slowly said to her: "Runrun, I do despise your dad. I'm angry with him, and I hate him. But I'll lend you the money to treat him. I don't want you to simply throw away your chance of being happy for the rest of your life. I heard that it was your own idea to be engaged with that young man and you do have feelings for him. You should not ruin those feelings for the sake of money."

Nuannuan did not tell her about her father being carried to Shang Xin Yuan to watch her because she knew that it would worsen her sorrow. The next morning when sending Runrun off, Nuannuan took six thousand yuan in cash and put it in Runrun's hand. Runrun dropped to her knees and burst into tears as she said: "My sister, I don't know what happened between my family and yours, but I can feel the grudge held between us. I never thought that you would help me."

Kaitian came to Chu Di Ju the following morning during breakfast time. Nuannuan was talking about the work plan with Shallot, with Dangen in her arms, when she saw Kaitian enter. She hesitated for a short while, thinking that he was here to see Dangen, and then she let the boy go. Shallot thought the same, and she said to Dangen: "Dangen, look who's here."

Dangen turned and saw Kaitian. He called out to his father. But the next thing he did was to return into his mother's arms. Kaitian put on a solemn look and said to Shallot: "Can you please take Dangen somewhere else to play for a while? I want to speak with his mum in private."

Shallot rose and took Dangen outside.

Nuannuan did not move. She sat and waited for him to speak. She knew he was here because of what happened the night before.

"I didn't know that you would do that for him," said Kaitian in a deep voice.

"I didn't do it for him. I was stopping a brutal act from happening," said Nuannuan as she gazed at the wall. She did not look at Kaitian. "You must remember, whatever you do, there's something above you watching."

"You're talking as if he had never done anything ruthless."

"I can't watch such things happen in front of me again. I can't let someone do it again in front of me."

"You're so politically correct – you sound like a county mayor. Our provincial governor would make a mistake if he didn't promote you to a county-level official. At least, he should let you become a township Party secretary."

"Spill it if you want to say something. Don't waste my time." Nuannuan abruptly stood up.

"I just want to know – have you grown fond of Zhan Shideng? If you have..." Kaitian spared no effort in taunting her with his sneering face.

"Kuang Kaitian, if that's all you have to say, you must leave now. Fuck off!" Nuannuan hit the table next to her hard, and it made a loud noise.

"Of course this is not what I'm here for. I just want to let you know that last night when I had people take that bastard Zhan Shideng home, he cried all the way like a sissy. Him aside, my true purpose of coming here is to warn you – you are doing no good to Shallot and Jiuding by teaching them to refuse my order of moving out of their houses and offering their land."

Nuannuan glared at him and said: "Stop skirting around the issue. Just say what you need to say."

"You can have a good think about it." Kaitian turned and left.

Nuannuan stood there and thought for a while. She considered Kaitian's intent to take their land. But after further thought, she did not believe that anyone could tear down another's house without consent. *Even Kuang Kaitian and Xue Chuanxin would not dare.* Therefore, she paid no further attention to Kaitian's words. After breakfast, she decided to follow her schedule and went with Uncle Tan to the forest valley to see the burial complex of Chu citizens.

Chu Wang Village was five kilometres from the forest valley, and the two arrived panting. Both of them were covered with sweat. Nuannuan heard the news from people in the village about the discovery of many graves of Chu, yet she did not pay much attention. She had no time to worry about what had happened thousands of years ago. She only came to please Uncle Tan. The excavation of the ancient graves was not yet complete. A couple of archaeologists were carefully digging the earth on top of the graves. Uncle Tan started by looking at the surroundings of the burial complex with joy. Next, he spoke with the archaeologists. They did not answer until they had listened to his professional opinions. Seeing them talking in excitement, Nuannuan left to dig up wild herbs on the small hill nearby since she could not understand the academic chat.

It was already late in the afternoon when Nuannuan and Uncle Tan started heading back. Though they had nothing but the pancakes Nuannuan made for lunch, Uncle Tan did not look tired. On the contrary, he said to Nuannuan in excitement as he walked: "The discovery of more than thirty graves of Chu citizens has supported the hypothesis that Danyang, the original capital of Chu, is exactly here. It has also proved the validity of my theory. The burial complex, the Great Wall of Chu and the ceremonial goods excavated in Chu Wang Village all serve as evidence. I'm very happy..."

Nuannuan listened to him with a smile. Though she could not understand him completely, she felt glad that the old man was happy.

"From the objects buried in the ordinary Chu people's tombs, it follows that they lived a tough life. Most of the objects are pottery kettles except for a few earthen tripods. Some of the tombs have absolutely nothing in them, which shows how hard their life was." Uncle Tan sighed.

"Uncle Tan, you can deduce the living conditions of the people based on the objects buried with them. Now that we've banned burial in the ground, let alone buried objects, how will people in the future learn about our lives?" asked Nuannuan.

"We've got many more techniques and media for preserving information than before..."

The two walked and talked on their way home. The sun was setting when they arrived at the village. Nuannuan was about to ask what the old man would like to have for dinner when she heard some quarrelling inside the village. She saw people running towards Shallot's house. The dogs, probably scared by the noise, started barking at the same time.

"What's happened?" Nuannuan hesitated in surprise.

Uncle Tan seemed astonished as well.

Nuannuan turned to him and said: "You should go back to Chu Di Ju." Then she started running towards Shallot's.

Nuannuan ran closer and saw that the houses of Shallot, Jiuding and several other families neighbouring Shang Xin Yuan had been torn down. There was no sign of Jiuding's fish restaurant either. The homeware of different households, with pots, chairs and freshly caught fish from Red Lake that Jiuding used to cook, were scattered about the ground. Bricks, bags of cement and sand were already piled up in the contracted farmland of the families. Jiuding and the others were squatting close by in silence while Shallot was cursing in tears: "You're killing us! Where do we live now?"

Kuang Kaitian shrugged and said: "I gave you the notice of demolition a long time ago, and I visited your houses several times to urge you to move. But you kept ignoring us and insisted on staying. You left Five Continents Group no choice but to demolish your houses. We have the consent from above to take over your land. What we did is legal and sensible. If you ask me, you should hurry up and take the compensation for removal and land occupation, and try to persuade the village committee to approve you some new land to build houses on." He waved the envelopes containing money in his hand.

Nuannuan remembered Kuang Kaitian's warning in the morning. It seemed that he had planned to tear down their houses beforehand. Overwhelmed by anger, she stepped up and glared at him as she asked: "Where do you think they can stay tonight?"

"They all have relatives and friends, and they can stay with them, or even with a neighbour. They should be building new houses soon. It takes no time to build a cottage. If they're fast, it'll take a dozen days. If not, a couple of weeks will–"

"What a monster you've become. And just for the sake of money."

"Hey!"Kaitian shouted. "Chu Nuannuan, why are you making a scene here? What does this have to do with you? Did I tear down your house? Did I take over your land?"

"I won't have you bullying people like this."

"How can you call me a bully? They've received compensation for removal and land occupation–"

"What can they do with such little compensation? Don't you know that it's nothing?"

"I don't care. I did this according to law and reason."

"Bah!" Nuannuan stopped arguing with Kaitian. She walked up to Shallot, helped her stand up and said to her: "Let's go, you can stay with me. Jiuding, you must find somewhere to spend the night too. It'll be getting dark soon. What can you do by simply staying here?"

As she finished her words, she saw Jiuding suddenly raising a brick in his hand. He walked towards Kuang Kaitian, who stepped back in fear and said: "Jiuding! What are you doing?"

"Since you won't let us live, we should die together," said Jiuding. Blue veins stood up on the back of his hand with the brick as if he had gathered all his strength.

Nuannuan stepped up and gripped Jiuding's hand. She said: "Jiuding, you can't do this. You didn't do anything bad to deserve this. If you do it, you'll be the bad guy. Brother Laosi, come. Pull him away."

Spotty Laosi hastened to take the brick away from Jiuding's hand and pushed him back into the village.

Huiyu wailed loudly. "Heaven, open your eyes and look at our little fish restaurant…"

Nuannuan let Shallot stay in a guest room of Chu Di Ju with the other three members of her family. Shallot was anxious and said to Nuannuan in tears: "Nuannuan, this guest room should be used for your business. You're losing money every day if we stay in here."

Nuannuan said: "There'll always be another way to earn more money. And you're my guests."

"I'll go to Shang Xin Yuan tomorrow to claim the small compensation. I can take it. We'll build two small cottages first and settle down. You can't twist a thigh with an arm – they're too powerful for us to fight."

"They must have prepared for your further attempts to appeal," said Nuannuan after some thought. "It doesn't matter. I'll write more letters to report them tonight. There's no way that they have bought over every official from above. The letters I wrote last time caused a police search, didn't they? Though it didn't work as I expected, they were scared. This time I'll write to more leaders in the municipal and provincial government. Not all of them are on their side."

Shallot shook her head and said: "I don't want to bring you more trouble. Kaitian is watching you."

"I can take care of myself. Go and take some rest."

Nuannuan stepped out of their room, only to see Uncle Tan still sitting on a rock in the courtyard. She hurried over and asked: "Why didn't you go to sleep?"

The old man sighed. "I can't. I heard what happened in your village. I think I'm also responsible for it. If I hadn't spread the news about the Great Wall of Chu, no tourists would have come here, and what happened wouldn't have happened."

"Uncle, it has nothing to do with you."

"It does. Things are all connected. It looks like nothing in the world has only advantages without disadvantages, including the tangible and intangible relics left to us by our ancestors. Not all the relics can make us better..."

"You'd better go to sleep now." She took the old man to his room without asking him first.

Nuannuan spent all night writing a dozen letters. The next morning, she had Hehe send them out as registered letters at the post office on the east bank of Red Lake with the excuse of taking Uncle Tan across the lake. Her original plan was to ask Uncle Tan to send the letters. However, she did not want to bring him trouble as he was a retired research fellow with no official title or power. So she decided to deal with the situation by herself and take all responsibility, sparing the old man any possible turbulence.

Shang Xin Yuan seemed quite prepared. The construction team came at noon the next day and started laying the foundations that very afternoon. The day after, a steady flow of steel, planks, bricks, bags of cement and sand was delivered. Nuannuan had no choice but to watch from a distance with Shallot, Jiuding and the others. Nuannuan knew that she could not stop them at that moment. All that she could do was wish that the letters she wrote could be read by the leaders from above so that people could be sent to stop them.

Nuannuan counted the days after she sent the letters out. One late afternoon, Kuang Kaitian paid an unexpected visit to Chu Di Ju as Nuannuan was serving dinner for the guests. She turned her head and pretended not to have seen him. Kuang Kaitian seemed relaxed. He waited for her to finish and followed her into her room. He said to her: "Let me show you something."

Nuannuan did not sound friendly. "What?"

Kaitian took his time to take a piece of paper out of his pocket. He passed it to Nuannuan and asked: "You wrote this, didn't you?"

Nuannuan took a glimpse and saw one of the reporting letters that she had Hehe send out. She was surprised and thought to herself: *How did it end up with him?* She reached out to take the letter, but Kaitian drew back his hand.

"You didn't expect it to end up in my hands, right?" said Kuang Kaitian with a deep laugh. "I told you not to work against me, but you didn't listen. You were so confident in your ability to bring me down. Me, the king. Don't you understand now? You can't escape my power. Even in your wildest dreams, you wouldn't be able to bring me down, and just with some letters. You have underestimated the power of Five Continents Group and me. You sent letters to the municipal and provincial governments, but it won't change anything. It wouldn't work even if you sent them to Beijing."

Nuannuan was speechless. She did not expect her letters to be handed to Kuang Kaitian. She was shocked and wondered who had given it to him. She wanted to find out to whom the letter was addressed, but Kuang Kaitian was grasping it firmly.

"I've told you many times not to meddle with things that do not concern you and instead focus on running your own business. I don't want to give you a hard time because we used to be married and my son Dangen is with you. More money will be good for you, for Dangen, and for the elders in your family. But you never listen. You've ignored my advice and persisted in going against Five Continents Group and me. I have no choice. You kept asking for trouble, so you can't complain about getting it."

"Kuang Kaitian, since I dare to act, I also dare to take all responsibility. Do whatever you need to do. I'd like to see what you think you can do to me. I didn't steal or tear down other people's houses and occupy their fields. I didn't force decent girls into prostitution either. What can you do to me? Do you think you rule

Chu Wang Village as the king? Do you think you can bully other people and do whatever you like because you rule here?"

"Just you wait," said Kuang Kaitian before he turned to leave.

"I will!" shouted Nuannuan. She sounded determined, but inside she felt more in shock. Her letters had been addressed to the upper-level leaders, but they ended up with Kuang Kaitian. It made her realise the influence that Kuang Kaitian and Xue Chuanxin were able to exert with their connections. She started worrying about the possible revenge that would come from them, and how it might affect Chu Di Ju.

After Kuang Kaitian had left, she sent for Shallot and asked her to be more careful about every tiny piece of work in Chu Di Ju so that no one could use any small mistake against them. Shallot was a smart woman, and she immediately understood what Nuannuan meant. She said to her: "Nuannuan, don't you worry. I know you fought against all odds to start and run Chu Di Ju. I'll never mess about with the business here – everything will be carried out according to the rules and regulations, and nobody will find fault with us."

Before anyone knew it, summer arrived. In the past few years, the golden seasons for touring Chu Wang Village on the west bank of Red Lake were spring and autumn. Now, due to the large number of people taking refuge from the heat, it became a tourist destination in summer as well because the temperature around the hill and facing the lake was much lower than elsewhere. In peak season, waves of guests came to Chu Wang Village by boat to cool themselves. To attract tourists to stay in Chu Di Ju, Nuannuan developed two new tourist attractions: "Overnight on the Hilltop" and "Lakeside Angling at Dusk". These were in addition to the existing attractions, such as the Great Wall of Chu, the triangle in the middle of the lake and Lingyan Temple. She bought some small tents, sleeping bags and fishing gear. The top of the back mountain was very cool at night, so she set up some of the tents with sleeping bags for the tourists who were willing to sleep there. Evening by the lake with a cool breeze was a good time for fishing. Therefore, she set up seats and fishing rods for the keen anglers. Chu Di Ju's business was prosperous even without the massage and sex services.

That evening, several young people arrived at Chu Di Ju. Shortly after checking-in, they asked impatiently for mahjong. Shallot tried to explain to them that because most guests in Chu Di Ju spent time sightseeing and few people asked for mahjong, they did not have a set. She also apologised and asked the guests to forgive her mistake. However, they did not yield and insisted that Shallot find a set of mahjong – otherwise, they would check out and move into Shang Xin Yuan. Shallot took the issue to Nuannuan. Nuannuan did not think too much about it, so she said: "If the guests really want to play, you can go to the shop nearby and buy a set for them. The tiles are quite durable, so we can pass them down to future guests who want to play."

Shallot nodded before taking the money to buy one set of mahjong tiles and handing it to the guests.

Before she went to bed that night, Nuannuan walked into the courtyard and heard the guests still playing mahjong in their room. Again, she did not give much thought to it and went back into her room to sleep. She slept so deep that the instant she was woken up by the noise, she thought it was just an argument between the security guard and one of the guests who had just come back from a late-night stroll by the lake. Therefore, she did not pay much attention and turned over. To her surprise, a gruff male voice rose with a loud knock on her door. "Open up!"

Nuannuan's sleepiness was driven away by the sudden noise. She quickly got out of bed and asked: "Who is it?"

"The police." The response sounded dry and forceful.

"The police?" Nuannuan hurried to put on some clothes and said to herself in curiosity: *What do the police want at this time of night?*

She got up and opened the door to look. A few police officers were standing in the dark courtyard. She was taken aback and wanted to ask some questions when the police officer standing in front of her door said to her: "We have received a report that your Chu Di Ju has been organising gambling. We came to check and caught you on this site. Look, these are the gamblers, their gambling tools and their money. What do you have to say?"

It was then that Nuannuan looked and saw the young people who had asked for mahjong were all squatting in the courtyard with cuffed hands. So it was their fault. Nuannuan suddenly felt assured and said in a calm voice: "They only arrived in the late afternoon…"

"Come with us to the police station and tell your story there," said the police officer as he waved his arm. Two female police officers walked towards Nuannuan. Her heart dropped, knowing that this was the trouble she had been expecting. She quickly nodded to Shallot and said: "Take care of things at home."

The police officers in the township police station kept asking Nuannuan the same questions: "How long have you been hosting gambling? How much is your commission? How many gambling tables do you have? Have you provided other illegal services to them?"

Nuannuan answered: "Those people only arrived last night, and it was the first time that someone had played mahjong in Chu Di Ju. I have never taken any commission or provided any assistance to any gambling."

The interrogation continued until the following day. The police officers were worn out and told her the results of the interrogation of the gamblers. They all confessed that they had gambled more than thirty times in Chu Di Ju, that there were over forty people at most who were gambling at the same time, and that Chu Di Ju charged fifteen yuan to each gambler per session.

Nuannuan shivered at his words, and her face turned pale. She had thought it was simply a misunderstanding, and she believed that the police would find the truth. However, after hearing what the police officer told her, she realised how severe things had become. This whole thing was not as simple as she had thought. The lies that those people were telling must be part of a conspiracy. If the police believed what they said, both her and Chu Di Ju would have no future. She felt cold sweat on her back. *I didn't do anything to those people, so why are they doing this? Was it because...* Her heart dropped again, and she thought of Kuang Kaitian and Xue Chuanxin. At that moment, she understood everything. Everything could be explained as she linked what the young people did with Kuang Kaitian and Xue Chuanxin. *How dare they do this to me.*

After the revelation, Nuannuan asked the police to find independent witnesses since what she said wasn't in agreement with the young people's confession. She said: "If Chu Di Ju sheltered gamblers for such a long time and the scope of gambling was that big, then it would be impossible for all the employees not to know about it. The neighbours would have heard about it. You can question them to find the truth."

A policeman said: "We've thought of all this."

It was not until the morning of the fourth day that Nuannuan was free to leave the police station on Juxiang Street. She hurried back to Chu Wang Village. Due to anxiety, rage and lack of sleep, she was very pale, and stumbled many times on her way back. She clenched her teeth, bowed her head and walked as fast as she could on the sandy road between the mountain and the lake.

Not far from Chu Wang Village, she suddenly heard someone amiably greeting her. "How are you?"

Nuannuan raised her head and saw Master Tianxin from Lingyan Temple.

He smiled at her, a small bucket in his hand. "How are you?"

Nuannuan stopped immediately. "Master, you're…"

"As usual, I'm here to release some lives," Master Tianxin replied unhurriedly as he shook the bucket in his hand. "I saw you staggering with your face pale. What's happened to you?"

The question brought tears to the eyes of Nuannuan, who was full of grievances. She told him what Kuang Kaitian and Xue Chuanxin had been doing with a teary voice. Master Tianxin sighed after hearing her misery and said slowly: "In my opinion, everything you told me stems from human greed, which is fathomless and boundless. You aroused the desire in the first place. I know what has been going on even though I am confined in the temple. It may not be wrong to arouse the desire, but you need to check it thereafter. You've failed to do that, and it's resulted in where you are now. It may be inappropriate to repress people's desires, but you must contain them after awakening them. You brought lots of tourists to our temple and changed our monks' lifestyle from farming to selling entrance tickets. As money came more easily, some young monks began to study English and desire mobile phones. The change may not be wrong, but I've noticed it nonetheless. For example, some monks started to regard our food as too plain and our gowns too shabby. I gave them timely warnings. As for your sufferings, I think you're resigned to what has happened and are enduring it. Everything will become history…"

Nuannuan didn't want to endure.

After leaving Master Tianxin, she hurried into the village and stopped in front of the gate of her Chu Di Ju. It had again lost its bustling atmosphere. No one was in front of the gate, which was locked by a large padlock. There was a big noticeboard leaning on the threshold that read: *Due to the shelter of gambling, business is suspended for rectification for three months.*

She stared at the noticeboard for a long while. On the inside, she was shouting: *Kuang Kaitian! Finally you have succeeded in sabotaging me!*

Seeing Nuannuan return, Shallot ran out of the side door. She opened the padlock on the gate and said: "After you left that day, Kuang Kaitian brought several people down along with the noticeboard about the suspension of business. He told me to close up after dawn and check out all guests before lunch. We can't take in any more new guests or send any tour guides to take guests sightseeing. Our boats must not go onto the lake, and we must not take anyone to camp on the hill or to fish by the lake. No more tea should be served to the seats by the pond. I had to follow his orders, and I stopped everything."

Nuannuan did not know what to say. She slowly walked into the courtyard.

"Nuannuan, I've been doubting those gamblers. How can this whole thing be such a coincidence? They arrived and asked for mahjong, and someone came to arrest them the moment they started playing. Not to mention the sudden suspension of business soon after they were arrested."

Nuannuan did not engage with the topic. She asked in a low voice: "You haven't paid the salary to our staff members, right?"

"No, I haven't. I thought I should wait for you to come back."

"Pay them now. Pay them two weeks' salary."

"Sure. I'll go—"

Before Shallot could finish, the sound of a bugle rose and interrupted her. The two turned their faces and saw through the holes of the brick wall that it was the start of *Farewell* in Shang Xin Yuan.

Shallot continued: "All the guests have gone there now. They've finished the first floors of the dozen or more villas they are adding, said to be in the European style. The expanded compound is several times bigger than Shang Xin Yuan's original one. It's supposedly going to have tennis courts and a fashion show stage. I heard that the new attraction building is named Lake View Hall. They demolished a few families' houses yesterday and took away a few acres of land. The villagers rage and curse them in silence."

Nuannuan stayed quiet. She turned to walk out of the gate.

"Where are you going? Are you going to find Kuang Kaitian?" said Shallot as she held Nuannuan's hand to pull her back. She was in tears. "My sister, I need you to make peace with him. They say that one step back will let you see a broader sky. Jiuding and I, we've decided to go and claim our compensation money from Shang Xin Yuan. Of course, it's not fair, but we're under their power and threats, so we must bow our heads to live. Now you must see we can't win by reporting them and going against them. I heard that Kuang Kaitian has recently earned the award of Distinguished Village Leader, and he is also the Party secretary now. He has a lot of connections in the township and the county. With the money and power of Five Continents Group behind Xue Chuanxin, I wonder whether there's any connection that they can't reach now. You're just a woman – you can't go against money and power combined. If you ask me, we should yield and let it go. We don't need to pay attention to them, and we won't report them any more. We'll suspend the business for three months. But after three months, we can be assured to run our business again. Don't you worry about me, or Jiuding and the other folk. It's our bad luck. We got in the way by being the neighbours of Shang Xin Yuan."

Nuannuan did not answer. Instead, she turned and walked towards Shang Xin Yuan.

At first look, Nuannuan could tell that the *Farewell* show was another success. Kuang Kaitian and a few female villagers who played the role of his maids of honour were chatting and laughing at Shang Xin Yuan's entrance. He looked satisfied. As soon as he took a cigarette from his pocket, a security guard lit it for him. He took a long puff and started blowing smoke rings from his mouth. As he was doing so, he noticed Nuannuan walking towards him. He rolled his eyes, stopped blowing smoke and put on a grim face. The women around him scattered when they saw Nuannuan coming. Kaitian turned to enter Shang Xin Yuan, pretending not to see her.

She walked straight into Kuang Kaitian's office but did not

speak. Instead, she glared at him. Kaitian did not say anything either. He glared back at her. However, after a short while, he turned his eyes away and asked in a calm voice: "What now? Do you need me for anything?"

"Kuang! You're so vicious!" said Nuannuan clenching her teeth. "I was so blind to fall in love with you before. I was such a fool to marry you against all odds."

"What are you talking about? Did I cross you? We don't interfere with each other any more. You can do your business, and I'll do my work. Are you here to ask for trouble? Is it your intention to make things awkward?"

"You're a pig. You don't speak or act like a man. Aren't you ashamed of sabotaging others? Aren't you scared of your bad karma? Aren't you worried that the Buddha will punish you?"

"What nonsense. Who did I sabotage?" said Kaitian, his eyes widened in anger. "Are you unhappy with my order to suspend the business in Chu Di Ju? I'm doing what a leader should do in the village. And it was your own fault. How can you shelter gambling? Don't you know it's against the law?"

"Bullshit! You know better than anyone else that I didn't shelter any gambling. You know better than anyone else where those mahjong people came from."

"Since you know what happened, you should also know that you must stop working against me. I've told you so many times not to mess with Shang Xin Yuan, but you never listen. Are you happy now that Chu Di Ju is closed and you have no source of income? Are you comfortable being held by the police? If you can learn a lesson from this, you can reopen after three months. If not, I'll make sure that your business will always be suspended. I'll make sure that your empty houses in Chu Di Ju rot for nothing and that you go back to your old days of farming from morning till night. Do you think you can fight with me, your leader? I'll tell you again that things have changed – now you're on my and Xue Chuanxin's territory. It's simple. You ought to be obedient. Don't say or do anything that you shouldn't."

"You bastard!" Overwhelmed by anger, Nuannuan picked up a cup on the desk and threw it at Kaitian.

Kuang Kaitian did not expect her to try to hurt him. Dodging out of the way, he rushed over, kicked Nuannuan and shouted out with an angry face: "You bitch! How dare you attack me? Don't you know who I am? I'm your leader. I'm the king of Chu Wang Village. I'll show you what a king can do."

Nuannuan could not stop his attack. She fell onto the floor after a few kicks, but Kuang Kaitian carried on. He moved forwards and kicked her relentlessly. Nuannuan tried to strike at his feet, but slowly she stopped moving. It was the blood from her mouth and body that stopped Kuang Kaitian from taking out his full rage. He calmed down and stood for a while, breathing heavily. Then, he walked to the door and shouted to two security guards outside: "Come and take this bitch Chu Nuannuan back to her house."

The two security guards entered. They were too stunned to move, seeing Nuannuan covered in blood. Kuang Kaitian shouted again: "What are you doing? Take her." The two men bent over to carry Nuannuan out.

Xue Chuanxin had been listening to everything from next door. He came out now and asked Kuang Kaitian in a low voice: "Will she be OK?"

Kuang Kaitian waved his arm and said: "What can happen to her? That bitch deserves a good beating. If you don't beat her, she'll keep being proud and never learn her place. How dare she work against me? Who does she think she is?"

Spotty Laosi was descending from the hill with a group of tourists he had taken to see the Great Wall of Chu. He was shocked to find Nuannuan covered in blood and being carried by two security guards.

One of the guards said hesitantly: "She... got the leader... angry..."

Spotty Laosi immediately realised that Kaitian had beaten her. Though a timid person, he yelled: "How can he strike her like this? Is he going to kill her? Where's the law?"

Kuang Kaitian, who was standing in the compound of Shang Xin Yuan, heard him. He rushed out and roared: "Spotty Laosi, what the fuck are you yelling about? Do you want me to revoke your tour guide licence and close your lotus soup shop? If you don't want to live in Chu Wang Village, then let me know."

Upon hearing this, Spotty Laosi didn't dare to utter another word. He vented his hatred by kicking a stone under his foot and cursing in a low voice: "You're a despot. But if you can do anything, why didn't you bite my dick?"

Shallot was washing the guest room bedding in the courtyard when the two security guards carried Nuannuan inside. She was shocked by the blood covering Nuannuan's body and let out a scream. "What happened?"

The two men did not dare to answer. They put Nuannuan on the bed and left.

Shallot hurried over and held Nuannuan in her arms. She asked in tears: "Nuannuan, did they hit you?"

Nuannuan could only give a weak, vague whisper of an answer: "Kuang Kaitian, that pig."

Hearing the words, Sister-in-Law Shallot gnashed her teeth, tears rolling from her eyes. "Sister Nuannuan, you're suffering for our sake. I..." She stopped short of saying anything before rushing to the Mei Pharmacy and leading Physician Mei to Nuannuan.

The physician checked Nuannuan's condition as he shook his head and sighed. "The injuries were caused by kicking. Who's so vicious?" Shallot didn't reply but urged him to treat Nuannuan. Physician Mei washed the wounds, massaged her here and there, and applied some ointment over her body. He then prescribed seven doses of a decoction of Chinese medicinal herbs. He advised that Nuannuan needed to rest quietly to recuperate, that she wasn't to move or get angry, and that she had to take the decoction regularly.

Shallot nodded. "I'll remember everything." Then she went to call Nuannuan's mother and grandmother over.

Seeing Nuannuan in such misery, Mum burst into tears. "God, who did this?"

Nuannuan's grandma didn't ask questions – she only breathed a deep sigh. "Nuannuan's element of personality is water, but unfortunately, she got married to a person with the element of earth, which conquers water. It's her fate."

Only then did Mum realise who the perpetrator was. It was Kaitian – the name's literal meaning is "open the fields". She looked up at Shallot and asked: "Did Kaitian beat her?" After Shallot nodded, Mum turned towards the gate, and as she walked, she shouted: "I'll ask him why he hit my daughter like this?"

Shallot grabbed her by her arm and said: "Aunt, Kuang isn't

reasonable any more these days. You can't reason with him. If you trust me, leave this to me..."

Nuannuan slept in pain over the next few days. Once in a while, she would open her eyes, and every time she looked, she saw Shallot sitting next to her. In her blurred memory, she knew that Shallot had been taking care of her. On the tenth day, Nuannuan finally woke up and was able to open her eyes completely.

Nuannuan said in a soft voice: "Shallot my sister, I can't thank you enough."

Shallot held her hands and burst into tears. She said: "Nuannuan, you were beaten by Kuang Kaitian because you wanted to help me and the other people. I can't take this. I have made up my mind. We will not sue or report on their deeds of tearing down our houses and occupying our land. We will yield on that. But he hurt you, and I won't yield on that. I'll avenge you."

Nuannuan shook her head and said: "Shallot, my sister. Kuang Kaitian and I did not end up like this simply because of what happened to you. Don't worry about me. I'll report him as soon as I can walk again. I'll go to the city, to the provincial office to report him. He and Xue Chuanxin can't have bought everything under the sky."

Shallot wiped her tears and said: "I can't see you suffer again. He's crossed the line. It's time for his punishment."

Nuannuan squeezed her hand and said in a weak voice: "He has power. No one dares to punish him without the support of the township office and the county office."

Shallot sneered and stopped talking.

At suppertime, Nuannuan sat against the headboard as Sister-in-Law Shallot fed her some rice soup. Suddenly, Zhan Shiti entered the room carrying Zhan Shideng on his back. Nuannuan and Shallot were both dazed for a few seconds.

"My brother insisted that I carry him here to see you," said Zhan Shiti awkwardly. He had never spoken to Nuannuan face to face like this since she married Kaitian.

"What are you doing here?" asked Shallot, who shielded Nuannuan warily. "She's injured now." She knew that Nuannuan had offended the Zhan family and assumed the brothers were up to no good.

Nuannuan gently pushed Sister-in-Law Shallot aside and said

with a weak voice: "I know what they're here for – they're here to laugh and poke fun at me. They must be delighted with the result of my marriage. Say what you want to say. I'm all ears."

But the brothers didn't say anything: Zhan Shideng had lost function, while Zhan Shiti clammed up his mouth with his head hanging low. Only a package dropped onto Nuannuan's bed from Zhan Shideng's moveable hand. After that, the brothers left as quietly as they had come. Nuannuan and Shallot were astonished. Shallot nervously opened the package and was surprised to see dried jujube dates, weighing over half a kilo. Nuannuan took the package and stared at the fruit. Tears trickled down her face...

Nuannuan was able to struggle out of bed after a couple of weeks, but she would succumb to dizziness after a few steps. Shallot was worried about her staying in bed all day, so she made a wooden cane for her to carry while walking around the courtyard. Several more days passed, and Nuannuan was eventually able to take care of herself. However, she could not move around much before she started panting heavily.

One morning, Shallot served Nuannuan breakfast and supported her to sit down in the courtyard. She then went back to her room and changed into the clothes that her husband used to wear when performing in *Farewell*. She said: "Nuannuan, my sister. Your brother Changlin has something else to do away from the village. So I will be in *Farewell* instead of him today. I'll row the boat for King Zi and earn my ten yuan."

Nuannuan smiled and said: "Go. But your clothes are for men."

"They are for men. I can be a man today."

Shallot turned to leave. On reaching the gate, she paused and turned her head before saying: "Nuannuan, this is my first time to act in the show, and I'll be the boatman of the King of Chu. I really want you to watch by the door to see how good I am and tell me if I resemble a boatman of Chu."

Seeing her serious face, Nuannuan tried her best to nod and smile as she answered: "Sure. I'll step out of the courtyard to check you out."

Nuannuan sat in the courtyard for a while after Shallot left. She wanted to see Dangen in the Kuangs' house next door. She had not seen Dangen since the attack. Dangen's grandparents seemed to know what had caused her situation, and they did not send Dangen over to see her in fear of the things that she might say to him. Nuannuan rose to walk towards the gate when she saw a man with a beard wearing smart city clothes. She thought he was a new tourist and hastened to explain to him that Chu Di Ju was closed at the moment and that they could not take him in. She told him to stay in Shang Xin Yuan. However, the man did not stop and walked right up to her. He asked in a gentle tone: "You must be Manager Chu Nuannuan. How is your injury?"

Nuannuan looked at him in suspicion. She asked herself: *Who is he? How does he know about my injury?*

Before she could ask who he was, Mr Han the accountant suddenly walked out from behind the wall. He shouted to the man with the beard: "You must be a tourist. Come to Shang Xin Yuan to watch the performance of *Farewell* about life in Chu. You'll like it."

The man turned and asked Mr Han: "When does it start?"

"Right now. Go." Mr Han kept rushing him.

The man with the beard nodded to Nuannuan and left with Mr Han.

Nuannuan leaned against the jamb of the gate and thought about the man's words. She felt more curious. At that moment, she could hear the bugles and the bamboo whistles, so she knew that *Farewell* had started. She remembered what Shallot had asked of her and slowly walked out on her cane.

It was a nice day. The sky looked clear, as though someone had cleaned it. There were no clouds, the sky was pure blue, and there was no breeze on the lake to raise any waves. The lake was as peaceful as a large mirror reflecting the pure blue sky. The boats of the King of Chu emerged from the reeds of the lake on this beautiful day, and they quickly approached the lakeside. Nuannuan saw Shallot wearing her Chu clothes as she stood on the stern of the boat carrying King Zi. She was rowing as hard as she could. The boat had brought a breeze that blew up the ridges of Shallot's clothes and played with her short hair. She kept rowing against the wind, and it made her soft figure look more majestic. Nuannuan kept her gaze on the stern of the boat. She knew that once she turned her eyes, she would see the man who was playing King Zi, the man who made her heart drop every time she thought about him. *Kuang, you're so vicious that you almost killed me with your kicking...*

Nuannuan did not look at the performance of the ritual led by

King Zi. She was so familiar with that scene that it had been imprinted on her mind. She kept her gaze on the king's boat rowed by Shallot, and she saw Shallot keeping herself busy on the boat after King Zi and his stewards disembarked. She would occasionally stand up, but after a short while she squatted down again until King Zi and his stewards got back on the boats while the music played. It was time for the farewell. The melody turned sad and profound as the boats slowly departed. King Zi stood on the boat and bowed to his motherland while the stewards were kneeling to salute. Shallot started rowing again. All the boatmen needed to do by then was to scull the boats back into the reeds. Everyone did that except for Shallot, who kept rowing the boat into the centre of the lake. The spectators around had noticed her, and they kept watching her in surprise. Nuannuan did not expect it either – she thought that Shallot was confused because her husband Changlin had not explained the role well enough to her. Nuannuan saw clearly that King Zi and his stewards were turning to look at Shallot. They were probably asking why she had changed the performance. To everyone's astonishment, the boat suddenly shook and broke into pieces, and all the people on that boat fell into the lake. When Kaitian fell, Nuannuan saw Shallot rush towards him. People watching on the land did not worry when the boat broke because they knew that everyone could swim in the village. It was not a big deal if someone fell into the lake. Naturally, Nuannuan did not worry either. She was a little bit concerned about Shallot, fearing that Kuang Kaitian would dock her payment because of the mistake. Everyone watched in silence. Seeing the locals calm and assured, the tourists did not act either. Nuannuan also caught a glimpse of Xue Chuanxin as he stood among the tourists with a confused look.

As the people who had fallen into the water were swimming towards the bank, Nuannuan searched for Shallot. She knew that Shallot was a good swimmer, so she should have reached the lakeside too. However, she was not among those who had made it back to shore. Nuannuan started looking for Kuang Kaitian, and she could not find him either. She turned to look at the lake, yet there was no one swimming in it any more. Nuannuan's heart was beating fast. She cried out: "No!" She was thinking fast and remembered how Shallot talked about getting revenge for her. She thought about how Shallot had behaved in the past days and suddenly understood why she had asked her to watch the performance and what her real intentions were. Nuannuan ran towards the lake and cried in a broken voice: "Help!"

The locals watching by the side of the lake also seemed to realise that a real problem was occurring. Several people hurried onto the boats to row into the lake.

Two people emerged from the lake as Nuannuan jumped on a small boat and cried: "No, no–"

It took Kuang Kaitian several circuits around the village lying on the back of a bull to wake up and spit out all the water he had taken in. Shallot had taken in water too. She was unconscious as the village people carried her on a wooden board to the hospital on Juxiang Street. Once he had woken up, Kuang Kaitian was carried into his office in Shang Xin Yuan. He closed his eyes, thinking of what had just happened to him. Full of resentment, he said to Xue Chuanxin: "That bitch Shallot held me so tight after I fell in. If I had not knocked her out, I would be dead. What are the fucking odds that the boat should break? I suspect that it was her who made it all happen. Neither she nor her husband will have anything to do with Shang Xin Yuan in the future..."

The next morning after breakfast, Nuannuan walked out on her cane. She had asked Jiuding to ride the bicycle and take her to the hospital in the township to see Shallot. Nuannuan was just sitting down on the back of the bicycle when she saw a motorboat riding the waves of the lake and stopping at the pier. Several people in plain clothes stepped out and stormed into the courtyard of Shang Xin Yuan. Nuannuan was curious. *Is there an emergency in Shang Xin Yuan?* As she was thinking this, Kuang Kaitian and Xue Chuanxin were pulled outside with their hands cuffed by those people in plain clothes. Both Nuannuan and Jiuding were astonished. Kuang Kaitian was shouting: "What do you want? I'm the leader of Chu Wang Village! How dare you do this to me?"

One of the men in plain clothes took out a piece of paper that looked like a warrant and showed it to Kuang Kaitian. He did not speak any more. Nuannuan felt a sudden surge of happiness: *The police! They must be police officers! Good heavens! The day has finally come!* Nuannuan could feel the strength returning to her body, and she quickly walked towards Shang Xin Yuan with her cane.

Xue Chuanxin shouted: "I'm a senior executive of Five

Continents Group in the capital city. You lowly police officers can't touch me. You think you can take me away now, but you'll have to send me back here and offer your respect later. Don't complain about what I'll do to you after this."

"Do whatever you like," said another man who was walking out of Shang Xin Yuan. His voice was loud and clear. "I'd like to see what you can do." He waved his hand, and the undercover police officers pulled Kuang Kaitian and Xue Chuanxin onto the motorboat. Nuannuan looked at the man who spoke and widened her eyes in surprise: it was the tourist with the beard who asked about her injuries the day before. He was a police officer.

"Manager Chu Nuannuan, how are you?" said the bearded man after he saw Nuannuan. He walked towards her amicably. "I must introduce myself – I'm a police officer from the municipal police department of Nanfu City."

"What are you doing?"

His voice suddenly dropped as he answered: "The leaders in my department sent me down here as soon as they received your report. But I came undercover as a tourist, and I've been staying in Shang Xin Yuan for several days. Now I'm authorised to announce to you that you can resume business in Chu Di Ju immediately."

Nuannuan forgot to answer or listen to the man. She was too busy wiping her tears away. It was not until the man stepped back onto the motorboat that she remembered to wave to him. The motorboat purred as it started and then headed towards the east bank. It kicked up a spray of lake water into the sky as it moved through the endless waves. The picture imprinted in Nuannuan's mind on that day was the figure of Kuang Kaitian standing in panic on the boat. He was looking back at Chu Wang Village. The village seemed further and further away from him...

One autumn morning a year later, Chu Street of Chu Wang Village opened with a ribbon-cutting ceremony. Tourists from all over the country entered the small street full of excitement. They travelled through a street filled with the culture of Chu from two thousand years ago. Full of curiosity, they gazed at the architectural designs of the authentic style of Chu, as well as the men and women passing by, all dressed in the clothes of Chu.

In front of a pottery vendor, Uncle Tan, whose hair had turned completely grey, was speaking with Nuannuan. "My wish has finally come true thanks to you. A look at this street will give us a glimpse into the lives of our ancestors. I'm so happy."

Nuannuan turned to look away from a group of foreign visitors in the distance and asked quietly: "What's the social status of a businessman in Chu?"

Uncle Tan answered with a smile: "Businessmen were already prominent among the four types of citizens. Ancient history has recorded the saying, 'Scholars, farmers, artisans and businessmen – none will abandon their profession.' This saying exactly represents life in the time of the Chu State…"

Another big event that day after the ribbon-cutting ceremony was a guided tour for more than fifty tourists from America and Europe. They went to see the misty triangle at the centre of the lake, with Nuannuan guiding the tourists to make sure that nothing went wrong. The clear water looked no different from usual when the boat stopped in the centre of the lake. However, after a few minutes, a curtain of mist rose from the water, as though a farmer's wife had just lit firewood from her kitchen under the water. The mist grew thicker and expanded to the last corner of the triangle in the centre of the lake before it slowly danced, rising into the sky. The foreign tourists were amazed by the strange scene, and everyone's eyes were wide open. Nuannuan spoke in English, which she had begun learning a short time ago. "Ladies and gentlemen, please look up to the mist, and you'll see whatever it is you wish for."

The tourists followed her instructions and raised their heads. It took no time at all before people started calling out in Chinese and English:

"I see two Mercedes Benzes…"

"I see a huge wine cellar…"

"I see an enormous manor…"

"I see a group of very, very beautiful women…"

Nuannuan raised her head to look above the mist too.

She had taken visitors here many times and had seen various interesting things, including a flock of sheep, a tractor, a motorcycle and a man whose face she could not quite make out.

What will I see this time? She gazed upon the mist without blinking. An image emerged and became clearer. A group of people were walking away. There were men, women and ceremonial flags. A man walking into the centre of the group was wearing the clothes of a Chu king, and he looked just like Kuang Kaitian as King Zi...

The group of people walked further and further away...

King Zi, is it you? If it's you, please keep walking. Go as far as you can...

As far as you can, away from me...

ABOUT THE AUTHOR

Zhou Daxin (1952 -) is a contemporary Chinese author and winner of several major literary honours including China's highest award for literature, the Mao Dun Prize.

Across his body of work – more than thirty novels and short stories – Zhou draws on his countryside roots and long military career for inspiration.

Yet Zhou's works also manage to transcend his upbringing. His piercing observations of Chinese society set characters in rural, urban and even allegorical environments, and touch upon challenging and often intimate humanitarian questions seldom dealt with by other authors of his generation.

This explains the success his stories have found in film and TV adaptations, and with international readers. More than half of his works have been adapted for the screen. One of the most popular, *Women from the Lake of Scented Souls*, directed by Xie Fei in 1993, became a Golden Bear winner at the Berlinale Film Festival, sharing the prize with Ang Lee's *The Wedding Banquet*.

ABOUT THE TRANSLATOR

Thomas Bray is a 2012 graduate of the University of Melbourne, with a 1st Class Honours degree in Organic Chemistry, and a 1st Class Minor in Chinese. Thomas has travelled extensively within China, including a three-month overland trip to the Pakistani border in Xinjiang.

He has had much proofing and editorial experience through his work at the Melbourne Law School's Asian Law Centre, and continues to expand his Chinese fluency through the Hamer Scholarship Program. He is currently studying Advanced Chinese Language at Nanjing University

ABOUT THE TRANSLATOR

Haiwang Yuan is Professor Emeritus at Western Kentucky University in the US, and Guest Professor of English at Nankai University, China. He is a writer, translator and translation consultant. He has authored and co-authored many books, including *Tibetan Folktales, Tales from the Other Peoples of China, The Magic Lotus Lantern, Other Tales from the Han Chinese* and *This is China: The First 5,000 Years*. Among two dozen of his translations are *Songs from the Forest, There is a Fish in the Desert, Open-Air Cinema* and *Illustrated Stories of Chinese Characters for Children*. He has consulted on the translation of two Sinoist Books titles.